Three sexy business magnates, each spending a month in a small California town, looking for something—and finding someone!

Matchless Millionaires

Three intense, sensual romances from three favourite Mills & Boon® Desire™ writers

D1387426

Matchless Millionaires

ANNA DePALO

ELIZABETH BEVARLY

SUSAN MALLERY

MILLS & BOON

First published in Great Britain 2012
by Mills & Boon, an imprint of Harlequin (UK) Limited,
Eton House, 18-24 Paradise Road, Richmond, Surrey TW9 1SR

MATCHLESS MILLIONAIRES © by Harlequin Enterprises II B.V./S.à.r.l
2012

An Improper Affair, Married to His Business and *In Bed with the Devil* were
first published in Great Britain by Harlequin (UK) Limited in separate, single
volumes.

An Improper Affair © Anna DePalo 2007
Married to His Business © Elizabeth Bevarly 2007
In Bed with the Devil © Susan Macias Redmond 2007

ISBN: 978 0 263 89680 0

05-0212

Printed and bound in Spain
by Blackprint CPI, Barcelona

AN IMPROPER AFFAIR

BY
ANNA DePALO

A former intellectual property attorney, **Anna DePalo** lives with her husband, son and daughter in New York City. Her books have consistently hit the Waldenbooks bestseller list and Nielsen BookScan's list of top one hundred bestselling romances. Her books have won an *RT Book Reviews* Reviewers' Choice Award for Best First Series Romance and have been published in over a dozen countries. Readers are invited to surf to www.annadepalo.com, where they can join Anna's mailing list.

For my aunt Angela Dagostino, and my editors,
Melissa Jeglinski and Jessica Alvarez

One

Cooling his heels in a backwater like Hunter's Landing wasn't Ryan's idea of a good time, but then, nothing was these days.

He was so close to victory he could almost taste it, and since revenge was a dish best served cold, he intended to take his time savoring the triumph.

In the meantime, he didn't intend to let his prey off the hook. Webb Sperling—CEO and chairman of the board of Sperling department stores, and the man he was forced to call his father—would never know what hit him.

Now he walked along one of the main shopping drags around south Lake Tahoe, keeping his eye out for a place where he might pick up a wedding gift. If he was stuck in Hunter's Landing for the month of June, he might as well figure out what amusements lay nearby.

There were precious few amusements to be had in Hunter's Landing itself, that was for sure. He figured the locals in such a quiet little place depended on their cable service for access to television, the Internet and the world.

Cable interested him. *Cable* had made him rich. His company, El Ray Technology, was among the bigger players in California's fabled Silicon Valley.

A store sign hanging from a metal bar up the street caught his eye. Distressed Success, it announced in flowery type.

His lips curved in sardonic amusement.

The sign summed up his life.

When he drew even with the store, he was able to see it was a tidy little shop devoted to home furnishings. Its facade was white with light blue and yellow trim, like an Easter egg, and both its store windows presented cozy tableaus of domestic bliss.

The window on the left showcased a table set for tea with mismatched cups and saucers. The table had a distressed finish and was covered with a chintz tablecloth and set for four.

The window on the right displayed an old-fashioned settee—something that looked as if it had been salvaged from a garage sale—strewn with an outrageous assortment of silk, beaded and tasseled pillows.

It was domesticity with a hint of sin, he thought, his gut tightening.

The look would have suited a room tinged with Eastern exoticism—or a madam's boudoir. Here, on the California border with Nevada, where regulated brothels were legal in some localities, the decor would have found a ready market.

Intrigued by the storefront, he decided to have a look inside.

A chime above the door announced his entrance.

"These raw-silk photo albums just came in last week—"

The woman's voice, with just a hint of huskiness, washed over him, along with the faint scent of a flowery blend.

He walked around a display table and came face-to-face with the owner of that voice.

She glanced up, smile in place, and he felt the air leave him as if he'd taken a sucker punch to the stomach.

Hello.

"Good afternoon…"

Her voice trailed off as they stared at each other.

He went tense, the elemental reaction of a male who's gone too long without a mate.

He looked at her hand, noticed she wasn't wearing a ring and felt his spirits lift.

Things were looking up for his enforced month-long stay in sleepy Hunter's Landing, he thought bemusedly.

Tall and curvaceous, she had hair that flowed past her shoulders in loose curls. He had to call it titian colored, for lack of a better word.

She was a latter-day Venus—a model for the goddess of love that would have made even Botticelli proud. She had a pale heart-shaped face and symmetrical features.

She was dressed in a brown velvet top, ruffled skirt and high-heeled sandals. The look was professional but with a hint of the bohemian, and it dovetailed with the image of her shop.

She stood with a well-dressed, middle-aged female customer, the two of them flanking a waist-high white counter upon which were arrayed a number of albums.

She cleared her throat and righted the smile that had wavered. "Please take a look around and let me know if you need anything."

She hesitated a second, as if she belatedly realized how the words could be interpreted, and he felt his lips twitch.

"I'll be able to assist you as soon as I'm done," she said.

He thought about how he'd like her to *assist* him and smiled with lazy assurance. "No problem. Take your time."

She looked momentarily uncertain, then turned back to deal with the customer in front of her.

The mood broken, he sauntered around the shop, at the same time taking the opportunity to study her.

Over the years, he'd had plenty of confirmation that women found him attractive. Still, his charm was rusty from lack of use. His last relationship—if a three-month fling could be called that—had ended nearly a year ago.

Her voice reached him from the back of the shop. "These are interleaved with acid-free pages—"

He eyed a floor lamp with a tasseled flower-print shade, then a wrought iron chandelier with beaded glass strands of blue and green.

He felt as if he'd entered a fantasyland, one with a profusion of colors and textures.

Still, her shop couldn't compare to her. *She* interested him as no woman had for a long time.

"—we also have some leather-bound albums you might like—"

Her voice caressed his mind like the stroke of a petal.

He'd definitely been too long without sex, he thought. *Too long without anything except work.*

And now, thanks to his old college buddy Hunter—who'd gone to his grave too young—he had too much time to think about it.

At Harvard, he and Hunter and five other guys had formed a small band—a fraternity unto themselves.

One night, across a table strewn with beer bottles, they'd vowed to make their own marks on the world, though they'd come from families of distinction and wealth. They'd vowed to come together again in ten years to celebrate their friendship and success.

But shortly before graduation, Hunter's sudden and shocking death from melanoma had ripped the group apart, and they'd eventually lost touch.

That is, until a few months ago, when he and the remaining Seven Samurai had gotten letters from a Los Angeles law firm representing the Hunter Palmer Foundation.

Before his death, Hunter had apparently made arrangements for a lodge to be built near Lake Tahoe, and now, reaching from beyond the grave, he expected his friends, as they reached their milestone decade past graduation, to honor the vow they'd made to one another.

By the terms of Hunter's will, if each guy spent a month at the lodge, at the end of six months, twenty million dollars would go to charity and the lodge itself would be bequeathed to the town of Hunter's Landing so it could be used as a restorative place by cancer survivors and patients.

Twenty million was a lot of moola, and not even Ryan, hard-hearted millionaire that he was, could say no.

So that was how he found himself in this predicament. He was trapped in Hunter's Landing at the precise moment he was closing in on the goal he'd worked years to achieve—making Webb Sperling pay and then pay some more.

His mouth twisted. Of course, leave it to Hunter to find a place called Hunter's Landing for his old college buddies to serve their time. Hunter had always had a peculiar sense of humor.

Three guys had gone before him to the lodge, Ryan thought, so they were already halfway through this ordeal.

Of course, all three of his old buddies had somehow managed to get themselves engaged or married, including Devlin, whose month at the lodge had just ended.

In fact, Ryan had shown up in Tahoe early—and had stayed at a casino last night while the caretaker was having the lodge cleaned in anticipation of his arrival—because Dev was getting married tomorrow and had asked Ryan to be his best man.

Ryan grimaced. Devlin had even referred to the lodge as the Love Shack.

Right.

He eyed Venus again. He'd settle for a good lay, since that alone would be a vast improvement over his recent love life.

"I hope you enjoy your purchase."

Venus's voice broke into his thoughts.

He glanced around to see her walking her customer to the door.

A jangle of bells marked the customer's departure and Venus paused to organize a display of books. Silence heralded the fact that they were alone.

He watched her line up the spines of some books and then adjust the angle of a photo frame.

Finally, after what felt to him like aeons, but what was certainly no more than a few moments, she looked up and fixed him with a smile.

"May I help you?" she asked, walking toward him.

"Looking for a wedding gift," he said. "I was passing by and the name of your shop made me curious."

"A lot of people have had the same reaction," she admitted. "The name's served as a good advertisement for the shop."

"You're a savvy marketer."

This close, he could see her eyes were hazel beneath perfectly arched brows. Her lips were full and glossy pink, her complexion creamy and unblemished. It was hard not too be knocked over by so much perfection.

"Thank you." She seemed to consider him. "Our style aims for shabby elegance so—"

"Shabby elegance?" The name wanted to make every male cell in him snort in derision. "That's an oxymoron if I ever heard one."

"Yes," she responded, "but it's also part of a hip trend—one of its hallmarks being furniture with a distressed finish."

"And here I thought the name of your store was a description of my life."

She laughed.

He liked her laugh. It had a musical quality to it and he wondered if he could get it to a huskier timbre in bed.

He lifted a clock from a nearby shelf, checked the price and raised his eyebrows. "People are willing to spend a lot of money to look poor."

She nodded. "Celebrities included." She added with a light laugh, "This *is* Tahoe, after all."

"There's a market for expensive mismatched china?"

"Yes," she confirmed, refusing to look the least bit insulted. "It's an art form to bring together disparate pieces to create a harmonious look. I'll hunt for something a client is looking for if one of my regular suppliers doesn't have it."

He supposed more than one customer had been seduced by Venus's sales pitch. "Any suggestion for a wedding gift for a couple that already has everything?"

His question brought a smile to her lips. "Young couple or old?"

"Young," he said. "He's a millionaire and she's about to become the wife of one."

"Lucky girl," she said, then looked around her shop thoughtfully.

He glanced around, too. Everything in her store

seemed designed to appeal to feminine tastes—to women, with perhaps the occasional husband in tow.

He was lost.

Her eyes alighted on something and she took a few steps forward. He followed.

"What about crystal candlestick holders?" she suggested.

The candlestick holders on a nearby shelf were about a foot high and had deep, crisscrossing cuts.

He knew he'd be sending a more expensive gift to Dev and his bride in the future, but he liked the thought of bringing something with him tomorrow, to add to the significance of the day.

Venus looked from him to the candlesticks and back. "Crystal is always appropriate, always timeless, always—"

"Sold," he said. "I'll take them."

She looked surprised but pleased.

He took one of the candlestick holders off the shelf and turned it over. The price was hefty, but he could well afford the cost, especially since the purchase would be worth every penny if it won him points with Venus.

After she took the other holder off the shelf, he handed the one he was holding to her.

As she took it from him, their hands brushed, sending a little electric charge through him—and, if he wasn't mistaken, judging by her sudden tension, through her, as well.

The moment was over in the span of a few seconds, however, and she quickly turned away toward the back of the store.

He followed her as she walked to the checkout counter.

"Is there anything else I can show you?" she asked over her shoulder.

Yes, you. He admired the view of her from the back. *Spectacular.* He thought about how she'd fit in his arms.

Aloud, he forced himself to say, "That's it for this time."

There'd be plenty of other occasions over the course of the coming month, if he had anything to say about it.

She went around the counter and he stopped in front of it.

He watched as she pulled the price tag off his purchase and then wrapped both candlestick holders in tissue paper.

The sight of her slim, manicured hands readying his purchase was arousing.

He needed to get a grip, he thought. Or better yet, get laid.

"Are you staying in Tahoe or just passing through?" she asked, interrupting his reverie.

"I'm staying in Hunter's Landing for a few weeks," he responded. Referring to his stay in terms of mere *weeks* somehow made the upcoming month more palatable.

"Oh, really?" She glanced up. "I live near there."

"Hunter's Landing is small and quiet," he said with a grimace.

He figured she probably assumed he was here for a vacation. He was dressed in khakis and a polo shirt for a change. His usual uniform consisted of custom-made suits and power ties.

"I like small and quiet," she responded.

Small. Quiet. She didn't sounded like a party animal, he thought. Maybe she was in a relationship and felt little need for the local bar scene.

She wore no ring, but there could be a boyfriend in the picture. Or, more likely, *boyfriends,* he amended, figuring men panted after Venus.

"Since I'm not familiar with Hunter's Landing," he said, "maybe you can tell me where I can find a good meal."

He was stretching the truth, since he'd grown up literally next door, on his family's estate in Clayburn, and he'd been to Tahoe on many occasions.

But not in recent memory. Lately he'd been bent on revenge, and Tahoe was too much of a local playground for Webb Sperling and his ilk.

On top of it all, the caretaker of the lodge had left the refrigerator there stocked with gourmet food, but Venus didn't have to know that.

She seemed to consider him, as if wondering whether he was putting the moves on her.

Desire washed over him in a wave.

Her top was a typical V-neck but, since her breasts were at least a C cup, almost anything on her would have looked sexy.

He could also see now, with more intimate inspection, that her eyes were amber shot through with green and gold.

Eventually, she said, "There's not much going on in Hunter's Landing."

Now there was an understatement.

"There's the Lakeside Diner," she went on, "and, of course, Clearwater's, which has a deck overlooking the lake."

Oh, yeah. He could picture a little romantic dinner, moonlight glinting off the water, followed by a retreat to the lodge. They'd sip some red wine and maybe take a dip in the hot tub, all the while listening to some mellow jazz. Then he'd peel off her clothes and they'd make love in the oversized master suite.

He tried to unfog his brain as she deposited his purchase in a ridiculous yellow bag displaying the Distressed Success name.

"Clearwater's sounds great…" He paused. "I didn't get your name."

"Kelly."

"Kelly." He held out his hand. "Ryan."

She shook his hand and he felt long, elegant fingers, her delicate palm tapering to a slim wrist.

The moment seemed to draw itself out, until she finally withdrew her hand.

"How would you like to pay for your purchase?" she asked.

As he pulled out his wallet, he wondered whether he'd only imagined that her voice had sounded husky. "AmEx okay?"

She smiled. "Of course."

Anything to make the customer happy, he thought. She was the consummate saleswoman and, having grown up as an heir to the Sperling department stores fortune, he knew something about the art form.

He handed her the credit card. "I'd enjoy having some company at Clearwater's." He'd eaten alone way too often lately. "Are you available for dinner tomorrow night, Kelly—? I didn't get your last name."

Tomorrow was Saturday. *Smooth, smooth.*

"It's Hartley," she said easily.

As she glanced down at the credit card he'd handed her, a weird feeling washed over him.

One of Webb Sperling's many mistresses had been named Hartley, and the woman had had a daughter with the name Kelly.

Kelly's smile died at the same time as the one on his lips froze. He watched as her eyes widened and her lips parted.

Damn it.

Recognition seemed to slam into her at the same time it did into him.

He cursed under his breath. To think, he'd almost got taken in by a bimbo, just like his father. *Almost,* though. Fortunately, he didn't have Webb Sperling's susceptibility to trashy women.

He'd worked hard his whole life to avoid comparisons to his father. Luckily, his looks came from his mother—a debutante from a rich family—who'd been a dark-haired beauty, right up until cancer had claimed her, just as it had his friend Hunter.

Beautiful, of course, was just the way Webb Sperling liked them, he thought cynically, staring now at Kelly.

Beautiful and money hungry. No wonder she'd thought Dev's bride was lucky to have landed a millionaire.

She'd chosen well for the location of her store. Tahoe catered to people with money to burn. Just like her mother, she seemed to have an unerring sense of where to find easy money.

If he had a say, though, Venus would be ruined.

"You're Webb Sperling's son," she said.

"And you're Brenda Hartley's daughter," he responded grimly.

How could she not have recognized him?

Easily, Kelly answered herself. She hadn't seen him in more than a decade, since before she'd left

Clayburn, and he'd become something of a press-dodging millionaire. From time to time, she'd read newspaper articles about his business dealings, but that was about it.

Of course, the intervening years had wrought a transformation in him.

Any hint of teenage lankiness was gone, replaced by lean muscle and the good looks of a movie star. Though she was tall and wearing heels, he easily topped her. And unlike Webb Sperling—who was blue-eyed and fair, though his hair had been turning white for years—Ryan was dark. With chocolate-brown eyes and dark hair, he had a face that was all Roman god.

She'd felt her breath leave her body when he'd walked in the door. When she'd been a teenager, she'd also found him overwhelming, though then she'd merely stolen glances of him from a distance.

Back then, she'd have been tongue-tied and dumb-struck if Ryan Sperling had deigned to speak to her. He was only two years older, but his wealth and rebellious bad-boy attitude had made him seem far removed from her in worldliness and sophistication.

She'd never had an actual crush on him—she'd been far too practical for that—but she'd been able to appreciate his seductive appeal.

Rumor around town had been that Ryan was aware of his father's affairs and resented him for it. Ryan's mother had fallen ill and died around the time that Webb Sperling had been involved with Brenda Hartley, and, soon after, Ryan had departed for college, not to be seen around Clayburn again.

She watched now as Ryan's lips curled. "Well, if this isn't a strange coincidence."

The look on his face hardened. Clearly, he was aware of the history their parents shared.

"Or maybe not so strange," he drawled.

She tensed. "How so?"

He rubbed his jaw. "I'm finding it hard to believe you didn't recognize who I was the minute I came into your store."

Her eyebrows knitted. "And why would I pretend not to know you?"

He shrugged. "Perhaps you were trying to impress me without seeming to, hoping I'd run back to tell the Sperlings what a tremendous little entrepreneur you are."

Her eyes widened. So he knew about her negotiations with Webb Sperling to get her designs into Sperling department stores.

She felt herself flush and an uncomfortable feeling swept over her. She was still uneasy about accepting a favor from her mother's loathsome former lover, even if she was desperate to realize her dreams for Distressed Success.

His lips curved without humor. "Sort of like a chef pretending not to know when a food critic is in the restaurant." He looked around her shop, his expression disdainful. "Except you calculated wrong, because I'm not in Webb Sperling's orbit these days."

So, she thought, Ryan's relationship with his father hadn't improved over the years. The rebellious teenager had transformed into an estranged son.

Aloud, she countered, "If that's the case, then how could you know about any discussions I *might* have had with Sperling, Inc.?"

Her negotiations with Sperling were still in their early stages. She had yet to see a contract, in fact.

"I have my sources."

She raised an eyebrow. The idea of Ryan engaged in corporate espionage struck her as funny, even under the circumstances. "A spy?"

"It's not spying when it's all in the family," he asserted.

"And you all get along so well," she shot back.

She knew the company that owned Sperling department stores was completely family owned, its shares divided among various Sperling extended family members.

"I'm not like my sordid parent," he said bitingly, looking her up and down. "That's more than I can say for you."

She bristled.

"On second thought, I should have recognized you. The similarity to your mother can't be missed."

She felt heat rise to her face again as her temper

ignited. She's spent years making sure she *didn't* become her mother. She'd worked hard to get where she was—and, unlike *some people,* she hadn't had the benefit of family money to back her up.

She couldn't do anything about the curvaceous figure and dark coppery red hair that she had in common with the loose-living, fun-loving Brenda Hartley. But these days, people around Tahoe knew her as the owner of a successful small business and as a respectable member of the community. And that's just how she liked it.

"Let me show you the door," she managed, gritting her teeth.

He tossed some bills on the counter, much more than the crystal candlestick holders were worth. "Consider this my contribution to the cause."

Two

"Phew! Who was that?" Erica said as she glanced back toward Distressed Success's front door, where she had just entered and Ryan had just departed. "Looked like Mr. Tall, Dark and Dangerous."

"Mr. Tall, Dark and Irritating is more like it," Kelly responded, wrinkling her nose. She was still steaming over Ryan's attitude.

Kelly had hired Erica, a cute blonde and married mother of two, to help her out in the shop part-time, and her assistant was just showing up for the day.

As Erica continued toward her, she looked down

at the bills scattered on the counter. "Well, it seems as if he liked what he saw."

"Yes," she agreed acerbically, "until he realized *whom* he was seeing. *That* was Ryan Sperling."

Erica's eyes widened.

"Yep," she said in confirmation, "Webb Sperling's son."

She glanced down at the counter. Ryan had left double what the candlestick holders had cost.

Damn Ryan Sperling, she thought. He made her feel unclean accepting his money, just as she felt unclean doing business with Webb Sperling.

"It's too bad he turned out to be someone you'd never want to get involved with," Erica responded. "He's the hottest guy to walk in here in months."

"I hadn't noticed." *Liar, liar.*

"What's he doing in Tahoe?" asked Erica, picking up the scattered bills.

She shrugged. "Taking a vacation, I assume. And with any luck, I won't be running into him again."

She filled Erica in on the encounter with Ryan.

Since being hired to work at Distressed Success three years ago, Erica had become her close friend. Though Kelly was cautious about what she told people regarding her past, she'd confided in Erica about her childhood in Clayburn and her mother's affair with Webb Sperling. More recently, Erica was aware of her negotiations with Sperling, Inc. and how they'd come about.

"From what you've told me," Erica said finally, "he wasn't too happy about your doing business with Webb Sperling."

"Well, there's nothing he can do about it."

Yet, despite how adamant she sounded, she found herself shaking off a feeling of unease.

"Still, maybe it's best if you got this contract with Webb finalized, sooner rather than later," Erica observed.

I couldn't agree more, Kelly thought.

"I'm going to get back to opening those boxes of merchandise that arrived yesterday," Erica announced.

"Thanks."

After Erica had headed back to the stockroom, Kelly found herself left alone with thoughts that she couldn't push away.

The encounter with Ryan Sperling had shaken her up more than she cared to admit to Erica. Ryan exuded power, even a little ruthlessness, and he made her nervous on every level.

By Ryan's own admission, however, he and his father were estranged, so there was little he could do to meddle in her negotiations with Sperling, Inc. Or was there?

She knew from press reports that Ryan had made a fortune gobbling up cable companies. She'd also read he'd inherited from his paternal grandfather a small minority of shares in the family business, but other than that, he had nothing to do with the Sperling retail chain.

On the other hand, Ryan seemed as if he'd be all too eager to upend his father's best-laid plans, particularly when they had anything to do with his former mistress.

Somehow, Ryan had known about her attempt to get her goods into Sperling stores and he'd seemed none too pleased at the prospect.

Kelly shook her head. Of course, she wouldn't be in this predicament if she hadn't said more than she wanted to her mother.

She still rued the day she'd confided in Brenda that she hoped to find a national retailer to carry designs under the Distressed Success name.

The last time her mother had breezed through Tahoe, Brenda had been short on cash *again* and looking for "a small loan," and, as usual, Kelly had offered up some money, knowing she'd never be repaid.

Brenda had taken the opportunity to look around Distressed Success and comment on the latest inventory.

"These jewelry boxes are gorgeous, tootsie," Brenda had said, holding an embroidered silk and stone-encrusted case.

"Thanks," she'd said, walking over. "I hired a manufacturer to produce samples from some designs I sketched. I'm selling some of the samples in the store, but I'm hoping to find an outside vendor for them, too."

She hoped if the samples sold well in Distressed Success, she'd have an easier time getting a big chain to carry them. Her dream wasn't to carry other designers' goods in her boutique, but to build up Distressed Success into a national, even international, brand using her own designs.

Brenda perked up. "A vendor?"

Her mother turned the jewelry box around in her hands, inspecting it. Her nails were long, manicured and fire-engine red, a color that matched her lips.

Not for the first time, Kelly wished her mother would tone it down. Brenda's makeup was perfect for television or for the Las Vegas showgirl she'd once been, but in the harsh light of day, it just looked garish.

Then again, Kelly reflected, since her mother's life often resembled a soap opera, the makeup wasn't completely inappropriate. Brenda continued to live in the fast lane, her devil-may-care attitude still going strong in her fifties.

Kelly sighed. As a teenager, she'd been embarrassed by her mother's loose living. Her mother had drunk, smoked and partied hard. And now it appeared some things were destined never to change.

"I'm looking to partner with a national chain," she said in response to her mother's inquiring look, "but there's a lot of competition for shelf space, especially in the more prestigious retailers."

She could only fantasize about getting her designs in Neiman Marcus or—

"What about Sperling?" Brenda said, her eyes sharpening.

For a moment, Kelly thought she'd spoken out loud, but then she realized Brenda was giving voice to what she herself had been thinking.

"I could contact Webb and—"

"No," she said emphatically. It would be a bad idea for either of them to let Webb Sperling back into their lives.

"It's settled," Brenda said animatedly, putting down the jewelry box. "I'll just give Webb a call and—"

"No."

But Brenda was already caught up in another one of her schemes. "Of course, he's still married to that cheap slut Roxanne—" Brenda's mouth curved in a hard smile "—but Webb and I keep in touch."

Kelly resisted rolling her eyes. As far as Kelly knew, Brenda and Webb hadn't been lovers in years. But one could never tell with those two, particularly since Webb was a known adulterer and Brenda had never looked a gift horse in the mouth.

Kelly mentally winced at the thought of her mother approaching Webb for a favor, then winced again as another, more ominous thought occurred and she wondered whether Brenda had *already* been approaching Webb from time to time over the years for "a small loan."

In the end, she'd convinced Brenda to back off the idea of contacting Webb Sperling—or rather, she thought she had.

Two weeks later, however, the phone call had come. Webb's tone had been too hearty, his attitude a tad oily.

She hadn't had the willpower to resist what was being dangled in front of her, particularly since all her dreams for Distressed Success were bound up in it.

Now, though, she'd unexpectedly come face-to-face with the avenging angel—someone who despised Webb Sperling and everything associated with him. *His son*.

Still, Ryan's attitude riled her. He had some nerve to judge her.

When they'd both been teenagers in Clayburn, he'd been the scion of the richest family in town and she'd been the daughter of the local sexpot and living in a run-down house in the cheapest part of town. Sure, her mother had had an affair with Ryan's father, but only because the senior Sperling liked his women brassy and trashy.

Her world and Ryan's couldn't have been more different—growing up, the only times she'd see him was when she'd occasionally spot him around town. He'd attended exclusive private schools, while she'd been a student at the local high school.

And though he'd had a reputation for hell-raising, his rebelliousness hadn't prevented him from getting into Harvard. She, in contrast, had worked her way through two years of community college to earn a degree in small-business admin- istration and management.

The same will to succeed, however, now made her pick up the phone sitting on the counter. She needed to put her mind at rest, or try to.

When Webb's secretary picked up, she said, "I'd like to speak with Mr. Sperling, please."

"Who shall I say is calling?"

"Tell him it's Kelly Hartley of Distressed Success."

"Please hold while I see if he's available," the secretary intoned.

After she'd endured an anxious wait of several minutes, Webb came on the line.

She'd been afraid he wouldn't be in since it was already Friday afternoon and her recollection from her days in Clayburn was that Webb liked his golf game.

"Kelly, what can I do for you, sugar?" Webb said heartily.

She hated being called sugar, but it appeared to be Webb's favorite endearment.

"Thank you for taking my call," she began.

"There's no need to be so formal, sugar. After all, we're old friends, aren't we? Next time, you just tell my secretary that it's Kelly calling."

Ignoring the invitation, she went on, "I thought

I'd check to see where matters stood as far as putting through orders for Distressed Success's designs."

Webb sighed. "You have to be patient, sugar. I've passed along your information to the right people."

"Yes, but—"

"You could say we have a sort of committee system around here for bringing in a new vendor," Webb said jocularly. "Lots of hoops to jump through."

She'd heard the speech before, but it had already been weeks since she'd heard from any of his people. "I know, but it's been a while since—"

"Listen, sugar, there's a meeting I need to get to. Say hello to your mama for me, you hear?"

Webb ended the call before she could argue any further.

Kelly bet his *meeting* was an appointment on the golf course.

"What's wrong?" Erica asked, walking back into the room.

"I called Webb Sperling to check on things, and got nowhere," she replied. "He told me to be patient, etcetera, etcetera."

"Still thinking about your run-in with Ryan Sperling?"

"Among other things."

Erica shook her head. "Don't let a man shake you up. Trust me, it isn't worth it—" she stopped and grinned "—particularly when you aren't even sleeping with him."

An image of her and Ryan making love flashed through Kelly's mind, sending a shiver of awareness shooting through her.

Appalled, she tried to banish the image.

She was sick, *sick,* to even be thinking of Ryan that way after he'd basically accused her of being a skank and made it clear what he thought of her business.

The guy was obviously a jerk with tons of baggage—baggage she didn't need. She already had enough luggage herself to ground a 747.

Erica waved a hand in front of her face. "Earth to Kelly. Come in, Kelly."

"Sorry," she responded, focusing on Erica again.

"Was it something I said?" Erica joked. "You know—" Erica looked at her shrewdly "—Ryan may be a jerk, but there's no denying he's a wealthy, good-looking jerk."

"Really?" she asked, injecting her voice with a healthy note of skepticism.

"Mmm-hmm."

"Hey, you're a married mother of two."

"And not dead."

"What would Greg say?" she pressed.

Greg, Erica's husband, was a hulking firefighter.

"Actually," Kelly added, her tone turning thoughtful, "the image of Greg pounding Ryan to a pulp holds some appeal." Until now she hadn't known she possessed a bloodthirsty streak.

"I think it would be an even fight," Erica responded. "Ryan Sperling looked like no pushover."

And that's what she was afraid of, she thought, pushing aside her unease once again.

She forced herself to switch gears. "Good news. How could I have forgotten to mention it when you walked in? I've been officially hired for the decorating job at the lodge."

Erica clapped her hands. "Fantastic!"

Kelly nodded. "I met with Meri again yesterday, briefly toured the rooms of the house that need decorating and signed a contract."

She and Erica had been discussing the lodge ever since the caretaker for the mysterious home—a woman named Meri—had walked into Distressed Success, taken a look around and talked to them about decorating some empty bedrooms.

Meri, a good-looking woman with an incisive mind, had been short on details about the lodge. It wasn't until Kelly had met with her on Erica's day off yesterday that she'd gotten any real particulars about the house—luxurious even by Tahoe standards—about which speculation had been rife among the locals during the nearly twelve months it had taken to build it.

"For some reason the lodge is now being transformed into a restorative place for cancer patients and survivors," she said to Erica.

Erica raised her eyebrows. "The plot thickens."

"Officially," she went on, "Distressed Success has been hired by the Hunter Palmer Foundation, which got the original building permits. The home has never been fully furnished, and now that it's going to be a restorative place, they need to complete the decor ASAP."

Erica cocked her head. "Why aren't they going with the original decorator?"

"The original firm is too busy right now to take on any more business." And happily, *she'd* turned out to be the beneficiary of the scheduling difficulty. "Meri wants this project completed in the next few weeks in order to cause as little inconvenience as possible to any future occupants."

Erica's brow furrowed. "Lots of work for you."

Kelly gave her a game smile. "No sacrifice is too great where Distressed Success is involved."

"You've got to lighten up," Erica grumbled.

"I will. *After* I put the *success* in Distressed Success. I want the Distressed Success name in every bathroom, every bedroom, every living room—"

Erica rolled her eyes. "Good grief. I'm working for a megalomaniac."

Kelly stopped and grinned. She'd almost forgotten how badly her day had started. Almost. "Sorry. I got carried away."

"So when do you start?"

"I'm visiting the lodge on Sunday, since the shop is closed then. Meri gave me the key to the front door yesterday. She shuttles back and forth to Los Angeles, and she wanted to make sure I'd have easy access. The house will have an occupant for the coming month, but he's been told about the decorating project."

Meri had been tight-lipped about who had been using the lodge, but rumor among the locals was that a man had stayed there in March, another in April and a third in May. Kelly assumed they'd been vacationers who'd paid to rent the place, and that the man due to check in this weekend was there for a similar stay.

"Do you need me to come along?" Erica asked.

Kelly shook her head. "Sunday is your time with the kids. Meri hired Distressed Success because we're local and this project needs to be done fast. Now that I've seen the lodge, I think I know what she's looking for."

Sunday couldn't come too soon for her. She was relishing diving into a new project. Just let Ryan Sperling try to stomp on her dreams!

Sunday morning, Kelly got up early and drove over to the lodge.

Although decorating the house would eat into her leisure time, she was eager to have another venue to showcase her designs. She had no illusions about how competitive the home-decor market was and she'd already spent years improving her designs.

As she got out of her car, she looked up at the famed log-and-stone house. At 9000 square feet, with a soaring sloped roof suspended on thick log columns, the home would surely satisfy any millionaire's luxury tastes. Multistoried, with covered decks on the main level, the house sloped down to the water on one side and had a spectacular view of Lake Tahoe.

Her feet crunched on the ground in front of her as she crossed to the house and traversed the porte cochere to the front entrance.

It didn't look as if anyone was at home, but she rang the doorbell a few times anyway. She waited a moment and, when she received no response, she let herself in with the key Meri had given her.

Stepping into the great room, she caught her breath, impressed all over again. A massive fireplace dominated one wall and large armchairs stood before it. An immense metal chandelier was suspended from the vaulted ceiling, which was braced with wood beams. Windows and French doors afforded a wonderful view of the lake, which glittered under the gaze of the morning sun, the sunlight catching and sparkling like so many diamonds scattered across the waves.

She turned around and looked back at the grand staircase that led to the upper level, where Meri had told her the master suite and guest bedrooms were located. Only two of these rooms had been furnished so far.

Hearing a click, she whirled around, realizing she was no longer alone.

"What the hell—"

Ryan Sperling, naked except for a gray towel riding low on his hips, stood silhouetted by the French doors leading to the deck outside. Droplets of water clung to his torso. Ryan's expression was thunderous, and Kelly sucked in a breath.

She drank in the sight of his smooth, muscled chest, flat stomach and hair-roughened legs, which ended at feet planted firmly on the plush carpeting.

She knew from her first tour with Meri that there was a hot tub on the deck. He must have been soaking in it.

"What the hell are you doing here?"

"I—" Shock rendered her momentarily speechless.

"If this is some desperate attempt to try to persuade me that Sperling department stores should be doing business with you," Ryan sneered, "forget it."

She couldn't believe his ego. He'd already informed her that he didn't have anything to do with Webb these days. Did he really think she'd seek him out as a supplicant for any leverage he *could* provide as far as getting her products into Sperling department stores? *Apparently so.*

Ryan's expression darkened even more. "If this is some sort of entrapment scheme, I've got some of the best lawyers in the country on retainer."

Her temper rose. "Not to worry. Entrapping *you* is the last thing on my mind."

He scowled. "How did you track me down?"

"Easy," she retorted, "I just followed the trail of fawning women."

He smiled mirthlessly. "I've got news for you. Women don't faint for me, they just press their phone numbers into my hand. But this is the first time one's gotten into my house unannounced."

"You'll have a hard time tossing me out," she said, letting a note of satisfaction creep into her voice.

"Why's that?"

"I'm the newly hired decorator."

Three

Ryan figured if he kept talking, he wouldn't get turned on.

Little Miss Sweet and Tart was the last woman he'd expected to discover inside the house, even if he'd had one heck of an erotic dream about her last night. In fact, for a second, when he'd first seen her, he figured he must *still* be dreaming.

He'd been ticked off this morning when he'd realized whom he'd been fantasizing about and that, combined with his current effort to hold those memories at bay, made him brusque.

"Meri said a decorator would be coming by," he

said icily, "but she also said whoever it was would ring the doorbell if she did."

"I *did* ring the doorbell," Kelly said defensively, "but I got no response."

"I was in the hot tub," he snarled, "and I didn't hear you. Then when I did, it took me a minute to get inside to answer the door."

"Clearly."

Great, Ryan thought. It was the first time he'd had a chance to relax in a hot tub since he didn't know when, and now he had to deal with *her*.

It didn't help she was wearing some ridiculous getup that nevertheless managed to be provocative. She had on a white crewneck T-shirt, a long, high-waisted black skirt and black suspenders. The outfit was finished off with midcalf-length black leggings and black pumps.

Her generous breasts were framed by the high waist of the skirt and by the black suspenders. Damn.

"I rang three times," she said.

"I heard only two."

Her chin came up. "Are you suggesting I'm a liar?"

He smiled mirthlessly. "The apple usually doesn't fall far from the tree."

"Same thing goes." She craned her neck. "Anyone out there with you?"

He frowned. *"No."*

She stopped trying to see outside and gave him a cool look. "Well, I'm surprised."

She went beyond irritating, he decided. And what's more, if she was the decorator, then she'd be hanging around the entire time he was here. The realization came as a blow.

"I didn't see a car," she said.

"It's in the garage."

"Oh."

He raked his hand through his hair. "How long is this damn decorating job supposed to last?"

Her lips tightened. "For several weeks, at least. And please try not to refer to it as 'this damn' anything. Some of us have to work or starve."

"Or depend on the generosity of our *friends,*" he sneered.

He figured Brenda Hartley's daughter could spot a sugar daddy as well as, if not better than, her mother. The two certainly looked alike. The pair shared the same voluptuous figure and dark-red hair—and the same siren voice calling men to their doom.

"Let's keep family out of this," she snapped.

"Can't," he responded. "You're trying to shake some more fruit from that tree."

"It's a business deal!"

"Nothing for Webb Sperling is merely business when an attractive woman is involved."

Her mouth fell open. "Are you suggesting I'm *putting out?*"

He raised his eyebrows and she sucked in an outraged breath.

"I don't put out for anyone," she bit out. "Besides, if the newspapers are to be believed, you're just one of many family members who owns a minority interest in Sperling, Inc., so there's not much you can do about my contract with Sperling stores."

"It's not a contract yet, *sugar.*"

Despite her bravado, he sensed her worry he might be able to do something to cause her deal with Webb Sperling to fall through. The hardened business executive in him knew better than to tip his hand, however.

"Look," she said, "I don't like this arrangement any more than you do. Let's just agree to stay out of each other's way. Next time, I'll ring the doorbell until someone responds or call in advance or whatever."

"Nice to hear, but there won't be a next time." He picked up the cordless phone sitting nearby. "I'm calling the caretaker and getting this project postponed or, better yet, cancelled."

The longer he stood in front of her nearly naked, the harder it was to keep thoughts of sex at bay, which fueled his ire, both at her and at himself.

"You wouldn't dare," she said, hurrying forward.

She stopped an arm's length away, visibly fuming as he dialed the cell number Meri had given him.

When Meri picked up after a couple of rings, Ryan spelled out the problem, his eyes on Kelly.

"But I don't understand," Meri said. "I explained

the decorating project to you previously by phone, and you had no problem with it."

"That was before I knew who you'd hired. Ms. Hartley and I have—" how the hell was he supposed to describe it? "—a history. Or rather, *we* don't, but a couple of family members do."

He had no idea why he was protecting the old man by not bringing his name directly into it. The bastard deserved to have his dirty laundry aired.

"Just think of us as friends of the bride and groom, respectively, after there's been a divorce," he told Meri smoothly, regaining some of his cool. "We're on two different sides of the fence."

The caretaker sighed. "Unfortunately, it's out of my hands. Ms. Hartley's been hired by the Hunter Palmer Foundation. The timeline for getting this decorating job done has been spelled out because we wanted to inconvenience the guests as little as possible. By the time you get all this sorted out with the lawyers for the Foundation, your stay will be over. I'm sorry."

Damn it. Into the phone, he said curtly, "Understood."

When he hung up, Kelly asked apprehensively, "Well?"

He contemplated her for a moment. "You're here for the duration—"

She looked relieved.

"—just make sure to stay out of my way. I want

you to let me know when you're showing up—and ring the damn doorbell!"

With those words, he stomped out of the room and up the staircase to the master suite so he could get some clothes on.

His stay in Tahoe was getting off to a rotten start. First, running into Kelly Hartley, and now finding out she'd be wandering around the lodge for the month.

And attending a wedding yesterday hadn't helped.

Having grown up observing his parents' bad marriage, Ryan had never been one for wedding celebrations. Still, he hadn't been able to say no when Dev had asked him to act as his best man. He knew he would have to go to Tahoe anyway to begin his month-long stay at the lodge.

Though even a harsh cynic about happily-ever-after like himself had to admit that Nicole and Dev were well matched, yesterday's wedding was about as close as he ever wanted to come to the altar.

As he made his way down the upstairs hallway, he glanced at a framed photo of Hunter that hung on the wall.

Damn Hunter. Why couldn't his old buddy have just given a big pile of cash to charity and been done with it? Why rope all his old college friends into this ridiculous lodge-sitting relay?

It didn't make sense.

Still, he'd agreed to come to the lodge, willing

to trust that his fraternity buddy had had his reasons. Hunter had in many ways been the deepest thinker in their group.

And the fact that honoring Hunter's will would benefit cancer patients and survivors had been an added incentive. Ryan had been a generous contributor to various charities to fight cancer his whole adult life.

On top of it all, because of his own mother's untimely death from breast cancer when he'd been seventeen, he was a sucker for honoring an old friend's dying wish.

Kelly watched Ryan leave.

Jerk.

Then a sinking feeling settled in her stomach.

She couldn't believe she had to decorate while he was staying here!

She'd been so full of enthusiasm for this project. Now her excitement lay like broken china on the polished wood floor.

And yet, she couldn't forget her initial reaction when he'd walked through the French doors wearing only a towel. Before he'd opened his mouth, heat had shimmered through her and she'd felt the instinctive primal pull of woman to man.

Ryan's chest had been dappled plains, his biceps pronounced and his legs all corded muscle—as if he worked out but wasn't obsessive about it.

There hadn't been an inch of excess on him. Well, except for, perhaps, *under* the white towel riding low on his hips and serving as a startling contrast to the warm tone of his skin.

She heated at the thought, then stopped short.

She had to remember who Ryan was and who she was.

She could *not* be attracted to Ryan Sperling.

She wasn't like her mother. She wasn't looking for a quick roll in the sack with a rich guy who'd throw a few trinkets her way and then toss her aside without a second glance. She'd built her life refusing to be that stupid, that careless…*that promiscuous.*

And *even* if she were to be, it would be unwise for her to get involved with Ryan Sperling, the son of her mother's former lover and a man who clearly disdained her.

She hated Ryan's contemptuous attitude.

What had he said? *The apple doesn't fall far from the tree.*

He knew nothing about her. Nothing about how hard she'd worked and how far she'd come.

And anyway, if she was mired in mud, so was he. He was the son of a consummate adulterer.

Added to that, she'd caught the momentary flare of attraction in his eyes when he'd spotted her today. Even knowing who she was, he hadn't been able to contain it.

Her lips curved without humor. Ryan Sperling

was attracted to her, as much as he might hate the fact. Her feminine intuition told her so.

With that thought, she headed toward the unfinished bedrooms. She spent the next half hour measuring the rooms and their respective bathrooms.

She already had some idea of the pieces she'd use to furnish the rooms, but she needed to make sure they'd all fit. She hadn't had time to take measurements on her cursory walk-through with Meri.

When she was done measuring, she stood in the middle of the last room, contemplating.

She knew she'd use Woolrich wool plaid for the curtains and some of the upholstery, accenting and contrasting with some flower and solid prints. She also needed an accent piece or two and had already thought of a deep red leather chair for this particular room.

The house, with its polished wood walls and multiple fireplaces, needed warm tones. Big, comfy furniture would add the finishing touch to its inviting feel.

Her planned theme would fit with the decor in the other rooms of the house, as well as be in keeping with local tastes. Though it wasn't the style she favored for Distressed Success, which had a more feminine appeal, it wasn't a big leap for her creatively, either. She'd lived in Tahoe for several years and become familiar with the local styles.

When her cell phone rang she responded absently. "Hello?"

"Hey," Erica said. "Just wanted to touch base. How are you doing?"

"You'll never believe who's staying here," Kelly responded, her voice lowering. The walls were thick, but she didn't want to risk Ryan overhearing her conversation.

"Don't keep me in suspense," Erica said with a laugh. "I have two kids at home. I may not live to see tomorrow."

"Ryan Sperling."

"What?"

"Under the circumstances, I think I can claim the shorter life expectancy," she said with morbid humor. "It's going to kill me to work here with him around."

Ryan had loved Hunter like a brother, but that didn't prevent him from cursing his old friend over the next few days.

He was holed up in the master suite, trying without success to ignore the noises coming from other parts of the house.

If Kelly hadn't been here, he would have been talking to his longtime lawyer, Dan Etherington, from the great room downstairs. Or while lounging on the outdoor deck. Or while ensconced in the office loft.

Instead, he was organizing a clandestine operation out of his temporary bedroom.

"Will he sell?" he said into the phone.

His father's cousin Oliver had been the last hold-out among the family members he'd approached with an offer to buy their shares in Sperling retail stores for an outlandish amount.

The others had gone quietly, tempted by a payday that would permit them to live out their days on a perpetual holiday in Saint-Tropez. They knew Webb Sperling's inflated ego would never permit him to take the family company public, allowing them to each make real money from the sale of their ownership stakes. A sale to another family member—even an estranged black sheep such as Ryan— was the only type of transfer that wasn't restricted by the bylaws of the corporation.

"He's finally been persuaded, it seems," Dan replied.

Ryan laughed mirthlessly. "Must be my charm."

Oliver had lived a life devoted to fast cars, fast women and fast cash for all of his fifty-nine years. The only thing that set him apart from Webb Sperling was the lack of a managerial position in the family company.

"The charm of your greenbacks is more like it," Dan responded drily.

With the acquisition of Oliver's share in Sperling department stores, Ryan would have finally and quietly acquired enough shares for a controlling interest.

Enough shares, he thought with a rush of triumph, to oust Webb Sperling.

His hand tightened on the receiver. He could taste victory and the flavor was sweet. Still, years of playing corporate hardball had taught him to rein in his emotions—and not count on anything until he was ready to spring the trap.

Though other family members, aside from Oliver, were already on board, Ryan was waiting to take the final step in purchasing their shares until he could count on Oliver's. He wanted to make sure Webb Sperling remained in the dark until the last possible moment, when he'd be presented with Ryan's ownership as a done deal.

He was also counting on the fact that there was no love lost between Webb and other family members to keep Webb clueless.

"People want to sell while they can," Dan went on. "You're benefiting from the impression among family members that Webb Sperling is content to sit on his laurels and isn't doing much to keep Sperling stores ahead of competitors."

"My father has been mismanaging things since he took the helm of the company a decade ago," Ryan responded. "For things to be different, he'd have had to show a discipline he's never possessed."

Webb Sperling had become CEO and chairman of the board of Sperling department stores upon the untimely death from a heart attack of his older brother—Ryan's uncle—who'd succeeded Ryan's grandfather.

The general impression in the corporate world was that Webb was an absentee CEO and that much of the work and decision making was done by those lower in command.

"Well, you finally hit the magic number for Oliver," Dan noted.

"Everyone's got his price," Ryan said cynically. "Now that Oliver's given us his verbal okay, I want the transfer of shares done ASAP. The last thing I need is for him to change his mind."

"I'm sending the paperwork to his attorney as we speak," Dan replied.

After ending his call with Dan, Ryan glanced around the room.

A noise from downstairs alerted him to the fact that Kelly was still in the house.

Damn it.

He felt trapped. It was a feeling he was unaccustomed to and he didn't like it.

Suddenly a loud thud sounded from another part of the house.

Ryan swore and strode to the door.

Four

Walking through the open doorway of one of the unfurnished bedrooms, Ryan pulled up short at the sight that greeted him.

Kelly sat on the floor surrounded by cardboard boxes, curtain rods, yards of fabric and an old wooden ladder.

She glanced up at him distractedly and he wasn't sure whether to be annoyed or amused. Women never looked through him. He could say without ego that he was a commanding presence.

She, on the other hand, looked young and fresh faced sitting on the floor, her hair pulled back in a ponytail and her face devoid of makeup. She was wearing jeans and a pink T-shirt that she looked like she'd been poured into.

After quelling a rush of lust, he reluctantly realized she wasn't too different from the way she'd been a few years ago. She was young and eager to make her mark on the world, full of bright dreams and hungry to see them to fruition.

He had to remind himself she was also a scheming little hussy, just like her mother.

"I heard a crash," he said.

He didn't want to admit to the alarm he'd felt when he thought she might have been hurt.

"I accidentally backed into a box that I'd left on the ladder." She shrugged. "It won't happen again."

"I'd be grateful for small favors."

Sexual awareness made his tone mocking. She'd been here three days in a row now, and her constant presence was starting to wear on him.

Every time she'd shown up, she'd been in some outfit guaranteed to entice, though never overtly sexual.

On Monday, she'd been wearing a short-sleeved striped shirt that resembled many of the ones *he* owned, except hers had had a bright white collar and cuffs. She'd paired it with midcalf-length black khakis and ballet flats.

On Tuesday, she'd been wearing an outfit he'd been at a loss even to describe. There'd been some sort of white peekaboo peasant blouse, a knee-length skirt, and peep-toe plaid sling backs.

Who the hell wore plaid shoes? he'd thought, right before the effect of her whole outfit had slammed into him like a fist of lust.

He knew she showed up at the lodge before or after her day at Distressed Success and, now that he knew how she dressed for work, he wondered that she didn't get more male customers. *Lots more.*

Today, mercifully, she was dressed a little more normally. Like him, she wore jeans—but that pink top was giving him ideas.

He looked around in a deliberate attempt to cool off. "*You* hauled in this stuff?"

She must have when he'd been on the phone.

"Yes," she replied.

"Tell me you're not planning to do this yourself."

"Have you got a better idea?" she asked, her tone defensive. "I need to stay on schedule with this project, and I need to get things done whenever I can get away from the shop."

"Who's holding down the fort?" he asked curiously.

"Erica, the employee who walked in when you walked out on Friday." She added, rising, "Not that it's any of your business."

"You're right," he agreed. "It's not."

He should leave. Now. There was no room for misplaced gallantry in his life.

"I'm about to hang curtains in here."

Her message couldn't have been more clear. She was waiting for him to leave.

"You're going to kill yourself trying to get this job done while keeping the shop open," he found himself saying.

He was acquainted with eighteen-hour days from his own climb to the top of the corporate world.

"I'll get it done," she said, seeming to want to cut off further discussion.

"I'll give you a hand."

She looked as shocked as he felt over his unintended offer.

After a moment, she said, "You're offering to help me?"

He shrugged. Heck, even *he* wasn't sure what motivated him. "There's not too much else to do while I'm here."

"Aren't you on vacation?"

"A *working* vacation," he replied. "I need to stick close to the phone and computer."

Until I oust Webb Sperling, he added silently.

He needed to be available for any communications from Dan, and though he had capable managers at his company, El Ray Technology, *he* had the final say as founder and CEO.

She folded her arms. "Okay, what do you know about hanging curtains?"

"I did volunteer work on low-income housing in

high school." He shrugged. "I went to a place where character-building activities were big on the agenda."

There hadn't been nearly enough of the character-building stuff going on in the Sperling family. But he'd managed to hammer and paint his way into Harvard.

She dropped her arms. "Why would you want to help me? After all, you'd be helping my business and you've already made it clear what you think of the direction that's heading in."

"Maybe I'm hoping to distract you so you'll forget all about Sperling, Inc.," he said with dry humor.

"I frown on corporate sabotage," she said disapprovingly, and he gave a snort of laughter at the earnest expression on her face.

"Aren't you on vacation, even if it is just a working one?" she persisted.

"Not quite a vacation."

In response to her inquiring look, he asked, "How much do you know about the lodge and why it was built?"

"Almost nothing," she replied. "But there was plenty of speculation among the locals when the house went up, and rumor has it there has been a different man staying here every month since March."

"Nathan Barrister, Luke Barton and Dev Campbell," he said, identifying them. "We were all good buddies and housemates at Harvard. Hunter Palmer was a close mutual friend of ours."

"The guy whose foundation built the lodge," Kelly stated comprehendingly.

"Yeah, he's dead." A wave of nostalgia, then sadness, unexpectedly washed over him. They'd all been young and full of hope back then. Much less cynical and hardened to the world.

"I'm sorry."

He fixed her with a bland look. "It's been ten years. He died of melanoma right before graduation. In his will, he set aside money to have the lodge built. If each of the remaining six of us spends a month here, the property will become a rest and recovery place for cancer patients and survivors."

"And that's where I come in with the decorating job," she finished for him.

He inclined his head, then added drily, "Except where you come in is during my damned month."

For the first time, though, he could see some humor in their situation.

Kelly watched as Ryan held up the curtain rod at the level they'd marked on the wall.

"Okay?" he said.

"Mmm-hmm," she responded. She really needed to get her mind off the way his rear end looked encased in those jeans and the way his green shirt stretched across the expanse of his broad back.

She was reluctantly grateful for the help he'd

offered earlier, but she still didn't completely understand why he'd offered it. Plus, he'd said nothing to
indicate his opinion had changed about her negotiations with Webb Sperling.

She just hoped the wheels of the administrative
process at Sperling, Inc. moved quickly from here
on out.

Ryan turned to look at her, and she started guiltily.

He cocked an eyebrow. "How am I supposed to
interpret 'mmm-hmm'?"

"Looks good." *Everything* looked good.

"Great," he said, taking the curtain rod off the
wall and stepping off the stepladder.

He set the rod on the floor and looked around.
"Now that we have the right height, I'll need a
screwdriver to get the rod in place."

"I'm capable of doing it myself."

"Yeah, I know, but humor me. I'd be bored
otherwise."

"Wouldn't you be bored if I *didn't* challenge
you?" she parried.

His eyes glinted. "With women, it depends on the
time and place, but since we *are* in the bedroom, I'd
have to concede you're right."

"Sexist pig."

He laughed. "I knew that comment would get a
rise out of you."

Despite the tremor that went through her in
reaction to his words, she decided to steer the con-

versation to safer ground, and gestured to a pink case on the floor. "It's in there."

He lowered himself to his haunches and opened the case, then looked up at her. "Tool kit?"

"At least we're getting in the game," she shot back.

She sold the woman-sized tool kits in Distressed Success and used one herself at home.

He flashed a grin. "I'll try to adjust."

She was fairly sure he meant to the tools and not to women being in the game but still, she asked, "Why should a woman have to beg and prod her husband or boyfriend to get some curtains hung?"

"I'm all for female empowerment," he said easily, taking the screwdriver out of the case and straightening.

"And yet, given a say in the matter," she shot back, "you'd pull the plug on Distressed Success in a second."

Any hint of humor disappeared from his face. "That's personal."

"How is what I do different from what you do?" she pressed. "You're an entrepreneur and I'm a boutique owner. We're both trying to grow a business."

"I don't try to fleece people with feminine wiles."

"No, you just twist their arm with your money and power," she retorted.

His expression tightened. "Are you going to try to convince me your deal with Sperling has nothing to do with your being the daughter of my father's former lover?"

She threw up her hands in exasperation.

"Look, we've got different perspectives on this issue and neither of us is going to convince the other."

"Agreed."

She watched as he climbed the wooden ladder and started to put a bracket in place for the curtain rod.

It shouldn't have been so sexy to watch him do a menial task, but it was. He was effectively acting as her handyman and she found it all incredibly arousing, no matter how infuriating she found his opinions.

She *really* needed to put their relationship back on a more professional footing, she thought.

"I need to pay you," she said into the silence.

He glanced at her, amusement stamped on his face once again. "Do you know how much I'm worth? The opportunity cost alone would put me out of your price range."

She flushed, but persisted stubbornly, "Still, I ought to compensate you…"

He turned back to put in another screw. "Okay," he said finally, "but I need a point of reference. How much do you charge for *your* services?"

"You couldn't afford me," she responded automatically.

He gave a bark of laughter and looked at her again. "Okay then, we're even."

On the contrary, she disagreed silently. They were far from *even* and she seemed to be losing ground with every passing second.

"All right, when I say lift, we're going to pick up this mattress and set it down upright on its shorter side at the foot of the bed."

Kelly blew tendrils of hair out of her face.

Ryan Sperling, she'd discovered over the course of the past four days, was a man used to issuing commands.

Still, she knew she ought to be charitable. He'd done physical labor uncomplainingly all week. He'd helped her put up curtains, lay down rugs, move furniture and hang pictures. He hadn't even balked when she'd announced today there was a change of plan and she wanted to put this bed in another room.

She watched now as Ryan planted his hands at his waist. "Let's pay attention."

"Right, sorry." There was no way for him to know what she'd been thinking about, but nevertheless heat rose to her face.

She grasped the handles at the sides of the mattress and watched as Ryan did the same on his end.

"Lift," he ordered.

When they got the mattress upright, he grasped it around its shorter side and maneuvered it to lean against the bedroom wall.

Kelly reflected that though Ryan's help had been invaluable these past few days, it had come at a price: their physical proximity was beginning to wear on her.

Just this morning, she'd been aghast to discover she'd dreamed about him. And it hadn't been a sweet dream, either. *No.* In her dream, he'd come to her, massaged her breasts and looked into her eyes with a look of desire. In her dream, he wasn't Webb Sperling's son and she wasn't Brenda Hartley's daughter.

And somewhat more disturbingly, these past few days she could feel his hot eyes on her when he thought she wasn't looking.

What's more, she'd become quite the expert at surreptitious glances herself.

It was clear, however, that his was an unwilling type of attraction. And she didn't know whether to be flattered or offended because she felt likewise.

Of course, it made no sense for her to be attracted to him. From the day he'd walked into Distressed Success, he'd made it clear he thought she was a slut—a floozy, who, like her mother, was one step away from earning her living in one of Nevada's famous brothels.

Wouldn't Ryan be stunned to learn the truth! she reflected. She only *wished* she was having as much fun as her supposed scarlet reputation warranted.

"Now the box spring," Ryan said, heading back toward the bed.

She sighed. "You're comfortable giving commands."

"Yeah, and having them obeyed," he replied with dry humor.

"It wasn't a compliment."

"I'd rather be respected than liked."

"Why can't you be both? Respected and—"

"—inspiring the warm fuzzies?" he finished for her, then shook his head. "Some of us aren't selling romance for a living."

"Well, I haven't heard that one before," she responded. "This is the first time someone has said Distressed Success is *selling romance*."

He gave her a droll look. "You should use it as an ad slogan. 'Distressed Success. We sell romance.' You'll have those workaholic guys beating a path to your door. Expand your demographic."

"Helping me again?" she said, matching his flippant tone. "At this rate, I'll be ready for the big time before your month is up."

"High standards I can respect," he responded. "They're what set a good business apart from its competitors."

"That's how I feel," she said in surprise.

"Then you've got a decent shot at making something out of your business." He looked down at the box spring. "Ready?"

A little while later, the bed now set up in the next room, Kelly sat down and flopped back on it.

Frowning, he braced his hands on his waist. "What are you doing?"

"Taking a break," she responded.

She surveyed him. He looked none the worse for this afternoon's exertions. In fact, he might as well have just come in from a stroll.

He looked at his watch. "We've got fifteen minutes before you need to get back to the shop. We can hang those two picture frames you wanted in the bathroom."

"Don't you ever stop?" she asked in exasperation. "Erica accuses me of being all work and no play, but I seem like a slacker next to you."

"Just trying to work off some edginess."

"What are you edgy about?" she asked curiously.

His face shuttered. "Nothing."

It clearly wasn't *nothing.*

"I've been jogging," he elaborated, "but I'm not getting the workout I'm used to back home."

"Let me guess. You normally rise at five in the morning to get on the elliptical trainer."

"And let me guess, *you* don't. Instead, you're having tea out of a mismatched cup and saucer."

She shook her head and smiled. "Tea's at four in the afternoon," she corrected. "Civilized."

Civilized, she thought, was what Ryan barely seemed, despite generations of money and breeding in the Sperling family tree. He emanated raw masculinity and barely leashed power.

He eyed her and she belatedly realized how she must look lying before him. She was wearing a sheer emerald green blouse over a snug-fitting beige tank, and had paired them with pedal pushers.

They didn't like each other, she reminded herself. They had just unexpectedly been thrown together this month, and had reached a de facto truce so they could be civil to each other.

His gaze trailed over her. "Yeah, well, don't worry. You're none the worse for not hitting the gym at five. Everything looks good."

Men, she thought, suddenly indignant. He was willing to look down at her, literally and figuratively, but that didn't prevent him from enjoying the view.

"How can you know me so well and yet think so little of me?" she blurted.

He didn't respond, but the look on his face was one of sexual awareness blended with irritation and it spoke of his inner battle.

All at once, she'd had enough. Enough of his scorn, enough of his disdain, enough of his attitude altogether. She'd spent a lifetime feeling answerable for her mother's actions and she'd had enough.

She patted the bed beside her. "Take a break."

He looked from her to the bed, his eyes narrowing.

She almost smiled, feeling a touch reckless—and strangely empowered.

"No, thanks," he said roughly. "Let's get a move on."

She arched a brow. "Does it bother you if I lie here?"

"In a word, *yes*."

His hand closed around her ankle, and he pulled her toward him.

She gasped and sat up, lowering her feet to the floor as she reached the edge of the bed.

"That's better," he said, his eyes gleaming.

She stood up and watched as his gaze went to the cleavage revealed by her V-neck blouse.

When his gaze finally came back to hers, time seemed to slow.

She searched his face. His expression was forbidding, but desire was nevertheless stamped on every feature. *He wanted to kiss her.*

Her lips parted and she felt a tingling awareness all over.

"You don't even like me," she said.

"Yeah, but right now, it's hard to care," he responded.

"This is a bad idea."

"I've had worse," he muttered.

"You're going to kiss me."

"Are you going to object?" he asked, bending toward her.

Her eyes fluttered closed and she sighed as his lips touched hers. His mouth was warm and soft as it moved over hers, shaping and stroking.

Her arms stole up to his neck and his came around her, so that they fit together snugly.

This, she thought, was what she'd wondered about ever since he'd walked into her shop, but the real thing was even better than she'd imagined.

She opened to him, allowing him to take the kiss deeper.

Within moments, liquid desire pooled between her legs and her breasts grew heavy and sensitive.

Her hand ran through his hair, anchoring him, as the heat they generated took them ever higher.

She moaned and shifted, and it seemed to fuel his response and need.

Abruptly, however, he lifted his head and he pushed her away.

"Damn it," he said harshly, his eyes glittering.

She felt off balance, but his reaction soon sunk in.

"Damn it," he repeated, running a hand through his hair, as if unable to believe his own stupidity. "You're the daughter of my father's former mistress. My father was sleeping with your mother while mine was dying!"

His words stung, dredging up feelings of being cheap and unclean—guilt by association with Brenda Hartley.

Her chin came up. "And that sums it up, doesn't it?"

"Those are the facts that you and I can't change," he countered.

"Except you're attracted despite yourself, aren't you, Ryan?" she tossed out. "And you hate yourself for feeling that way."

She turned then, grabbed her purse and bolted from the room.

When she made it down to the lower level of the house, she could hear Ryan's footsteps upstairs.

"Kelly!"

Without heeding his attempt to catch up with her, she yanked open the lodge's front door and walked rapidly to her car.

Moments later, as she pulled out of the drive with a spray of gravel, she let the humiliation sink in.

She would not be that vulnerable to Ryan Sperling again, she vowed.

She, of all people, should have known better.

Five

That night, Ryan nursed a beer at the bar of the White Fir Tavern. As he took a swig of his drink, he looked around him morosely.

The White Fir was your typical rustic roadside bar, except it claimed to have been in existence since 1930. A steady trickle of upscale tourists through its doors lent it some pretension. The wood surface of the bar was so dark and beer stained, it was practically black. An unused pool table stood to one side, along with a fifties-style jukebox.

The place was about half-full, and between the steady drone of conversation and the wail of Chuck

Berry, the waitstaff could be heard calling out orders to the short-order cook.

Ryan glanced behind him. The short blonde at the middle table looked familiar from the day he'd stomped out of Distressed Success. What had Kelly called her—Erica?

She sat now with a big, equally blond guy. A husband or boyfriend, he figured.

Given the way things had gone with Kelly earlier in the day, he wasn't inclined to introduce himself to one of her friends.

In any case, Erica didn't appear to recognize him. Or if she did, she preferred to keep her distance. Maybe Kelly had already confided in her and Erica was calling him ten kinds of rat under her breath.

He shook his head. If women just got over the loyalty thing, he thought wryly, they could rule the world.

On the other hand, *his* major problem appeared to be a lack of self-discipline. He couldn't believe he'd let loose and kissed her.

He needed to have his head examined—or get laid. The second approach had its appeal, but the only woman he was interested in at the moment was Kelly and going to bed with her would only worsen the problem, not lessen it.

He wished to hell his month at the lodge were over. Of all the places in the world, Hunter would have to have chosen Kelly's backyard to build his damn house, and *he'd* have to have chosen the month when she'd be working there, parading her tempting butt in his face.

He took another swig of his beer. He needed to stay away from her.

No more helping out with her decorating. It had been a mistake from the beginning to offer his assistance. He could see that now.

Too bad the only thing he could still see was the memory of Kelly lying across a bed like the greatest temptation.

"So how's it going over there at the lodge?" Erica asked.

"Fine," Kelly said curtly, setting down a lamp with more force than necessary.

It was Friday morning and they were straightening up inside Distressed Success in anticipation of opening the store at ten.

Erica quirked a brow. "Just 'fine'?"

"He's a pain in the butt," she blurted. There was no need for her to explain who *he* was.

Erica laughed. "I thought he was helping you."

"He is."

Beside her, Erica stopped setting out new inventory and searched her face. "And?"

"Yesterday, he kissed me."

Erica's eyes widened, then she grinned. "I

guess he's taken to heart the saying about loving your enemy."

Kelly arched a brow.

"Keep your friends close and your enemies closer?" Erica asked.

"This situation is *not* funny." She'd been brooding all last night over how she was going to face Ryan again. How was she ever going to be able to work at the lodge anymore?

Erica pretended to consider. "Let's see…wealthy, gorgeous guy puts the moves on you." She nodded knowingly. "Yup, definitely not funny."

"Afterward, he regretted it," she said in a rush, reliving the moment. "He couldn't believe he'd committed the unpardonable sin of being attracted to a Hartley. I guess the parallels to his father and to Webb's affair with Brenda were too much for him."

"Jerk," Erica agreed cheerfully. "I should tell you some of the insensitive things Greg said to me when I first met him."

Kelly frowned. "Are you defending Ryan Sperling?"

"No," Erica responded. "He's an arrogant jerk who deserves to be taken down a peg."

"Exactly."

"Still," Erica said, tilting her head, "you haven't told me how *you* felt when he kissed you."

"I—"

The truth was…the truth was, it had been wonderful. She'd felt dizzy with sensation. Aloud, she said, "Does it matter? It ended badly."

"Repressed sexual desire," Erica responded knowingly. "Ryan slipped the leash yesterday and he's pissed off. Still, it's not good to repress emotion."

Kelly sighed impatiently. Sometimes she forgot that she and Erica had bonded over the fact they were both the children of free spirits. Erica was the youngest child of 1960s flower children who'd spent time in Haight-Ashbury, and she…well, *she* was the daughter of Brenda Hartley.

"Ryan's not repressing anything," Kelly replied. "It was just a kiss. Unplanned and spur-of-the-moment." And out of control. "I've been at the lodge all week and he's helped me out. That's it. In the evenings, he takes himself off to who-knows-where."

"The White Fir Tavern," Erica said.

Kelly looked at her blankly. "What? How do you know that?"

"It's where I meet Greg after work so we can drive home together. Greg and I have seen Ryan eating dinner or having a drink at the bar a couple of nights this week."

So *that* was where Ryan went when he left the lodge alongside her in the evenings. She'd wondered where he was going, even though she'd told herself not to.

"Both times there've been women hitting on him, too," Erica supplied.

She felt a stab of jealousy.

Stop it, stop it, stop it, she told herself.

Still, she steamed over Ryan's double standard. Apparently, he was willing to paint *her* as a wanton hussy while *he* hung out with the swinging singles crowd at the White Fir Tavern.

She, meanwhile, had spent her evenings the way she usually did—quietly at home, *alone.* Often, she was simply trying to catch up on billing and other correspondence for Distressed Success.

Erica shrugged. "You'd think Ryan would expect to see you there, offering lap dances to the male patrons, from the things he's said to you."

"Yes," she mused, "he would, wouldn't he?"

This wasn't the smartest idea she'd ever had, Kelly conceded.

Still, now that she was here, she had no choice but to brazen it out.

Inside the White Fir Tavern, she spotted Erica and Greg sharing a table near the center of the pub.

The second thing she noticed was Ryan, sitting at the bar holding a beer, turned mostly away from her and the entrance.

Kelly noticed Erica's eyes widen when she saw her.

She'd told her assistant to go on home, since she just needed to finish closing up shop for the day. Instead, she'd gone to the back of the store and changed clothes before coming on over to the White Fir Tavern herself.

She knew Erica and Greg would be there, maybe sharing a quick drink or some finger food before heading home to the kids and relieving the babysitter, who happened to be Erica's mother.

Of course, the other person Kelly knew she'd find at the White Fir Tavern was Ryan.

But as she moved toward Erica's table, she refused to look around because she didn't want to lose her nerve.

And judging from the look on Erica's face, Kelly knew exactly how she must appear. Her whole outfit begged for attention, from the bronze halter top to the black skirt and three-inch spike heels.

She got plenty of looks from the male patrons—admiring, appreciative and lustful.

As she approached Erica, Greg turned around, too, and his arrested expression put both courage and fear in Kelly's step, since it was probably a good indication of what Ryan's reaction would be.

"Hi," Kelly said brightly, stopping at their table.

"What are you doing?" Erica asked in a low voice.

"Just what we discussed," she responded. "Living up to what's expected of me."

Greg looked from Kelly to his wife. "Anyone care to fill me in?"

Erica nodded her head toward the bar. "It's about the guy over there who's staying at the lodge this month while Kelly is decorating. Ryan Almighty Sperling. He thinks Kelly is a—" she paused and threw Kelly an apologetic look "—slut. Kelly has taken it into her head to make a point."

Kelly watched as Greg looked up at her. "Well, I'd say she made it, all right." His glance moved beyond her, and his lips twitched. "And to the guy at the bar, too."

"Good," she said emphatically, though she felt the hairs at the back of her neck prick. "I'm going to get myself a drink."

She sauntered to the bar, taking care not to look directly at Ryan, though she could sense the heat of his gaze.

"Jack and diet," she instructed the White Fir Tavern's bartender, a genial-looking man in his sixties.

The bartender's eyes crinkled and he set down a napkin before her. "Coming right up. Lady knows what she wants."

She smiled. "Today I do. Thank you."

"What the hell are you doing here?" Ryan said roughly.

She took her time turning to face him.

His expression was grim as his eyes raked her, pausing at her cleavage, where her breasts threatened to spill from the restraint of her halter top.

"What am *I* doing here?" she challenged. "I thought *you* were the newcomer."

His lips thinned. "You know what I mean."

"I'm acting the way you expect me to," she said with defiance. "Isn't this where you thought I'd be?"

Given his opinion of Hartleys, he should think she'd fit right in here among the women hanging out at the White Fir Tavern—and pawing him, if Erica was to be believed.

The bartender set her drink down before her and she picked it up and took a sip, scanning the room. More than a few men continued to look her way—and enjoy.

Ryan threw some bills down on the counter and said grimly, "I'm settling the tab for both of us."

Kelly threw him a flirtatious look, then turned to walk away.

Without invitation, Ryan followed.

She stopped at her table and gestured at Erica and Greg. "Have you met my friends? Erica and Greg Barnes—" she waved a negligent hand in Ryan's direction "—this is Ryan Sperling."

Erica smiled and Ryan and Greg shook hands.

She and Ryan sat down at the small round table. Erica turned to Ryan. "So, Kelly mentioned you're staying at the lodge while she's decorating."

"Yes, I am." Ryan shot Kelly a look, but she refused to turn his way. "Just for the month."

"How do you like Tahoe?" Greg asked.

"I haven't been here in several years," Ryan responded, shooting her another look. "It's interesting coming back. Some things have changed and others are really *familiar.*"

While Erica and Greg continued to make desultory conversation with Ryan about the local area, the atmosphere at the table continued to carry an undercurrent of tension.

After some time, a young waitress in a low-cut top came around to take an order of drinks. The waitress smiled invitingly at Ryan, who looked as if he didn't mind the attention, and Kelly thought sourly that bare boobs were apparently acceptable on anyone *not* named Hartley. She put in an order for a green-apple martini—one of Brenda's favorites. After that, she remained determinedly distracted, smiling an invitation at the men who happened to look her way.

Eventually, though, Erica and Greg announced they had to get back to the kids.

When everyone rose from the table, Erica leaned close. "I hope you know what you're doing."

Kelly smiled reassuringly. "I'm having the time of my life, can't you tell?"

With a look of semiserious warning, Erica turned toward the door and Kelly took the opportunity to walk back to the bar and settle herself on a stool, leaving Ryan alone at the table.

Ryan's presence had been keeping men away, she thought irritably, and it was time she did something about it.

After she'd ordered another fabulous martini—

why hadn't she discovered them earlier in her life?—she smiled at the attractive man sitting next to her. She'd noticed he'd looked her way occasionally since he'd walked into the bar fifteen minutes ago, and now she met those looks straight on.

He looked to be around thirty, with sandy-blond hair and blue eyes. If it had been wintertime, she would have said he was a ski bum, drawn to the slopes nearby. Tahoe attracted those with money to burn to its slopes, lake and nearby casinos.

"Buy you a drink?" he offered.

She smiled back. "Thank you." Then she leaned closer, conspiratorially. "You're more likable than the other guy who offered to buy me a drink tonight."

She used the term *offered* loosely. Ryan, in typical high-handed fashion, had announced he was settling the bill and that was that.

The man next to her smiled back. "I noticed you the minute I walked in."

She learned his name was Tate and he was another money-to-burn fun seeker vacationing in Tahoe.

All the while, however, she could feel Ryan's eyes boring into the back of her head.

She took another sip of her drink, her third, and thought she had a nice little buzz going.

She cast a sidelong look at Tate, then one at Ryan, who still sat sullenly, beer in front of him, at the table they'd shared with Erica and Greg.

The contrast between the two men couldn't have been more apparent. One was a blond thrill seeker, the other a dark angel with a mission. And the more she talked and flirted with Tate, the more she thought she preferred the former.

She smiled languidly at her bar buddy. He was a nice man, she decided with a warm rush. He was full of effusive compliments that bolstered her confidence, *unlike* another man she could name.

She leaned in, resting her hand on Tate's arm.

Ryan's jaw hardened.

She was tipsy and getting more inebriated by the minute.

Of course, the smooth-talking charmer Kelly was flirting with was enjoying every second of it. Likely, he was waiting for the moment when she was so far gone he could convince her to head home to bed with him.

On top of it all, the guy had thrown him a couple of amused looks, as if he knew he was an interloper and was enjoying the fact.

Ryan's hand flexed on his drink. He itched to slug Prince Charming.

He knew the type. Growing up under Webb Sperling's roof had taught him to identify it.

He told himself he didn't care, but then Kelly leaned toward the guy, laughing, her eyes too bright, and Ryan downed the last of his drink and rose.

As he walked toward the bar, he told himself he was just irritated *this* was the thanks he got for toiling for her all week.

"Are you here with someone?" Charming said to Kelly, noting his approach.

"No—"

"Yes," Ryan cut in, "she's with me."

Kelly swung around. "No, I'm not." She looked beyond him. "Where are Erica and Greg?"

"They left," he responded flatly.

"Oh, right."

He looked at her closely. She'd clearly passed *tipsy* and was well on her way to *ditsy*.

He turned then and sized up the guy she was with.

There was a reason, he thought, that the initials for Prince Charming were *P.C.* The guy looked as if he never put a foot wrong—as if he knew exactly how to ingratiate himself with women.

"Tate Henderson," the guy said, offering his hand.

"Ryan Sperling," he responded, ignoring the hand.

Tate's face registered surprise. "Ryan Sperling? The guy behind El Ray Technology?"

"None other," he responded curtly.

Tate, however, became more animated. "I've heard of you. You're a legend in the cable world, not to mention a favorite on Wall Street. Those shares you offered—"

Kelly stifled a yawn with her hand.

Ryan glanced at her. He was putting a damper on her tête-à-tête with Tate and she clearly wasn't happy about it.

Ryan didn't mind invoking his wealth and power when it suited his purposes, and *now* definitely suited his purposes.

Ryan signaled the bartender and leaned forward, wedging himself between Tate and Kelly to order another drink, tonic water that he intended to sip while he kept an eye on Kelly's Brenda Hartley impersonation.

Turning back after he'd ordered, he took the opportunity to murmur to Tate, "Sweetness is on her way to Happyland. I'm here to make sure she gets home safely—and alone."

Tate raised his eyebrows. "What's she to you?"

"There's a family connection."

The other man's lips quirked up. "It's always something like that."

Tate downed the rest of his drink, then leaned back to reach into the pocket of his jeans.

"Leave it," Ryan said. "I'll settle the tab."

Tate gave a brief nod of acknowledgement and slid off his bar stool as Ryan stepped back from the bar.

Kelly frowned. "Where are you going?"

"It's been a pleasure, *sweetness*," Tate responded, tossing an amused look at Ryan.

Kelly's frowned deepened. "You're leaving?"

Tate glanced at Ryan. "I'd ask *him*."

Ryan and Kelly both watched as Tate moved off toward the door, then Kelly swung to face Ryan.

"You chased him off," she accused.

"No chasing was involved."

"Thanks a lot," she muttered. "It's none of your business."

She took another swallow of her drink, then looked surprised when she came up short.

Ryan watched as she signaled the bartender.

"Don't you think you should go easy?" he asked.

"I'm not talking to you."

He sighed and settled down on the bar stool beside her, opposite the one where Tate had been sitting. Clearly, she wasn't going to make this simple.

"If you're looking for some action, why don't you go after the guy you really want?" he challenged.

She surveyed him. "I don't want you."

He arched a brow. "That wasn't the case when you were moaning in my arms."

Her lips pursed. "Go away."

"Can't. That option isn't available to you."

They sat without talking for close to an hour. She made vain attempts to flirt with other men, but Ryan knew his presence—like a dragon at the gate—would keep them away.

He'd have to put a stop to this at some point soon. She was obviously a drinking lightweight and, despite the sex-on-heels outfit, she seemed un-accustomed to the bar scene.

Finally he watched as she finished her drink and tossed a look his way.

He looked back at her.

"You're cute, you know?" she said, her voice a little slurred.

He arched an eyebrow. "Some have said so."

Now *this* was an interesting turn in the conversation.

She tilted her head and touched his hair. "You've got wonderfully thick, dark hair."

He stiffened at her touch, and want shot through him.

"Such deep, dark eyes." She sighed, then pronounced, "Mysterious."

She looked back at his hair and said sadly, "You'd have *beautiful* hair if you kept it longer than almost military length."

An unbidden smile tugged at his lips. Nobody used a soft, frilly word like *beautiful* for him. And though he knew it was the alcohol talking, he felt his body grow taut in response.

She leaned toward him but, when it seemed as if she was about to lose her balance, his hand shot out to steady her, clamping down on her thigh—and staying there.

They both looked down, then she looked up and met his gaze.

"Nice hands, too," she said huskily.

He could see the lovely rays of golden-brown in her hazel eyes and his hand tightened on her leg.

Then he caught himself. He wasn't here so she could hit on him. He was here so he knew she got home okay.

"Let's go," he said.

She sat back. "Go?" she echoed. "Well, that's direct."

"You're slurring your words." He called over the bartender, then covered their tab plus a hefty tip.

She hopped off the bench, showing off mile-long legs and he sent up a prayer for resistance he didn't have.

Then, because she teetered on her heels, he took her arm. And when that didn't seem to do the trick, he bent in one quick motion and swung her into his arms.

She gasped and he could feel every luscious curve of her pressed into him.

He moved toward the front door, and one of the other patrons opened it for him.

He glanced down at her as he walked over the gravel drive to his car. "You know," he said wryly, "I think I like you better drunk."

"You know, I think I like you better when I'm drunk." She frowned, concentrating. "Wait. Did I say that right?"

He smiled. "It came out okay."

She looked at his car. "A black Mercedes. I

wasn't surprised you drive a Mercedes. You've always had money."

He ignored the comment about money. Dangerous territory, he decided, right before he set her down—against the car, just in case.

He got the front passenger door open. "In you go."

She looked around, perplexed. "Where's *my* car?"

"Doesn't matter. You're in no shape to drive."

"Hmm…I guess I agree?"

Then, because she chose to just stand there and he was getting impatient, he picked her up and put her in the front seat.

He reached across her for the seat belt and strapped her in, all the while brushing against her, picking up her scent and testing his endurance even more.

"What's the perfume you're wearing?" he asked roughly.

She smiled. "Sin."

"Of course."

He closed the passenger door and went around the front of the car.

On the drive over to the lodge, she was chatty. She yawned a few times, too, tiredness winning out over the alcohol.

"You're not as bad as you seem," she observed after an interlude.

Her words came out sleepy, and he glanced at her, taking his eyes off the road for a moment. She was striving to keep her eyes open.

"You're doing a good deed by staying at the lodge. Hunter Palmer was your friend and you'll be helping sick people."

"It's my good deed for the decade," he disavowed. "I'm as low and slimy as you think."

If she was calling even *him* nice, she must really be tired or wasted or both.

Six

When they got to the lodge, Ryan pulled into the garage and got Kelly upstairs to the guest suite next to the master bedroom.

Once there, she sat on the bed and looked around. "This room is so pretty. I hope I can do as good a job with the rooms I'm decorating."

"I'm sure you will," he reassured her.

"Do you think so?" she asked hopefully.

He nodded.

There was not much else he could say. The room they were in looked fine to him. Maybe it was because he came from money and took it all for granted, but he'd never been too interested in the aesthetics of his surroundings.

He regarded Kelly. "Are you okay getting undressed and into bed by yourself?"

She flopped back onto the bed so that she was lying in it. "Of course."

He sighed, then reached out and grasped her hands to pull her back to a sitting position. "Okay, sweetness, let's really get you ready for bed."

With her cooperation, he got her shoes off, tugged off her skirt and breathed a sigh of relief when it turned out she was wearing a strapless bra beneath her halter top.

Undressing her was pure torture. He was just glad she was too tired and inebriated to turn up the heat on him even more.

"I'm just like my mother," she said as he tossed her clothes onto a nearby chair.

He stopped because her comment came out of nowhere. "What?"

She looked forlorn. "I'm being undressed by a man I met in a bar."

He wanted to point out that they'd known each other before tonight and that he had no intention of taking her to bed—he just wanted to put her *in* one.

"No matter how hard I try," she said sorrowfully, "I can never escape my mother's past."

Now *that* he could relate to. Hell, he'd been

trying to escape his legacy for more years than he could count.

Aloud, he said, trying to offer some solace, "You're not the only one."

He pulled back the bedcovers and she slid her legs underneath them. Without delay, he tugged the covers up, hiding her tantalizing body from view.

She sank back against the pillows and closed her eyes, and he expelled a breath.

In a moment, however, her eyes opened again. "You forgot to take off my bra."

He clenched his jaw. "I didn't forget." He mentally ran through explanations. "There are no pajamas here for you to wear, so you'll have to sleep in your bra."

The logic wasn't great, but he hoped in her current foggy state, she'd let it pass.

"Hmm," she said, and in the next second, sat up and reached behind her.

Her luscious breasts sprang free.

He couldn't help himself. He took it all in hungrily.

Her breasts were round and firm and capped with tight, dusky pink nipples.

Kelly dropped the bra to the side and lay back down, pulling up the covers as she did so.

"I've never had a man look at them like that before," she murmured, her eyes drifting closed. "But then, I've never been to bed with a man before, either." After a moment, she added more faintly,

"Well, one guy. Once or twice. But he didn't stay the night."

His mind churned with questions, but her peaceful expression told him she'd fallen asleep.

She had dropped quite a few bombshells on him tonight, but damned if she hadn't left the biggest for last.

Kelly woke with a headache.

She moaned and pressed her head into the pillow.

Some of the events of the night before came back and she reflected that she'd drunk more at the White Fir than she'd ever put back at one go in her life.

Making a note to herself that those apple martinis were potent stuff, she finally opened her eyes and looked around.

It took a moment to register she was in the already-furnished guest suite at the lodge.

Her heart seized and she bolted to a sitting position…then moaned again and cupped her forehead.

Ryan had driven her back to the lodge.

With dread, she peered under the covers, and discovered she was naked except for her panties.

She groaned, remembering how she had bared her breasts to Ryan, and how he had fixed his searing gaze on them.

How was she *ever* going to look him in the eye again? Last night made the kiss they'd shared in one of the lodge's bedrooms seem insignificant in comparison. She had bigger problems to think about now—starting with needing to get to work.

She checked the bedside alarm clock. It was seven. Enough time, she thought with relief, for her to get out of here, home to change and then to work at Distressed Success.

Her mind skittered across the fact that she wasn't sure she remembered *everything* she'd said and done last night. What if she'd forgotten something significant?

She winced, then willed herself out of bed and got in the shower. Fortunately, the adjoining bathroom was stocked with towels and toiletries, and the shower helped clear her head.

Afterward, stepping back into the bedroom, she threw on the previous evening's clothes because she had nothing else to wear. She left her panties off, however, and stuffed them in her purse.

She reflected that she *really* was turning into her mother if she was walking around without underwear.

She shook off the thought as she towel dried her hair. Last night *was* an aberration. She was going to go home and resume life as usual.

But first she had to get out of here without a confrontation with Ryan.

When she was done fixing her hair and straightening up the bedroom, she slung her purse over her shoulder, took a deep breath and headed toward the door.

Outside in the hallway, she found herself tiptoeing without meaning to.

She told herself that she didn't want to awaken Ryan if he was still asleep. It was only after seven in the morning. Closer to eight, really, but who was around to quibble with her?

She stole down the stairs, then crept toward the front entrance.

"Good morning."

She jumped and turned.

Ryan stood there, an amused expression on his face. He was holding a cup of coffee, and looked relaxed and showered.

"Er— good morning."

He was dressed in jeans and a gray T-shirt, and looked not only clean, but refreshed. It wasn't fair, she reflected, that he should look so put together, while she felt rumpled and tawdry.

"You weren't leaving without saying goodbye, were you?" Then without waiting for an answer, he added, "Coffee?"

She regarded him suspiciously because he looked to be in a good mood.

He *should* be furious with her. He'd definitely seemed so last night. She had gotten wasted, hit on another guy and given him the cold shoulder. Then he'd had to drive her home.

"Um, thanks," she responded, "but I'd prefer just to head home."

He looked her over. "You're looking good this morning…all things considered."

She wanted to tell him that her outfit felt like dessert: Some things were best indulged in before regrets took hold.

His eyes came back to hers and now she could see the flicker of amusement in their depths. "I guess you didn't have a choice but to jump back into last night's clothes."

She looked down at what she was wearing, trying to brazen it out. "What, this? I find a halter top a freshening change from work clothes, don't you?"

"I wouldn't know," he murmured, then looked at her purse. "I guess the underwear is optional."

She followed his gaze and realized with embarrassment that her panties peeked out of her open bag.

Could life get any more humiliating?

"No underwear," he said wickedly. "Just how I like it."

She flushed. He was enjoying teasing her, and unfortunately she was giving him the reaction he wanted.

He seemed to be *flirting* with her, though *that* didn't make sense.

Last night, she'd proven every preconception he'd had of her and then some. She'd acted like her mother and worse.

"Aren't you angry at me?" she blurted.

He tilted his head. "What for?"

"For last night," she tossed out. "I had too much

to drink and you had to get me—" she almost said home, but caught herself "—back from the bar."

There had been more to last night than merely getting drunk, of course, but she left the rest unsaid.

He shrugged. "We all make mistakes. I may have been too harsh."

"You mean, last night?"

He shook his head. "Since running into you at Distressed Success."

A strange skittishness seized her at his admission, but she attributed it to vestiges of her flirtation with the wild side the evening before.

"How much do you remember about last night?" he asked.

The answer seemed to matter to him. "More or less all of it," she hedged.

"Everything?" he probed.

"Enough to know we *didn't* sleep together!" She was sure she'd remember *that* much.

He looked at her thoughtfully, then seemed to switch gears, lightening up and nodding toward the back of the house.

"C'mon," he said. "I'll fix you a cup of coffee, then drive you."

She sighed. "Okay."

She couldn't protest too much. The way her head felt, coffee sounded wonderful.

As they walked toward the back of the house, he asked, "How were you planning to get back, by the way? Your car's back at the tavern." He smiled briefly. "Or were you planning to strand me by car-jacking my car?"

"I knew there were a couple of mountain bikes in the garage," she responded reluctantly.

He looked at her inquiringly.

"I was planning to bike to the gas station down the road," she elaborated, "and then call a cab service to take me home."

He grinned. "You were going to ride a bike wearing a skirt and no underwear?"

She felt herself blush. "I admit it wasn't one of my better ideas."

Minutes later, they got into his car, coffee in hand, and began the drive over to the tavern.

"What about grabbing some breakfast nearby?" he asked.

"I need to get Distressed Success open by ten." His attitude had changed completely this morning, and she still wasn't sure what to make of it.

He glanced at her. "You're the boss. Give yourself permission to show up late."

She cupped her forehead and joked weakly, "I think my interlude of acting irresponsibly ended last night."

"Coffee, and lots of it," he advised, then added, "What about dinner tonight then? You mentioned Clearwater's once and I haven't tried it."

She hesitated. "Thanks, but—"

"—you want to thank me for putting you to bed last night?"

She couldn't argue there. "All right," she said, giving in.

"I'll pick you up. Seven, okay?"

"Perfect."

Less than two hours later, Kelly arrived at Distressed Success just on time. After Ryan had driven her back to the White Fir Tavern, she'd driven home, changed and made her way to the shop.

She watched as Erica pulled up in her car just as she got the front door open.

"Hi," Erica said as she came in moments later. "You're right on time."

"You sound surprised," Kelly responded, flicking on some lights.

Erica gave her a look of open curiosity. "Well, I admit to wondering how last night went…."

"You mean, my moment of glory as the red-haired sex goddess?"

Erica grinned. "Even Greg was surprised, and, let me tell you, after two kids and twenty years in the fire department, it takes a lot to shock that man."

"I got completely and utterly inebriated."

Erica's eyes widened. "Drunk?"

"I was a drinking virgin until last night," she confirmed grimly, putting down her purse and taking off her jacket.

Erica looked at her closely. "Well, you don't look too much the worse for wear."

"Thanks to coffee, and lots of it," she responded, echoing Ryan's earlier statement.

"I knew we should never have left you! I said as much to Greg, but he said Ryan was around to keep an eye on you."

"Oh, he kept an eye on me all right," she said ominously, remembering the way he'd gotten an eyeful of her breasts. "He drove me back to the lodge—" Erica's mouth fell open "—and put me to bed in one of the guest suites."

Erica gave a laughing gasp.

Unflinchingly, she went on with the rest of the story. "I tried to sneak out this morning, but he heard me, plied me with coffee and drove me back to my car—which was still parked in front of the White Fir—and completely failed to take advantage of me in the process."

"Good gracious!"

Kelly sucked in a breath. "I set out to make a point and I fell flat on my face—"

"No, not completely," Erica said, shaking her head. "Instead of confirming you're like your mother, last night might just as well have convinced him of the opposite. After all, you couldn't hold your liquor—" Erica gave her a semiapologetic smile "—and you didn't leave the bar with anyone. I mean, other than Ryan."

Kelly frowned. "He ran the guy off."

Erica raised her eyebrows. "Ryan ran off a guy you were talking to?"

"Not talking to," she corrected. "*Flirting with.* And yes, he ran him off, though he denied it. I don't know what he said to Tate."

At least she *thought* his name had been Tate. Last night continued to be a headache in more ways than one.

Erica laughed. "I ought to tell you my story of Greg running off a guy *I* was flirting with soon after we met."

Kelly sighed and Erica looked at her sympathetically.

"Is it possible that Ryan isn't the black-hearted ogre you think he is?" Erica asked. "Greg liked him."

"Greg's a guy." Then she admitted, "Ryan *was* extraordinarily nice this morning. I couldn't really understand why…"

"Mmm-hmm."

"He wanted to have dinner tonight at Clearwater's."

"And you said?" Erica asked.

"I said yes."

Seven

That night, using directions Kelly had given him, Ryan discovered that Kelly lived in a town house midway between the lodge and Distressed Success.

Her place was in an older development, with a parking space out back and a neat little garden in front.

He rang the doorbell, and when she opened the door, he felt the air whoosh out of him.

She wore a bottle-green velvet jacket that gathered under her breasts and revealed plenty of cleavage. A slim brown skirt and knee-high, high-heeled boots completed her outfit.

He was glad now that he'd dressed more formally

for tonight. He had on beige pants and a striped dress shirt beneath his blazer.

"You look fantastic," he said as his eyes ate her up.

She smiled at him and stepped aside. "Come on in. I just need to grab my purse."

When he'd stepped inside, he immediately realized her house was a showcase for Distressed Success's style.

The front door led directly into a large room with a living-room area at one end and a dining room at the other. A kitchen sat off to one side.

The dining room had a table and sideboard in some sort of distressed finish. A chandelier with multicolored beads that reflected the light hung above the table.

The living room contained a sofa and love seat at right angles to each other. They were covered with a profusion of pillows in different prints and shapes. An etched-glass cabinet stood against one wall and a fireplace was set in another. A tasseled rug partially covered the wood floor.

"If your decorating project at the lodge turns out as well as your house," he said, turning toward her, "I'd say you're well on the path to success."

"*Distressed* Success," she deadpanned.

"Is there any other?" he countered.

She smiled. "I'd offer to show you the rest of the house, but I think we'll be late."

Looking into her eyes, he said, "Next time."

The moment drew itself out between them and he could tell she was thinking about what meaning to attach to his words.

All of them, he wanted to tell her.

Kelly cleared her throat, breaking the mood. "Let me just turn off the lights and make sure I've got my house keys."

As she switched off lamps, he reflected that she'd surprised him last night and proven him wrong, and he wasn't a man used to being surprised—or wrong.

She'd only slept with a guy once or twice. She'd floored him with the admission, though she'd given no sign since that she even remembered what she'd said.

He realized now that she must have been even more affected by growing up with Brenda Hartley than he'd been by being Webb Sperling's son.

Last night she'd even referred to not being able to shake off her mother's history. Now he knew how it had affected her in surprising ways.

Of course, it all meant he'd been wrong about her—wrong to accuse her of being like her mother and wrong to think he had her all figured out.

Sure, the way she'd dressed and acted last night had been at odds with her sexual inexperience, but she seemed to have set out to teach him a lesson.

She'd said she was just living up to the behavior *he* expected of her. Or just maybe, he mused, it was the behavior she was expecting of *herself* that she had fought against.

It also occurred to him now that she might have gotten her start as a designer by making the most of a modest budget while she was growing up. His recollection was that Brenda Hartley was not supposed to have had much money, and rumor around town was that she'd also been an indifferent parent.

When Kelly drifted back to his side, he asked, "Ready?"

She smiled. "Yes."

On the drive over to Clearwater's, they chatted casually about local events. When they got to restaurant, he made sure they were shown to a table with a prime view of the twinkling lights on and around Lake Tahoe.

They talked about innocuous subjects such as the weather and skiing. She'd learned to ski only when she'd moved to Tahoe, he discovered, while he did black-diamond runs to work off steam.

After the waiter arrived and they'd placed their order—she, a salad and veal française, he, a shrimp cocktail and the surf and turf—he sat back and contemplated her.

She had extraordinary features. Her bone structure was exquisite and the combination of full lips and hazel eyes with shades of topaz added a hint of exoticism.

"Why are you staring at me?" She looked back at him with a hint of uncertainty.

"You're beautiful," he said simply. In her case, it was a statement of fact, not flattery.

She looked as if she didn't know how to react. "Thank you," she said eventually.

"I also think you're not completely happy with the fact," he added.

Her eyes lowered to hide her expression. "I don't know what you mean."

"I mean," he said, refusing to let her off the hook, "you don't seem entirely comfortable being Brenda Hartley's daughter."

"About as comfortable as you are being Webb Sperling's son."

He nodded briefly. "I accept that," he said, then he eyed her. "Have you been in touch with him recently?"

"Who?" she asked, cloaking her expression again.

"You know who. Your mother's former lover." He said it unflinchingly, forcing them both to face the fact baldly.

"Why would I tell you?" she countered. "You obviously don't approve."

"I don't like watching anyone make a deal with the devil."

"Some have called *you* ruthless and worse. I *do* read the newspapers like everyone else, you know."

He changed tactics. "Webb Sperling is a philanderer and worse."

She remained silent.

"When I started hearing rumors he was having an affair with your mother," he went on, "I knew it wasn't the first time he'd cheated. But my mother had just gotten diagnosed with stage-three breast cancer. I figured the least the bastard could do was keep his pants zipped while she went through chemo."

She still said nothing, though this time she looked as if she wanted to.

"Did you know about the affair?"

The answer was irrelevant to him now, but curiosity made him ask.

She nodded finally. "My mother has a history of choosing the wrong men at the wrong time, starting with my father—actually, maybe even before that." She paused, then added, "I didn't know him, by the way."

"Your father?"

She nodded again. "Brenda wasn't positive about his identity, but she thought he was an out-of-town salesman visiting Vegas while she worked at a casino."

"Yeah, well, I was legitimate, at least," he drawled. "Webb made sure of *that*. There was no way he was jeopardizing his claim on my mother's millions."

"I saw Webb a couple of times during the affair," she admitted, then wrinkled her nose. "He and Brenda weren't the most discreet of couples."

His lips lifted in sardonic amusement. "You call her *Brenda?*"

"Don't you use *Webb?*"

A dry chuckle escaped him. "Another thing we have in common."

"Brenda didn't like to be reminded she was a mother," Kelly said. "It was bad enough I spelled the end of her aspirations to be a showgirl. Of course, since I'm twenty-eight now, she'd much rather I lied these days and said we were sisters."

"Given what you look like, I don't blame her for that."

"Thank you. At least you got to escape Clayburn and go to Harvard."

"Yeah, except I discovered there's no use trying to outrun your past."

"Easy for you to say," she replied. "You've always had money, power—"

"—and you never have," he finished for her.

"Exactly."

"You know," he said, "I remember driving by the house you lived in with your mother."

She looked surprised. "I didn't even know you knew I existed."

"I knew who you were, all right. The rumor mill in Clayburn made sure of that. As a point of pride, though, I pretended not to recognize you."

"So why did you drive by the house?"

He shrugged. "Curiosity. I was mad as hell with my father that day and drove around aimlessly—"

"—yes, I remember you'd tear through town when you were on break from prep school—"

"—and at some point I figured I'd check out where his latest tart was living."

At her raised eyebrows, he added, "It's what I was thinking at the time. *Tart.*"

"Believe me, I've heard worse said about Brenda."

"Ditto about Webb."

He noticed that a tentative camaraderie had taken hold. "I saw you that day in front of the house, walking home in your ice-cream shop uniform."

"I bet you hated me on sight."

"No," he responded slowly, "I was too consumed by anger at Webb to see past to anything else."

"I *never* saw you come into Sloanie's, and it had the best ice cream in town!"

"I didn't want to run into you." He laughed shortly. "Besides, something as wholesome as ice cream would have ruined my bad-boy image."

"I recall," she said drily. "I'd spot you around town from time to time. Of course, I knew you were Webb Sperling's son, but even if I hadn't, your Jaguar convertible would have been a dead giveaway you were the son of the richest family in town."

He smiled rakishly. "I loved that car."

In the next moment, the waiter arrived with their food, and the conversation moved on to other topics.

But a newfound level of understanding existed between them and Ryan was sure he wasn't the only one who felt it—just as he was sure he wasn't the only one to feel the undercurrent of sexual energy.

Afterward, he drove her home. When he pulled up in front of the town house, she offered, "Would you like to come in…for coffee? Or—" her eyes laughed at him "—tea?"

He felt his lips quirk. "Tea sounds great…for the novelty value."

Inside, they took off their jackets and she deposited her purse on an entry table before heading toward the kitchen.

He followed, and they chatted about current events while she boiled water in an old-fashioned teakettle, packed loose tea into a holder and pulled down some cups and saucers.

When she'd prepared two cups of tea, they walked back into the living room and sat on the couch.

The conversation touched on Tahoe and growth nearby in California, and he recounted amusing bits of Silicon Valley lore.

After a while, he looked around and commented, "This is like being allowed into the inner sanctuary."

"Would you like a tour? You didn't get to see it all before we left for dinner."

He nodded. He was looking forward to uncovering some more of the mystery that was Kelly Hartley.

Besides the living room, dining room and kitchen, the lower level of the house had a laundry room and a small bath with scented candles and a little stained-glass cabinet.

When they went upstairs he discovered the upper level had three rooms and a full bath. There was a guest bedroom with a neat, canopied double bed. Next to the guest bedroom, there was a study that functioned as a workroom and that contained a desk, a sewing machine and shelves full of bolts of fabric.

They came to her bedroom last, and as Ryan sauntered in, he realized he'd been wrong. *This* was the inner sanctuary.

A metal four-poster bed occupied most of the room and was covered with brown-and-aqua bedding. A chandelier with blue glass droplets was suspended over the bed. A floor lamp with a poplin shade stood in one corner. Along one wall stood a mirrored dresser. Along another, there was a vanity table and stool. The room was finished with built-in white shelving behind the bed that held books and photos.

Ryan turned back to Kelly. "It's like seeing your style in its purest form. Wow."

She looked embarrassed but flattered. "Thank you, *I think*."

"You're welcome."

She glanced out the window. "I just noticed. There's a full moon."

He stood beside her and peered out. "So there is. How about that?"

He glanced down at her and was struck anew with the urge to kiss her.

At the same time, she turned to look up at him, her eyes shadowed.

Slowly, he raised his hands to cup her shoulders and turn her to face him fully. Then he lowered his head and brushed her lips.

She sighed against his mouth and he took the kiss deeper, taking the edge off a hunger that dinner had done nothing to sate.

Eventually, his lips drifted away from her lips to explore the delicate shell of her ear and the hollows of her throat.

She swayed into him and sighed again, her arms locking around his neck.

Finally, however, and with difficulty, he raised his head. With Kelly, he'd have to go slow. He took a deep, head-clearing breath and asked, "What are you doing tomorrow?"

Tomorrow was Sunday, and he knew Distressed Success would be closed.

"I'll be at the lodge," she replied huskily. "Working."

"Good."

He had a surprise for her and, fortunately, the weather for tomorrow called for sunny skies and a clear view.

* * *

"I should be working. This is crazy." Kelly pulled loose strands of hair away from her face in a futile battle with the wind.

Though she had her hair tied back in a ponytail, she knew she'd be struggling to get out knots later on.

Ryan grinned in response to her words, his hair whipped by the wind.

He stood by the sails of the boat, and Kelly thought she'd never seen him so carefree. She could well imagine how he might have been a pirate in another life.

She'd shown up early this morning at the lodge because it was Sunday and she didn't have to be in the shop today. She'd intended to put in a full day's work, setting up additional furnishings that had been previously delivered.

Ryan, however, had had other plans. After they'd worked for three hours, he'd taken the vase she'd been holding and announced they were playing hooky for the rest of the day.

It turned out he'd already had a picnic basket packed and, what's more, he'd rented a sailboat.

She had taken one look outside at the glorious weather and had found it impossible to resist.

Now here they were on the vastness of Lake Tahoe—blue skies overhead accentuated by the occasional lazy puffy white cloud, wavy aqua waters below dotted by the occasional watercraft.

Ryan had rented a sloop, which had a single mast and two sails. Because she'd been on a sailboat just once before in her life, Ryan had taught her the basics of trimming the sails and handling the helm before they'd left the dock.

Once they'd gotten under way, however, Ryan had done most of the work. Except for handling the helm when Ryan trimmed the sails, she was able to sit and enjoy the ride.

"Where did you learn to sail?" she called to him now. Then before he could answer, she added, "No, wait. Let me guess. You took Sailing 101 at prep school."

He flashed a grin. "Good guess, but in fact, I learned to sail right here on Lake Tahoe. It's a place where we vacationed when I was younger."

He'd been to Tahoe regularly?

She tilted her head. "That first day at Distressed Success, you acted as if you were unfamiliar with the area. You asked me where you could find a good meal—"

"I was hitting on you."

A tremor of sexual awareness ran through her as something indefinable, but palpable and strong, passed between them.

Silhouetted against the blue sky, he was breathtakingly handsome. He wore khaki pants and a polo shirt paired with a windbreaker and reflective sunglasses. He looked as if he could have been in an ad for Ralph Lauren.

She hadn't known they'd go sailing, but she was glad now that she put on pants and espadrilles that morning. A windbreaker that they'd found for her at the lodge protected her from cold and damp.

As Ryan again busied himself with the sails, she reflected on the events of the weekend. She hadn't intended to reveal so much during their meal at Clearwater's. Still, she could understand Ryan's anger better now, as well as identify with it since Brenda, like Webb, hadn't been the most responsible parent in the world.

Finished with what he was doing, Ryan came toward her and jumped down to where she sat. "Time for lunch. I'm famished."

She laughed. "I can't believe you prepared a whole picnic basket!"

He grinned slyly. "Gourmet everything…courtesy of the concierge service at one of Tahoe's poshest nouveau places."

Eight

Kelly found that the next week passed in a blur of work, decorating and, above all, Ryan and more Ryan.

By the following weekend, she realized somewhat surprisingly that her work at the lodge was nearly done. She also knew she couldn't have done it without Ryan's help.

She hadn't heard anything more from Webb Sperling, but she pushed the thought aside.

She had time, she told herself. Deep down, though, she knew she didn't want to upset her newfound accord with Ryan.

As she prepared to leave the lodge late that Sunday afternoon, Ryan surprised her by saying, "Why don't you come on in? We'll sit on the deck and watch the sunset."

"I should be getting back." The words flew out of her mouth in automatic response.

"Why?" he asked bluntly. "We both know Distressed Success is closed on Mondays." He smiled. "In fact, since you'll want to be working here tomorrow, it makes sense for you to stay the night."

She felt a strange fluttering sensation in her stomach, then caught the teasing glimmer in his eyes.

"After all," he drawled, "you're already familiar with the guest bedroom."

She held her palms up. "I didn't bring any clothes—"

His smile widened. "Do you really want to hear my solution to that problem?"

She felt herself heat in response. She still wasn't used to his teasing.

The past week had been wonderful, but he hadn't tried to kiss her again. He hadn't done anything, in fact, that could be interpreted as a come-on, even by her fevered imagination.

She, on the other hand, had become attuned to his every breath, every expression, every stretch of hard, lean muscle.

Ryan reached out and touched her arm. "Hey," he said soothingly, "come on. Let's just open a bottle of wine and contemplate the meaning of the universe."

She relaxed a little. "Okay."

Minutes later, they stepped out onto the deck, Ryan holding two wineglasses in one hand and a bottle of red wine in the other.

She tried not to look at the hot tub, remembering how she'd first spotted him at the lodge.

"I can vouch for its relaxing properties," he murmured.

"What?" she asked, startled.

"The hot tub. It's great." He paused, a glimmer in his eyes. "Want to try?"

"No, thanks!"

Her response was immediate and automatic. Just the thought of getting into a hot tub with Ryan Sperling sent her senses into overdrive.

"Don't tell me you've never been in a hot tub," he teased.

"Some of us weren't born into the hot-tub-and-wine set." Then she added, relenting, "In any case, I have nothing to wear."

His eyes crinkled. "Why let a lack of clothing stand in your way?"

At her look of forbearance, he shrugged. "Can't blame a guy for trying." He paused, then added thoughtfully, "I could lend you one of my undershirts and a pair of boxers. You could even keep your bra and underwear on underneath."

His lips twitched. "I *know* how important underpants are to you."

She wondered how much of his sexually charged

teasing she could withstand, then asked suspiciously, "And what will you be wearing?"

"Swim trunks."

"I shouldn't agree to this."

He grinned. "But you are."

They headed back inside. He handed her some clothes and, after they'd both had time to change, she met him on the deck again, padding outside in bare feet and shivering in the cool night air.

Soft jazz filtered out from iPod speakers set up on a table.

He stood holding two full wineglasses and swept her a look from head to toe, his gaze heating. "I had no idea my shirts and boxers could look so sexy."

She flushed. It felt impossibly intimate to be wearing his clothes, albeit over her own.

He'd already started the hot tub, and the tub's jets created frothy water, illuminated from below by recessed lights.

It looked so inviting, she thought as she shivered again.

He set the wineglasses down on a small tray at the side of the tub, then straightened and held his hand out to her. "Come. Let's warm you up."

He warmed *her* just by looking at her with his hot eyes, she wanted to say. Instead, she put her hand in his and stepped into the tub.

"Careful," he cautioned, but she knew she was being anything but—*with him, with anything.*

He followed her and settled on an underwater ledge across from her.

She sighed as the hot tub's jets pounded her gently, massaging her muscles. She closed her eyes and leaned back, relaxing against the tub's side.

"Better?"

"Mmm-hmm."

After a few moments, during which she heard him lift and sip from his wineglass, he instructed, "Look up."

She did, and gazed at the inky black sky. Dozens of little stars twinkled back at her.

"My guess is that you haven't had much time to stargaze in your life," he commented.

"Mmm-hmm."

"Neither have I."

She looked down at him, and asked, "Why do you think Hunter wrote a stipulation in his will that you and his other college buddies have to stay at the lodge?"

"Why didn't he just give the money to charity, you mean?"

She nodded.

"We'd made a promise to one another all those years ago, on a night after too many beers. We'd vowed to become huge successes—on our own, not riding on our families' coattails—and then reunite in ten years. Once Hunter got sick, the rest of us forgot that crazy night. But Hunter never did."

He looked heavenward. "Maybe he knew we'd need to do *this*. And somehow he knew it would be up to him to get us to come here just to take a moment and look up at the stars."

"I guess he was right, because it's been a while since you've taken time to look at the stars."

"Ages," he answered absently, then he lowered his head to look at her. "How about you?"

"Ages," she concurred.

A companionable silence followed. She sipped her wine and looked off into the dark trees, then out at the dark waters of Lake Tahoe.

Finally, she asked, "So you and Hunter were close friends?"

He shrugged. "Yeah. I didn't have siblings, so all six of the guys from college were like brothers to me." A wry smile touched his lips. "We called ourselves the Seven Samurai."

She laughed. "Who came up with that name?"

"Blame it on too many late nights chowing down on bad pizza and watching Kurosawa movies. We studied hard, but partied harder."

"You talk about it as if it's one of the better times in your life."

"It was."

"Did you find it difficult being an only child?"

"Did you?" he countered.

"It was more difficult being Brenda Hartley's daughter."

He raised his wineglass in silent salute. "I felt the same way."

"It was as if the college partying days never ended for Brenda," she elaborated, "except she never went to college…."

"But you did," he prompted.

"Yes," she said, looking at him in surprise. "How did you know?"

He shrugged. "A good guess."

"I worked my way through community college in Reno to get a degree in business administration."

The conversation moved to the challenges of starting a business. Kelly found herself fascinated by the tales he had from his climb to the top of the cable-communications world.

After a while, he said, "Now I have a question for you that I've been wondering about. Why did you settle around Tahoe or, more specifically, Hunter's Landing?"

She sighed. "How I got where I am is a lot less interesting than how you got where you are."

"I'm all ears."

She regarded him. He really did seem genuinely curious. "I knew I had to get out of Clayburn," she said eventually. "I knew I didn't want to go to Vegas, but Reno wasn't too far. Once I found a job in Reno, I enrolled at a community college and, on weekends, I'd take cheap day trips to Tahoe."

She shrugged. "I fell in love with the area and,

since there's a big tourist trade here, not to mention lots of seasonal residents, it seemed like the perfect place to try to open a business."

"You've got good instincts," he said.

They'd both finished their wine by this time and the music had died away, replaced by the stillness of the night.

She looked around. "I could lie in here forever, but I'd be a wrinkled prune!"

"Ready to head in?" he asked.

"I think so."

They'd been having such a relaxed, quiet conversation, she'd started to forget they were barely dressed.

Now, however, she was nervous about emerging from the tub.

He placed the wineglasses and wine bottle to one side on the deck and rose. Water sluiced from his body as he climbed out of the hot tub, and awareness shimmered through her as she got a close-up of sheer male virility.

He turned then and made to help her.

She took his outstretched hand and stood up, stepping on the tub ledge, then out onto the deck.

He picked up a couple of towels and handed one to her.

"Th-thank you," she said, and attributed her stutter to chattering teeth caused by the cold.

Except when her eyes accidentally met his, she'd noticed he was looking fixedly at her body.

She looked down at herself, and realized what he saw.

His white shirt was dripping wet and clung to her like a second skin, defining all her curves. Her nipples, made hard by the cold air, were pronounced against the thin cotton of her bra and his shirt. She looked more top-heavy than she did under her own carefully chosen clothes.

She shivered, and his eyes narrowed.

He dropped his towel and slowly reached up and brushed back wisps of her hair.

Then instead of withdrawing his hand, he trailed the back of it along the curve of her jaw, down her neck and lower….

His hand traced the curve of her breast, then moved up to touch a lock of her hair. "Tempting curves, siren hair."

She sucked in a breath.

He looked as if he was still waging a battle with himself, caught between desire and something else.

"I should hate you," she whispered. It was a desperate last bid to avoid what was happening between them.

"No, you don't. Not really. Not anymore," he whispered back.

"I *want* to hate you."

"I wanted to hate you, too," he admitted without a trace of apology, "but I can't. I want you."

He looked into her eyes, his full of desire, then cupped her neck and drew her near.

He searched her face for a moment before he bent his head and touched his lips to hers.

As she let go of her towel, she thought that this moment had been inevitable since the first time he'd walked into her shop.

If he hadn't discovered who she was, and she hadn't found out who he was, they'd probably have reached this point long before now.

His lips claimed hers in a deep, searching kiss. Her body came up flush against his, molding to him, seeking welcoming heat where before there had been just cold.

Her hand moved to the back of his head, pulling him down to her, and she kissed him back, feeding their passion.

A voice inside her head insisted this was wrong. But the voice of scruples was faint, drowned out by the strength of their desire.

He made her feel vibrant and alluring and full of life. The clothes between them warmed from the heat of their desire.

Moments went by before he finally lifted his head and breathed deep.

"I want you," he stated baldly.

"Yes."

He searched her face. "Yes?"

"Make love to me," she breathed, throwing caution to the wind.

It was all the encouragement he seemed to need.

He bent and scooped her up in his arms. "Let's get inside. It's freezing."

He stepped into the house and crossed the great room to the staircase. He took the stairs deliberately, not showing the least exertion from carrying her up.

When they got to the upper level, he went down the hall and into the master suite, setting her down near the bed.

As he lowered her feet to the floor, she brushed against him, doing a slow slide to a want that went bone deep.

"Kiss me," he said, and she complied because it was the only thing she felt she could do.

The kiss went on and on. Their labored breathing filled the stillness of the room and their bodies moved against each other, straining to be closer.

Liquid warmth pooled between her legs.

He pulled his lips away from hers finally and groaned against her mouth. "I want you badly."

"Yes." She felt the same way. A faint tremor shook her hand as she raked it through his hair.

He sat back on the bed and bent to take the tip of one breast into his mouth, groaning as he did so and bending her backward.

She gasped and grasped his shoulders in order to

anchor herself. The sensation of him heating her wet and tender flesh was delicious. "Ryan…"

When his mouth moved away, she was burning with hunger for him.

He pulled the shirt over her head and she raised her arms to assist him. Then he tugged down the boxers she was wearing—*his* boxers—and did the same for her panties. Both pieces of underwear dropped to the floor. Then he pulled her down on the bed for another searing kiss.

When her hand accidentally brushed against him, she stroked his erection and he groaned. Finally, when it seemed as if he couldn't take any more, he pulled his swim trunks off.

She wrapped her hand around him without invitation and his breath hissed out.

A faint smile touched her lips. It felt wonderful to have Ryan Sperling in her grasp, literally, and on his knees, figuratively.

"What are you smiling at?" he asked.

"Nothing," she denied, but caught the sudden urge to tease him. "Just thinking about giving you pleasure…having you in the palm of my hand—"

He tilted his head, his eyes heavy lidded. "Oh, yeah?"

In the next instant, he pushed her back on the enormous bed and came down beside her, anchoring her.

She squealed and he nuzzled her breasts.

"That first day at Distressed Success," she said, striving to keep her train of thought, "before I knew who you were, I was immediately attracted to you."

He lifted his head, his expression roguish. "I wanted you like crazy."

Her eyes widened. "You did?"

He nodded. "I already admitted I was hitting on you. Of course I had the hots for you."

"I thought—"

"What?" He smiled. "You think I hit on every young female entrepreneur selling mismatched china?"

She pretended to look offended.

With a grin, he looked at her bra and slid a finger under the band. "Are you going to take this off for me?"

"It's front closure."

"In that case—" He raised himself up and undid the clasp between her breasts, allowing them to spill free.

"You're beautiful," he said reverently, tracing the outline of one breast.

Then he kissed her and caressed her all over, bringing her to a fever pitch. When he dipped a finger into her damp heat, she went dizzy with sensation.

"Ryan," she said hoarsely.

But he pressed, making rapid little movements, like the beating of butterfly wings.

She moaned, mindless with pleasure.

Then, all at once, she went up and over and into

the vortex, her grip on his arm the only thing anchoring her to the world.

He pressed his mouth against her damp heat, making her gasp again and jerk, even as her fingers threaded through his hair.

She felt the tension within her build again and she trembled against him. Turning her head to one side, she pulled a pillow toward her, trying to muffle the way he made her feel.

Within moments, however, he pulled the pillow from her grasp.

"I want to hear you," he said hoarsely.

And then he enjoyed her until she felt liquid fire dance along her nerve endings.

Her release was fiery and rapid, bringing tears to her eyes.

She lay limp afterward and thought dimly that her limited experience had not compared to this…had not prepared her for Ryan Sperling.

He pressed kisses to her inner thighs, then levered himself up off the bed. He pulled open a dresser drawer and retrieved a foil packet.

"Because you just never know when you'll need it," he explained.

"I'll do it," she responded, and watched his eyes flare.

She'd never done this before, but he made her feel daring and bold.

She took the foil packet from him, but when he

lay back on the bed, instead of rolling the protection on him, she pleasured him with her mouth.

He tensed with surprise, then relaxed and groaned. "Kelly…"

She heard the warning in his voice but, knowing she was undermining his control, she kept on going.

"I'm about to lose it," he said hoarsely.

When she raised her head, he gave her a quick hard kiss.

"Bold in bed," he said, smiling. "I like that."

It took them a long time to roll the protection on him. In the end, neither of them could wait any longer.

He rolled her under him and parted her thighs. Then, holding her gaze, he slid into her slowly and came down into her arms.

The buildup was slow—and he toyed with her, increasing her pleasure—but when her release came, it was in a rush of sensation so that she gasped and cried out, grasping his hips as she moved against him.

His release came on the heels of hers and he spilled himself inside her.

She held him afterward, knowing that in this moment he was totally hers.

Nine

When Kelly woke the next morning, she glanced over and blinked. Ryan looked back at her, his hair tousled.

She'd done that, she realized, heat rising. Last night, she'd raked her fingers through his hair, and so much more.

"Good morning," he said.

"Morning," she said, suddenly unsure of herself.

She tried to glance at the clock on the bedside table.

"It's only eight," he said. "Plenty of time for you to get to work, which, in any case, is right here." He smiled. "Lucky you. You can just roll out of bed and be on the job."

Last night had been what she'd imagined sex was supposed to be. She'd pictured it in her mind countless times. And it had finally become a reality with Ryan Sperling.

"Last night was incredible," he said, as if reading her mind.

A pleasurable thrill shot through her. It had been wonderful for her, too, but she wasn't as experienced in bed as she was sure Ryan was.

"It'd been a while for me," he stated.

She looked at him in surprise. *She* was the one who'd been all but celibate most of her adult life.

"Really? Why?" she asked.

"You could say I've been consumed with other things…"

"It's been a while for me, too," she admitted.

"Yeah, I know." Under the bed sheets, his hand trailed along her leg.

He knew? Had she been so obviously rusty and inexperienced last night? She felt heat stain her cheeks.

She looked at him quizzically. "How did you know? Was I so obviously a novice?"

He shook his head and gave her a quick kiss. "No, but that night at the White Fir, when I got you home, and before you drifted off to sleep—"

She felt herself tense. She'd wondered whether she'd forgotten some key details from that night.

"—you mentioned you'd been with only one guy before, and then only a couple of times."

"I did?" Apparently, when she was tipsy, she relished divulging her innermost secrets.

His lips quirked. "You'll recall your conversation was a little, ah, disjointed, that night. I got you into bed and a second before you fell asleep, you said something about never having spent the entire night with a man before, though of course—" his eyes crinkled "—I was getting you into bed only in the most literal sense."

Her brows drew together. "So you knew this when you slept with me last night?"

A smile rose to his lips again, even as the heat rose to her face.

"Yeah," he said.

His words landed with the force of an explosion— at least to her. Looking at him, she knew he had no clue.

The rat, she thought.

He'd known all along just how inexperienced she was. No wonder he'd changed his tune after that night at the White Fir.

What had he claimed as the reason behind his change in attitude? The realization that *we all make mistakes?*

Well, *she'd* made a mistake—starting with sleeping with him last night!

She threw back the bedcovers and got out of bed.

"Where are you going?" he asked.

He continued to look guileless—his tone and expression relaxed and satisfied—and it fueled her anger.

She grabbed her clothes from where she'd put them on a nearby chair last night and decided to give him a clue.

"So I was an easy target?" she demanded. "Ripe for the picking because you knew I'd gone so long without, hmm?"

He sat up, suddenly alert. "No. I explained I haven't had any, either—"

She waved a hand. "Yes, I know. *In ages.* All the more reason for you to have been thrilled to find a soft target. I just fell into your lap, didn't I?"

He smiled roguishly. "Well, if you want to put it that way—"

"No wonder you seemed so willing suddenly to overlook the fact I was Brenda Hartley's daughter!"

"Don't dare bring your mother into it," he said, no longer joking as he rose from the bed.

She stomped to the nearby bathroom and slammed the door and locked it.

"Damn it, come back here so we can talk about this!"

She ignored him.

"Kelly!" He knocked on the door and twisted the knob. "Come on out."

Methodically, she dressed, while he continued to knock and pound.

"All right," he said eventually. "I'm not having

this conversation through the bathroom door. I'm going downstairs to make some coffee and wait for you to calm down."

She *was* calm, she wanted to tell him. In fact, she was thinking more lucidly than she had all weekend.

He hadn't mentioned he knew her sexual history, or lack thereof, until *after* he'd gotten her into bed.

She thought he'd started seeing *her*—really seeing her—for the whole of who she was. Instead, he'd seen no more than a potential bed buddy, convinced by nothing more than her sexual history.

She couldn't believe she'd started falling for him. She was such an idiot.

She dressed quickly, then took a deep breath. She would march out of the house without letting Ryan persuade her otherwise. He couldn't be trusted.

She would just have to chalk up today as a loss as far as finishing the job at the lodge went. Later, she could figure out how she was going to finish up her decorating work without coming into contact with Ryan. She'd just have to come to an arrangement with him to be at the lodge while he was out.

Taking another deep breath, she opened the bathroom door and looked around.

The room was empty and her eyes strayed to the huge bed. The rumpled and twisted sheets were a reminder of last night.

Resolutely looking away, she stole out of the room and crept down the stairs.

This was the second time she was trying to sneak away, and while she was prepared for Ryan to intercept her, she preferred not to have a scene.

When she'd made it down to the lower level, she sighed with relief.

She quietly opened the front door…and her heart leapt to her throat.

"Brenda?" Her question came out as a gasp.

Her mother, who had been surveying the drive, turned to face her.

Brenda's bright red lips curved into a smile. "Hello, tootsie. I was just about to ring the doorbell."

Kelly felt her heart race. No, no, no, she wanted to scream. Not here, not now.

"What are you doing here?" she squeaked.

Brenda's smile dimmed. "I went by your house, but you weren't there. When I tried your cell and couldn't reach you, I called Erica. She was out with the kids, but Greg told me you might be here."

"I—"

"Aren't you going to invite me in?"

"Kelly."

Ryan's voice sounded behind her and, as if in a nightmare, Kelly watched Brenda look past her, just as she herself turned to see Ryan coming into the foyer.

All three of them froze.

Ryan stared at the woman in the doorway, and his lips thinned. Even if he hadn't seen her before, it wouldn't have been hard to figure out who she was. She looked like an older version of Kelly.

He'd come to iron things out with Kelly—because last night had been fantastic, and because now that he'd found her, he wasn't letting her go. Instead, he was confronted by one of the last people he wanted to see.

"Brenda," Kelly said, "this isn't a good time—"

Ignoring her, Brenda sashayed in, looking from her daughter to Ryan and back. "I see I'm interrupting something."

She looked Ryan up and down in frank appraisal, making his skin feel tight with angry tension.

"What makes you think so?" Kelly asked, addressing her mother.

Ryan could have told her that her high-pitched, slightly hysterical voice was a dead giveaway.

Brenda lifted her hand, with its fire-engine red nails, and rubbed a lock of Kelly's hair between her fingers.

"Bed hair," she said succinctly.

Kelly flushed, then looked helplessly at Ryan.

He approached slowly, aiming for a casual stance. "Kelly's sister, I presume?"

Brenda gave a tinkling laugh, as if she found his question highly amusing. "I see you inherited your father's charm."

She turned to her daughter. "I admit being surprised, however, that you picked Webb's son as your…playmate."

Kelly drew in an audible breath. "You know who he is?"

Brenda flashed a hard smile. "I make it my business to keep up with all of Clayburn's current and past illustrious citizens." Then she looked at Ryan again. "However, the photos I've seen of you in the local papers don't do you justice."

If the comment had come from anyone else, Ryan figured he'd have been flattered. But this was Brenda Hartley. Clayburn's erstwhile sexpot. His father's former mistress. *Kelly's mother.*

The last thought brought him up short.

Kelly looked as if she were in agony.

Brenda apparently noticed, too, because she flashed a saucy smile at her daughter. "There's no need to look panicked, Kelly. I'm just glad you're having some—" she paused and gave Ryan a sweeping look "—fun. I was starting to worry about you, toots."

"Why are you here?" Kelly asked, looking as if she wanted the ground to open up and swallow her.

Brenda focused her attention back on her daughter. "Why, to see you, of course!" She leaned in and kissed the air next to Kelly's cheek. "And you know, I may need the teeny, tiniest—" she indicated how much by a small space between her index finger and thumb "—little loan."

Brenda glanced at Ryan, her expression shrewd. "On the other hand, maybe these days you can afford more than a *little* loan...."

Ryan decided he'd heard enough. It was time he took over the situation.

"Come on in, Brenda," he said.

"We're just leaving, actually," Kelly said quickly.

"No, you're not."

Brenda clapped her hands. "Oh, I love a man who takes charge."

His eyes clashed with Kelly's, before he looked back at Brenda. "Coffee?"

"I'd love some," Brenda responded.

"Okay, then *I'm* leaving," Kelly said.

He shrugged and turned toward the back of the house. He had some negotiating to do with Brenda Hartley, and if Kelly wasn't around, so much the better.

Brenda started to follow him toward the back of the house.

"Fine," Kelly said in exasperation behind them. "In that case, I'm going back upstairs to take a shower. Let me know when your coffee break is over."

Back in the kitchen, he gestured Brenda toward a seat at the counter and removed the coffee carafe from its holder.

"How do you take it?" he asked.

"Black, no sugar."

"I figured."

He checked himself, waiting for the hate to kick in.

For years, he'd loathed Brenda Hartley for having an affair with Webb.

Somewhat surprisingly, however, all he felt at the moment was a cool detachment. He was prepared to deal with her in the same way he'd dealt with everything that had stood in his path to date—with unemotional, clear-eyed calculation.

He set a coffee cup down in front of Brenda and asked without preamble, "So why'd you take up with Webb?"

She sipped her coffee and took her time responding. "He was rich—" she gave a throaty laugh "—and good in bed."

"He's slime. His wife was dying."

Brenda shrugged and suddenly she looked every one of her years. "For men like Webb, life's too short to forgo the kicks." She wagged a finger suddenly. "But don't think he's the only married man to wander. At least he was generous with the perks."

"I just bet he was," Ryan replied drily, leaning back against the counter and folding his arms. "But that generosity ended a long time ago and now you're back to scavenging."

Brenda's brows snapped together. "I do *not*—"

"How much?" he interrupted.

She stopped. "How much what?"

"How much do you need from Kelly?"

Brenda sat back, a slow smile spreading across her face. "I like a man who's willing to talk business."

* * *

The next morning, when Kelly showed up for work at Distressed Success, Erica was waiting for her.

"Well," Erica said, as Kelly set about getting ready to open the store for business, "how did your date with Ryan go?"

"Where do I begin?" Kelly responded drily. "Brenda showed up as I was trying to sneak out of the lodge and away from Ryan yesterday morning."

Erica's eyes widened and her jaw dropped. It was one of the few times Kelly had seen her at a loss for words.

"Wow…I'm not sure I know where to begin," Erica said slowly. "Brenda's in Tahoe? *You slept with him?* And what do you mean you were sneaking away?"

Kelly filled her in on the events of the weekend, omitting, however, some of the more salacious details. She ended with, "No wonder he changed his tune after that night at the White Fir!"

"Well," Erica said, "you're sure leading a more exciting life than I am. Mine's a merry-go-round of work and kids. Yours is more interesting than watching the afternoon soaps."

"I'd opt for *boring* in a heartbeat."

Erica laughed. "Not with a yummy beefcake like Ryan Sperling around, you shouldn't."

"Haven't you heard what I said? His whole aim was to try to get me into bed."

"Yeah, that was more or less Greg's primary goal in life when we first met."

Kelly looked at Erica, a seed of doubt was sown. Her friend had been married close to ten years, she had more experience with men and she didn't look nearly as condemning of Ryan.

"Are you saying Ryan isn't wrong?" Kelly asked.

"No, he's a rat," Erica responded cheerfully, "but he's a *man*, so the behavior's understandable—predictable, even."

"Thanks for the tip," she said drily.

"Since Brenda is in town, remind me to hide some of the new stock that came in," Erica replied. "Last time she was here, she made off with a new jewelry box and a small vase."

As it turned out, Kelly spent the next days having Brenda as her houseguest—and trying to forget Ryan Sperling.

Luckily, she was forced to spend a significant amount of time at Distressed Success. Brenda, fortunately, was more than happy to entertain herself with the attractions of Tahoe and its casinos.

As she got ready for work on Thursday morning, Kelly thought with relief about the fact that her work at the lodge was nearly done. The furnishings had arrived for all the bedrooms, and except for waiting for an odd piece or two and hanging up a few more pictures, she was finished.

Just as she and Ryan were *finished,* she thought with remaining anger—and a pang or two. Soon, she'd never have to see him again. Her job at the lodge would be done and his month in Hunter's Landing would be up.

He hadn't tried to contact her since she'd left the lodge three days ago and, as much as she hated to admit it, it hurt that he hadn't. She could only suppose that now that he knew she was clued in to his game, he'd moved on to other amusements.

Three days ago, when she'd come back down the stairs at the lodge after freshening up, she'd encountered Brenda in the foyer.

Not wanting another confrontation with Ryan, she'd asked sharply, "Ready?"

"Aren't you going to kiss Ryan goodbye?" Brenda had responded, a gleam in her eye.

"We'll be seeing each other again soon, I'm sure," she'd hedged. "He'll understand."

"Take it from me, tootsie," Brenda had advised. "If you want to keep a man, *never* leave without saying goodbye."

Thinking about Brenda's words now, Kelly sighed. The advice said it all about her relationship with her mother.

She glanced toward her bedroom doorway as Brenda appeared, as if on cue.

"I'm heading out," Brenda announced.

"What?"

Brenda had gotten back so late last night, Kelly hadn't seen her—she'd already been asleep.

She glanced down now at the carry-on bag at her mother's side. "Where are you going?"

Brenda laughed. "Home. You didn't think I was staying forever, did you?"

Clayburn was home again to Brenda these days, though her mother led such a peripatetic existence, Kelly wondered how long the current state of affairs would last.

She finished buttoning the jacket of her green pantsuit. "I'm just surprised, that's all. You said nothing about leaving yesterday."

Her mother waved a hand negligently. "You know I prefer living life in the moment. It makes things so much more *interesting*."

Kelly helped her mother take her luggage outside, then paused beside Brenda's car.

"You never told me how much you needed," she said, remembering suddenly Brenda's request when she'd shown up at the lodge earlier in the week.

"How much I needed for what?"

Kelly sighed. "When you arrived, you mentioned you needed a small loan."

Brenda gave a throaty laugh and waved a hand dismissively. "Oh, *that*. It's not necessary anymore."

Kelly frowned. "What do you mean it's not necessary? Did you win at the slot machines?"

Brenda laughed again. "Well…I suppose that's what I *should* say."

"Should?"

Brenda leaned in and lowered her voice, though no one else was around. "Your *boyfriend* asked me to keep this quiet, but what the hell? You *should* know." She seemed to pause for dramatic effect, her eyes alight. "He *gave* me the money."

"Ryan?"

Brenda straightened, a satisfied look on her face, and she patted Kelly's cheek. "You have that man eating out of the palm of your hand. I always knew you were a smart girl."

"How much did he give you?" she blurted.

Part of her didn't want to know—dreaded knowing, actually—but the other part knew she had to find out.

Brenda hesitated. "Five thousand."

"Dollars?"

Brenda laughed again. "What else is there? I knew he could afford more, but I also knew asking for more might make him suspicious. After all, I did say I needed a *small* loan from you."

"How could you?" she asked, the question coming out like a wail. "How could you take money from him?"

Brenda sighed impatiently. "Why should I have turned him down?"

"Didn't you think you might be creating…obligations for me?"

"Well, considering you're already sleeping with him," Brenda replied tartly, "I don't see how *that* could be the case."

Kelly opened and shut her mouth. It was useless. Arguing with Brenda was like banging her head against a brick wall. They came at things from two different sets of assumptions—two different worldviews. She should have learned that by now.

"How did he get the money to you?" she demanded. "Not even someone as rich as Ryan carries around that much cash."

"He had his people wire some money to me."

"No wonder you had to stay in the area for a few days!"

"Listen, tootsie," Brenda replied dismissively, "I've really got to go." She checked her watch. "I have someone waiting for me at the casino."

As Brenda gave her a quick kiss, Kelly thought that without a doubt the *someone* was male and with money to burn.

After she'd deposited her mother's suitcase in the trunk of her ancient Mercedes—which she knew for a fact Brenda had bought for a song at some dismal used car lot—she watched her mother pull away from the town house.

Then she went back inside, closed the front door, and braced her hand against the wall for support.

What had Ryan done? *And why?*

She tried to sort through her jumble of emotions.

On some level, she *was* grateful. After all, Brenda would have asked her for the money, otherwise.

But she was also *upset.*

She didn't want rich men doing favors for her. It made her feel like Brenda. It made her feel cheap.

Oh, sure, she'd sort of accepted a favor from Webb Sperling. But that was different. It was an even exchange. She had confidence in the strength of her designs—it was just a question of getting her goods into the hands of the right buyers.

This situation with Ryan was different. She felt bought. He'd out-and-out paid off her mother.

For her, her heart whispered, before she could avoid it.

And that was the other reason this situation was different, she told herself. Because it was Ryan, not Webb, who was involved. Part of why she'd felt so betrayed when she'd realized what his motivation had been for sleeping with her was that it *did* matter to her what Ryan thought of her.

She had her pride, she told herself—even though her heart whispered again, telling her that there was something more than *pride* involved here.

Somehow, she had to repay him.

She racked her brain, then smiled as an idea eventually came to mind.

As soon as she got to work, she had a call to make to Webb Sperling.

Ten

"Since Oliver is on board, we're set to go," Dan said.

Ryan watched his attorney pull paperwork out of his briefcase. They were sitting in the lodge's office loft, the morning sun coming in through the windows.

Dan had driven over from Silicon Valley, where El Ray Technology was based, as soon as the sun had come up. Now, he set contracts out on the table before them.

"Everyone has signed," Dan explained, "so I just need your signature before I—" he smiled fleetingly "—send out some big checks."

"I want this wrapped up ASAP," Ryan said, checking his watch. "It's already Thursday. I'd like to make this transfer public by early next week *before* someone leaks the news to the press."

He wanted to call the shots in this situation. He'd decide when and how Webb Sperling found out that the trap had been sprung.

"There's a confidentiality clause in all the contracts—"

"Yes, I know," Ryan said, cutting him off, "but we're talking about the Sperlings here. Any one of them is capable of wreaking havoc at the last minute."

"It'll be done," Dan replied, as Ryan leaned forward and began to sign. "I know you want to start concentrating on other things—like El Ray's acquisitions in foreign markets."

El Ray was in the beginning stages of courting cable companies in South and Central America for a partnership or buyout. All the more reason, Ryan thought, to get this issue of Sperling, Inc. wrapped up and for this idyll in Hunter's Landing to come to a close.

"In the meantime," Dan continued, "I've already drafted a letter to Webb, warning him his executive authority has ended and that all pending contracts negotiations and other matters are to be suspended."

Ryan thought about Kelly's contract. There was a time not too long ago when he would have made it a priority to pull the plug on Distressed Success as soon as he got control of Sperling, Inc.

He doubted Kelly had had a chance to sew up a

deal with Sperling stores—she certainly hadn't given any indication to the effect during the time they'd spent together.

Knowing his father, Ryan figured he'd just passed the matter along to underlings and gone on with his golf game or whatever the heck else he did these days.

As Dan began to drone on about the contract particulars, Ryan's mind stayed on Kelly.

It had been three days since he'd last seen her. Three days since the confrontation with Brenda.

In that time, he'd been tied up with his bid to get control of Sperling, Inc. In addition, he hadn't wanted to go by Kelly's place to hash things out if Brenda was still hanging around.

And, he admitted, he'd expected Kelly to put in an appearance at the lodge before now, no matter how much she might want to continue to avoid him.

She'd surprised him, however, by managing to stay away from the decorating job for three consecutive days.

She was probably occupied with her unexpected houseguest, he told himself. But another part of him acknowledged that there was no reason to think she'd softened toward him since Monday.

Yes, her sexual inexperience, once he'd found out about it, had put a whole new spin on things. But contrary to what she believed, it wasn't her inexperience in and of itself that had attracted him. Rather, it was because it was further, definitive proof of what he'd been seeing signs of all along, but hadn't allowed himself to acknowledge: Kelly was far different from her mother.

He had no intention of leaving Hunter's Landing without telling her so—just as soon as this damn issue with Sperling, Inc. was concluded.

He was going to have it out with her *and* have her. *Again and again,* until they were both mindless with pleasure.

"Have you heard?" Erica asked, when she showed up for her shift around lunchtime on Tuesday.

"Heard what?" Kelly replied distractedly.

She was doing some record keeping at her desk in her office at the back of Distressed Success.

She'd promised herself today would be the day she faced the music by going back to the lodge. She'd also just run out of excuses, because Erica had shown up and could cover for her at the shop.

"Ryan Sperling has taken over Sperling department stores and ousted his father from his role as CEO and chairman of the board!"

Kelly's head jerked up. "What? Where did you hear that?"

"I heard it on the radio on the drive over," Erica said. "You called Webb just in time."

Kelly pulled out her computer keyboard, and with trembling fingers, she did a Google search for Ryan Sperling and Sperling department stores.

A slew of hits came up, including a bunch of local news stories from the last few hours.

She clicked on the first site listed and, when the article came up, scanned it rapidly.

It appeared Ryan had bought ownership shares in Sperling, Inc. from various family members, giving him a majority stake.

His first order of business had been to remove his father from the chairmanship of the board and to strip him of his title of CEO.

She sank back against the chair weakly, trying to digest the import of Ryan's takeover, her mind racing. Out front, she heard the shop door open and close, and knew they had another customer.

Rotten timing, she thought, then rose and said to Erica, "I'll get this one."

At the very least, the customer might help take her mind off the bombshell that had just landed in her lap.

She walked out to the front of the store, a polite smile on her face. "Can I help—"

She came to a halt.

There facing her was none other than Webb Sperling.

Webb Sperling fixed her with a dim smile as he looked her up and down. "Hello, Kelly. You're the spitting image of your mother."

Kelly felt her own smile fade.

Webb's eyes were pale—a washed-out blue, she remembered thinking once—and he looked as if he'd put on a good fifteen or twenty pounds since she'd last seen him more than a decade ago. At around six feet, he was tall and imposing—but also paunchy and balding, his complexion florid.

"What are you doing here?" she blurted.

Rather than answer, he sauntered farther into the store. "I suppose you've heard the news."

"This morning," she responded shortly. What did one say to someone who'd just lost control of his company and been ousted from his position? *Condolences? I'm sorry?*

Webb glanced around. "Nice little boutique you have here."

"Thank you," she said, "but I doubt it's what brings you by."

"Actually," he drawled, "I'm on vacation in the area—"

A *forced* vacation, Kelly thought.

"—and I thought you'd be able to tell me where to find Ryan. This morning, he wasn't at the fancy log house he's staying at nearby."

She tensed. "Why do you thing I would know?"

"There's no need to be coy, sugar," Webb responded. "Brenda's filled me in on the fact that you and Ryan are lovers."

She sucked in a breath and the look on Webb Sperling's face said he knew he'd struck a direct hit.

She opened her mouth to reply just as the front door opened and Ryan walked in.

Webb turned, coming face-to-face with the man Kelly had thought never to see in her shop again.

"Well, well," Webb drawled, "I see I'm interrupting a rendezvous."

"What the hell are you doing here?" Ryan shot back.

Webb's lips twisted. "Isn't it obvious? I'm here to congratulate you on your recent coup."

"The element of surprise was part of my plan," Ryan responded coolly.

"If you'd just waited, it would have all been yours one day."

"It's mine now." Ryan's jaw hardened.

"You always were the impatient type."

Kelly looked back and forth from father to son, fascinated despite herself by the exchange.

"I'd been planning on retiring," Webb mused, looking out the store windows. "Roxanne wants to be able to travel and not be tied down by business." He looked back at Ryan. "We may even spend part of the year right here in Tahoe."

"Is that the story you're spinning for the press?" Ryan said scornfully.

"It's the truth."

Webb adopted a look of such open sincerity, Kelly almost believed him herself despite the fact that his declarations were obviously a face-saving gesture, now that he'd been unceremoniously ousted from Sperling, Inc.

No wonder the man had been such a successful and clandestine adulterer for years, she thought— he created his own reality.

"Like hell," Ryan retorted, then his eyes shot to her. "When did he get here?"

Her gaze met and clashed with his. "Just now."

He looked back at Webb. "Where's the wife?"

"Roxanne?"

"If she's the one you're still married to," he responded icily.

"She's back at the hotel. I didn't think she needed to be here."

"More likely, you didn't want her finding out any unsavory details she might not be aware of already," Ryan sneered. "After all, a visit to the daughter of your former mistress might set off alarm bells, particularly for a woman with a well-honed sense of self-preservation like Roxanne."

Kelly almost laughed.

Webb managed to look wounded, then cagey. "The apple doesn't fall far from the tree. According to Brenda, you're screwing her daughter."

Ryan's eyes blazed. "My relationship with Kelly has nothing, *nothing,* in common with yours and Brenda's, no matter what the hell that relationship is these days."

Webb's eyes gleamed. "Brenda and I have stayed

close friends." He threw a quick glance at Kelly. "I recommend it with one's former lovers, by the way. You
never know when they'll prove useful, especially
when a family *affair* looks to be repeating itself."

Ryan's expression turned stony. "You're out," he
gritted. "Out of a job, out of Sperling, Inc. and out
of here."

Webb laughed. "You're quite protective of your
little chickadee." He looked Kelly up and down,
then murmured, "I can understand the attraction."

Ryan's fists clenched, but Webb turned toward
the door.

"Roxanne and I plan to take an extended
European vacation," Webb informed them.

"Of course," Ryan replied acidly, "you'll want to
take a long vacation until all of your socialite friends
move on to the next piece of gossip." He paused, then
added, "Is that why you were tracking me down? To
let me know how you were going to spin this?"

"And there are the thoroughbreds to be raised
and traded, of course," Webb went on, as if he
hadn't heard.

"The horse farm never interested me."

"You took after your mother's side of the family
in that way," Webb replied, shaking his head as he
walked to the shop's entrance, "but it's heartening
to see you've inherited my taste in women."

With that parting shot, Webb opened the store's
front door and left.

Ryan turned back to face her.

Before he could say anything, however, the door to the store opened again and a customer walked in.

Kelly smiled—with relief, really—at her unexpected customer, and moved forward. "May I help you?"

As she walked past Ryan, she murmured, "We can't talk now."

Moments later, as she was directing the customer to a display of furniture knobs, she noticed Ryan leaving.

She sighed, then watched as Erica emerged from the back room.

"You heard?" she asked in a low voice.

Erica nodded. "But with all the fireworks going off around here, I was afraid to come out of the storeroom."

"I wish I'd been back there with you."

That night, Tahoe received buckets of rain. It was one of the most powerful thunderstorms in recent memory.

Kelly sat in her living room, contemplating the rivulets of water cascading down her windows.

She sat, still in her work clothes, worn out by the drama that had played out at Distressed Success earlier.

Even if she'd been brave enough to face Ryan

tonight—even if the storm hadn't kept her home—she wouldn't have known what to say to him.

Yes, he was maddeningly self-assured, arrogant even, with looks that were too sinful to waste on a hard-nosed corporate raider. But he was more than that.

She thought about the way he'd taken time to help her decorate the lodge, patiently waiting while she contemplated something, happy to move things if she changed her mind completely.

She remembered how he'd gotten her back safely and tucked into bed the night she'd put away too much at the White Fir.

She thought about the wind ruffling his hair that day on the sailboat on Lake Tahoe.

She even thought about, yes, how he'd given money to Brenda.

And she realized that, whether she liked it or not, she had fallen for him. It was why she'd been so hurt when she'd thought he'd slept with her just because she might have been an easy lay, convinced by nothing more than her sexual experience that she was *okay*.

She wanted to be *more* to him. She wanted him to appreciate all of her. Her temper had had time to cool these last few days, allowing her to realize as much.

Tears threatened suddenly, but she held them back.

It was useless to feel the way she did, because Ryan didn't feel the same way about her. To him, she was just a fling during his enforced stay in Tahoe.

There was no way Ryan could want a more permanent association with the woman who remained, unalterably, Brenda Hartley's daughter.

She even *looked* like Brenda. He wouldn't want to wake up over the years, look over at the next pillow and be reminded again and again of the woman that his father had been sleeping with during his mother's last months.

The sound of the doorbell startled her from her reverie and she wondered with some unease about who could be ringing her doorbell in the middle of a thunderstorm.

She peered out her living-room window.

Dimly, she could make out a man's form.

He must have seen a movement, because he turned to face her and she saw it was Ryan.

Her heart began to pound.

She got up and moved to the door, unlocking and opening it.

"Yes?" she asked.

Droplets ran down from the brim of his hat.

"Can I come in?" he asked.

Without responding, she moved aside and he stepped inside.

While she closed the door to the wind and wet, he pulled off his hat and jacket.

Turning back to him, she said, "Let me take those."

He handed them to her, and she deposited them on a nearby coatrack.

After that, she folded her arms and walked farther into the house. He followed.

She turned when she reached the middle of the living room. "Can I offer you a drink?" She nodded at her cup. "I just made a pot of tea."

It seemed ridiculous to be offering him a drink, but it served to cover the terrible tension.

"Thanks, but I'm fine." He looked at her closely. "You look tearful."

She'd been so surprised by the sound of the doorbell, she hadn't thought about her appearance.

"Allergies," she fibbed.

He walked toward her. "I don't think so."

"I can't imagine why you're here," she said quickly.

"Can't you?" he responded obliquely.

Her chin came up. "Come to tell me that your first order of business as the new head of Sperling, Inc. is to cut off Distressed Success?"

"I think you know the answer to that question."

Her lips parted.

His expression remained indecipherable. "I'm not willing to walk away from the bargaining table—yet."

She wrapped her arms around herself. She longed for the return of her midnight lover of tender caresses and passionate kisses, but the man in front of her wore a mask of inscrutability.

"Provided you can meet a few conditions," he said, "I think we're in business."

Her heart pounded. "Such as?"

"The first thing anyone would need to know," he said, "is whether you have any brand recognition."

Her spirits sank. "Well, not really—"

"It doesn't have to be nationwide," he supplied helpfully. "It could just be local. Say a small place like Hunter's Landing?"

She nodded. "People in Hunter's Landing definitely recognize Distressed Success."

The truth was, it was a laughably small place to rely on for brand recognition.

"What about meeting demand?" he asked. "Who are your suppliers?"

She felt a spark of hope. Here she was on firmer ground. "I have some manufacturers right here on the west coast. I know they're reliable. They've produced samples for me ahead of schedule in the past. Plus, I found them on recommendations and I know they produce goods for some of the major department store brands."

"Even Sperling stores?"

"Even Sperling," she confirmed.

"What about gross-profit margins?" he went on. "Department stores usually look for around forty-five percent, but—" he stopped and looked at her thoughtfully "—that's negotiable."

"How negotiable?" she asked suspiciously.

"What are you making at Distressed Success?"

She hesitated. "I'm getting around sixty in the shop right now."

He looked impressed. "Superb."

"Location is everything," she allowed. Then emboldened, she decided to put down some qualifications of her own. "You could achieve the same in Sperling stores, but I'd have to be assured of proper product placement—good sight lines, and some swing areas."

"Done…but I need an exclusive deal."

"What kind of exclusive deal?" She tried to read his expression again, but couldn't.

"You partner with me only. No relationships with other parties."

Eleven

She felt a flutter in her stomach, then wet her lips.

His eyes zeroed in on the action and flared, before his eyelids dropped to conceal his expression.

"With an exclusive deal—" she cleared the catch in her voice "—I'd expect…more."

He shifted closer. "Name your terms."

"Are we still talking about Sperling, Inc. and Distressed Success?" she asked, huskily.

The tension was unbearable.

"I don't know," he said, raising his hand to cup the side of her face, his fingers delving into her hair. "Are we?"

"Aren't you worried about partnering with me?"

She searched his eyes. "I am Brenda Hartley's daughter. I even look like her."

"I *like* the way you look." His fingers caressed her scalp, making her want to purr. "And for the record, you're nothing like your mother in the ways that count. You're no more like Brenda because you have red hair and hazel eyes than I'm like Webb because I've become head of Sperling, Inc."

"People may be surprised to hear we've… hooked up," she whispered.

His eyes lowered to her mouth. "We might as well make a big splash."

"We're from different worlds—"

"We're alike, you and I," he contradicted, smiling wryly as his eyes met hers again. "We've both spent our whole lives making sure we *didn't* become our parents."

"You do have a point there," she conceded.

"See," he joked, "that's a great first step—admitting I'm right. I foresee a beautiful…partnership."

Her laugh came out weak and breathless.

He leaned forward and placed light kisses on her nose, the corner of her mouth, her lips….

"You know," she joked, "this is inappropriate…if I'm giving a presentation to become your business partner."

"But not," he responded in a low voice, "if you're interviewing for the position of wife."

Her heart flipped over. "What did you say?"

Instead of responding, he kissed her, long and deep.

When he finally pulled away, he said, "Marry me and let's have kids."

"*Yes.*" Tears pricked the back of her eyes. "I called up Webb last week and told him I was no longer interested in getting my designs into Sperling stores."

"I know," he said quietly, catching a tear with the pad of his thumb.

"*You know?*"

He nodded. "The first thing I did when my ownership became official was to call up the managers at Sperling headquarters and find out where your contract was in the pipeline."

She smiled through her tears. "So you could torpedo it, I would have thought."

He shook his head, his expression wry. "So I could move it along. Imagine my surprise when I found out the negotiations had stalled…at *your* request."

"I wasn't sure you'd believe me if I told you I'd pulled out *before* your takeover became public."

"I would have believed you, because you're too important to me. My *first* order of business was to find out what had happened to your contract." He smiled ruefully. "Imagine how perplexed the people at Sperling were when the new majority owner's first questions were about a contract that most of them had never heard of and that had worked its way down the food chain."

She blinked back tears.

He sobered. "Why did you do it? Why pull out when Sperling was the key to your going national?"

"Pride," she said. "Brenda told me that you'd given her some money."

Ryan cursed under his breath. *"She told you?"*

"Yes."

"And you drew the worst possible conclusion," he guessed.

She nodded. "I wanted to repay you. I didn't want you to think I was some—" her vision got blurry again "—some floozy you could b-buy."

"Aw, honey." He grasped her upper arms and started kissing away tears that had seeped out. "That's not why I did it. I wanted Brenda to go away, so we could concentrate on straightening things out between us. I'd just had the most incredible weekend of my life."

"That's just it," she said, hiccupping. "Your paying off Brenda, coming on the heels of my finding out you'd known all along about my sexual history or lack thereof, made me think that sex was all you wanted from me."

"Honey, if all you want from *me* is sex, I'll die a happy man."

She gave a watery laugh.

He sobered again. "The more I fought against my attraction to you, the more I fell under your spell. It became impossible to ignore how alike we are."

"Two people trying like crazy *not* to be their parents?" she supplied.

Her comment elicited a smile. "Actually, your sexual inexperience made me realize you'd been just as affected, if not more so, by growing up as Brenda Hartley's daughter as I was by being raised as Webb Sperling's son."

"The first guy I slept with was a fellow college student," she supplied. "Then he met Brenda and announced our relationship couldn't possibly go anywhere. He had serious plans to storm the corporate world, and an in-law like Brenda would have been a liability."

"Idiot."

She smiled. "Between that and the sex not being all that terrific to start with, Tyler sort of soured me on relationships for a long time. After growing up with Brenda, it had been a leap of faith for me to get involved with him to begin with."

He nodded. "My parents had an unhappy marriage, and when I arrived in Hunter's Landing, you were the last woman I would have said I'd get involved with. But you made me love you."

"I love you, too," she said shakily.

He leaned in for another kiss, one that quickly turned hot and full of promise.

She pulled him closer, her fingers splaying and delving into his hair as he plundered her mouth.

When they finally broke apart, they both took labored breaths.

"I need—"

"Make—"

They both stopped and Ryan grinned.

"Bed," he said simply.

Somehow, they made it up the stairs and to her bedroom.

She went to him then and stood by the bed, sandwiched between his legs.

He went to work on the buttons of her blouse, kissing each inch of skin as it was exposed.

She sighed and held him to her. Outside, the storm continued to rage, beating against the windows, but inside they were locked in their own world.

He peeled the blouse from her, then gazed into her eyes. "I've been a fervent admirer of your breasts."

She laughed. "I *thought* I saw you looking—"

"It was impossible not to."

"And yet you resisted me."

"It was a losing battle."

Then his mouth nestled in the dark valley created by her cleavage, placing moist kisses there.

Kelly gave a low moan.

When he released the clasp of her bra, her breasts fell into his hands like ripe fruit, tight and firm, and he kneaded them until she felt warmth spread within her.

Her skirt hit the floor next and his hand smoothed up and down the side of her thigh.

"Fantastic legs, too," he murmured.

"Being on my feet all day gives them plenty of exercise," she demurred.

"You're the total package. Beautiful inside and out."

She was sensitized to react to his every word... his every look...his every touch.

He undid his shirt, then stood, and between increasingly passionate kisses, he let her help him off with the rest of his clothing.

Her hand grazed his erection, stoking their need as their breathing became heavy with desire.

Once he'd lowered her panties and she'd stepped out of them along with her slipper-footed mules so that they both were naked, he tumbled her onto the bed next to him and began to caress her.

She arched to his touch, feeling him bringing her to life with every masterful stroke.

When he reached the spot at the juncture of her thighs, her world tilted, her breathing coming in audible gasps.

He licked and she was on fire.

He refused to relent, however, until she trembled and shook against him, cresting on a wave of deliverance and emotion that left her spent and replete at the same time.

He moved next to her then, driving need stamped

on his face, heavy on the scent of his skin and etched in the tension of his muscles.

"Protection," he rasped, looking around at the jumble of his clothes.

"You know I haven't been with anyone since—"

He went still. "It was a long time for me before you and I've been tested."

"Me, too."

"Are you sure?"

Her heart opened. "Would it be so bad if we got started on kids sooner rather than later?"

"Heck, no," he said.

"I want it all," she said, "the career, kids, you." Then there was no talking as he gathered her against him. He positioned himself and slid into her on a wave of mingled moans and sighs, and together they began to ride the wave.

She hung on to him, her hands low on his hips, meeting his thrusts, which sent them higher and higher, until they came at the same time.

She called his name as she felt him groan harshly against her neck.

Afterward, they lay together in bed, hearing the storm wreak its havoc outside.

"I can't believe you drove here in this weather," she said in disbelief.

His hand smoothed up and down her arm. "My month is almost up. I came as soon as I dealt with the fallout from my takeover of Sperling, Inc. I knew I had to resolve what was between us before I left."

"Just think," she responded, "if you hadn't been forced to spend a month at the lodge, we would never have met."

"I didn't come to Hunter's Landing looking for a woman," Ryan said, placing a light kiss on her lips. "In fact, it was the furthest thing from my mind. I was closing in on Webb—just about at the point where I had enough shares lined up to oust him—and I was pissed off about being forced to take off a month to cool my heels."

Kelly turned toward him fully. "Why *were* you set on taking over Sperling, Inc.? I mean, I know you dislike Webb, but—"

"It wasn't just revenge for what he did to my mother, though that was part of it," Ryan admitted. "He was mismanaging the stores, squandering the family heritage."

"And now that you have control, what do you plan to do?" she asked curiously.

"Sperling has been treading water at best under Webb's leadership," he responded. "Sales and profits have been lackluster. I'm planning on taking the stores more upscale and improving customer service. We need to stock cutting-edge fashion. There's no point in trying to beat discount merchants at their own game."

It was exactly what she'd do, Kelly thought, then

realized she shouldn't be surprised by Ryan's business acumen. After all, he was the man who had thumbed his nose at taking his rightful place in the family company and had instead, in ten short years, built one of the most dynamic, profitable cable companies around, buying up competitors for a song and turning them around, in part with the synergies created by his own burgeoning empire.

"So now you're a retail mogul as well as a cable-company tycoon," she teased.

"Yeah," Ryan conceded, "but I'm planning to delegate most of the work for the stores." He arched a brow. "Are you interested in helping?"

Kelly laughed. "I went looking for just an outlet for my designs, and wound up with the whole chain at my disposal."

"Honey, you have *me* at your disposal."

Kelly felt a quiver run through her. "Just a few hours ago, I was sitting on the couch thinking we were over."

He gave her a quick, fiery kiss. "My victory over Webb didn't give me the satisfaction I thought it would. Instead, I spent my time thinking about *you*. Thanks to Hunter's will, I've had time to figure out what's meaningful."

"I wonder if that was Hunter's motive all along," she mused.

"I've wondered the same thing," Ryan admitted. "He knew me and the other guys well. There was no way he could have predicted what our lives would be like ten years on, but maybe he had an inkling, since we were all hard-charging types, that we might need a little incentive to force us to take a breather, to assess how far we'd come and where we were going."

"You mean, he might have had a clue you'd turn into a driven corporate shark?"

"Maybe." He grinned good-naturedly. "I don't know how seriously the rest of us took that pact that we'd made to reunite in ten years. I'd forgotten all about it before my stay at the lodge. Maybe Hunter knew that would happen—that it would be up to him to make sure the Samurai weren't lost forever. Now I can't wait till I see the others. We have a lot to thank Hunter for."

"And thanks to you," Kelly said, "I realized we can't run from our past—"

"—but we can run toward our future, together," he finished for her.

And then there was no more talking, as he showed her exactly what some of their future would hold.

Ryan looked around the lodge one last time. It had been a hell of a month. He'd walked in seeking one thing and he was walking away with something else entirely.

Something better. Purer. Love in an unexpected

package, in an unexpected place. And he was a better person for it.

He sat in the great room, looking out at the midday sun, contemplating the note in front of him. It was part of his plan to begin building bridges to his old college buddies.

"What are you doing?" Kelly said, walking into the room and coming to sit on the arm of his chair.

"Composing a note to Matt Barton." He tapped the top of his pen against the coffee table. "He's due to arrive soon to start his month at the lodge."

Kelly smiled. "Telling him what a wonderful time you had here?"

"This place really is the Love Shack," he responded, then grinned. "All four of the guys who've spent a month here have wound up finding the One. And you know what they say. Forewarned is forearmed."

Kelly swatted him playfully.

They were about to embark on a trip to Napa Valley, where they planned to have an intimate wedding. Then they were heading back to the real world, so he could get back to work at El Ray Technology.

Kelly was already helping him get Sperling, Inc. back on track, offering advice about how the stores could be revamped. She was also placing production orders for her designs, so that they could be found in Sperling stores in the coming months.

Kelly had asked Erica to run Distressed Success for her in the meantime, and had hired a couple of local college students to help out. She wanted to keep the shop open while she expanded nationally.

Kelly leaned forward. "What did you write?"

Ryan picked up the piece of paper and read it aloud: "Matt, good luck, bud. I'm passing on a piece of advice. You're about to begin your month at 'the Love Shack.' Remember the universal truths about women we came up with on New Year's Eve our senior year? They tie you down and won't let you do anything dangerous? Scrap 'em. Here are the new universal truths about the One: She'll set you free. Loving her is the most dangerous thing you'll ever do. Ryan."

"Aww…"

Ryan smiled. "Don't get all weepy on me. Knowing Matt, he'll read it and think it's a load of BS."

Kelly looked at him archly. "I'm surprised there was nothing in your universal truths about sex. You know, seven college guys, lots of testosterone…you must have been thinking about it all the time."

Ryan grinned. "Yeah, well…I didn't want to say the sex *doesn't* get boring. Some things a guy wants to keep to himself."

Kelly slipped off the chair arm and into his lap, looping her arms around his neck. As she pulled his head down to hers, she murmured, "Come here and I'll prove that part to you right now."

"I guess our departure *can* wait," Ryan responded as they set about proving the universal truths they'd both discovered in the last month.

* * * * *

MARRIED TO
HIS BUSINESS

BY
ELIZABETH BEVARLY

Elizabeth Bevarly is the RITA® Award-nominated, nationally bestselling author of more than five dozen books. When she's not writing, she's watching *Project Runway* and *What Not to Wear*, but only for research purposes. She's also confident that she'll someday find a story in *House Hunters International*, so she watches that religiously, too. In the meantime, she makes do with her real life of ready-to-wear from Macy's and college exploratory trips around the Midwest with her husband and soon-to-be-a-senior son.

For all my Desire™ readers over the years.
Thanks for joining me on the ride.

One

As Kendall Scarborough watched her boss close his cell phone, stride to the northernmost window of his office and push it open, then hurl the apparatus into the wild blue yonder, she found herself thinking that maybe, just maybe, this wasn't a good day to tender her resignation. Again. But she would. Again. And this time she would make it stick.

And how fitting that one of her last tasks for Matthias Barton would be ordering him a new phone. Again. At least phones were easier to program and format to his liking than were PDAs and MP3 players, a number of which also lay at the bottom of the reflecting pool in the courtyard of Barton Limited—which just so happened to be situated directly below the northernmost window of Matthias's office. In fact, there were at least five years' worth of PDAs and MP3 players and other small appa-ratuses…apparati…little gizmos…in the pool, Kendall knew. Matthias Barton was, without question, one of the finest minds working in big business today. But when it came to itty-bitty pieces of machinery, he was reduced to, well…throwing a lot of stuff out the window.

She straightened her little black-framed glasses and plucked out the pen that was perpetually tucked into the tidy, dark blond bun knotted at the back of her head. Then she withdrew a small notepad from the pocket of the charcoal pin-striped, man-style trousers she'd paired with a tailored white, man-style shirt. All of her work clothes were man-style, because she was convinced they gave her petite, five-foot-four-inch frame a more imposing presence in the male-dominated society of big business. After scribbling a few notes—not the least of which was *New phone for Matthias*—she flipped the notepad closed and stuffed it back into her pocket.

"Kendall," he began as he closed the window and latched it, then turned to make his way back to his desk.

"Got it covered, sir," she told him before he said another word. "We'll go with VeraWave this time. I'm sure that service will suit you much better than the last one."

To herself, she added, *And the one before that. And the one before that. And the one before that.* It was just a good thing Barton Limited was headquartered in a city like San Francisco where new phone services sprang up every day. The year wasn't even half over, and Kendall had already been forced to change cellular companies three times.

"Thank you," Matthias told her as he seated himself behind his big mahogany desk and reached for the small stack of letters she'd typed up that morning, which were now awaiting his signature.

His attire was, of course, man-style, too, but she didn't

think that was what gave him such an imposing presence—though certainly the espresso-colored suit and dark gold dress shirt and tie, coupled with his dark hair and even darker eyes, didn't diminish it. Matthias himself was just larger than life, be it sitting at the head of the massive table that bisected the boardroom of Barton Limited, or slamming a squash ball into the wall at his athletic club, or charming some bastion of society into a major investment at a dinner party. Kendall had seen him in each of those situations—and dozens of others—and she couldn't think of a single moment when Matthias *hadn't* been imposing.

He'd intimidated the hell out of her when she'd first come to work for him straight out of graduate school, even though, back then, he'd barely been out of grad school himself. In spite of his youth, he'd already made millions, several times over. Kendall had been awed that someone only five years older than she—Matthias had only recently turned thirty-two—was already light-years ahead of her on the corporate ladder. She'd wanted to observe his habits and policies and procedures and mimic them, thinking she could achieve the same rapid rise and level of success through emulation.

It hadn't taken long, however, for her to realize she would never be in Matthias's league. He was too focused, too intense, too driven. His work was his life. He needed it to survive as much as he did oxygen or food. Over time, she'd gotten used to his ruthless single-mindedness when it came to achieving success, even if she'd never been able to understand it. And not just any old run-of-the-mill success, either. No, Matthias Barton had to be the absolute, no-close-seconds, unparalleled *best* at everything he set out to do.

Not that it mattered now, Kendall told herself, since she

wasn't going to be a part of his pursuit—or his success—
much longer. She had a pursuit—and success—of her own
to accomplish, and she should have started years ago. With
her MBA from Stanford, she'd been overqualified for the
position of personal assistant when she'd taken the job
with Matthias. But she'd known that working for someone
like him for a couple of years, even as a personal assistant,
would offer her *entrée* into an echelon of big business that
most recent grads never saw. She'd learn from a legend and
make contacts up the wazoo, swimming with the prover-
bial sharks. But "a couple of years" had become five, and
Kendall was savvy enough around the sharks now to be
able to grill them up with a nice wasabi sauce.

It was time to go.

"Okay, where were we?" Matthias asked.

"Well, sir," she began, "you'd just, um, concluded your
call with Elliot Donovan at The Springhurst Corporation,
and I—" She inhaled a deep breath, steeled herself for
battle, and said, in a surprisingly sturdy voice, "I was about
to give you my two weeks' notice." To herself, she added
silently, *And this time, I'm going through with it, no matter
how hard you try to change my mind.*

His head snapped up at her announcement, and his bit-
tersweet chocolate eyes went flinty. "Kendall, I thought
we'd already talked about this."

"We have, sir, several times," she agreed. "Which is
why it shouldn't come as a surprise. Now that your
wedding to Miss Conover is off—"

"Look, just because Lauren and I canceled our plans,"
Matthias interrupted, "that doesn't mean I don't still need
you to take care of things."

His now-defunct wedding to Lauren Conover had just

been the most recent reason he'd used for why Kendall couldn't leave his employ yet, but she was still surprised he would try to use it again. Technically, the wedding hadn't been canceled. There had just been a change of date and venue. Oh, and also a change of groom, since Lauren was now planning to marry Matthias's twin brother, Luke.

"Anything left to do will be taken care of by Miss Conover and her family," Kendall pointed out. "If there's anything left to do."

And she doubted there was. Matthias hadn't spoken much about his broken engagement, but Kendall hadn't been surprised when she'd heard the news. Well, maybe the part about Lauren's falling in love with Luke Barton had been a little surprising. Okay, a lot surprising. But even without Luke's intervention, the marriage, as far as Kendall was concerned, would have been a huge mistake. Matthias had proposed to Lauren Conover only because he'd wanted to merge his business with her father's, and Lauren Conover had accepted the proposal only because…

Well, frankly, Kendall was still trying to figure that one out. She'd met Lauren only a few times, but she'd never gotten the impression that Lauren was in love with Matthias—or even in like with him. Obviously she hadn't been in love, because she wouldn't have fallen for his brother, identical twin or not, if she had been. Personality-wise, Luke and Matthias Barton couldn't be more differ-ent from each other—save the fact that Luke was as driven professionally as his brother was. At least, that was what the office scuttlebutt said. Kendall had never met the other man in person.

There was no question that the match between Luke and Lauren was indeed a love match. With Matthias, however, any life he'd envisioned building with Lauren had been more about business than pleasure, more about ambition than affection. There were times when Kendall wondered if the man could care about anything *but* building his business.

Matthias said nothing for a moment, only met Kendall's gaze levelly. "But there are other things I'm going to need you to—"

"There is nothing," she quickly, but firmly, interjected, before he had a chance to create and/or fabricate a host of obligations that anyone could see to. "We're coming up on the slowest time of the year for Barton Limited," she reminded him. "I have you up to speed on everything for the next month. Now that the Stuttgart trip is out of the way, you don't have any international travel scheduled until the fall. No conferences until September. Nothing pressing that whoever you hire to take my place won't have plenty of time to prepare for. And since you'll be spending the entire month of July at your friend's lodge, anyway, that makes this the perfect time for me to—"

"I'll need you more than ever at Hunter's lodge," Matthias interrupted. "Even with all the preparation I've done—"

You mean *I've* done, Kendall thought to herself, since it had been she, not Matthias, who'd made all the arrangements.

"—it's still going to be difficult, being away from the office for that length of time. It's essential that I take someone with me who knows what's going on."

"Then I'd suggest you take Douglas Morton," Kendall said, naming one of Barton Limited's newest VPs.

"Morton needs to be here," Matthias said. "*You* need to be with me."

So now he was going to use the mysterious month at the

mysterious lodge to keep her on her leash, Kendall thought. She knew his upcoming trip to his friend's lodge on Lake Tahoe was much more than a trip to his friend's lodge on Lake Tahoe, even if she had no idea exactly why. All she knew was that, in January, he'd received a letter out of the blue from some law office representing the estate of a friend of his from college. The man had passed away, but before going had imparted a dying wish he wanted fulfilled by his old friends. They were each to spend one month in a lodge he owned on the lake.

Why? Kendall had no idea. But Matthias had driven her crazy for weeks, trying to rearrange his spring schedule so that he could spend his assigned month of April in Lake Tahoe. Then, when he'd been unable to reschedule a trip to Germany in April, he'd driven her even crazier rearranging everything she'd spent weeks rearranging so that he could switch months with his brother Luke—whom he hadn't even spoken to in years at that point—who had been assigned July.

There were seven friends in all, Kendall knew, dating back to Matthias's time at Harvard, all of whom had gradually lost touch with one another after graduating. Matthias hadn't wanted to talk about it in detail, and Kendall had respected his wishes. She'd also managed the impossible, reworking his schedule and obligations—twice—so that he could abide by his friend's last wishes and spend his month in Lake Tahoe.

It would have been so much better if he'd been able to stick with the original plan. Not only because she would have saved herself a lot of trouble, but because Lake Tahoe was where Kendall would be going to complete the necessary training for her new job—starting the first week of

July. She was dreading the possibility—however remote—that she might run into Matthias there so soon after severing ties with him. He was bound to be unhappy about her leaving. Even more so once he discovered who her new employer was.

"I can't be with you, sir," she reiterated. Inhaling a deep breath, she told him the rest. "I've been offered a position elsewhere that I've already accepted. They want me to take part in a week-long training seminar that starts the first of July—two weeks from today," she added for emphasis. "And I'll report for work at the company immediately after completing my orientation."

Matthias said nothing for several moments, only leaned back in his chair and crossed his arms over his expansive chest. Then he looked at her in a way that made Kendall feel like her backbone was dissolving. Fast. Finally, he said, "You've already accepted a position somewhere else?"

She nodded. And she hoped she sounded more confident than she suddenly felt when she told him, "Um, yes?"

Oh, yeah. That sounded totally confident. There was nothing like punctuating a statement with a question mark to really hammer home one's point. Provided one was a four-year-old child.

"Mind telling me where?" he asked.

Kendall braced herself for his reaction, reminding herself to be forceful and assertive and end her sentences with a period. Maybe even an exclamation point where necessary. By golly. Or, rather, By Golly! "With, um, OmniTech Solutions?" she said. Asked. Whatever. Oh, hell. "I'm going to be their new VP? In charge of Public Relations?" When she realized she was still speaking in the inquisitive tense, Kendall closed her eyes and mentally willed her age back up to twenty-seven-and-a-half. If she kept this up, Matthias wouldn't let her have her milk and cookies for snack later.

When she opened her eyes again, she saw that his dark brows had shot up even farther at her declaration. Question. Whatever. Oh, hell.

"OmniTech?" he asked. Using the proper punctuation, Kendall couldn't help noticing. Unlike *some* people. "Who the hell recruited you to work for OmniTech?"

Strange that he would assume she was recruited, she thought, and that she hadn't gone looking for the position on her own. Even if, you know, she had been recruited for the position and hadn't gone looking for it on her own. "Stephen DeGallo," she told him. And she applauded herself for finally grasping the proper rules of punctuation. Now if she could just do something about the sudden drop in volume her voice had taken….

Although she wouldn't have thought it possible, Matthias's eyebrows arched even higher. "The CEO of the company recruited you to come work for him?" he asked with obvious disbelief. "As a vice president?"

Kendall didn't see what was so unbelievable about that. She was perfectly qualified for the job. Tamping down her irritation, she repeated, "Yes, sir."

Matthias narrowed his eyes at her. "Stephen DeGallo never hires from outside the company. He always promotes from within. He doesn't trust outsiders. He likes to surround himself with people he's trained to think like he does. You know. Suck-ups."

Kendall ignored the comment. Mostly because she couldn't help thinking that, after five years of working for Matthias, she was even better qualified for the job of suck-up than she was vice president in charge of public relations. "Stephen said—"

"Stephen?" Matthias echoed, this time punctuating the comment with an incredulous expulsion of air. "You're already calling him by his first name?"

"He insisted. Sir," Kendall added meaningfully, since Matthias had never extended her the invitation to address him so informally, even after being his right-hand woman for five years. Before he could comment further, she hurried on, "Stephen said I had impeccable credentials. And I do," she couldn't help adding. "In case you've forgotten, I have an MBA from Stanford, and I graduated with highest honors."

Matthias actually smiled at that. "Oh, yeah, I'll just bet DeGallo's impressed with your…credentials." He leaned back in his chair even more, folding his arms now to cradle his head in his hands. It was a position Kendall knew well, one that was meant to lull the observer into a false sense of security before Matthias struck with the velocity and toxicity of a cobra.

"You realize," he said, "that the only reason DeGallo offered you the job is because he's competing with Barton Limited for the Perkins contract, and he's going to expect you to tell him everything you know about the work we've done so far to win it."

The barb hit home, just as she knew Matthias had meant for it to. Instead of reacting to it, however, Kendall only replied calmly, "That would be highly unethical, sir. Possibly even criminal. Not only could Stephen *not* be expecting me to provide him with any such information, but he must know I'd never betray you that way."

"Wouldn't you?" Matthias asked easily.

Kendall gaped at him. Now that was a reaction she *hadn't* expected. "Of course I wouldn't. How can you even ask me something like that?"

She realized then how right she'd been to accept the new position. If Matthias could suspect she was capable of turning on him so completely, so readily, then he truly didn't view her any differently than he did the phones he tossed out the window. He'd also implied she wasn't qualified for her new job, even after the countless times she'd proved how valuable an employee she was.

Clearly, it was time to go.

"Fine, then," he said, dropping his arms and sitting up straight again. "But, Kendall, haven't you learned anything from me in the time you've been at Barton Limited? Big business isn't the gentleman's game it was a generation ago. No one's going to do you any favors. Why should you do any favors for them? For me? When it comes to business, you think of yourself first, others not at all. Feel free to report to OmniTech tomorrow if you want. Since you'll be going to work for one of my competitors, I can't risk having you around the office any longer and potentially compromising the work we're doing here. Your two weeks' notice won't be necessary. You're fired. Clear out your desk immediately. I'll have Sarah call security and they can escort you out of the building. You have ten minutes."

And with that, he turned his attention back to the stack of papers requiring his signature and began to sign each without another glance in her direction.

Kendall had no idea what to say. She hadn't expected this from Matthias at all. She'd thought he would react the way he'd reacted every other time she'd tried to resign, with a seemingly endless list of reasons why she couldn't go, none of which was in any way legitimate. Never in a million years would she have thought he would fire her, even if she was going to work for one of his competitors. Barton Limited had scores of competitors. She would have been hard-pressed to find a position with a company that *didn't* compete with Matthias in some way. She'd thought he would view her acceptance of a new job the same way she did: as business. Instead, he seemed to have taken it…

Personally, she marveled.

Immediately, she told herself that was impossible. Matthias Barton didn't get personal. About anything. He was just reacting this way because he was worried she would compromise his pursuit of the Perkins contract. That, she thought, *wasn't* surprising. That he would think of his business first, and others…well, as he'd said, not at all. She just wished he had enough faith in her to realize that she would never do anything to sabotage him or his work.

Clearly, it was *so* time to go.

With a briskly muttered "Yes, sir," Kendall spun on her heel and exited Matthias's office, giving him the same courtesy he'd extended to her and not looking back once. She wasn't the kind of person to look backward. Only forward. That was the reason she'd come to work for Matthias in the first place, because she'd been thinking ahead, to a better future. Now that future was the present. It was time to start thinking forward again. And that meant never giving another thought to…

Well. She could barely remember Matthias Thaddeus Barton's name. Or how his espresso eyes flashed gold when he was angry. Or how that one unruly lock of dark hair fell forward whenever he had his head bent in concentration. Or how one side of his mouth turned up more than another whenever he smiled that arrogant smile…

Matthias looked at the closed door through which Kendall had just exited and silently cursed it for ruining the view. Not that there was anything especially scenic about Kendall Scarborough. With her librarian glasses and those mannish, colorless clothes hiding what was doubtless a curve-free body, anyway, and with her hair always bound tightly to her head, she wasn't likely to be showing up as a trifold with staples taped inside the locker of a dockworker. Of course, that had been the first thing to grab his attention during her interview five years ago, because the last thing he'd wanted or needed in a personal assistant was someone he might want to get personal with.

Not that *personal* to Matthias was all that personal, but the risk for screwing up was always there, since he had, in the past, been swayed by beauty, with disastrous results. He was understandably wary around beautiful things and beautiful women. But he'd never been able to resist either.

He'd thought he'd solved his problem by arranging a marriage with Lauren Conover that would have provided him with not just a suitable wife for a man in his position, but a beneficial merger with her father's company, as well. Lauren was beautiful, smart, accomplished and chic, but there hadn't been a spark of any inconvenient passion between them. The two of them could have lived in a beautiful home, had beautiful children and a beautiful life, without Matthias ever having to get too deeply involved with any of it. It had been so perfect. Until his brother, Luke, had come along and, as had been a habit with Lunkhead since their childhood, screwed up a perfectly good thing.

But it wasn't Lunkhead Luke who had screwed up things with Kendall, Matthias reminded himself. Kendall, who was exactly what Matthias *did* want and need in a personal assistant: pragmatic and professional, enterprising and efficient. In the five years she'd worked for him, she'd been his calendar, his clock, his coordinator. His bartender, his astrologer, his conscience. His butcher, his baker, his candlestick maker. His tinker, his tailor, his spy.

That last word hit Matthias hard, since it was precisely what he'd just accused Kendall of being for someone else. Even though he knew she wouldn't. Even though he knew she couldn't. Although there was no question that Stephen DeGallo's motive in hiring her had been driven by his hope—hell, his certainty—that he could persuade her to share information about both Matthias and Barton Limited that would work to his benefit, Matthias couldn't honestly see her turning on him that way. He'd just been so surprised by her announcement that she'd already accepted a job somewhere else—and with his biggest competitor—that he hadn't known what to say.

Whenever she'd tried to tender her resignation before, Matthias had always been able to talk her out of it. And he'd always talked her out of it because he'd needed her here. Hell, he knew she was overqualified for her position. That was why he'd given her so many raises over the years that she was now making almost twice what her predecessors had made. Yeah, okay, maybe she could be doing more with her degree and her savvy, he conceded reluctantly. But she didn't have to do it for OmniTech.

There was no way Stephen DeGallo had recruited

Kendall for her résumé. He didn't see her the way Matthias did—pragmatic and professional, enterprising and efficient. She was just an opportunity to mine the practices and policies of Barton Limited. Nothing more.

He expelled a disgruntled breath of air as he continued to look at the closed door. Well, he'd just have to get along without her, wouldn't he? He'd just hire another personal assistant, that was all. Someone else who was pragmatic and professional, enterprising and efficient. Someone else who would be his calendar, clock and conscience. That shouldn't be so hard, right? He'd put Kendall on it right away.

His finger was actually on the buzzer to call her in before he realized what he'd been about to do. Ask Kendall, the woman he'd just fired—not to mention insulted—to hire a replacement for herself. He shook his head and chuckled at himself for the gaffe, even if he couldn't find anything especially funny about it. Man. If he didn't know better, he'd almost think he couldn't do *anything* without Kendall. And that, he knew, was nuts.

He was a captain of industry. He had made his first million less than a year after graduating from college, and he'd multiplied it dozens of times over since. He headed a Fortune 500 Company that employed thousands of people all over the world.

So he'd lost his personal assistant, he thought. So what? Personal assistants were as easy to find as cheap champagne on New Year's Eve. He'd hire another one tomorrow. Have the person trained well enough by the time he left for Tahoe that they would at least have the basics down. Actually, the timing, as Kendall had said, was perfect. He could use the month in Tahoe with his new assistant to mold him or her to his liking.

Matthias would get along just fine without Kendall Scarborough. Hell, yes, he would.

Hell, yes.

TWO

Kendall made the trip to Tahoe courtesy of OmniTech, enjoying the brief flight in first class. A rental car awaited her on arrival, a luxury sedan that was quite the posh way to travel, compared to her little economy car at home. Maybe on her new salary, she could ultimately buy something like this, she thought as she settled into the leather seat and pushed the button to open the sunroof. As the balmy summer air tumbled into the car, she donned her sunglasses, fastened her seat belt over her white oxford shirt and khaki trousers and tuned the radio to the jazz station. Then, feeling like a corporate executive for the first time in her life, she pulled out of the rental lot at the airport basking in contentment.

Until she thought about Matthias Barton. Then her contentment fled. And what she'd hoped would be a peaceful, introspective drive that was filled with planning for her future at OmniTech suddenly turned into a grueling marathon of disgruntlement instead.

But then, thoughts of Matthias—never mind disgruntlement—had been regular companions over the two weeks that had passed since she'd last seen him. So as she merged onto the highway, Kendall did her best to think of something—anything—else. How she needed to replace the hardware on her kitchen cabinets. The fact that women's shoe manufacturers still hadn't figured out how to wed style with comfort. Why the sky was blue and the grass was green. The atomic weight of boron. Where the contestants of *Survivor* should go next—though, admittedly, it probably wasn't polite for her to say aloud where *she* thought they should go. Whatever it took to keep from hearing again those two little words she'd never thought she'd hear Matthias say to her.

You're fired.

She still couldn't believe he'd done it. After giving him five years of her life, years she could have spent building her own career instead of bolstering his, he'd cut her loose in the most insulting way possible. She'd seen him fire plenty of people during the time she'd worked for him, but they were people who'd deserved the boot. Employees who had been, at best, ineffective, and at worst, dishonest. People who had cheated him, or lied to him, or stolen from him. Now Kendall, who had never missed a day on the job, and whose work ethic had been irreproachable, had been relegated to their ranks.

But even that wasn't what bothered her the most. What bothered her the most was her own reaction to having been fired. She told herself she should be angry with Matthias for the way he'd dismissed her. She should be resentful.

She should be outraged. She should be reporting him to the Equal Opportunity Commission. Instead, what she felt was hurt. Hurt in the same way a little girl feels hurt when she's always picked last for kickball. And hurt feelings were *not* something a consummate professional like Kendall should feel.

Matthias was right about one thing. She hadn't learned as much from him as she'd thought she would when she accepted the position, if she couldn't be the focused, unflinching businesswoman she'd envisioned becoming. She could be as ruthless and determined as Matthias was, she told herself. She *could.* And she would be, too. Starting the moment she passed through the doors of the Timber Lake Inn.

That must be a new hotel in Tahoe, Kendall thought as she exited onto the road that would take her to her final destination. She'd never heard of it before. It was kind of an odd name for a conference hotel, too. They must be trying to make business travel sound less businessy or something.

She glanced at the numbers on a shop window to get her bearings and calculated that the hotel was another eight blocks down, toward the lake. She hadn't been to Tahoe since college, she realized as she drove, smiling at the shops boasting kites and artwork and jewelry and clothes. In the winter, there would be skis lined up everywhere, but during the summer, there were water toys and rafts instead. People dotted the streets in their bright summer colors and sunglasses, lolling at café tables and sauntering in and out of stores. The weather was perfect for being outdoors, the air kissed with just a hint of the cool breeze gliding off the lake, the sky a faultless blue streaked with gauzy clouds.

Kendall smiled at the promise inherent in the day. It was a good omen. She had been right to leave Matthias's employ. Stephen DeGallo's offer couldn't have come at a better time. Funny how things just worked out perfectly sometimes. She had a full week to spend in one of the most beautiful places on earth, learning about a new career that, she hoped, would be hers for the rest of her life. Her future at OmniTech was wide-open. If she worked hard and did everything right—who knew?—she might even become the CEO of the company herself someday. Stephen DeGallo was a confirmed bachelor in his late forties with no family he was bringing up through the ranks, and he was known for rewarding his workers with generous benefits and bonuses. Even if he never groomed Kendall for his own position at the company, there was every reason to believe he might someday install her as the head of one of the scores of businesses he owned. Unlike Matthias, who had never offered any indication that he would ever consider Kendall for anything more than his assist—

Dammit. She was thinking about him again.

She pushed Matthias out of her brain—again—and looked for another street number. Two more blocks.

When she braked for a red light, she used the opportunity to get her bearings. A glance at her watch told her it was just coming up on three o'clock, precisely the time she'd anticipated arriving, knowing her room would be ready by then. She was supposed to meet Stephen and the other trainees at six for an informal dinner, so they could all get to know one another, and training officially began at eight in the morning. Dress would be casual, but Kendall had packed a couple of suits in with her trousers and shirts, just in case. She was, after all, a consummate professional.

Of course, she was in Lake Tahoe, too, so she'd also included blue jeans and T-shirts and shorts and sandals, her preferred attire for relaxing. She wasn't such a workaholic that she didn't take advantage of her off time. Unlike Matthias, who—

Dammit, she was doing it again.

The light changed green, so she banished thoughts of Matthias—*again*—and urged the accelerator down lightly, taking the last two blocks slowly. The lake was in view now, but she didn't see any hotels large enough to qualify for corporate lodgings up ahead. She took her eyes off the road long enough to glance down at the passenger seat, where she'd laid the directions and a map, to confirm she had the address right. Maybe she'd written it down wrong, she thought. Because this block and the one beyond it was nothing but more quaint shops and cafés and cozy B and Bs.

Just as she neared the end of the last block and began to look for a place to turn around, she saw a sign with an arrow pointing to the right that read Parking for Timber Lake Inn. Braking quickly, she was able to make the turn just in time.

But the drive led to the entrance of a tidy, cheerful little bed-and-breakfast. Kendall frowned, wondering where she'd gone wrong, then noted a sign above the door that identified it as the very hotel she'd been looking for. Huh. That was odd. The place looked more like a honeymoon hotel than it did a corporate facility. Stephen DeGallo must like to use places like this to make his new hires feel more comfortable. Yet another way in which he differed from Matthias, who, Kendall was sure, would have scheduled an orientation for…

Well, actually, Matthias would have trained people in the buildings where they would be working, she thought. Or rather, he'd have *other* people training his new employees in the buildings where they would be working. It would be more professional that way. More businesslike. God forbid he should ever want anyone to feel any other way.

When Kendall realized she was thinking about Matthias *again,* she shoved the thought away *again*—harder this time—and pushed open the car door. By now a bellman had emerged from the hotel and was descending the stairs to help her with her bag. Instead of the liveried uniform he might have worn at a larger hotel, however, he was dressed in khaki shorts and a polo bearing the logo of the Timber Lake Inn stitched on the breast pocket. Coupled with his shaggy blond hair and ruddy complexion, he looked as if he should be standing at the edge of the ocean toting a surfboard instead of lugging bags for a lakeside hotel.

"Dude," he greeted her with a smile, reinforcing the image. "Welcome to the Timber Lake Inn. I'm Sean. I'll get your bags."

"Thanks," Kendall replied with a smile of her own as she reached into the car to pop the trunk open. "I'm Kendall Scarborough. I'm here for the OmniTech orientation session."

Sean nodded. "Well, wherever that's going on, you can probably get there by walking. We're pretty centrally located here."

The comment puzzled Kendall. "It's going on here," she said. "At the hotel."

Sean's eyebrows shot up at that. "Whoa. First I've heard about it. But then, I was on vacation last week and just got back today. All I knew about going on this week was the Tyson-Gerhart wedding and the Truckee Ski Club reunion. Those have got us booked to full capacity."

Kendall looked at the hotel again. It didn't look big enough to host those functions and a training session. Not that she'd expected the OmniTech orientation to be a huge event, but since it would run for a week, and since Stephen DeGallo himself would be part of it, she'd just assumed the company would be training quite a few people. A business that size employed hundreds in San Francisco alone, and Kendall had been under the impression that this session would include new hires from all over the Northwest. There must be more to the hotel than the two stories she could see.

Sean collected her bags and she followed him into the lobby, which immediately made her feel comfortable. It was everything a place called the Timber Lake Inn should be, from its knotty pine walls to the huge creek stone fireplace on the opposite side of the room. The hardwood floors were covered here and there by woven rugs in Native American geometrics, and wrought iron fixtures hung from the exposed log ceiling. A wide staircase to the right of the reception desk led up to a line of rooms on the second floor, but none of them seemed to be meeting rooms. As if to illustrate that, one of the doors opened and a couple exited, looping their arms around each other and cuddling like newlyweds.

Nothing about the place suggested it was used for business events. In fact, the place looked…well, cozy. That was the only word that came to Kendall's mind.

The word returned when she entered her room…until she discovered it was actually a suite appointed with more pine walls and more exposed ceiling beams and more Native American rugs. In the main room, French doors opened onto a spacious balcony that offered a glorious view of the lake, which was picked up again in the bedroom by a broad picture window. The bathroom boasted a jacuzzi and small television, and there was a wet bar tucked into the far side of the living room. An enormous basket of fresh fruit and wine sat at the center of the dining table, and a massive bouquet of flowers, fragrant and splashy, was perched on the desk. Envelopes bearing her name—her *first* name—were tucked into each.

"Still think DeGallo wants you only for your MBA and your business savvy?"

Kendall spun around with a start at the question to find Matthias leaning in the still-open door to her room. Her lips parted in surprise, but not entirely because of his unexpected arrival. He looked…different. And not just because he was casually dressed in clay-colored trousers and a navy-blue polo, where she was more accustomed to seeing him in suits. She'd seen him dressed for non-business-related functions before, everything from rugby in the park to black-tie opening nights. It wasn't Matthias's clothing that looked off today. It was Matthias.

His clothes were a little wrinkled, his hair was a little shaggy, and his eyes were a little shadowed, as if he wasn't getting quite enough sleep. In fact, his whole face looked a little shadowed, a little leaner, a little rougher. And Matthias had never been "a little" anything. He was an all-or-nothing kind of man, emphasis on the *all*, especially where his physical appearance went.

She ignored the little pang of concern that pinched her at seeing him in his less-tidy-than-usual state. It was none of her business if he was working too much. None of her business if whoever he'd hired to take her place wasn't keeping him on track the way she had. She wasn't her boss's keeper. Especially since Matthias wasn't even her boss anymore.

"What are you doing here?" she asked by way of a

greeting, congratulating herself on keeping her voice steady, clear and indifferent. "I mean, I know why you're in Tahoe. But what are you doing *here?* At my hotel?"

He raised a shoulder and let it drop, then pushed himself away from the doorjamb. As he strode into the room, he told her, "I made better time driving from San Francisco than I thought I would, so I'm a little ahead of schedule. I don't have to meet the caretaker for another hour, so I thought I'd drop in and say hello."

Kendall eyed him suspiciously. It wasn't like Matthias to "drop in" on anyone, for any reason. And he must have gone to some lengths to find out where she would be staying and when she would be arriving, because she hadn't shared any of that information with him. Not to mention they hadn't exactly parted on the best of terms. They hadn't spoken to or seen each other since he'd had her escorted out of the building like a common thief. If he was here now, it had to be because he wanted something.

So she asked him, "What do you want?"

Matthias looked at Kendall and wondered which of dozens of answers to that question he should give her. He wanted a lot of things, actually. He wanted the Perkins contract. He wanted the Barton Limited stock to go through the roof. He wanted to be worth a billion dollars by the time he was forty. Hell, he even wanted world peace, since it would create so many new business-friendly governments. And, okay, he wanted a new personal assistant, too, since, so far, everyone he'd interviewed had been, at best, unqualified and, at worst, a lobotomy gone tragically wrong.

Mostly, though, he wanted Kendall to open her eyes and see what was so obvious to him. Talk about a lobotomy. What had happened to the pragmatic, professional, enterprising, efficient woman he'd hired? Looking at Kendall now…

Well, actually, looking at Kendall now, Matthias wondered what she'd done to herself. The dark blond hair she normally had twisted up out of her way hung loose, cascading past her shoulders in a thick, silky mass. Wow, it was a lot longer than he'd thought—not that he'd ever thought much about Kendall's hair. But it was long. Thick. Silky. Had he mentioned silky? And long? And thick? Her glasses were gone, too, and he noted with some surprise that her eyes were huge without them. And green. He'd never noticed that Kendall had green eyes. Really green eyes. Pale green. Like bottle glass. And every bit as clear.

"What do you want, Mr. Barton?" she asked again, bringing his thoughts back to where they needed to be.

It was a good question, he thought. He wished he had a good answer to go with it. But the fact was, he still wasn't sure why he was here. Yeah, her hotel was on his way, but even if it hadn't been, he would have driven the extra miles to see her. He'd done a little checking this week—okay, he'd done a lot of snooping—to find out where Kendall would be staying and the particulars of this "week-long orientation." But his mole at OmniTech—yes, Matthias had one there, just as he was sure DeGallo had one at Barton Limited—hadn't been able to uncover much about it.

Which had just hammered home to Matthias that the guy was up to no good. Had there been a legitimate orientation seminar going on, it would have been a matter of company record. As far as Matthias could tell, however, Kendall was the only new hire of any consequence that Stephen DeGallo had made recently. As he'd told her two weeks ago, the guy didn't hire outside the company for the kind of position he'd offered her. And any alleged orientation there might have been for her position should have taken place on-site—not in a cozy, romantic little hotel overlooking Lake Tahoe.

"I've come to offer you your job back," he said, surprising himself as much as he'd obviously surprised Kendall. He really hadn't been intending to do that at all when he drove into town. He'd just been planning to…

Okay, he wasn't exactly sure what he'd been planning to do. But now that he thought more about it, offering Kendall her job back made sense. No one he'd interviewed had come close to matching her qualifications. Matthias was confident that if he made her the right offer, she'd come back on board. Everyone had their price. Kendall was no exception. She'd just been feeling unappreciated, he told himself. He hadn't emphasized enough how valuable she was to Barton Limited. Oh, sure, he'd given her raises and more benefits. But any good employee needed ego stroking, too. Just because Kendall had never seemed like the kind of person who wanted that kind of thing didn't mean it wasn't important to her.

He didn't know why he hadn't thought about that before. At least not consciously. Evidently his brain *had* been considering it *sub*consciously, to have thrown out the offer to hire her back. That was probably what had been behind Matthias's driving into town to find her in the first place. He'd been planning—subconsciously—to renegotiate the terms of her employment and invite her back.

Yeah, that was it. It had to be. Why else would he have come?

Kendall, however, didn't seem to be as open to the idea of her return to Barton Limited as Matthias was, because she didn't answer him right away. In fact, she was looking at him as if she was kind of indignant.

No, it must be grateful, he told himself immediately. Indignity, gratitude…those got mixed up all the time. They had a lot of the same letters in common. After all, why would she feel indignant?

"I have a job," she said tersely.

Or maybe she'd said it sweetly. Those got mixed up a lot, too. Matthias was sure of it. The letter thing again.

"And I'm very excited about it," she added.

No, definitely terse, he thought. And not a little shirty.

Instead of replying, he strode across the room to the broad panoramic windows that looked out over the crystalline blue water of the lake and the bright blue sky above it. The day was glorious, the view crisp and clean, the dark green mountains on the other side of the water streaked with purple shadows from the forests of trees, the sun dappling the water as if it were scattering diamonds. This place was as far removed from the skyscrapers and concrete of San Francisco as it could be, and the last thing anyone should think about here was work. Which was why Matthias so seldom visited places like this. And which was why—one of many *whys*—he knew Stephen DeGallo was up to no good.

He sensed more than heard Kendall as she came up behind him, and was unprepared for the feeling that washed over him when she came to a halt behind him. He'd been edgy since leaving San Francisco, as he always was when he traveled. Travel was such a waste of time, and Matthias was always impatient getting from point A to point B so he could get on with business. This time, however, the feeling hadn't lessened once he'd arrived at his destination.

He'd still been feeling anxious when he entered Kendall's room. But when she stood beside him then, he was suddenly overcome by a feeling of calmness. Peacefulness. A strange sense of well-being that he hadn't felt for…

Well, a couple of weeks, anyway.

She said nothing as she gazed out the window, only studied the same view Matthias was considering himself. But he knew there must be some part of her brain that was questioning DeGallo's motives by now. She was a smart woman. She had good instincts. It was what made her so good at what she did.

"Look at that view," he said anyway, trivializing with a cliché what was a staggeringly beautiful piece of work. "You don't see views like that in the city." He turned to face Kendall before adding meaningfully, "Where most job orientations take place."

She slumped a little at the comment, expelling a tired-sounding sigh. But she said nothing to deny his more-than-obvious allegation.

"And look at this room," he said further, turning again and sweeping both arms open. "Who gets a place like this when they're undergoing orientation for a new job?"

Kendall sighed again, still sounding weary, but turned her body in the same direction as his. "New vice presidents for the company," she told him. "That's who. Stephen just wants to make a good impression, that's all."

Matthias dipped his head in concession, however small, to that. Then he strode to the table where there sat a bouquet of flowers more massive than *any* man *any*where had ever sent to *any* woman for *any* reason—be it declaring his love or groveling for forgiveness. He plucked the card from a particularly luscious-looking bloom and began to open it.

"Matthias, don't—" Kendall began.

He halted, snapping his head up at that, not because she had told him to stop, but because she had addressed him by his first name. Never, not once, during the five years she'd worked for him had she called him Matthias. Because never, not once, had he given her the okay to do it. And the fact that she had stepped over that line now so thoroughly, without his permission…

Hmm. Actually, now that he'd heard her call him Matthias, he realized he kind of liked the way his name sounded coming from her lips. In fact, he kind of liked the way her lips looked right now, having just said his name. Parted softly in surprise, and maybe embarrassment, as if she hadn't intended to call him Matthias, and now she wasn't sure what to do to take it back, or if she even wanted to take it back. What was strange was that Matthias didn't want her to take it back. In fact, he wanted her to say it again. Even more surprising, he realized the context in which he wanted to hear her say his name had nothing to do with her job, and everything to do with, well, other reasons people came to Lake Tahoe.

"Don't," she said again, more softly this time. Omitting the use of his name.

This time, too, she extended her hand toward the small envelope he still held tucked between his index and middle fingers. Not sure why he did it, Matthias pulled his hand toward himself, out of her reach. She took another step forward, bringing her body to within touching distance of his, then hesitated. But she didn't drop her hand, and for a moment, he thought—hoped—she would trail her hand after his to retrieve the card. He even found himself looking forward to her fingers tangling with his as they vied for possession. And although it was clear she was grappling with the possibility of that very thing herself—or maybe because she was grappling with it—she dropped her hand to her side again, ceding to him with clear reluctance.

The victory was strangely hollow, but Matthias shouldered it anyway. Opening the envelope, he withdrew the card, then scanned the sentiment upon it. He wasn't sure if it was DeGallo's writing, but it was masculine and forceful, and he suspected DeGallo himself had indeed penned the words. The task hadn't been left to an assistant to complete, which was what Matthias would have done in the same situation.

Then again, Matthias would never have been in this situation. Oh, he might have wooed someone away from one of his competitors specifically to learn more about that competitor's practices, but he would have been straightforward about it. He wouldn't have set up the new hire in a honeymoon suite with a breathtaking view of a romantic environment and called it orientation. And he wouldn't have sent flowers—with *any*one's signature.

He shook his head as he read aloud the sentiment DeGallo had written. "Kendall," he said, "Can't wait to have you navigating our PR waters. Welcome aboard!" He looked up at Kendall then, but she was staring at the wall. "Navigating our PR waters?" he repeated. "Was that the best he could do?"

Now Kendall turned to look at Matthias, her huge, clear green eyes penetrating deep enough to heat something in his chest. "Well, there *is* a lake out there," she said lamely. "Besides, what would *you* have said to welcome a new employee?"

"I would have said, 'Get to work,'" he replied. "And I would have said it to that new employee's face. I wouldn't go through all this ridiculous pretense to make her feel like she was more important than she actually is."

Two bright spots of color flared on Kendall's cheeks at that. She nodded brusquely. "Of course you wouldn't," she said. "Because no one is important to you. You think the success of Barton Limited is because of you and you alone. You have no appreciation for how many people it takes to make a company prosper, and you have no clue how to take care of the ones who are doing the best work. And if you're not careful, then—"

She halted abruptly, her eyes widening in what he could only guess was horror that she'd just leaped like a gazelle across the line she had previously only overstepped. Matthias narrowed his eyes at her, his own lips parting now in surprise. Kendall had never challenged him like this before. Hell, challenged? he asked himself. Compared to her usual self-containment, she'd just read him the riot act. With a bullhorn. Sure, she'd taken exception in the past to some of his decisions—okay, edicts—but she'd always pointed out her concerns with discretion. And deference. But this reaction was completely unlike her. Totally unexpected. And extremely…

Matthias stopped himself before allowing the impression to fully form. Because the impression had nothing to do with his reaction to Kendall as an employee, and everything to do with his reaction to her as a…a person.

"Is that what you really think?" he asked, deciding to focus on that instead of…the other thing.

She hesitated only a second, then nodded. And then, a little less forcefully than she'd spoken before, she added, "Yes. Sir." And then, a little more forcefully, she altered her response to, "Yes. Matthias."

There it was again, he marveled. That ripple of heat that should have been disapproval of her familiarity by using his first name, but which was instead…something else. Something he told himself to try to figure out later, because he really needed to respond to Kendall's allegation that he was so self-centered. But because of the way she was looking at him, all clear-green-eyed and hot-pink-cheeked and tumbling-silky-haired, all he could manage in response was, "Oh, really?"

A moment passed in which neither of them spoke, or moved, or even breathed. Then Kendall's lips turned up almost imperceptibly, into a smile with what only someone who had the vast experience Matthias had with the emotion could identify.

Victory.

Kendall Scarborough had it in her head that she'd just won whatever the two of them had been engaged in. Now if Matthias could just figure out what the two of them had just engaged in, maybe he'd know what to do next.

Kendall, however, didn't seem to be having the same problem he had. Because she settled her hands on her hips in a way that was at once relaxed and challenging, and she asked again, "Was there some reason you came here this afternoon, Matthias? Is there something you wanted?"

He honestly had no idea how to answer her. Because for the first time in his life, Matthias didn't know what he wanted. He was too off-kilter looking at Kendall and thinking about Kendall and listening to Kendall saying his name and marveling at how Kendall had thrown him so off-kilter.

But he didn't want to look foolish, either—that would have been another first he would have just as soon done without. So he reached into his trouser pocket and removed a small gadget he'd purchased for himself the day after she'd left his employ. Something called a... Well, he couldn't remember what it was called now, but it was supposed to be even better than the... Whatever that other thing was he used to use for keeping track of his appointments and obligations.

Then he held it out to Kendall and replied, "Yeah. Do you have any idea how this thing works? I keep getting e-mail from some deposed prince in Nigeria who needs my help freeing up some frozen assets he's trying to get out of the country, and I'd really like to help him out, because he promised me a more than generous share once he's fluid again. Plus, this woman named Trixie just got a new Web cam she wants to show me, and I'm thinking it might be technology I'd like to invest in."

He looked at Kendall, who was looking back at him as if he'd just grown a second head. "What?" he said.

She crossed the room in a half-dozen long strides and opened the door. Then she pointed to the hallway beyond with one finger. "Out," she said. "Now."

His mouth dropped open in surprise. "What, you're not going to help me?"

"I'm not your assistant anymore, Matthias."

Oh, as if he needed reminding of *that*. "But—"

"Out," she repeated. "Now."

He shook his head in disbelief. But he did as she asked him to. Told him to. Demanded he do. The door was slamming shut behind him before he'd even cleared it, missing his backside by *that* much. He spun around, and went so far as to lift a fist to pound on it again. But he stopped himself before completing the action.

There was a better way to go about this, he told himself.

He just had to figure out what it was. Because Kendall *was* making a mistake, thinking OmniTech was the place she needed to be. Where she needed to be was with him. Or, rather, with Barton Limited, he quickly corrected himself. Now all he had to do was figure out a way to make her realize that, too.

Three

Kendall leaned back against the door through which Matthias had just exited and tried to get a handle on everything that had just happened.

She'd thrown him out, she marveled. She'd looked at the BlackBerry in his hand, incredulous that, just when they were starting to have an exchange that felt evenly matched, he would ask her to program the little gizmo the way she had so many others when he was paying her to be his underling, and then she'd asked—no, *told*—him to leave. Even more stunning than that was the fact that Matthias had done as she asked—no, *told*—him to and had left. Without a word of argument. Without a word of exception. Without a word of reproach.

Okay, and without a word of farewell, either.

The point was that Kendall had taken charge of a situation with Matthias and she had mastered it. Eventually. Just because there had been a few moments in between that had been filled with strange bits of weirdness didn't diminish the enormity of that achievement.

But just *what,* exactly, had that weirdness been about? she asked herself now. There had been times during their conversation when Matthias had looked at her almost as if he were seeing someone else, someone he didn't quite know, someone with whom he wasn't entirely comfortable. Someone he wasn't sure he liked. It had been…weird. And her response had been weird, too. She'd suddenly been aware of him in a way she hadn't been when she'd worked for him. Or, at least, in a way she hadn't allowed herself to think about when she worked for him.

She let herself think about it now.

The day Matthias had announced his engagement to Lauren Conover, Kendall had experienced a reaction that had surprised her. A lot. And she'd realized that day that her feelings for her boss might perhaps, possibly, conceivably go a little beyond professional. Because where she had never minded the other women who came and went in Matthias's life—because they always came and went—when he'd made a move to join himself permanently to someone else, Kendall had felt a little…

Well, weird.

At first, she'd told herself it was just disappointment that such a smart man would do something as stupid as arrange a marriage of convenience for himself. Then she'd told herself what she felt was annoyance that, because of his engagement, he wanted her to arrange so many events for him that had nothing to do with work. In fact, she'd run through a veritable grocery list of feelings in response to

Matthias's announced nuptials: denial, then anger, then bargaining, then depression…

Hang on a minute, Kendall thought now. Those were the stages of grief. And no way had she felt *that*. No way had she been *that* far gone on her boss.

Ultimately, however, she had been forced to admit the truth. That maybe, perhaps, possibly, conceivably, she had developed…feelings… for her employer. Feelings of attachment. Feelings of allegiance. Feelings of… She closed her eyes tight and made herself admit it. Feelings of…affection.

The recognition that she had begun to feel things for her boss that she had no business feeling—even her allegiance wasn't for things that related to work—was what had cemented her conviction that she would, once and for all, tender her resignation. Even after his engagement to Lauren was canceled, she'd known she had to go. She couldn't risk falling for Matthias, because he would never care for her in any way other than the professional. He didn't care about anyone in any way other than the professional. That the offer from Stephen DeGallo had come on the heels of the cancellation of Matthias's wedding had just been an exclamation point to punctuate the obvious. She had done the right thing by leaving Matthias. Or, rather, she hastily corrected herself, by leaving Matthias's employ.

She just hoped taking the job with Stephen DeGallo had been the right thing to do, too.

Some lodge, Matthias thought as he pulled into the drive of what looked more like a boutique hotel than a private residence. Had it not been for the fact that he'd been here once before—three months ago, when his brother, Luke, was in residence—he wouldn't have been sure he was in the right place. He turned off the ignition and exited the car, hauled his leather weekender out of the backseat and made his way to the entrance where the caretaker was waiting for him.

The woman was dressed in a pale yellow straight skirt and a white sleeveless top, a canvas gimme cap decorated with a logo he didn't recognize pulled low on her forehead. Coupled with her sunglasses, it was hard to tell what she looked like, but what he could see was pretty, in a wholesome kind of way. The ponytail hanging out of the cap's opening was streaked dark blond, and she had some decent curves, so it wasn't surprising that Matthias found himself comparing her to Kendall…and thinking how nice it would be if it was Kendall who was here to greet him instead. Not because he wanted to spend a month here with Kendall, of course, but because if Kendall was here, he could get a lot more work done, that was all.

"I assume you're Mary?" he asked the woman by way of a greeting. "I'm sorry I'm late."

She seemed to deflate a little when she got a good look at him, and only then did he realize she had seemed kind of expectant as he strode up the walk. Maybe she'd thought he was someone else, since his own appearance probably wasn't easy to discern, either, thanks to his own sunglasses.

She nodded. "I'm the caretaker." Without further ado, she extended a key that dangled from a rather elaborate key chain and added, "Here's the key. Just leave it on the kitchen table at the end of the month. I've stocked the refrigerator and cabinets, and there's some carryout from a local takeaway gourmet. But if it's not to your taste or you'd like something specific, there are menus for some restaurants in Hunter's Landing on top of the fridge. I can recommend Clearwater's and the Lakeside Diner for sure. Or if you do the cooking thing, there's a market just east of where you turned off to find the lodge."

Her voice was soft but dispassionate, and she spoke as if she were reading from a script. And not very dramatically, at that. "Tahoe City is about a half hour north, the Nevada state line about twenty minutes east. If you want to gamble," she added, as if wanting to clarify.

"Not like that," Matthias told her. When he gambled, he liked for the stakes to be much higher than mere cash.

Mary nodded. "Would you like for me to show you around the place? Explain how everything works?"

"I assume it's all pretty standard," he replied. Not to mention he had no intention of seeing how anything worked. That way lay madness.

"Standard, yes," Mary told him. "But there are quite a few amenities. Hot tub, Jacuzzi, gourmet kitchen, plasma TV…"

He held up a hand to stop her. He wasn't the type to indulge in any of those things. He had too much work to do. "It won't be necessary," he told her. "Thanks, anyway."

"Then, if you won't be needing anything else?" she asked.

Well, there was nothing he needed that she could provide, anyway, he thought. So he told her, "Nothing, thanks."

"Emergency numbers are on the fridge, too," she said. "Including mine. Hopefully you won't need them, either."

She hesitated before leaving, studying Matthias's face for a moment as if she were looking for something. Then, suddenly, she said, "Goodbye," and turned to walk down the front steps. For the merest, most nebulous second, she seemed a little familiar somehow. He didn't know if it was her walk, her voice, the way she carried herself or what, but there was…something about her that reminded him so much of someone else. He just couldn't quite put his finger on who.

And then the impression was gone, as quickly as it had materialized. Mary was gone, too, having climbed back into her car and backed it out of the driveway. Matthias jingled the key in his hand absently, shrugged off his odd ruminations and turned to unlock the front door, closing it behind himself once he was inside. Out of habit, he tossed his battered leather weekender—the one he'd traveled with since college—onto the nearest piece of furniture. No small feat, that, since the place was huge, with a foyer the size of a Giants dugout, and the nearest piece of furniture was half a stadium away. He didn't care if he knocked something over in the process. He was still pissed off at Hunter for making all of them rearrange their lives for a month to come here and do whatever the hell it was they were supposed to do.

But then, he was still pissed off at Hunter for dying, too.

Of course, if he were honest with himself, Matthias would have to admit that he was more pissed off at himself than anyone else. He hadn't meant to lose touch with the Seven Samurai over the years. It had just…happened. Time happened. Distance happened. Work happened. Life happened. People grew up. They grew apart. They went their separate ways. Happened all the time. He and Hunter and the rest of them had all been kids when they'd made pacts and promises to stay friends forever. Hell, Matthias hadn't even kept in touch with his own brother. Then again, when your brother did things like accusing you of cheating him in business and stealing your fiancée, it was understandable why you'd allow for some distance.

As soon as the thought formed in his head, Matthias pushed it away. He was being unfair to Luke. Really unfair this time, and not the phony-baloney unfairness of which his brother had always accused him. Their father hadn't exactly been a proponent of fairness, anyway. He had pitted the two of them against each other from the day the twins were old enough to compete. Which, to the old man's way of thinking, had been within seconds of their emerging from the womb. If there had been some way to make the boys vie for something against each other, Samuel Sullivan Barton found a way to do it. Who could win the most merit badges in Cub Scouts. Who could sell the most wrapping paper for the school fund-raiser. Who could score the most baskets, make the most touchdowns, pitch the best game. As children, they'd been more like rivals than brothers.

It had only gotten worse after their father's death and the terms of his will had been made public. Samuel had decreed that whichever of the boys made a million dollars first, the estate would go to him in its entirety. Matthias had won. Though winning had been relative. Luke had accused him, unjustly, of cheating and hadn't spoken to him for years. It hadn't been until recently that the two men had shared anything. And then what they'd shared was Lauren Conover, the woman who'd agreed to be Matthias's wife. It had been the ultimate competition for Luke…until he'd fallen in love with the prize. And although Matthias had come to terms with what had happened, things between him and his brother still weren't exactly smooth. Or simple. Or settled.

Man, what was it about peoples' last wills and testaments that they always sent Matthias's life in a new direction?

He sighed as he leaned against the front door and drove

his gaze around the lodge. In college, they'd said they wanted to build a cabin. But "cabin" evoked an image of a rustic, no-frills, crowded little shack in the woods with few amenities and even fewer comforts. This place was like something from *Citizen Kane*, had the movie been filmed in Technicolor. The great room ceiling soared up two stories, with expansive windows running the entire length of one wall, offering an incredible view of the lake. The pine paneling was polished to a honeyed sheen, the wide planked floors buffed to a satin finish. At one end of the room was a fireplace big enough to host the United Arab Emirates, a sofa and chairs clustered before it that, ironically, invited an intimate gathering of friends.

The place was exactly the sort of retreat Matthias would have expected Hunter to have. Handsomely furnished. Blissfully quiet. Generously outfitted. And yet there was something missing that prevented it from being completely comfortable. Something that Hunter had obviously forgotten to include, but Matthias couldn't quite put his finger on what.

He pushed himself away from the door and made his way to where his weekender had landed—just shy of actually hitting the nearest piece of furniture he'd been aiming for. His footsteps echoed hollowly on the hardwood floor as he went, an auditory reminder of just how alone he would be while he was here. Matthias wasn't used to traveling alone. Kendall had always come with him on business trips, and even though they'd naturally had separate quarters, he'd seen her virtually from sunup to sundown. Of course, this wasn't, technically, a business trip. But he would have brought Kendall along, had she still been in his employ, because he would be working while he was here. And Kendall had been a big part of his work for five years.

Five years, he thought as he grabbed his bag and strode toward the stairs that led up to the second floor. In the scheme of things, it wasn't such a long time. But it comprised the entirety of Kendall's work life. He was the only employer she'd had since graduating. He'd been her first. Her only. He'd been the one who had introduced her to the ways of business, the one who'd taught her how to achieve the most satisfaction in what she did, the one who'd shown her which positions to take on things that would yield the most pleasurable results. And now, after he'd been the one to initiate her in all the intricacies of the working relationship, another employer had wooed her away.

"Oh, for God's sake, Barton," he muttered to himself as he climbed the stairs. "You're talking about her like she's an old lover."

He waited for the laughter that was bound to come from entertaining a thought like that, but for some reason, it didn't come. Instead, he was overcome by a strange kind of fatigue that made him want to blow off work for the rest of the day and instead go do something more—

The thought made him stop dead in his tracks, halfway up the stairs. Blow off work? Since when had he *ever* blown off work? For any reason? And how could anything be *more* than work? Work was everything. Talk about something that should have made him erupt into laughter.

But he didn't laugh at that, either. Instead, he realized he'd left his laptop out in the trunk of the car. Worse, he realized that, even if he'd remembered to bring it in with him, he wasn't completely sure how to get to all the files he needed to get to. That had always been Kendall's job. Knowing how to pull up whatever needed pulling up and pulling it up for him. Hell, half the time, she'd taken care of whatever needed pulling and then pushed it back down again.

He was going to have to hire a temp for now, he told himself. Surely there was a temp agency close by. Tahoe City maybe. Too bad Kendall wasn't here. She would have found just the right person, and she would have had the person here five minutes ago. But how hard could it be? he asked himself. He just needed to find the phone book, and he'd be good to go.

So where did people keep their phone books, anyway…

By the time she entered the bar of the Timber Lake Inn that evening, Kendall had accepted the fact that it, like everything else in the establishment, would be cozy. Sure enough, it was. Like the rest of the hotel, it was pine-paneled with hardwood floors and Native American rugs, but the lighting was lower than in the other public rooms, softer and more golden, and very… Well, there was just no way around it. Romantic.

Matthias was right. This wasn't the sort of hotel any businessman in his right mind would use for business functions. Nevertheless, she was confident Stephen DeGallo had his reasons for using it. *Besides* trying to lull Kendall into a false sense of security, which Matthias had implied— hah—was the case. Or to lull her into anything else, either. For all she knew, the Timber Lake Inn was the only hotel in Lake Tahoe that had had any openings when Stephen scheduled the orientation. And the fact that Lake Tahoe itself was such a cozy, romantic destination that was kind of an odd choice for a business orientation had nothing to do with anything. It was centrally located, that was all.

She shook the thought almost literally out of her head

and smoothed her hand one final time over the chocolate-brown trousers and cream-colored shirt she'd donned for the evening. Stephen had said the evening would be casual, and what she had on was casual attire. It *was*. Even if it was the same kind of thing she'd worn to work every day when she was with Matthias. Ah, *working for* Matthias, she quickly corrected herself. And the reason she'd wound her hair up into its usual workplace bun and put on her usual workplace glasses wasn't because she was trying to overcompensate for the cozy, romantic environment. It *wasn't*. It was because she just hadn't felt like going to any trouble. She had low-maintenance hair. So sue her. And even though she didn't need her glasses all the time, what with the low lighting and everything, she figured she'd need them.

So there.

She scanned the bar for a group of people who looked as if they were training for new careers, but saw only couples at a handful of tables here and there. Cozy couples. Romantic couples. In fact, one couple was being *so* romantic Kendall wanted to yell, "Jeez, people, get a room!" Glancing down at her watch, she realized she was a little early, so maybe she was the first member of the OmniTech orientation group to arrive. Then a movement in the corner of the room—the *farthest* corner—and the *darkest* corner, she couldn't help noticing—caught her eye, and she realized it was Stephen DeGallo, waving at her.

She lifted a hand in return and made her way in that direction, picking her way through the tables as she looked around for anyone else who might be joining him. And somehow, she refrained from muttering, *Jeez, people, get a room* as she passed by the overly demonstrative couple.

Nor did she toss a glass of ice water over them, which was another thought she hadn't quite been able to quell.

"Kendall," Stephen said warmly when she was within earshot. "Great to see you again. Glad you made it in one piece."

"It's great to be here, Stephen," she said as she extended her hand in greeting. "Thanks again for giving me this opportunity. I'm very excited about working for OmniTech."

He grasped her hand in both of his, not really shaking it, per se, just holding it for perhaps a moment longer than was necessary, something that made her think about Matthias's warning again. Which she immediately pushed out of her brain. Stephen was just being friendly. And she was just being overly sensitive, thanks to Matthias's ridiculous ideas about Stephen only wanting her because of her ties to Barton Limited. This was what happened when you were employed by a workaholic for so many years. You forgot that normal people could be casual and friendly, even in professional situations.

And Stephen's smile did put Kendall immediately at ease. Although he wasn't a handsome man, he was by no means unattractive. He was slim and fit, and was dressed according to his own edict—casually—in a pair of softly faded blue jeans and a white polo shirt. His blue eyes held intelligence and good humor, and his dark blond hair was just beginning to go gray, threaded here and there with bits of silver. What he lacked in handsomeness, he more than made up for in charisma. He was just one of those people who had a gift for taking charge of a situation without being overbearing, and making people feel better that he had.

Kendall had done her homework after his offer of employment, so she knew quite a bit about him. In many ways, he was as devoted to his company as Matthias was to Barton Limited, but where Matthias's extracurricular and social activities all still seemed to involve his work, Stephen DeGallo was a man who enjoyed his leisure time. He was a champion yachtsman and active in a charitable foundation he had started ten years ago that mentored gifted, but underprivileged high school students.

He was not just a good businessman, but a good guy, Kendall had discovered. And her admiration of him was due to both.

She seated herself in the chair he held out for her, folding her elbows on the table and weaving her fingers lightly together. Then she gave him her most businesslike smile. "Am I the first to arrive?" she asked, even though the answer was obvious.

"Actually," Stephen said as he folded himself into the chair opposite hers, "right now, you're the *only* one who's here."

Kendall told herself she just imagined the note of vague discomfort she thought she heard in his voice. More of Matthias's influence on her nerves, she was sure. Still, it was odd that no one else had arrived yet.

"Don't tell me I'm the only one who got here on time," she said.

"No, of course not," he told her. "The others just aren't scheduled to arrive until Wednesday."

Wednesday? Kendall thought. That was two whole days away. "Oh," she said, the word sounding more disappointed than she'd intended.

"The others are training for management positions," he said by way of an explanation. "You're the only VP candidate this time around. So I thought it would be nice if the two of us could have a couple of days where I could go over some of the policies and procedures that won't be pertinent to everyone else's training."

That made sense, Kendall thought.

"But first, a drink," he said, motioning to a waiter who had been hovering within range. "What would you like? I discovered a wonderful California pinot noir recently that's absolutely delightful."

"Thanks," Kendall told him, "but I'll just have a bottle of sparkling water."

He threw her a look of mock effrontery. "But we're celebrating your joining the OmniTech team," he objected.

"Which is why I ordered *sparkling* water," she said with a smile.

He smiled back, dipping his head forward in acknowledgment. "Then I'll have the same," he told the waiter. "Now then," he added as their server departed, "I thought we could spend much of tonight talking about how—"

"Stephen DeGallo!"

Kendall flinched at the sound of the booming, all-too-familiar voice, but managed to otherwise keep her irritation in check. Well, enough that no one would notice it, anyway. Though she had to admit that Stephen didn't look any happier about the interruption than she was. Nevertheless, good businessman—and guy—that he was, he smiled as he rose to greet Matthias. Kendall turned in her chair to acknowledge her former employer, but remained seated, hoping that small act of discourtesy would illustrate her pique in a way that wasn't quite as impolite as other actions might have been. Actions like, oh…Kendall didn't know. Tripping him as he strode past her to shake Stephen's hand. Calling him a big poophead. Stuff like that.

She noticed Stephen didn't grasp Matthias's hand in

both of his the way he had hers—in fact, he gave Matthias's one, two, three firm, manly shakes and released it. Then again, Matthias was a rival, so naturally, Stephen's greeting to him wouldn't be as familiar as his to Kendall had been. Similarly, it was understandable why Stephen's posture, too, with Matthias would be more assertive, more straight-forward, more businesslike, than it had been with Kendall. Wouldn't it?

Yeah. Sure. Of course.

"Matthias Barton," Stephen greeted him. "Long time, no see. What have you been up to?"

"Besides competing with you for the Perkins contract?" Matthias replied. "Not much."

Well, he'd recently lost his personal assistant of five years, Kendall thought irritably. Or so she'd heard. That was kind of major.

As if he'd read her mind, Matthias turned to her then and feigned tremendous surprise—though, Kendall thought, not very well.

"Why, Kendall Scarborough," he said with overblown amazement. "What are you doing here? I haven't seen you since…" He pretended to search his memory banks—again, not exactly an Academy Award-winning performance—then snapped his fingers. "Since you gave me your two weeks' notice to go work for some fly-by-night company."

She sighed wearily. "Well, except for this afternoon in my room, when you offered me my job back."

Now Stephen was the one to look surprised, Kendall noted. Only his was obviously genuine. Then he smiled, and looked at Matthias again. "Really?" he asked the other man.

Matthias looked a little uncomfortable now, and this time, he wasn't pretending. "It was just a formality," he said. "I always offer my exes the chance to come back, once they come to their senses and realize what a mistake they made, leaving Barton Limited."

Kendall couldn't prevent the snort of laughter that escaped her at that. Yeah, right. Matthias had the longest memory of anyone she'd ever met, and he never forgot a slight—real *or* imagined. If someone elected to leave the company for any reason, he had that person's personnel file expunged within the hour, as if they never existed. And he certainly never went looking for that person to offer them an opportunity to return.

Not until this afternoon, anyway, she reminded herself.

But the only reason he'd come looking for her, she further told herself, was because he hadn't known how to program his new BlackBerry. The offer to take her back had obviously been off-the-cuff, and had doubtless been extended for the same reason. He thought she was the only one who knew how to program one of those things. He didn't realize anyone could do it for him. Well, anyone except Matthias Barton.

"Well, Barton," Stephen said now, "had you appreciated Kendall's possibilities, the way I do, then maybe you wouldn't have lost her in the first place."

Kendall started to smile at that, then stopped. Something about the way Stephen had said it made it sound kind of unprofessional. Just what had he meant by *possibilities?* That was kind of a strange word to use. Why not *abilities?* Or *talents?* Or *expertise? Possibilities* made it sound as though he considered her a blank slate or unformed mass that he could turn into whatever he wanted.

"I assure you, DeGallo," Matthias replied, "that Kendall was one of my most prized possessions at Barton Limited. I hope you realize what an asset she'll be to OmniTech."

All right, Kendall thought. That did it. Forget about blank slates and unformed masses. Matthias had just made her sound like a new computer system. Possession? Asset? Just who did he think he was?

"Prized possession?" she echoed indignantly.

Matthias looked down at her and must have realized immediately from both her voice and her expression—and, most likely, the quick drop in temperature among the small group—what a colossal gaffe he'd just made. "Uh…" he began eloquently.

"If that's the case," she continued while he was still off balance, "then you better go over my operating instructions while you're here. I wouldn't want Stephen to think he acquired a defective machine."

The look Matthias gave her then was almost convincingly distressed. Almost. "Kendall, that's not—"

This time his words were cut off by Stephen's light, good-natured laughter. "Sounds to me like she works just fine," he said. "In fact, this particular model is promising to work better than I initially hoped."

Matthias's lips thinned at that. "Yeah, she's a piece of work, all right," he muttered.

She smiled sweetly. "And now I'm working for someone else."

Matthias opened his mouth to respond, but this time was prevented by the arrival of their server, who placed tall sweaty glasses of mineral water in front of Kendall and Stephen. Then the waiter looked at Matthias and asked, "Will you be joining this party?"

Even Matthias, Kendall thought, wouldn't be crass enough to crash her meeting with Stephen. And he didn't. Instead, he told their server that no, he was on his own and didn't want to interrupt anyone's dinner, so would just take a seat at a table by himself. Then, even though there were at least a dozen empty tables in the restaurant, he pulled out a chair from the table immediately beside Kendall's and Stephen's, and seated himself without a care.

Unbelievable, Kendall thought. Evidently, Matthias was that crass, after all. If not in blatantly joining them, then certainly in doing his best to destroy any chance the two of them might have for speaking freely about her new obligations as vice president. There was no way Stephen would discuss the policies of his company in the presence of one of his competitors, even superficially. He confirmed that by shrugging philosophically when Kendall looked at him—not that she needed any confirmation.

So instead of talking about her new job over the course of dinner, Kendall and Stephen instead discussed superficialities like the weather, books, current events and a favorite TV show they had in common…with Matthias throwing in his own commentaries here and there, completely uninvited.

It was going to be a long orientation.

Four

The temp Matthias ordered from a Tahoe City agency—once he found the phone book after thirty minutes of looking for it—arrived promptly at eight o'clock the morning after his arrival. Unfortunately, he'd done something wrong when he tried to set his alarm clock the night before—no, the alarm clock was defective, that was the problem—because it was the ringing of the front doorbell that alerted him to the arrival of his early-morning appointment. Not Kendall, who would have normally alerted Matthias to that. Kendall, too, would have been infinitely less intrusive about her reminder than the doorbell was.

Damn, he thought as he looked groggily at the clock and realized it had stopped working completely. He lifted his watch from the nightstand and grimaced when he saw the time. He never slept this late. And he'd never been unprepared for an appointment. Shoving off the covers, he jackknifed into a sitting position and scrubbed both hands briskly over his face to rouse himself. He grabbed a plain white T-shirt from the bag he hadn't even begun to unpack, shook it out quickly and thrust it over his head as he descended the stairs. And he thought dryly how lucky he was that it matched his sweatpants so well, otherwise he might have to be embarrassed about his attire. It was only as he was reaching for the doorknob that he realized he'd forgotten to put on shoes, so would be greeting his temporary employee barefoot. Somehow, though, he couldn't quite rouse the wherewithal to care.

The young man on the other side of the door looked surprised by Matthias's sudden appearance—and, doubtless, by his slovenly appearance—but quickly schooled his features into indifference. He obviously hadn't overslept, because he was well-groomed and dressed impeccably in a pale gray suit and white dress shirt, his necktie the only spot of color on his person—if you could consider pale yellow a color. He was young, early twenties at most, his blond hair cut short, his gray eyes nearly the same color as his suit. He looked to Matthias like something from a middle school poster advertising Junior Achievement.

"Mr. Barton?" he said.

Matthias ran a quick hand through his dark hair to tame it as best he could. "Yeah, that's me," he replied. Quickly, he amended, "I mean, yes. I'm Matthias Barton."

"William Denton," he said, extending his hand. "From DayTimers. I'm your new temp."

"Whoa, whoa, whoa," Matthias said, holding up a hand. "I haven't hired you yet."

This was clearly news to young William. "But they said

you need an assistant for the month you'll be spending here in Hunter's Landing," he said.

"I do need an assistant for the month," Matthias told him. "But I'm not going to take any Tom, Dick or William they send my way. I need to make sure you have all the qualifications I need for an assistant."

Young William smiled confidently. "No worries there, Mr. Barton. Temping is just my summer job. I earned my BS from the Haas School of Business at UC Berkeley in May, and I'll be returning in the fall to start work on my MBA. I'm more than qualified to take on this position."

Matthias's back went up at the kid's presumption. "Are you?" he asked coolly.

William Denton's confidence seemed to waver a bit. Nevertheless, he replied, "Yes. I am." As an afterthought, he added, "Sir."

Matthias nodded, settling his hands on his hips in challenge. They'd just see about that. Without even inviting William Denton into the lodge, he barked, "What are the major managerial and organizational challenges posed by electronic commerce?"

William Denton blinked as if a too-bright flash had gone off right in front of his eyes. "I...what?"

Matthias shook his head, sighed with much gusto, and asked, "All right, if that one's too tough, then how about this. True or false. In the simple Ricardian model, trade between similar economies is unlikely to generate large gains from that trade."

William Denton's lips parted in response to that one, but no words emerged to answer the question. Until, finally, he said, "I...what?"

Man, Matthias thought, this guy was never going to

amount to anything if he couldn't answer the most obvious question in the world. "All right, here's an easy one," he said. "Multiple choice. The current ratio and quick ratio are the best indicators of a company's what? A. liquidity, B. efficiency, C. profitability or D. growth rate."

William Denton's mouth began to work over that one—kind of—but his brain didn't seem to be cooperating.

Matthias shook his head in disappointment. "I'm sorry, Mr. Denton, but I just don't think you have what it takes to—"

"Wait!" he interrupted. "I know the answer to that one!"

"Unfortunately, your time is up," Matthias told him. "Tell DayTimers I'll be in touch."

And with that, he pushed the front door closed and turned away. From the other side, William Denton called out, "A! It's A! Liquidity! Right? Am I right?"

He was right, Matthias thought. But it was too little, too late. The person he hired as his assistant was going to have to be a quick thinker and unafraid to speak up, in addition to being knowledgeable and savvy. Like Kendall. William Denton just didn't have what it took to fill her shoes.

Oh, well. Another candidate lacking even the most rudimentary business skills. Another interview shot to hell. Matthias would just have to look for someone else.

Padding barefoot to the kitchen, he absently pushed the button on the coffeemaker, then went to retrieve the phone book from the same cabinet where he had discovered it the day before. Bypassing DayTimers this time—since, if William Denton was the best they could do, they were obviously a fly-by-night operation—he selected the next agency on the list. After arranging for a prospective temp to come to the lodge later in the day, Matthias turned to pour himself a cup of coffee—

Only to discover that the carafe on the hot pad was empty. In fact, the hot pad wasn't even hot. He was sure he'd filled the machine with both water and coffee the night before, but lifted the top, anyway, to make sure. Yep. Coffee on one side. Water on the other. Just like the directions said. He checked to make sure the machine was plugged in. Yep. It was. He made sure the cord was attached to the coffeemaker, as well, ensured that the light switch on the wall nearest the appliance was switched to the on position, in case that was necessary, inspected everything he could possibly inspect to see what the problem was. To no avail. He pushed the on button again. Nothing.

Dammit.

Matthias wasn't one of those pathetic caffeine addicts who couldn't function without their crack-of-dawn coffee and suffered ugly mood swings when denied. No way. But, like any civilized human being, he liked to enjoy a cup or two in the morning, maybe three if he had time, possibly four or five, if he had a meeting or something, and, okay maybe another jolt or two or three in the afternoon when he needed it. He didn't *have* to have coffee. He just wanted it. A lot.

He stared at the coffeemaker intently, drumming his fingers irregularly on the countertop, willing the machine to work. With great deliberation, he pushed the on button again. Nada.

Damn. His gaze lit then on a short stack of papers he'd placed on the countertop the night before. It was the last assignment Kendall had completed before she'd tendered her resignation, a contract she'd typed up for an agreement between Barton Limited and a new consulting firm with whom he'd be doing limited business for the rest of the year. He smiled, and reached for the phone again, punching in a number he knew by heart.

"Kendall," he said when she answered her cell phone. "It's…" He started to say "Mr. Barton," but halted. "Matthias," he identified himself instead. "There's a problem with the Donovan contract you typed up before you left. Can you spare a couple of hours this morning to go over it?" He listened to her objection, then said, "I realize that. But this is a problem you're responsible for, one you need to rectify. And it's urgent. When can you be here?" He grinned at her reply. "Good. I promise not to keep you any longer than I absolutely have to. And, Kendall," he added before she had a chance to hang up, "I saw a coffee shop in town. Would you mind swinging by it on your way?"

Kendall stewed as she waited for Matthias to answer the doorbell she'd just rung, and switched the enormous cardboard cup of coffee from one hand to the other as it began to burn her fingers. It had been awkward, to say the least, explaining to Stephen DeGallo on her first official day of training why she needed to take part of the morning off. And although he hadn't exactly been happy about the request, he'd told her to go ahead, that they could meet again after lunch.

Lunch, she thought now, that she should have been having with her new boss, not the one she'd left behind.

As if conjured by the thought, Matthias opened the door, smiling with what looked like profound relief when he saw her. She softened some at his expression, flattered that, in spite of everything, he still seemed to need her. It was always a nice feeling to have.

Then he reached for the massive cup of coffee in her hand, popped off the top and lifted it toward his face, inhaling deeply to enjoy a long, leisurely sniff. Carefully, he lifted it to his mouth and sipped, closing his eyes as he savored it. Then he opened them again, stared down into the dark brew and said, "Oh, God, that's better."

That was when Kendall realized it was the coffee for which he was grateful, not her. And she wondered again why she'd bothered.

Because she was conscientious about her work, she told herself. It had nothing to do with Matthias needing her. If there truly was a problem with the Donovan contract that was her fault, then it was, as he'd said, up to her to rectify it. Although she couldn't imagine what she'd done wrong. She'd triple- and quadruple-checked the document before she'd given it to Matthias to look at. And why was he just now looking at it, anyway? she wondered. It was supposed to have gone back to Elliot Donovan two weeks ago.

And what was up with his appearance? she wondered further. Okay, she knew he was on vacation, but she'd never seen him looking like this. Here it was, almost ten o'clock in the morning, and he looked as if he'd just rolled out of bed. His black sweatpants were rumpled from sleep, as was the white V-neck T-shirt stretched taut enough across his chest that she could see the dark hair beneath— besides what was visible around the neckline. A day's growth of beard shadowed his face, his dark hair was shaggy and uncombed and his brown eyes were hooded and soft. He looked…

Well, actually, Kendall thought as a coil of something warm and electric unwound in her belly, he looked kind of…hot.

No! Not hot! she immediately corrected herself. Slovenly. Yeah, that was it. Seeing him looking the way he did made her think of some lazy hedonist lolling in bed on a Sunday morning. Some dark-haired, sleepy-eyed pleasure monger, waking slowly and stretching his brawny arms high over his head, then smiling down at the woman lying next to him, who—Hey, how about that?—looked a lot like Kendall, then gliding a slow finger across my…I mean, *her*…naked shoulder, then leaning down to trace the same path with his mouth before rolling me…I mean, *her*…over onto her back and sliding his hand beneath the covers, down along my…I mean, *her*…naked torso and settling it between my…I mean, *her*…I mean…I mean…I mean…

She stifled a groan and stopped thinking about how Matthias looked. Until he lowered the cup of coffee again and ran his tongue along the seam of his lips to savor the lingering taste of it, wherein all Kendall could do was think about how it would feel to have his tongue running along the seam of her lips, too.

Oh. No.

The Donovan contract, she reminded herself. That was why she was here. Not for…anything else. "So, um…what's the, uh…the problem with the, ah…the Donovan contract," she finally got out.

For a moment, he looked at her as if he had no idea what she was talking about. Then, "Right," he finally said. "Come on in."

He stepped aside to let her enter, and as Kendall pushed past him, she tried not to notice how the fragrance of the coffee mingled with a scent that was distinctly Matthias, something spicy and woodsy whose source she'd never been able to identify. It was probably from the soap or shampoo that he used, though she'd never known another man to smell the way he did—or as good as he did. And smelling him again now, after being deprived for two weeks…

She sighed. What was the matter with her this morning? She was reacting to Matthias as if he were an old boyfriend she hadn't been ready to break up with.

She reminded herself again that she was nothing more to him than a former employee, and that he was nothing more to her than a former employer. She'd come here because of a professional obligation, not a personal one. The sooner she fixed whatever she'd done wrong with the Donovan contract, the sooner she could get back to work. Her new work. At her new job. With her new boss. One who appreciated her business degree and knowledge. One to whom she owed the greater obligation now. Matthias was her past. No, Barton Limited was her past, she corrected herself. And OmniTech Solutions was her future.

Period.

She spun around as Matthias closed the front door. "What's the problem?" she asked point blank.

Instead of answering her, he tilted his head toward the sweeping staircase behind him and said, "This way."

She rankled at the order, but followed him, noting how beautiful the lodge was. Wow. Whoever'd furnished the place had great taste. And they knew a thing or two about making a home comfortable without making it too feminine. Although the colors were bold and the fabrics a little masculine, Kendall would have felt perfectly content staying here herself. And the view of the lake beyond the picture windows was spectacular.

She wondered again about the details of the bequest that required him to be here. It must have been a pretty major requirement to make him take an entire month away from the office. Especially in a place like Lake Tahoe, where there were so few corporate concerns, and no one she could think of that Barton Limited did business with. Then again, in the whole time she'd worked for him, she couldn't remember him ever taking a vacation of more than a couple of days. So maybe it would do him good to be here for a month. Maybe he'd learn to relax a little. Realize there was more to life than work.

Yeah, right, she thought. And maybe the next World Wrestling champion would be named Stone Cold Sheldon Abernathy.

As her foot hit the stairway landing, her gaze lit on a photograph that was hanging there, and Matthias's reasons for being in the lodge became clearer. Unable to stop herself, Kendall halted for a moment, smiling at the picture of the—she quickly counted—seven men, all college-aged, one of whom was obviously Matthias. But one was his twin brother, Luke, too, so she wasn't sure, at first, which was which. Then she noted the way one of the boys' smiles curled up a little more on one side than the other, and she knew, without question, it was Matthias. Interestingly, he was the one with the longer hair, and was the more raggedly dressed of the two. Funny, because Matthias had always talked about his brother as if Luke were the black sheep of the family, the rebel, the one who wanted to make waves. Looking at the photograph, however, it was Matthias who better fit that description.

"The contract is in the office," she heard him say from some distance away.

Looking up, she saw that he had continued to the second floor and was striding down the hall without realizing she had stopped. "Hey!" she called after him, surprising herself. She'd never said *Hey!* to Matthias before. It had always been *Excuse me, sir* or *Pardon me, Mr. Barton,* something that had been in keeping with their relationship—which had always been fairly formal. It was just that, being here in this beautiful, comfortable lodge with him, seeing him in sweats and a T-shirt and finding a picture of him from his youth, formal was the last thing she felt.

He spun around at the summons, at first looking as surprised by the casual address as she'd been. Then he saw what she was looking at and...

Huh, she thought. She would have thought he would smile in much the same way as he was smiling in the photograph. Instead, he looked kind of annoyed. Probably because he didn't want an employee—even a former one—seeing him as anything but the businessman that he was.

Well, tough, she retorted silently. If that was the case, he shouldn't have made her drive down here. And he certainly shouldn't have answered the door in his jammies.

He walked slowly back down the hall, and then the stairs, until he stood beside her, hooking his hands on his hips in a way that made him look very put out. "What?" he asked. Interestingly, he didn't look at the picture, even though he had to realize that was why she'd called him back.

Unfortunately, she suddenly realized she wasn't sure what she'd intended to say when she'd called him back. She'd mostly just wanted to look at him now and compare him to the boy in the photograph. So she pointed to the picture and said, "Who are these guys you're with?"

It was with obvious reluctance that Matthias turned to look at the picture. He studied it for only a moment, then turned back to Kendall. "Friends from college. We called ourselves the Seven Samurai."

"Akira Kurosawa fans, were you?" she asked, proud of herself for knowing the name of the director of the film made half a century ago.

"Actually, I think Hunter was the only one of us who even saw the movie. He's the one who named us. God knows why."

"Which one is Hunter?" Kendall asked.

With even more reluctance than before, Matthias lifted his hand and pointed at the young man who was laughing right at the camera. He looked the happiest of the bunch, and gave the impression, even on film, of being their ringleader.

"Where is he now?" Kendall asked.

Matthias hesitated a telling moment before revealing, "He died."

Something hard and cold twisted in Kendall's belly at hearing the flatness of Matthias's voice. Even more than he sounded sad, he sounded…tired. As if the weight of his friend's death was too much for him to bear.

"What happened?" she asked softly. "He was so young."

"Melanoma," he said. "This is his lodge, even though he never lived to see it completed."

"I'm so sorry, Matthias," she said quietly. Impulsively, she extended a hand and curled her fingers over his upper arm, giving it a gentle, reassuring squeeze. His skin was warm beneath her fingers, solid, strong. But in that moment, he didn't seem any of those things himself. "I didn't mean to bring up bad memories," she told him.

He shook his head. "Actually, since coming here, I've had one or two good memories," he told her. "Things I'd forgotten about." He did smile then, albeit sadly. Still, it was better to see that than the look of desolation that had clouded his features a moment ago.

She waited to see if he would elaborate on his memories, but he didn't. And Kendall didn't want to pry any further than she already had. Even if she was massively curious about the other young men in the picture. And even more curious about the young Matthias.

"So the rest of you will share the house now?" she asked.

"None of us owns the place," he told her. "But each of us is spending a month here before it goes to its rightful owner. Which will be the town of Hunter's Landing."

Kendall smiled. She hadn't made the connection until now. "So Hunter came from here? Or he's named after the place?"

Matthias shook his head. "No, I think he just stumbled onto the town and liked that it shared his name. And since it was on the lake, he thought it was the perfect spot for the lodge. We'd all talked about doing something like this in college, building a big party house we'd share someday, but after graduation, we never followed through. We were all too *busy*," he said, the last word sounding as if it left a bad taste in his mouth. "Busy *working*," he added, emphasizing that word in a way that was even less complimentary. Which was strange, since Matthias was the kind of man for whom busyness was one of the seven virtues and for whom work was sheer Nirvana. "Too busy working for useless things like following dreams," he concluded softly.

His expression had gone soft, too, as he spoke, Kendall noticed, and when he turned away from the picture to look at her again, there was something in his eyes she'd never seen before. Melancholy. It was almost tangible.

"So do you still see the other Samurai?" she asked. "Besides your brother, I mean?"

Who, she had to admit, he hadn't seen much of. It had only been a couple of months ago that the brothers had even spoken to each other after years of estrangement. And then only because Matthias had needed Luke to switch months at the cabin with him so he could take his trip to Stuttgart. It had been that or break the terms of the will, and Matthias hadn't wanted to do that. Neither had Luke, which was the only reason he'd gone along with the switch. Ultimately, once everything with Lauren Conover had been smoothed out, the Barton brothers had renewed their relationship. But it was still, Kendall knew, a little strained at times.

Matthias looked at the picture again, seeming to take in each of the men one by one. "I haven't seen any of them for years," he said. "Though we'll all be here for the dedication in September."

"What dedication?" Kendall echoed.

He nodded, still looking at the photograph. "Once each of us has spent a month here, the house will go to the town, and I think the plan is to turn it into some kind of medical facility or something. Anyway, there's going to be a big ceremony with the mayor and chamber of commerce or something. All of us will be here, too."

She smiled. "Sounds like Hunter was a good guy."

"The best," Matthias immediately replied. "He was the very best of all of us." This time, when he smiled, there was genuine warmth, and genuine happiness, in the gesture. Then the smile fell, and he grimaced a bit. "I'm sorry. I'm keeping you longer than I meant to."

Actually, Kendall thought, *she* was the one who was holding up things by asking all these questions. *She* was the one who would make herself even later than she'd intended getting back to Stephen DeGallo. Funny, though, how she hadn't given Stephen a thought since entering the lodge.

"Hey," she said again when he started to turn away, more softly than she had the first time.

He spun around again. "What?"

She smiled and pointed to him in the photo. "You looked good with long hair."

He looked at where she was pointing and asked, "Are you so sure that one's me? It could be Luke."

She shook her head. "No, I know it's you."

Now he crossed his arms over his chest, as if in challenge. "How do you know?"

She wasn't about to tell him she knew him by his roguish smile. So she said, "I can tell by the twinkle in your eyes."

Oh, bravo, Kendall, she congratulated herself. *Telling him that was so much better than telling him you recognized him by his smile.*

Matthias arched his eyebrows at the comment, his eyes… Oh, damn. They were twinkling. "Really?" he asked with much interest. Way more interest than he should be showing, actually.

"I mean…" Kendall started to backtrack.

But he wasn't going to let her. "You think my eyes twinkle? Since when?"

"Well, since you were in college, anyway," she hedged. She pointed at the photograph again. "Obviously."

"No, I mean, since when did *you* notice it?" he asked.

If she were going to be honest, she would have to admit that she first noticed it when he interviewed her for the job. Naturally, she wouldn't tell him that. "I don't know," she hedged again. "And really, it's not like they twinkle a lot or anything."

He smiled. "They must, if that's how you knew it was me in the photo and not Luke."

"Okay, I lied," she said. "That's not how I knew it was you in the picture."

His smile grew broader. He was enjoying this, she thought. Enjoying seeing her uncomfortable. Enjoying putting her on the spot. She eyed him carefully. Or was it that he was enjoying the fact that she'd noticed his eyes? she wondered.

Nah, she assured herself. He couldn't have cared less what she noticed about him. He was just having fun at her expense.

"Then if it wasn't my twinkling eyes," he said, "what was it?"

She sighed with exasperation. At herself, because if she'd been put on the spot, it wasn't Matthias who'd put her there. She'd gone willingly by opening her mouth in the first place. Oh, hell, she thought. She'd already blown it. So she answered honestly this time, "It's your smile, okay? I could tell it was you because of your smile."

A smile that bloomed full force when he heard that. Honestly, Kendall thought. There should be a vaccination for the way Matthias could make a woman feel by turning on the full wattage of his smile.

"Really?" he asked. "What's so special about it?"

"Oh, you're just fishing now," she told him.

"Damned right. It's not every day a beautiful woman compliments a man's smile."

It was for him, Kendall thought. She was sure of—

Then the rest of what he said hit her. "You think I'm beautiful?"

His smile faltered at that. "Did I say that?"

She nodded. Vigorously. "Yes. You did."

He shifted his weight from one foot to the other, clearly not feeling as confident as he'd been a second ago. "Are you sure?"

"Yes. I am." What, did he think she didn't notice it when a man said she was beautiful? Especially a man like him?

"Well, I…" he began. "I mean…" he continued. "It's just…" he hedged this time.

"What?" Kendall demanded.

He jutted his thumb over his shoulder and said, "The Donovan contract. We really need to take a look at that."

She opened her mouth to object, but Matthias had already spun around on his heel and was headed down the hall. Knowing it would be pointless to continue—for now—Kendall followed him.

She found herself in an office decorated as nicely as the rest of the house, all warm wood paneling and hardwood floors and bold colors and boxy, but comfortable, furniture. There was a desk on which sat Matthias's laptop—she'd recognize it anywhere, even without the San Francisco Giants wallpaper—a chair, some shelves and a massive bulletin board onto which someone had tacked and taped more old photos of Matthias and his other six Samurai.

Then her gaze lit on a handwritten note that was tacked up alongside them. "Matt," it began—Matt? Kendall thought.

Good luck, bud. You're about to begin your month at "the Love Shack." Remember the universal truths about women we came up with on New Year's Eve our senior year? Scrap 'em. Here are the new universal truths about The One: She'll set you free. Loving her is the most dangerous thing you'll ever do.

It was signed, "Ryan."

Matt? Kendall thought again. She couldn't imagine anyone calling Matthias *Matt*. Then she remembered the way he'd looked in the photograph and altered her opinion. She supposed, once upon a time, he could have been a *Matt* after all. But what was with this "love shack" business?

"Here it is," Matthias said, picking up the document in question and dispelling any further ruminations she might have had on the love shack thing. "There are actually three places where I found errors," he added as he flipped up the top page.

Three? Kendall wondered. How could there have been that many? She'd gone over it a million times.

"The first one is on page two," he said.

She moved to stand beside him, so she could see what he was talking about, and tried again to ignore the luscious fragrance that was coffee and Matthias Barton.

He pointed to the middle of the second paragraph and said, "You left out a comma here."

Certain she'd misunderstood, she looked up at him and said, "What?"

He pointed again. "A comma," he repeated. "You left one out here. This is a compound sentence. There should be a comma before *and* here. And then on page three," he said, quickly turning the next page, "in the first paragraph here, this semicolon should be a comma, too. I'm sure of it. And on the last page," he continued, flipping back to that, "you didn't make the signature line long enough.

There should be at least another quarter inch there, to allow space for Donovan to sign. His first name is Elliot. You don't want to add insult to injury, not giving the man enough room to sign his name."

Kendall couldn't believe her ears. *This* was the problem with the Donovan contract? A comma? A semicolon? A signature line? For *this,* she'd risked hacking off her new boss? For *this* she'd driven a half hour one way? For *this* she'd bought him coffee using money out of her own pocket?

But even more offensive than all that was the fact that he was completely wrong. There was absolutely no need for a comma where he said there was—that wasn't a compound sentence—and the semicolon was perfectly fine. As for the sig line, she'd seen Elliot Donovan's signature before, and a more cramped bit of writing didn't exist anywhere. There was more than enough room for the man to sign his name.

She narrowed her eyes at Matthias. "You brought me all the way down here for a comma, a semicolon and a signature line?"

He clearly didn't see anything wrong with that. "It's details like that, Kendall, that people notice."

"Not unless they're wrong. Which these aren't," she told him.

He looked surprised at that. "Really?"

"Really."

"You're sure?"

"I'm sure."

"Oh. Well. Then I guess I brought you down here for nothing."

If looks could kill, Kendall thought, Matthias would be radioactive wind just then.

"But now that you're here," he said, "why don't you stay for lunch? The caretaker left some great stuff in the fridge."

There were so many ways Kendall could have answered his question—not the least of which was head-butting him, something she very much wanted to do just then—so she settled on a simple, "No. Thank you," and hoped he would hear the edge in her voice. And then, you know, fear for his life.

Instead, he smiled and asked, "Then how about if I offer you your old job back, and then you won't have to worry about getting back to Stephen DeGallo on time, because you'll already be where you need to be."

At that, Kendall decided that head-butting was too good for Matthias. What he really deserved was being hit with a brick. No, two bricks. Oh, what the hell. The same number of bricks it took to build the British Museum. However, she again managed to reply, "No. Thank you." And then she added, "Now, if you'll excuse me, I have to, as you said, go where I need to be. Which is *not* here."

And with that, she spun on her heel and exited the office. Without looking back once. Without even saying goodbye.

Five

Matthias watched Kendall through the front window of the cabin as she descended the steps toward her car.

He'd told her the truth about having good memories of Hunter and the rest of the gang since coming to the lodge. But he'd been plagued by even more bad ones. Not just of Hunter's death, but of how he and Luke had let their own relationship fall apart. Hunter had been the one in college who'd somehow managed to help the brothers turn their competition with each other into affection for each other. When he died, it was almost as if the bond that had held Matthias and Luke together died, too.

Matt and Luke, he corrected himself. Back then, he hadn't been Matthias. He'd been Matt. A regular guy, an easygoing student, the kind of kid who liked keggers and Three Stooges movies and games of pickup rugby in the park. It had only been after college, when he'd heard the terms of his father's will, that he'd begun to go by his given name of Matthias. Matthias had sounded more studied than Matt, more serious, more seasoned. Matthias had sounded like a grown-up. And, thanks to the terms of his father's will, Matt had been forced to grow up fast.

Even in death, the old man had pitted the twin brothers against each other, decreeing that whoever was able to make the first million would win the estate in its entirety. The one who didn't would be left with nothing. When the attorneys had read the stipulation to him and Luke, Matthias had been able to picture their father in the afterlife, leaning back in his celestial Barcalounger, rubbing his hands together with relish and saying, "Let the games begin."

And at first it had kind of been a game. Luke and Matthias had each good-naturedly joked that they would leave the other in the dust. Both had started their own companies, and then got down to business. Literally. For the first couple of months, they'd gone at it as they had every other competition they'd indulged in over the years, be it for a game, or a grade, or a girl. Then, little by little, Matthias had started edging ahead. A deal here, an acquisition there, and the money had begun to pile higher. A hundred thousand. Two hundred and fifty thousand. Half a million. Until that final deal that had cinched it for him and ensured he would win.

The problem was that the final deal had been tainted— unbeknownst to Matthias at the time—by some shady dealings inside his own company. Luke, suspicious, had cried foul and accused Matthias of cheating, an accusation Matthias resoundingly denied for years. An accusation that had split the brothers to the point of not speaking. Until Matthias discovered—only recently, in fact—a rat in his own corporation who had double-dealed him and Luke both and then disappeared with his own ill-gotten gains. And even though the two brothers realized now that they'd both been taken advantage of back then—even though the lines of communication were open now—things still weren't quite settled. Yeah, Matthias had helped his brother win the woman he'd once planned to marry himself. That the help had come in the form of a punch to Luke's eye had just been cake. But Luke had apologized for being an ass. Matthias, in turn, had apologized for being an ass *and* not trying harder to keep the lines of communication open.

Those lines were open now, he reminded himself. But things with Luke still weren't where they should be. He supposed there would never again be a day when they were the carefree college kids Hunter had helped them to be. But they could be brothers again.

And they would, he vowed. He would start calling his brother on a regular basis and make sure they saw more of each other. Hell, they both lived in San Francisco. It wasn't as if it was a hardship for them to see each other.

Kendall had folded herself into her car by now and started the ignition, and was looking over her shoulder as she backed out of the drive. She stopped to wait for a dog to trot past before pulling out, and when she did, for some reason, she looked back up at the house. Her eyes immediately connected with his, but she'd donned sunglasses, so it was impossible to read her expression. Matthias lifted a hand to wave it in halfhearted farewell and, after a moment, she lifted a hand in response. But she didn't wave, and she didn't smile, so the gesture felt more final than it should have.

And then she was rolling out of the driveway and putting

the car in gear, and heading down the road that would take her back to the highway. She didn't turn around again, even when she braked for the stop sign. Matthias watched her car until she was out of sight, then stood at the window a little longer, watching the empty place in the road where last he'd seen her. He told himself to get busy, that he had a lot of work to do today. He reminded himself he had another temp coming by in a few hours.

He reminded himself of a lot of things as he stood at the window looking at the place where Kendall wasn't. But all he could remember was the way her hand had felt, curled tentatively over his arm when she'd expressed her sympathy over Hunter's death.

She was going where she thought she needed to be, he told himself, recalling the words he'd used first, and which she'd turned back on him in an entirely different—and erroneous—way. But she was wrong. She didn't *need to be* with Stephen DeGallo, a man who would only use her long enough to pick her brain about Matthias's business and then manufacture some excuse to let her go. The man didn't like people working closely with him whom he hadn't brought up himself from scratch. Matthias knew DeGallo fairly well—What was the old adage? Keep your friends close, your enemies closer?—and Kendall, to DeGallo's way of thinking, was tainted. She was used goods, sloppy seconds. No matter how much she liked and trusted the guy, DeGallo would, once he got the information from her he wanted, consider her a liability, and he would let her go.

And *that,* Matthias told himself as he continued to watch the empty street, was why he needed—no, *wanted*—Kendall to come back to work for Barton Limited. Because

DeGallo didn't appreciate her the way Matthias did. Because DeGallo wouldn't offer her the security and benefits Matthias would. Because DeGallo didn't care about her any more than he would care about a new printer or phone system or hard drive.

It *wasn't* because of the warmth that had spread through him when she'd curled her fingers around his arm. And it wasn't because of the way she'd looked at him as he'd talked about his old friends, as if she wanted to hear more—about them *and* him. And it certainly wasn't because the lodge had come alive while she was here and felt dim and somber now that she was gone. That was ridiculous. Houses didn't live and they didn't have feelings.

Then again, there were those who would say the same thing about Matthias.

He sighed heavily and pushed a handful of hair back from his forehead. He didn't have time for this, he thought. He had work to do and an interview to perform. Because as much as he knew Kendall wasn't where she needed to be, she was the one who would have to realize that. In the meantime, he needed—no, wanted—someone else.

Even if no one else would ever come close to her.

By the end of the week, Matthias had run through every temp agency in the Tahoe area without finding even a marginally acceptable candidate to replace Kendall, even temporarily. The one who had just appeared at his door was his very last hope, and already he knew she wasn't going to work out, either. She had no concept of how to dress for a job interview, even one conducted in a nonoffice environment. She'd actually paired a crisp white shirt with a pair of pin-striped trousers and flat loafers, and had knotted her dark hair on the top of her head like a tennis ball. Her little black glasses were tailored and elegant, and her makeup—if she was even wearing any—was understated and clean.

What the hell was she thinking, showing up for a job interview looking like this? She was even more over-the-top and under-a-rock than the first guy had been.

He expelled a restless sigh and gestured halfheartedly toward the living room, indicating she should take a seat on one of the chairs beside the fireplace while he folded himself perfunctorily into the other. The sooner they got this interview over with, the better. Then Matthias could…

Well, okay, he could be alone. At least he wouldn't be wasting his time interviewing people who obviously had no clue how to interact in the world of big business. Instead, he'd be wasting his time dreading the fact that he'd have to set up another interview with someone who would almost certainly be as unqualified to fill Kendall's position as this woman was.

"So, Ms…." He glanced down at the résumé the temp agency had e-mailed him to inspect in preparation for her arrival. "Ms. Carrigan," he finished. "I see you're a graduate of Stanford Business School."

She smiled a small, unobtrusive smile that made Matthias flinch, so blatantly inappropriate was it for a job interview. "I am," she said. "I graduated in May with honors."

Yeah, yeah, yeah, Matthias thought. Honors schmonors. If he had a dollar for every honors degree places like Stanford and Harvard issued, he could paper the whole top of his desk.

"And what interests you about the position as my personal assistant?"

She sat up straighter, crossed her legs at the ankles,

wove her fingers together loosely in her lap, then tilted her head thoughtfully to one side. Matthias mentally shook his own head and somehow refrained from rolling his eyes. Her entire posture just screamed indolent slob. What an incredible waste of time this was.

"May I speak frankly, Mr. Barton?" she asked.

"Of course," he told her. Adding to himself, *Making presumptions already?*

"Ultimately," she began, "I'd like to move higher on the corporate ladder, but I think this would be a good entry level position for me, because it would offer me the opportunity to learn from, well, if you'll forgive my momentary gushing, a legend in the business world."

Suck-up, Matthias thought. But he kept his expression bland.

"University courses," she continued, "can only go so far in imparting information. I'm hoping that by coming to work for you fresh out of college, Mr. Barton, I could gain some professional experience that would enhance what I learned in the classroom at Stanford. At the same time, I'll do an excellent job keeping your schedule organized and making sure you have everything you need at any given moment. All modesty aside, my organizational skills are exemplary, and as you can see from the letters of recommendation I've supplied from five of my professors, I routinely led my classes when it came to completing assignments promptly and neatly."

Bighead, Matthias thought. Megalomaniac was more like it. Not to mention she was barely articulate enough to string two words together.

"I see," he said. "Well, that's all good information to have, and I appreciate your coming in today." He stood and extended his hand to her. "I have your résumé. I'll be in touch."

She was obviously surprised by the quickness with which he'd concluded the interview, but there was no reason for Matthias to waste any more time—hers or his. The woman had absolutely nothing to recommend her and was in no way suitable.

What was up with business schools these days? Matthias wondered as he watched her leave. Between Tahoe and San Francisco, he'd interviewed more than two dozen people to fill Kendall's position, and each person had been worse than the one before.

Well, there was nothing else for him to do, he thought. He couldn't afford to wait for Kendall to come to her senses. He'd just have to do or say whatever it took to get her back. Give her another raise, better benefits, whatever it took. Never mind that he'd already tried to do that. Twice. Never mind that he'd failed. Twice. Matthias Barton hadn't risen to the level of success he had by taking no for an answer. Unless, you know, no was the answer he wanted to hear. No *wasn't* a word he'd heard often from Kendall. Until, you know, recently. He was sure if he made her the right offer, she'd come around. Everyone had their price. Even Kendall. All Matthias had to do was find it.

Fortunately for him, he knew exactly where to look.

Kendall had been waiting for Stephen in the dining room of the Timber Lake Inn for fifteen minutes when she looked up at the restaurant's entrance once more, hoping to see her new employer there, and instead saw Matthias. He was dressed casually again, this time pairing his khaki trousers with a chocolate-brown polo that lovingly molded his broad chest and shoulders. She was surprised to see that he'd left his shirttail out, a casual affectation he normally didn't adopt. Then again, there was something about him tonight that suggested it wasn't an affectation at all.

She waited for the irritation that should have come at seeing him, but instead, she was filled with a strange sort of relief. Her orientation this week hadn't been quite what she'd thought it would be, filled as it had been with mostly one-on-one meetings with Stephen. Meetings that had taken place more often in restaurants than in a conference room at the hotel—conference rooms that were better suited to serving high tea than conducting business, anyway. Worse, the meetings had seemed to veer off course on a fairly regular basis, shifting from the policies and procedures of OmniTech to Kendall's experiences working with Matthias.

She didn't want to believe Matthias was right about Stephen DeGallo's only hiring her to uncover information about him. But after the way the week had gone, with her having to sidestep every effort Stephen made to shift the conversation to Barton Limited, Kendall couldn't quite dissuade herself of the idea that Matthias knew what he was talking about. At best, her new employer's training methods were unconventional. At worst, her new employer's intentions were underhanded. Either way, Kendall wasn't sure she was working for the right man. Either way, she wasn't sure she was where she needed to be.

Matthias caught her eye just as she completed that last thought, and a thrill of something hot and electric shuddered through her. She recognized it as sexual, but was surprised by its strength. Surprising, too, was how much it differed from the sexual responses she'd had to men in the past. Because joining the physical sensations that were rocketing through her body was an emotional reaction that was blooming in her heart. She had feelings for Matthias she hadn't had for other men. And they were stronger, she realized now, than she'd allowed herself to believe.

But this was *Matthias,* she tried to remind herself. As recently as a few weeks ago, he'd been Mr. Barton. Yes, she'd known she was attracted to him. But she'd thought removing herself from him would put an end to that attraction. Remove the appetite by removing the temptation. But the only thing removing the temptation had done was make her hungrier.

As long as she'd been working for him, Kendall's ethics hadn't allowed her to cross the line into intimacy. Office romances, she knew, were a Very Bad Idea, no matter how you played them. So as long as she was working for Barton Limited, her conscience had allowed her to find her boss attractive, but hadn't permitted her to act on that attraction. By leaving the office environment, any obstacles that had stood in the way of her feelings for him had disappeared. Simply put, now that she wasn't his employee anymore, her conscience and her brain—not to mention her heart— were letting in things they had locked up tight before.

Not good, she thought as he came to a stop behind the chair across from her and curled his fingers over the back of it. Because how wise would it be to let herself start feeling things—things beyond attraction—for a married man? Especially when what the man was married to was his business?

"Hi," he said. And with that one word, her troubled thoughts completely evaporated.

There would be plenty of time for thinking later, she told

herself. Especially if Stephen DeGallo never showed up. Where was he, anyway? It wasn't like him to be late. Then again, why did she care when Matthias was here?

That thought, more than any of the others she'd had this evening—this week—told her more than anything else could about herself. And her feelings. And her wisdom. Or lack thereof. What told her even more was how she quickly smoothed a hand over her ivory shirt and brown trousers before running it back over her head to make sure her hair was in place. Somehow, she knew she wouldn't have bothered for Stephen. Nor would she have removed her glasses to get a better look at him, as she did with Matthias now.

"Hi," she replied, tucking her glasses into her shirt pocket.

"Meeting DeGallo?" he asked.

She hesitated before telling him she feared her new boss had stood her up. Because then Matthias would ask her why, and she'd have to tell him she didn't know, unless maybe it was because Stephen had decided she wasn't a team player, even without first letting her into the dugout. So she only said, "Actually, I'm here alone." Which was true. She was alone. She just wasn't *supposed* to be alone.

And boy, was that a loaded statement she would just as soon not leave hanging. So she hurried on, "What are you doing here? Again?"

She hadn't meant for that *again* to sound as pointed as it had. Matthias either didn't notice or chose to pretend he hadn't heard it himself, because he only smiled and replied, "I actually came here to see if you wanted to have dinner with me. When you didn't answer my knock at you door upstairs, I took a chance that you'd be down here."

She nodded sagely, but said nothing.

He looked at her expectantly, but said nothing.

It occurred to her that he was waiting for her to invite him to sit down. Then it occurred to her that, with her luck, the minute she did, Stephen DeGallo would walk through the door with a perfectly legitimate reason for being so late, and whisk her off to a PowerPoint presentation of some of OmniTech's most arcane secrets, then apologize for it taking so long to invite her into the loving bosom of his inner sanctum.

And she thought, Ew. That sounded really gross.

Not to mention it was almost certainly *not* going to happen. At least, not that last part. But there was still a possibility that Stephen would show up with a legitimate reason for being late, and it wouldn't look good for her to be sitting here with Matthias.

"If you're waiting for Stephen," he began, as if he were able to read her thoughts.

"I'm not," she quickly interjected.

"Good," he said. "Because I saw him driving off with a breathtaking blonde as I was coming into the inn."

She gaped at him. "You did not. We had a dinner…" She started to say "date," realized that hammered home even better—or, rather, worse—what her orientation this week had felt like, and immediately corrected herself by finishing, "Appointment."

"So you *were* expecting him," Matthias said, a note of unmistakable triumph in his voice.

She flattened her mouth into a thin line to keep herself from saying anything else.

"Looks like your new boss stood you up, Kendall," Matthias said. "Which isn't a very sound business plan on his part." He hesitated a beat before adding, "The man's an idiot if he doesn't realize how lucky he is to have hired you."

The momentary thrill of surprise and pleasure that came with Matthias's compliment was quickly replaced by other things she felt for Stephen DeGallo. Resentment, frustration, disappointment. She was sure the two of them were supposed to have met for dinner here tonight. Positive. In fact, he'd told her barely three hours ago that he'd see her at six-thirty in the dining room.

She looked at her watch. It was ten till seven now. There was little chance the man would be this late when he was staying at the same hotel. Obviously, he'd discovered something—or someone—in the last few hours who had seemed a more profitable return on his investment.

She braced herself for Matthias's *I told you so,* but all he said was, "How about I buy you dinner instead?"

She told herself to say no, that all she really wanted to do was go up to her suite for some room service and a long bubble bath. Then she realized that was the last thing she wanted to do. She was tired of going to her room alone at night. Tired of wondering what Stephen's motives were in hiring her. Tired of not knowing if she'd made the right choice in coming to work for him.

Work, hah, she thought. Nothing she had experienced with Stephen DeGallo so far had felt anything like work. It had felt like…

Bribery, she thought. And snooping. And something kind of smarmy and icky.

She sighed again, but this time there was less resentment, frustration and disappointment in it. They were replaced instead with a sad sort of resolution that she had made a mistake. Not in leaving Matthias's employ, but in taking the job with OmniTech. She'd talk to Stephen tomorrow, ask him point-blank if he'd offered her the job because he'd expected her to tell him about the workings of Barton Limited. If he had, she would tender her resignation immediately. And if he hadn't…

Well. She'd wait to make plans until the two of them had had a chance to talk. In the meantime, she had another choice to make. And she told herself she'd better make the right one this time.

But instead of responding to Matthias's dinner invitation the way her brain told her to—by declining—she listened to her heart instead. Even knowing her heart was wont to get her into trouble. Hey, it wasn't as though her head had been doing such a good job lately.

"Dinner would be nice," she told him.

He smiled, and the heat inside Kendall sparked a little hotter. "Not here, though," he told her. "The steak I had the other night left a lot to be desired."

That wasn't the only thing at the Timber Lake Inn that was like that, Kendall thought.

"But I do know just the place. It's a bit of a drive, but you'll love it. Nice ambience, and the food is excellent. And the service can't be beat."

Before giving her a chance to agree or decline, he moved behind her chair and gave it a gentle tug. Then he lowered a hand to help her out of it. Without thinking about what she was doing, Kendall curled her fingers over his, marveling at how the heat inside her began to purl through her entire body.

This wasn't good, she told herself again as she rose. She should have told Matthias she couldn't go to dinner with him. It would be a mistake to think anything that might happen between them would ever go anywhere. Even if the two of them did get involved—and oh, wasn't she presuming a lot there?—whatever happened would flare up and fizzle out, probably in a very short time. Matthias Barton wasn't a man for relationships. He wasn't even a man for affection. The only thing he would ever love to distraction was his business.

As long as Kendall reminded herself of that—over and over and over again, she told herself—she would be fine. Right?

Of course, right.

<u>Six</u>

"You'll change your mind about this place, Kendall, the minute you taste your first glass of wine."

Matthias realized his concerns were unfounded when he turned from unlocking the lodge's front door to see Kendall gazing back at him with a smile. "That's okay," she said. "I like this place. It's nice. It makes you feel comfortable as soon as you enter."

So she'd noticed it, too, he thought. Interesting.

"Not to mention it's Friday night," he added. "Every decent place along the lake is going to be packed by now. We wouldn't get seated until after ten."

"It's nice that you have this place for a month," she said as she circled around him into the foyer. "It'll do you good."

It had already done him good, Matthias thought. And just by inviting Kendall inside, the good had become better.

"Remind me after it gets dark to go out onto the deck,"

he said as he closed the door behind them. "There's a tele-scope out there. It's incredible, the things you can find in the sky out here."

She smiled. "You've been looking through a tele-scope at night?"

He eyed her warily. "You sound surprised."

"I *am* surprised," she told him. "Matthias, you've never taken time out of your days—or nights—for something like that."

"Sure I have. I do it all the time."

She shook her head. "No, you don't."

"Yeah," he countered, a little more defensively than he would have liked. "I do."

Still smiling, she crossed her arms over her midsection. In-evitably, he noticed how, when she did that, the outline of her bra was just discernible enough through the pale fabric of her shirt to allow him to see that it was lace. He never would have pegged Kendall as the lacy lingerie type. She seemed like the Hanes-all-over type. Hell, there'd been times when she was working for him that she seemed like the boxer short type. And during one particularly daunting week, the jockstrap type. But now that he realized she *was* the lacy lingerie type…

Hmm. Actually, he found the idea kind of arousing. He also found himself wondering if she was the type to match bra to panties. Or, better yet, bra to thong bikini.

"Name one frivolous thing you do in your spare time," she challenged.

Figuring Kendall meant *besides* pondering the myster-ies of her underwear, he opened his mouth to rattle off a dozen things he did for enjoyment, then realized he couldn't think of even one. Other than looking through the telescope, which he'd done only since coming here.

Finally, "I play squash," he said. "And tennis. And I play an occasional round of golf."

"And you use them all for networking and wheeling and dealing."

Yeah, okay, she had a point. So sue him.

He bristled at her suggestion that he was a man who found no enjoyment in life outside his work. Mostly because he couldn't honestly deny it. "Frivolity is over-rated," he finally said. "And there's no point to it. I like working. It gives me pleasure. I don't need anything else in my life."

Her smile fell at that, and he realized he had been speaking with more vehemence than he intended—not to mention more than he felt. She'd just hit a sore spot with him, that was all. Why did everyone criticize people who were enthusiastic about their work? So what if he defined himself by how successful he was, and how hard he worked? So what if he was the kind of person who *would* be lying on his deathbed worrying that he hadn't worked enough during his life. There was nothing else in his life but work. Why was that such a terrible thing?

Kendall dropped her hands to her sides, her smile gone now. An awkward moment followed where neither seemed to know what to say. So Matthias forced himself to relax and said, "So how about dinner?"

For a minute, he thought—feared—she was going to decline and ask him to take her back to the inn. Finally, however, she nodded.

He roused a smile for her, tilting his head toward the kitchen. "Come on," he said in a lighter voice. "I'll have it on the table in ten minutes."

It actually only took about half that time, since all

Matthias had to do was remove food from containers in the fridge and arrange them on two plates. Opening the wine was the most time-consuming part of the task, but the cork left the bottle of Shiraz with a nice crisp *pop*. He poured them each a glass and carried those, too, to the table.

Kendall surveyed the food on the plate—a strip steak, green beans and new potatoes he'd picked up at a gourmet carryout place about ten miles down the road—a little warily.

"It's cold," she said.

"No, it's tartare," he countered as he sat in the chair on the side of the table that was perpendicular to hers. To show her it was fine, he lifted his fork and knife and sliced through the tender beef, then halved a potato with the side of his fork. "See? Looks delicious, doesn't it?"

"Tartare means uncooked," Kendall corrected him. She pointed at the plate. "This has been cooked. It just hasn't been heated up. I mean, even the vegetables are cold. Why don't you just pop the plates into the microwave for a couple of minutes?"

He sighed heavily. "The microwave is broken," he admitted. "And so is the oven," he added when she was about to mention that.

She looked over her shoulder at the appliances in question, the former set into the cabinets above the latter. "They look brand-new," she said as she turned back around again.

"Yeah, well, whoever built this place obviously cut corners on the appliances, because none of them work. But trust me, food like this tastes great cold."

Kendall smiled. "In other words, you've been eating your meals cold all week because you can't figure out how the microwave or stove work."

His back went up at that—figuratively *and* literally.

"No, I've been eating my meals cold because the microwave and stove *don't* work."

She gazed at him with an expression he couldn't decipher, then stood and picked up both their plates. She strode over to the microwave, set one plate on the stovetop as she opened the door and inserted one, then picked up the other and put it in beside the first. Then she looked at the keypad—which Matthias knew was completely incomprehensible to anyone except the rocket scientist who designed it—punched a few buttons with a beep-boop-beep and the microwave suddenly came alive.

He rose from his chair and crossed the kitchen to where Kendall stood. "How did you do that?" he demanded. "That thing hasn't worked since I got here."

"Well, it's fine now," she said. Then, with another little smile he wasn't quite sure how to figure out, she asked, "What else have you been having trouble with?"

"Why do you assume I've been having trouble with anything else?"

"Well, you did just mention that none of the appliances work."

"Right." He'd forgotten about that. He thought Kendall was insinuating that he had problems with small appliances. Which was completely ridiculous. He was, after all, a captain of industry. Now, if someone would just promote him to colonel of technology, he'd be all set.

He pointed over his shoulder, at the most pressing of his concerns. "The coffeemaker," he said.

She nodded knowingly. "I should have figured that out when you cooked up that bogus contract problem to trick me into bringing you coffee."

"I never—"

But she ignored him, only smiling more sweetly, as if in sympathy. "Poor Matthias. Not getting his morning coffee every day. It's a wonder you're not a drooling mess."

"Drooling mess?" he echoed. "I've never been a drooling mess. Over coffee or anything else."

"Of course you haven't."

He eyed her narrowly but said nothing. Hey, he knew he wasn't a slave to caffeine. He could quit any time he wanted. Caffeine addicts were weak. He was strong. Hell, there were days when he didn't even go near a Starbucks. He just, you know, couldn't remember the last one, that was all. Besides, real caffeine junkies drank cheap, grocery store coffee, and they drank it all day long. Matthias bought only the premium gourmet blends, and he drank only in the morning. Except on days when he needed a little extra something to get him through the afternoon. Hey, he could afford it. He still looked good. He was still healthy. Besides, there had been plenty of studies that said it was good for you. Plus he had all those issues with his father, and coffee helped take the sting out of those.

Ah, hell. What were they talking about?

"Then I guess you don't care that I have a coffeemaker like that myself," Kendall said, "and know how to fix it. If there is, in fact, anything wrong with it," she added in a way that he knew was meant to ruffle him.

It did.

"It doesn't work," he repeated, more emphatically this time. "I've done everything. Even the clock on it is wrong."

She patted him on the shoulder—something that sent a strange ripple of warmth through him—and crossed to the counter where the coffeemaker sat. Mocking him. Again, she pressed some buttons that made a couple of quick beeps. Then she pushed the big red button Matthias hadn't wanted to push himself, fearing it might trigger a nuclear strike over North Korea, and a little green light came on. But there was nothing to indicate the machine was working, no whirring of the grinder, no hiss of water as it heated, no gurgle of coffee as it dripped into the carafe.

"See?" he said. "It doesn't work."

"I set the timer for you," she told him, sidestepping his insistence that it didn't work. And it didn't work, Matthias was sure of that. "As long as you fill it with coffee and water every night, it'll start brewing at six-thirty in the morning."

He gaped at her. "How did you do that?"

She pointed to the little green light. "I set the clock to the correct time, then pushed the button that says, 'Timer.' The machine walks you through the steps after that."

Matthias hooked his hands on his hips and said nothing, only stared at Kendall in wonder, trying to figure out how the hell he was supposed to manage for the rest of his life if she was working for someone else. Because he had no choice but to admit then that he needed Kendall. *Really* needed her. What was beginning to scare him was that he was starting to suspect it wasn't only in the office where he had that need.

She smiled at him and extended her hand. "Okay, give it to me," she said, her voice tinted with laughter.

He shook his head in confusion. "What are you talking about?"

"Your new BlackBerry," she said. "The one you brought to the hotel earlier this week. I'll program it for you."

Damn, he thought. She *would* ask about that now. "It's not necessary," he told her.

She arched her brows in surprise. "You programmed it yourself?"

"Not exactly."

"Then give it to me and I'll do it for you."

He expelled an exasperated sound. "I can't."

"Why not?"

"Because it's at the bottom of Lake Tahoe."

Kendall looked at him in disbelief for a second, then she started to laugh. It was a nice laugh, Matthias thought. Full and uninhibited without being an obnoxious bray. He tried to remember the last time he'd heard Kendall laugh...and realized he never had. Not until this evening. She'd always been so serious at work. So pragmatic and professional. So enterprising and efficient. He'd always thought she was so straitlaced. So somber. It had never occurred to him that there was a woman lurking beneath her gender-neutral attire.

He watched her as she made her way back to the microwave to remove their now-warmed dinners. She was dressed as she always dressed for work—dark trousers, pale shirt, her hair pinned up on her head. But she was more relaxed now than she'd been when she worked for him. She smiled more. Laughed. Spoke to him familiarly. Called him Matthias. When she wasn't working for him, she was...different. Softer. Warmer. More approachable.

He began to feel a little warmer himself as he watched her carry their plates back to the table. Though not particularly soft, he realized with no small amount of surprise. He wondered what she'd do if he...approached.

"The steak formerly known as tartare," she said as she set his plate back on the table with a flourish. "Have at it."

Matthias smiled at her wording. *Have at it* could mean anything. And there were a lot of *its* he wanted to have. Fortunately, he and Kendall had a nice long leisurely evening ahead of them.

* * *

Kendall shook her head as she watched Matthias fiddle with a knob on the telescope, wondering what had come over him this week to make him so…so…so…

Human.

Tonight, he'd been… She smiled as a word came to her. She tried to push it away, so wildly inappropriate a description for him was it, but it wouldn't budge. There was just nothing else that was as accurate. Tonight he had been…*adorable.* All evening long. Never in her wildest dreams would she have thought she would use such an adjective to describe him. When she'd been working for him, he'd been a lot of things—gruff, focused, no-nonsense, intense—but never, ever adorable.

The closest she'd ever seen him come to being soft had been when he'd returned from this very lodge two months ago, after seeing his brother Luke for the first time in years. For a few days after his return, Matthias had seemed distant and distracted and, well, soft. But the softness had still been tempered with an edge, thanks to whatever had happened between the two men while they were here. They'd even brawled at one point over something. Although Matthias hadn't confided in Kendall what the fight had been about, he'd come back from that trip with a black eye that she'd naturally asked him about.

But even with all the changes that had come over him on that occasion—as temporary as they'd been—he hadn't seemed like a normal human being, any more than he ever seemed like a normal human being. He'd still been a powerful force to be reckoned with.

Tonight, though, that force was a soothing breeze. Just like the one rolling off the lake that nudged a stray strand of hair into Kendall's eyes. She brushed it back as she continued to watch him by the telescope, tucking it behind her ear, though, instead of bothering with trying to poke it back into the bun. By now, several such strands of hair had escaped and blew freely about her face. Short of freeing her hair and starting all over again, there wasn't much she could do about them. Not to mention there was something about the languid, peaceful evening—and okay, something about Matthias, too—that prevented her from wanting to be her usual buttoned-up self.

The broad deck stretched along the length of the back of the house, dotted here and there by sturdy wooden furniture and the occasional potted greenery. The sun hung low over the mountains behind them, spilling a wide, watery trail over the lake as it left the sky, bisecting the rippling water with a shimmer of gold. The temperature had dropped with the sun, tumbling from the eighties into the sixties, and she knew that, with full nightfall, it would go lower still. She wished she'd thought to wear a jacket. But then, she hadn't planned on leaving the hotel, had she?

Which was ironic, she thought now, because suddenly she didn't feel like going back to it.

It was just surprisingly pleasant being with Matthias now, when they were on more equal footing. No, she wasn't a corporate bigwig or hotshot industrialist, as he was. Not yet, anyway. But neither was she his assistant anymore. She could speak to him as an equal now, and did. What was nice was that he spoke to her as an equal, too.

But then she realized that wasn't exactly right, either. Because equals in business spoke to each other about business. And she and Matthias hadn't even touched on that tonight. Over dinner, they'd discussed Lake Tahoe and the lodge, the small town in Washington state where Kendall had grown up, Matthias's favorite dog when he was a boy, and how they'd both been high achievers throughout school. The sort of things people talked about when they were getting to know each other. Personally, not professionally.

"Okay, here we go," he said now, drawing her attention back to the matter at hand. "I found Venus. Come have a look."

Kendall drained the last of her wine and set her empty glass on a table next to his, then covered the half-dozen steps to where he stood by the telescope.

"You'll see it better once the sun has completely set," he added, "but even now, it's a beautiful sight to behold."

When she came to a stop beside him, he moved to one side, far enough that she would have room to look through the telescope, but still close enough that he could give her instructions, or a hand, if she needed one.

"Look through here," he said, pointing to a piece that jutted up from the enormous scope.

The thing must magnify a billion times, she thought.

"And you can focus in and out with this," he added, pointing to a knob next to the one he'd been turning to find the planet. He looked at her and smiled. "It's amazing the detail you get with this thing. When I look at the moon at night, it's like if I just stretched out far enough, I could fill my hand with moondust."

Fill my hand with moondust, Kendall repeated to herself, marveling at the phrase. Had Matthias actually said that? It was just so…so…so un-Matthias.

He seemed to realize that, too, because he suddenly looked uncomfortable. His gaze, which had been focused on hers, ricocheted off, and he began to look at everything on the deck except her. Finally, his focus lit on something behind her, and he pointed in that direction.

"Our glasses are empty," he said. "I'll open another bottle of wine." Then, still not looking directly at her, he dipped his head toward the telescope and said, "Enjoy the view. I'll be right back."

She took him at his word, but instead of enjoying the view through the scope, she instead enjoyed the view of Matthias as he strode over to collect their glasses, then made his way back into the lodge. His shirttail flapped in the breeze, rising at one point to give her a lovely view of a surprisingly nice derriere. Since it had generally been covered by a suit jacket whenever she was around him, she'd never had the chance to notice what a nice tush Matthias had. Or maybe she just hadn't allowed herself to notice, because she was working for him. Now, however, she noticed.

Boy howdy, did she notice.

Almost as if he'd heard the thought forming in her brain, Matthias spun quickly around and caught her ogling him. Heat flooded her face at being caught in such a flagrant position, and she waited for the icy look she was sure he'd shoot her way. But the look he gave her wasn't icy. In fact, it was kind of hot. For a moment, his expression didn't change. Then, gradually, an almost invisible smile curled his lips. The kind of smile he didn't want anyone to see. The kind of smile someone who knew him well—like Kendall—couldn't miss. Then it was gone, and he was turning again to make his way back inside the lodge.

But something in his smile lingered, even after he was gone. And it lingered inside Kendall. A thrill of warmth that had sparked in her belly when she first saw his smile, then gradually eased through her entire system, warming her even as the breeze off the lake began to grow cool.

Too much to drink, she decided. She and Matthias both had obviously overindulged on the wine. Funny, though, how she'd never considered two glasses of wine—spread out over two hours, with dinner—overindulging before.

Absently, she curled her arms over her midsection—because she was cold, she told herself, in spite of the warmth spreading through her, and not because she was trying to hold the feeling inside a little longer. She looked up at the bright speck in the sky with her naked eye, then bent toward the eyepiece of the telescope. It took her a moment to get in the right position, but eventually, she found what she was looking for.

Wow, she thought when she saw the yellow planet streaked with bits of orange and pink. It really *was* gorgeous. But she was still surprised that Matthias would think so, too. That he would even care there were planets up there. Looking at the sky just seemed like such a frivolous thing for him to do. That he'd been spending his evenings at the lodge out here on the deck, contemplating the mysteries of the universe, instead of in the amply equipped office getting work done, spoke volumes. And it wasn't in a language he'd ever been able to master before—that of leisure enjoyment.

Something warm and heavy slipped over her shoulders then, and she glanced up from the telescope to find Matthias settling a jacket, clearly one of his, over her shoulders.

He smiled at what must have been her obvious surprise at the gesture and said, "The temperature's dropping. I don't want you to get cold."

There was certainly no chance of that happening,

Kendall thought, as long as he looked at her the way he was looking at her now. She smiled gratefully and murmured her thanks, then pressed her eye to the eyepiece of the telescope once again.

"So what do you think?" he asked.

"You're right," she told him. "It's as if you could just reach right out and touch it."

"When it gets a little darker, I'll see if I can find Jupiter, too," he told her. "It's even more incredible. You can actually see the big red spot with this thing."

Kendall pulled her head back and looked at Matthias again. In the few minutes he'd been inside, the evening had grown noticeably darker, and now the flicker of candlelight danced in his hair, setting little gold fires amid the dark tresses. He must have lit the ones scattered about the tables and the railing while she was so rapt over the image of Venus. His gaze fixed intently on hers as he extended a glass of wine toward her, and she took it without really paying attention, automatically lifting it to her lips for a sip. It tasted different from the last glass, its flavor smoother, more mellow, more potent. Or maybe, she thought, it was just Matthias who was suddenly all those things. She'd better pace herself, or he'd go right to her head.

"So," he said, the word coming out slowly and softly, "how are things going with the new job? Do you like OmniTech so far?"

Kendall was surprised he would ask. Not just because of the whole former employer-employee thing, but because the evening had just been so pleasant and enjoyable with the absence of any talk that was work-related. Still, she knew Matthias wouldn't have asked if he didn't expect an answer. An honest one, at that.

"Actually," she said, her own reply coming out even slower and more softly than his, "so far, it's not exactly what I expected."

His expression changed not at all, but he asked, "How so?"

She shrugged, nudging back another strand of hair that blew into her face and pulling his jacket more snugly around herself. "Well, for one thing, Stephen's idea of orientation seems to be asking me a lot of questions about my old position at Barton Limited and dodging any questions *I* ask about my *new* position at OmniTech."

She waited for a smug *I told you so,* but Matthias's reply was instead a very careful, "I see."

Even though he didn't ask for more information, she found herself continuing anyway. "Orientation will be over after tomorrow, and I know almost nothing about Omni-Tech, save the history of the company and its mission statement and where its national and international offices are located and—" She halted abruptly. "Anything I could find out myself by an online search."

Matthias sipped his wine, but again said nothing, just waited for her to continue, should she want to. The sky behind him was smudged dark blue, the fat full moon hovering over his left shoulder. The only other light came from the candles flickering inside the hurricane globes on the tables, but it was enough to allow her to see his expression. Unfortunately, she couldn't tell by his expression what he was thinking, and that bothered her a lot. Not that she wanted to know what he thought about her situation with OmniTech, but because she wanted to know what he thought about *her.* If he considered her naive for not realizing what he had about Stephen DeGallo, or foolish for having disregarded his warning, or ridiculous for clinging to the idea that she had made the right choice.

Especially since she was no longer clinging to that idea. With every new meeting she had with Stephen, her suspicions about the man and his motives grew stronger. His having blown off their dinner meeting tonight—regardless of his reason for doing so—had only cemented her fear that what Matthias had told her was true. Stephen DeGallo had hired her because he'd hoped she would give him insight into Matthias's business. Which, of course, she would never do. Her job performance at Barton Limited was pertinent to Stephen only in so far as assuring him she had achieved enough experience to perform the job for which he had hired her, that her record was stellar, and that she was committed to her professional obligations. Period.

Now that he had realized she had no intention of playing corporate spy, he was no longer interested. She wouldn't be surprised if, before her alleged orientation even ended tomorrow afternoon, he manufactured some reason to let her go. Thanks to reorganization, the position for which he'd had her in mind was no longer viable. Or he'd discovered something in her work history that presented a conflict of interest. Oh, he'd find some way to make it sound plausible. He might even give her a generous severance package—though she doubted it. But there was certainly reason to believe her new position at OmniTech wouldn't be hers for long.

She looked at Matthias. "You were right," she said, forcing herself to admit the truth. "I think the only reason Stephen hired me was because he assumed I would share what I know about Barton Limited with him."

Matthias eyed her warily now. "Did he ask you about the Perkins contract?"

She shook her head. "Not specifically, no. Not yet, anyway. But he did ask an awful lot of questions about you and the company. I wouldn't be surprised if the particulars of the Perkins contract was next on his to-do list."

"And what did you tell him about Barton Limited?" Matthias asked, his voice revealing nothing of what he might be thinking about.

She smiled. "I told him about the history of the company and its mission statement and where its national and international offices are located. You know. Anything he could discover by doing an online search."

Matthias smiled back. "That's my girl."

Something about the way he said it, so soft and intimate, sent a ripple of awareness shimmying through her unlike anything she had ever felt before. The breeze chose that moment to pull another strand of hair from the knot at the back of her head and nudge it across her eyes. She started to reach up to brush it away, but Matthias intercepted her, dipping his index finger beneath the disobedient tresses and brushing them back from her forehead. Then he surprised her even more by moving his hand to the clip that held the mass of hair in place and pulling it free.

"You might as well just leave it loose," he told her as he completed the action. "The wind is only going to pick up as the evening goes on."

Which, Kendall thought, was all the more reason to keep her hair anchored. Matthias obviously thought differently. Because as her hair tumbled down around her shoulders, he dragged his fingers through it the way a stylist would, pushing it back over her shoulders, then forward again, then back, as if he wasn't sure how he liked it best. But where a stylist would keep his touches dispassionate and economical, Matthias took his time, stroking the straight, shoulder-length tresses again and again. Kendall finally had to reach up and circle his wrist with her fingers to stop him. When she did, he immediately halted, his gaze connecting fiercely with hers.

For a moment, neither of them spoke, neither of them moved, neither even seemed to breathe. Matthias dropped his gaze from Kendall's eyes to her mouth, then looked into her eyes again. She felt her lips part almost of their own volition, though whether it was because she intended to say something, or for another reason entirely, she wasn't sure. The moment stretched taut, and still neither spoke or moved. Then, for one scant, insane instant, it almost seemed as if he were dipping his head toward hers, tilting it slightly, as if he intended to…

Kiss her? Kendall thought frantically. Oh, surely not.

But her heart began to hammer in her chest all the same, and heat flared in her belly, and her pulse rate quickened, and her entire body caught fire, and then…and then…

And then Matthias suddenly, but gently, pulled his hand from her grasp and leaned back again, and the moment full of…whatever it had been full of…evaporated. He looked down at his glass and lifted it to his lips, filling his mouth with the dark red wine, savoring it for a moment before swallowing. Kendall was still too keyed up and confused by what she was feeling to say anything, so she watched him instead, noting how his strong throat worked over the swallow, feeling warmth spread through her belly as if she were the one who had drunk deeply from her glass.

When Matthias looked at her again, his expression was bland and unreadable, as if there had been nothing about the last few minutes that was any different from the millions of minutes that had preceded them. As if wanting to emphasize that, he asked a question guaranteed to dispel any strange sensations that might be lingering.

"So what do you plan to do about Stephen?"

Kendall wished she had an answer for all the questions—both spoken and unspoken—that had arisen this evening, but most especially for that one. Her future, at the moment, was shakier and more open than it had ever been before. And she wasn't the sort of person who found the unknown exciting. On the contrary, she couldn't function if she didn't have a thorough, well-thought-out plan. The only plan she had at the moment, though, was to have another sip of her wine. Which she did.

Then, "I don't know," she finally said. "I feel like Stephen hired me under false pretenses, and I don't want to work for OmniTech if that's the case. I'd like to be hired on the merit of my knowledge and potential, not because I might have juicy gossip."

"You could resign," Matthias said.

She studied him in silence for a moment, wondering why he'd made the suggestion he had. Was it because he wanted to be proven right? Or was he looking out for Kendall's best interests? Or was it simply because he wanted to stick it to Stephen DeGallo?

Not long ago, she would have assumed it was either the first or last of those reasons. Now, however, she couldn't help thinking maybe he really did want to help Kendall do what was best for herself.

"It will probably be a moot point," she said. "If he decides I'm not going to be beneficial to him in the way he first thought, I wouldn't be surprised if he manufactures some excuse to let me go."

She raised a shoulder and let it drop, hoping the half shrug hid the turmoil roiling inside her. What was weird was that the turmoil was less a result of the prospect of being unemployed, and more the result of the way Matthias continued to look at her.

He dropped his gaze into his glass again, swirling the dark wine around the sides of the bowl in thoughtful concentration. "Well, if you do decide to resign," he began, "or if Stephen is stupid enough to let you go, I have a position at Barton Limited that needs filling." He glanced up at Kendall again, fixing his gaze on hers. "If you think you'd be interested. You'd be perfect for it."

For some reason, his offer of her old job back didn't rankle her as much as it had before. Maybe because this time he wasn't being such an arrogant jackass about it. No, this time, his tone was solicitous, his body language inquisitive. This time, it was indeed an offer, not an order. But Kendall was no more interested in accepting it now than she had been before. She still wanted—needed—more than to be Matthias Barton's assistant. She was too smart and too ambitious, and she wanted to do more—with her life and herself.

"Matthias, I can't be your assistant anymore," she told him. "We've been through this. I need something that will challenge me to be the best that I can be."

"I'm not offering you your old job back," he told her. "I'm offering you a new one."

Kendall wasn't sure if she should be suspicious or not. Ultimately, she decided on being cautious. "What kind of position?"

He turned toward the deck railing and leaned over to

prop his arms on it, then gazed up at the moon as he spoke. "There's no title for it yet. But I'm getting ready to acquire a technology company that's been failing due to mismanagement and carelessness. I'm going to need someone to work side by side with me getting it whipped into shape."

Kendall told herself not to make anything of his body language—that he was looking at the moon and might be, figuratively anyway, offering her something that didn't exist—and consider what he was saying. "Tell me more about the company," she asked carefully.

He did, describing its rise and fall and the problems that had led to its faltering. She nodded as he spoke, turning over in her mind the possibilities and potential, and the various avenues they could take to put the company back on its feet. When Matthias finished, she asked, "What's the salary and benefits for this position?"

"Quadruple what you made as my assistant," he told her.

Her eyebrows shot up at that. That was two times more than the position at OmniTech.

"Full medical and dental," he added, "contributions to an IRA and 401(k). And, if you want, we can talk stock options."

"I want," she said readily.

By now he had straightened again and was lifting his glass to his mouth. But he stopped so abruptly when Kendall said what she did that some of the ruby wine spilled over onto his hand. Hastily, he took the glass in his other hand and tried to shake the wine from his fingers, then looked around for something to wipe the rest of it off. Kendall, always prepared, pulled a clean handkerchief from her trouser pocket and handed it to him. He set his glass down, wiped his hand clean, then, out of habit, she guessed, deftly tucked the scrap of cotton into his own pocket.

When he looked at her again, he seemed agitated about something. But all he said was, "Then let's talk."

Kendall met his gaze levelly. "Okay. I'm listening."

Seven

The coffee shop where Stephen had scheduled their "morning meeting," which he'd deemed "unavoidable" on a Saturday because Kendall's "orientation" had "fallen behind" this week—yeah, Stephen, since some people blew off "essential dinner meetings" to instead chase after breathtaking blondes—was located a couple of blocks away from the inn. But it was every bit as quaint and charming. Even though it was early—and also *Saturday,* in case Kendall hadn't mentioned that part—there were a number of people out and about, ambling down the walkways, waiting for the shops to open and sipping their morning lattes. But, unlike Kendall, who was dressed in her usual business trousers and shirt—in this case beige for the former and cream for the latter—everyone else sported vacation clothes, mostly shorts and T-shirts or loose cotton dresses coupled with sneakers or sandals. Because they, unlike Kendall, didn't have to work today. On account of it was Saturday. In case she hadn't mentioned that part.

She looked longingly down at her pointy-toed, three-inch ivory pumps, then at the beat-up Birkenstock sandals on a woman passing by, and she sighed. Someday, she thought, she was going to be the big cheese at her own successful corporation. And the first policy she planned to put in place was a Casual Friday. Then she'd add a Casual Thursday. And a Casual Wednesday, Tuesday and Monday, too. And then she'd decree that no work ever took place on the weekend.

She knew her business philosophy was an unconventional one. Most corporate big shots had gotten where they were by working overtime, downtime, double time and time and a half. She knew it was traditional to keep employees toeing a conservative line in all things business-related. And she knew power suits made a more imposing impression than well, beat-up Birkenstock sandals. But she also knew that the *real* secret to success was loving what you did for a living.

And Kendall loved big business. She just wasn't that crazy about all its trappings. She didn't think the image was as important as other people did. As far as she was concerned, actions spoke louder than power suits. She would rather have a force of casually dressed, happy, productive employees working for her than she would a bunch of polished corporate drones. It wasn't enough to be smart and energetic in today's business world. Creativity was absolutely essential. And creative people were *not* a suit-wearing tribe. So Kendall was going to cut her workforce a little slack.

She toed off one pointy-toed high heel and let it drop to the sidewalk. And she would cut herself some slack, too.

Matthias hadn't had a title or description yet for the job he'd offered her, but she wasn't worried. No matter what it was, she would do it well. She would play by his rules for as long as it took to get the business off the ground, and then she would tailor it to her policies and procedures and put her own personal stamp on it. Matthias, for all his conservative bluster, had always been an open-minded and farsighted businessman. It was part of what had made him so successful. He would allow—no, expect—Kendall to be her own woman with whatever he gave her to direct. And she couldn't wait to get started.

As if cued by the thought, Stephen DeGallo turned the corner just then, catching Kendall's eye and raising a hand in greeting. He was having a Casual Saturday, she noticed, wearing faded jeans with a brightly patterned tiki shirt and, she noted with some wistfulness, sandals.

"You didn't have to dress for work," he said by way of a greeting as he sat down across from her.

Kendall eyed him with what she hoped looked like terseness, since terse was suddenly how she felt. "Well, since we're *supposed* to be *working*," she said meaningfully, "I dressed for work."

"But it's Saturday," he said with a smile. Then he looked past her and waved to catch a waiter's attention. "You don't have to be all buttoned-up and battened down. Live a little."

Yeah, like you did last night, huh, Stephen? Kendall had to bite her lip to keep the words from tumbling out. Instead, she was the picture of politeness when she asked, "What happened to you last night?"

He looked genuinely puzzled. "Last night?"

She nodded. "We were supposed to have a dinner

meeting. To discuss which OmniTech health-care plan would be best for me."

He shook his head. "No, we're doing that this afternoon."

Kendall turned her head and tugged lightly on an earring. "No, it was supposed to be last night, Stephen. In fact, when we parted ways yesterday afternoon after our session on the new sweetheart agreement you made with one of the subsidiaries I'd be working with, you distinctly said, 'I'll see you at six-thirty.' But I waited twenty minutes, and you never showed."

He looked a little taken aback, presumably by her tone, which, she had to admit, wasn't the sort of voice one normally used with an employer. Particularly a brand-new one. No, it was more the tone of voice one used with a dog who had just peed on the carpet.

His eyes went flinty. Then he smiled, a gesture that fell well short of making him look happy. "I meant six-thirty *tonight*," he said.

"No, you meant Friday," she countered with all confidence. "I don't make mistakes like that."

"Neither do I."

"You did last night," Kendall told him pointedly. "Or maybe you just found yourself…preoccupied by a better prospect. A blond prospect."

His smile disappeared, and his eyes hardened even more. "What I do in my private time is none of your business, Kendall."

"It is if it affects my job."

He expelled a soft sound of undisguised contempt. "What job?" he demanded. "You're fired, effective immediately."

Not that Kendall minded, since it would save her the trouble of resigning and get her out of OmniTech more quickly, but she felt compelled to ask, "On what grounds?" Mostly because she didn't want to leave any loose threads hanging. And, okay, also because she wanted to goad him.

"What grounds?" he asked incredulously. "How about insubordination for starters? You're also completely unsuited to the position I hired you for."

Ridiculous, she thought. She was perfect for the job of vice president. And in a few years, once she got her legs, she'd be perfect for the job of CEO. After that, she wasn't sure, but she might take over the universe. At the moment, she felt perfectly capable—she was that confident of her abilities.

Evidently, Stephen didn't have such an inflated opinion of her, however, because he continued, "You're also withdrawn and uncooperative, and you're *not* a team player."

Kendall nodded at this. By his definition of those words, he was right, and she told him so. "In other words, I'm ethical to the point that I won't roll over on my former employer and tell you all his best-kept business secrets."

Stephen's mouth shut tight at that, but he said nothing.

"That's why you hired me, isn't it, Stephen? Because you thought I'd speak freely about Matthias Barton. You thought I'd make you privy to all his personal quirks and habits and reveal the details of any of his dealings that I might have been in on."

For a moment, Stephen said nothing. Then he sneered at her and said, "As if Matthias Barton would allow his *secretary* to be in on any of his dealings. I don't know what I was thinking to assume a nobody like you would have any insight into a rival corporation."

Kendall smiled sweetly. "For one thing, Stephen, secretaries are the backbone of any good business. They're not nobodies. For another thing, you're wrong. I know more about Matthias's business than Matthias does. He'd tell you himself he couldn't operate without me. So much so, that he's offered me a job. An executive position," she added confidently, even though she was confident of no such thing. Matthias had made clear that the job—whatever it was—*was* important. Essential. Valuable. And it was hers, the moment she was free of Stephen DeGallo.

Which was going to happen more quickly than she initially thought.

"You can't fire me, Stephen," she told him as she stood. "I quit." Much better than resigning, she thought. As she slung her purse over her shoulder, she added, "Thanks for the coffee. And the reality check. I assure you both were *much* appreciated."

And then she turned and strode confidently down the sidewalk, back toward the Timber Lake Inn. She had an unexpected day off, she thought with a smile. Well, okay, maybe not all *that* unexpected. She'd planned to tell Stephen this morning that she wouldn't be coming to work for OmniTech, and she'd been fairly sure he would terminate her on the spot. She'd just thought it would go a little more smoothly, that was all. She truly hadn't meant for things to end as abruptly as they had, or with as much chilliness.

But Stephen *had* deliberately skipped their meeting last night, something that had illustrated his disregard for her as both a person and an employee. And he *had* hired her under false pretenses to begin with. It hadn't exactly been a situation that lent itself to air kisses and toodle-oos. If she'd been too pushy or blunt—

Her steps slowed and her back straightened. She smiled. If she'd been too pushy and blunt, then it just meant she was a solid businesswoman. Any man who'd been pushy and blunt would have been applauded and called assertive and candid. So she was going to applaud herself, too.

Boy, what a couple of days for changes and epiphanies, Kendall thought. So far, she'd accepted a new power job, resigned from an old dubious job, told her sleazy ex-employer what a sleazy ex-employer he was, discovered what an assertive businesswoman *she* was, and now she could go back to her hotel and—

She halted in her tracks, her confidence fleeing completely. Because she realized then that her hotel wasn't her hotel anymore. Stephen DeGallo wasn't going to foot the bill for her room now that she wasn't in his employ. And he'd probably cancel her return ticket to San Francisco, not to mention the rental car. And with it being the peak of the summer tourist season, finding a flight *or* car right away might prove to be a bit daunting.

She was going to have to check out of the Timber Lake Inn. She had nowhere else to go and no way to get there.

She sighed and gave her forehead a good mental smack. So much for being the assertive, candid businesswoman who could take over the universe at will. In a matter of hours, Kendall was going to be living on the streets.

Matthias was reading a political thriller he'd found in one of the spare bedrooms when he heard the front doorbell ring. He set it facedown on the sofa and went to answer, automatically brushing the dust from his jeans and pin-striped, untucked oxford, even though the house wasn't old enough to have accumulated any dust, and even though, if it did, Mandy or Mindy or Maureen or whatever the hell the caretaker's name was would make quick work of it.

Mary, he remembered as he stepped into the foyer.

Mary, who had seemed strangely familiar for some reason, even though, at the moment, Matthias couldn't even remember what she looked like. For all he knew, it was she who was at the front door right now. He hadn't seen her since the day of his arrival. Not that he'd expected to. He wasn't even sure if she lived here in Hunter's Landing. But something about her had made him think she had a vested interest in the house and would check on it from time to time to make sure none of the Seven Samurai was trashing the place with wild parties and wilder behavior.

Even though the days of their trashing anything—like the furniture they'd nailed to the ceiling in the dorm their freshman year—had long since passed. These days the Seven Samurai, in addition to no longer being seven, were no longer the soldier of fortune types they'd fancied themselves when they'd assumed the nickname for the group as young men. They'd all made their fortunes in one way or another, and now they were all too busy trying to protect those fortunes and make them grow larger to have time for wild parties and wilder behavior.

And why that realization made Matthias's mouth turn down in consternation, he couldn't have said.

But his mouth turned up again when he opened the front door, and his step felt lighter—even if he was standing still—when he saw that it wasn't the caretaker who stood on the other side, but Kendall.

Her appearance surprised him. Not so much her appearance on his doorstep, but rather her *appearance* on his doorstep. She was dressed in the kind of thing he'd never seen her wear before—blue jeans that were faded to the point of being torn in places, and a pale lavender T-shirt that was brief enough to allow a glimpse of creamy flesh between its hem and the waistband of her jeans. Even more surprising than Kendall's appearance, however, was her luggage's appearance, since, by virtue of its appearance, it was apparent that it would be visiting, too. It was scattered about her feet in a way that made it look as if she'd just dropped it there in frustration before ringing the bell.

She sounded frustrated, too, when she said, by way of a greeting, "Can I ask you a favor?"

Matthias tried to tear his gaze away from that very alluring strip of naked flesh…and failed miserably. Still gazing at the hem of her shirt, he mentally willed it to leap up again the way it had—all too briefly—when she'd shoved her hands into her back pockets. And somehow he conjured the presence of mind to reply to her question. Unfortunately, that reply was a very distracted, "Huh?"

She shifted her weight from one foot to the other, an action which, although not the one he was mentally willing her to complete, nevertheless had the desired result. For another scant second, that band of naked flesh widened, causing the heavens to open up and a chorus of angels to sing, "Hallelujah, hoo-ah."

"Can I ask you a favor?" Kendall said again.

But she said it without moving her body, unfortunately, so her shirt stayed in place. Then again, that at least allowed Matthias to be coherent enough to answer her question this time. Kind of. At least he got out an "Mmm-hmm" that sounded vaguely affirmative in nature. The problem was, by then, he couldn't remember what the question was that he was answering.

His reply seemed to be fine for Kendall, though, because

she continued, "Would it be possible for me to crash here for a couple of days?"

The question was unexpected enough to command a much larger chunk of his attention. So unexpected, in fact, that he wouldn't have been more surprised if Kendall had just asked him if it would be possible for him to pull the Empire State Building out of his pocket. Then again, the way he was beginning to feel watching the comings and goings of her shirttail, that might not be such an unreasonable request in a few more minutes.

He managed to cover his reaction well, though—he hoped. And through some herculean effort, he also managed to bring his gaze back up to her face. "Problems at the inn?" he asked.

She shook her head. "Problems at OmniTech."

Hey, that sounded promising, he thought. "What kind of problems?"

"I sort of quit. Effective immediately."

He was wrong. That wasn't promising. It was perfect.

Before he could say anything more, she hurried on, "But I sort of didn't take into consideration until too late the fact that, by quitting, I was also ending any reason for Stephen to pay my hotel bill. In the time it took me to walk from the café where we had our morning meeting back to my room, the lock had already been changed on my door. The only reason I was able to get my stuff out was because housekeeping showed up, and the housekeeper was nice enough to let me change my clothes and pack while she was in there cleaning."

Thank God for small favors, Matthias thought. Inescapably, his gaze had dropped to her midsection again when he'd noticed—how could he miss it?—that as Kendall had spoken, she had used a lot of hand gestures, and the hem of her little T-shirt rose and fell with every one, once even high enough to allow him a peek at a truly spectacular navel. So spectacular, in fact, that he enjoyed a quick impression of dragging a line of openmouthed kisses across her flat abdomen before dipping his tongue into the elegant little cleft for a taste....

Until he remembered it was Kendall's navel he was tasting in his fantasy. Kendall, he reminded himself emphatically. This was *Kendall* he was thinking about, for God's sake. *Kendall*'s midsection. And *Kendall*'s navel. All of them were strictly off-limits because... Because... Because...

Well, because she was Kendall, Matthias told himself. That was why. A trusted employee. A trusted employee he didn't want to compromise with some kind of messy workplace involvement. A trusted employee with an excellent work record. A trusted employee with strong business ethics and sound professional judgment.

A trusted employee with silky dark blond hair that was tumbling free around her shoulders in a way that made him want to reach out and touch it. A trusted employee with enormous green eyes a man could drown in. A trusted employee with a luscious navel he really, really wanted to taste.

"So if the offer of that new position is still open," his luscious, tasty, trusted employee said now, "I'd like to come back to work for you."

The word that should have registered most in that sentence was *work*. But Matthias's brain had gotten so caught up on *position* that it never quite made the leap to *work*. And the position that came to mind just then, although it definitely involved Kendall, had absolutely nothing to do with work. Well, okay, maybe there would have to be a little work involved—it was kind of an unusual position—but that work would have definitely been a labor of lo—

Lust, he hastily corrected himself. A labor of lust.

"Matthias?"

His name, spoken in her voice, a voice so rife with concern, made him push the thoughts out of his head completely. "What?" he asked.

She eyed him curiously. "Is everything…okay?"

He nodded. "Yeah, fine," he said with some distraction. "I was reading when you rang the bell, and I guess my mind just hasn't caught up with the rest of me."

Actually, that wasn't true, he knew. His mind had not only caught up, it had raced right past him and was now in an entirely different time zone. The Navel Zone. Where time moved at a totally different pace than it did in Lake Tahoe.

"So is it okay if I crash here for a couple of days?" she asked again. "I had to change my flight back to San Francisco, and I couldn't get one out until Monday. I tried to find a room at another hotel, but all the good ones are booked solid, and—"

"It's fine, Kendall," he interrupted her. "Of course you can stay here. There's plenty of room."

Though the minute he said that, somehow, for some reason, the huge lodge suddenly felt very crowded.

"Thanks," she said, breathing a sigh of unmistakable relief.

She bent to retrieve her bags, but Matthias intercepted her, scooping up all three before she had the chance. When he looked at her again, he could tell she was surprised by the gesture. Or maybe it was just that she was usually the one doing things for him, not the other way around.

It hit Matthias then, like a two-by-four to the back of

the head, how very true that was. When she was working for him, Kendall had done so many things for him to keep him on track. Granted, that was what he paid her for, but still. What had he ever done for her in return, other than pay her wages and benefits? Yeah, there had been the Godiva chocolates for her birthday every year and the gourmet food baskets every Christmas. But those had been things he'd had his secretary order for her—and he hadn't even picked them out himself.

Then again, Kendall had never seemed to expect anything more, he told himself. Then again—again—that was no excuse for not showing his appreciation more often.

Note to self, Barton. Show Kendall a little appreciation this time around. As a reluctant afterthought, he made himself add, *And appreciate something* besides *her navel.*

It would be a tough job, but he was pretty sure he could do it.

She followed him up to the second floor where Matthias had a choice of guest rooms in which to house her. Not asking himself why he did it, he made his way immediately to one near the master bedroom, where he was sleeping himself. The room was furnished in varying shades of green and gold, the stout four-poster covered with a light-weight patchwork quilt, the hardwood floors broken up here and there with rag rugs. It was what Matthias had come to think of as the Rustic Room. Though it was every bit as luxurious as the rest of the house. The wide windows opened onto a thick patch of pine trees, beyond which was a spectacular view with a finger of lake on one side. At night, he thought, she could do what he'd been doing—lie in bed and listen to the wind gliding through the trees, and wait for the melancholy hoot-hoot-hoot of a solitary owl.

Hey, it wasn't as if there was much else to do around the lodge at night. At least, there hadn't been before.

"Why don't you stay more than a couple of days?" he asked impulsively as he tossed Kendall's bags onto the bed.

When he turned, he saw that she had stopped in the doorway, and she didn't look as if she planned on coming in anytime soon.

"I mean, you quit OmniTech," he pointed out unnecessarily, "and I'm not going to be coming back to San Francisco for a few more weeks. I don't expect you to report to the office before I get back myself. When was the last time you took a vacation?"

She threw him a funny look. "I just had one. Two weeks between leaving Barton Limited and going to work for OmniTech."

"Oh. Right. Well, what did you do during those two weeks?" he asked. "I bet you didn't spend them out of town, did you?"

"No," she admitted. "I did some work around my condo that I'd been putting off for a while."

"Well, there you go," Matthias said. "You need a vacation. I have a vacation home. At least for a few more weeks."

She crossed her arms over her midsection and dropped her weight to one foot. "And besides," she said, "you brought a lot of work with you from the office, and you could use someone to help out with it while you're here. Right?"

He gaped at her, shocked that she could think such a thing of him. What shocked him even more was that what she'd just accused him of had never once crossed his mind. "Of course not," he denied. "Yeah, I brought work with me, but I'm getting it done just fine by myself."

Well, except for how his laptop kept eating his files and

how he couldn't figure out how to open Excel and how every time he tried to send e-mail on the desktop in the office upstairs, a box kept popping up with all kinds of weird symbols in it that he was reasonably certain were the equivalent of digital profanity. Really bad digital profanity, too. Other than that, everything was fine.

She smiled at him in a way that made him think she knew exactly what kind of problems he was having. Then she surprised him by saying, "Okay, I'll stay a couple more days. It is a beautiful place. And I could use some downtime."

Matthias wasn't sure what to make of the ripple of pleasure that wound through him at her acceptance of his invitation. So he decided not to question it. In fact, he decided not to think about it at all. Because Kendall's smile grew broader then, and she crossed her arms in a way that made her little T-shirt ride up on her torso again, giving him another delicious glimpse at that navel. The ripple of pleasure turned into a raging tsunami at that, and he was suddenly overcome by the absolute conviction that his life would never get better than it was in that moment, standing in the same room with Kendall and her navel, knowing she would be around for a few more days.

But he was wrong. Because what she said to him after that multiplied his pleasure tenfold and nearly sent his body into paroxysms of ecstasy.

Because what she said then was, "You know, I need to run into town to pick up a few things. Why don't we look for a new BlackBerry for you while we're there? And I'll get it all nice and programmed for you, just the way you like it."

That was when Matthias knew, without doubt, that Kendall Scarborough was the only woman in the world who would ever be able to make him happy.

"But, Matthias," she added, more soberly this time, "you have to promise me you won't contact that guy in Nigeria or the woman with the Web cam."

He narrowed his eyes in confusion. "Why not?"

"Just don't. Trust me."

Strangely, he realized he already did. Implicitly. Though, thinking back on their history together, maybe that wasn't so strange after all. What was strange was that, suddenly, for some reason, he realized he also trusted Kendall in ways that went beyond the professional. But what was strangest of all was that he found himself wanting her to trust him, too. In ways that had nothing to do with the professional.

"C'mon," she said. "You'll have to drive. Let's pick up some groceries, too. I'm tired of hotel food and carryout. Let's cook tonight."

Eight

They weren't able to find a BlackBerry for Matthias in tiny Hunter's Landing. They did lots of other things there— shared a banana split at the ice-cream parlor, played air hockey at the arcade, selected fresh produce at the farmer's market and enjoyed a late-afternoon beer at the pub—but the little community was fresh out of sophisticated gadgetry by the time they arrived. Interestingly, Matthias wasn't even halfway through the banana split when he forgot all about it. And when Kendall made mention of it again halfway through the afternoon beer, he had to take a minute to remember that, oh, yeah, that was one of the reasons they'd gone into town, wasn't it? Because by then, he was enjoying himself so much with Kendall that he couldn't even remember why he'd wanted a BlackBerry in the first place.

Nor could he remember the last time he'd played air

hockey. Probably because he had played with Luke, and it had probably been one of those death matches the two of them never seemed able to avoid. With Kendall, they hadn't even kept score. Matthias couldn't remember the last time he'd had a banana split, either, and he'd certainly never shared one before, thanks to the I-got-mine mentality he'd grown up with under his father's misguided tutelage. Even the afternoon beer was unusual for Matthias. He never took time out of his day to engage in things that had no purpose other than to make the day a little nicer.

And the thing was, the day would have been nicer even without all those things, simply because Kendall was a part of it.

Why had he never realized before how much he liked having her around? he wondered as they drove back to the lodge, chatting amiably the whole way. She'd worked for him for five years—five years—and not once had it occurred to him that the reason his life was as good as it was was due in large part to Kendall's simple presence in it. All that time, he'd thought he valued her for her efficiency and organizational skills. It was only after she'd left that he'd realized she'd brought so much more to his life.

He *liked* Kendall. He liked her a lot. Not just as an employee, but as a person. As a friend. As a companion. The two of them had an easy camaraderie with each other after all these years that he hadn't even realized had developed. A give and take, an ebb and flow, an itch and scratch that was as well orchestrated and choreographed as a Broadway show. And now he understood that that camaraderie transcended their working relationship. Today, they'd enjoyed an ease of conversation Matthias didn't share with people he'd known twice as long as Kendall.

And last night, out on the deck with the telescope… That had been one of the most enjoyable evenings he'd ever had.

Even as they unpacked and put away their groceries, they spoke easily and moved in concert with each other as if they did this all the time. The preparation of dinner, too, was another perfectly executed team effort, as was the cleaning up afterward. As Matthias opened a second bottle of wine, Kendall reached into the cupboard for two fresh glasses. As he poured, she dimmed the lights, and, together, they retreated to the lodge's lush living room.

The sun was setting over the mountains, leaving the lake midnight-blue and smooth as silk. Matthias watched Kendall head for a lamp, then hesitate before turning it on. He understood. The lighting outside this time of evening was just too beautiful not to appreciate it. When she moved to the massive windows to look out on the vista, he joined her. But it wasn't the lake and mountains that drew his eye. It was Kendall's expression as she looked at them, all soft and mellow and contented. The way he felt himself.

"This place is truly gorgeous," she said.

He nodded, still looking at her. "Gorgeous," he echoed.

"I can't believe your friend had it built and isn't able to be here to enjoy it."

Matthias sighed, turning to look out at the view now. "Oh, I imagine Hunter's enjoying it, wherever he is. I think he's enjoying seeing the effect the place has on all of us. Somehow he knew all those years ago what kind of men the Seven Samurai would turn out to be."

"And what kind of men did you all turn out to be?" she asked.

Matthias inhaled a deep breath and let it out slowly. "Men who are too busy building our empires to remember why we wanted to build them in the first place. Men who work so hard, we've forgotten how to live."

But he realized as he said it that that hadn't been true of him today. Today, Matthias had forgotten all about work. Today, he'd forgotten all about empires. Today, he'd thought only about Kendall. And today, more than any other day of his life, he had *lived.* He'd lived, and he'd enjoyed living. He'd enjoyed it a lot. More, even, than work.

From the corner of his eye, he saw Kendall turn toward him, but he continued to gaze out the window, looking for…something. He wasn't sure what.

"You miss him, don't you?" she said softly.

He nodded. "It happened so quickly. By the time the doctors found the cancer, it was too late to do anything to save him."

"It must have been hard on you and your other friends."

Hard wasn't the word, Matthias thought. "Devastating," he said instead. "It tore us apart, in more ways than one. Hunter was the glue that kept us together. I think that was his gift—that he knew people. Knew what made them tick. Knew what made them behave the way they did. I mean, look at what he did for me and Luke."

"What?" Kendall asked. "I thought you guys didn't get along."

"We don't. Didn't," he immediately corrected himself. "But in college, we did. Somehow Hunter made us see past all the animosity and one-upmanship our father generated in us. Luke and I were friends—real friends—in college. But after Hunter died…"

He didn't continue. What had happened to Matthias and Luke was complicated and unsettled, and he didn't want to talk about anything complicated or unsettling tonight.

So he only said, "We all drifted apart after college. We all did well, at least professionally, but we lost each other."

He did turn to look at Kendall then. "Until now," he said, smiling. "This lodge, Hunter bringing us all here, it's getting us together again. There's going to be a reunion in September, once Jack has fulfilled his obligation to spend the month here." Although he had no idea what possessed him to do it, Matthias added, "Would you like to come back with me for that?"

Her eyes widened in surprise at the invitation. And truth be told, Matthias was surprised he'd extended it. But once said, it seemed perfectly natural. Perfectly normal. Something about having Kendall there with the friends from his past—the people who had always been more important to Matthias than anyone else—felt right.

She nodded slowly, smiling. "I'd love to come," she said. "It would be nice to meet all your old friends. And your brother, too."

Matthias wasn't sure why he did what he did next. Something about the moment, about the lodge, about the woman, just made it feel right. Dipping his head toward Kendall's, he covered her mouth with his and kissed her.

Lightly at first, gently, a part of him fearing she might pull away. But she didn't pull away. She tilted her head to the side a little, to make it easier for him, and then she kissed him back. Slowly, sweetly, almost as if she'd been expecting it, and as if she wondered what had taken him so long.

Kendall wasn't sure when the line between her and Matthias disappeared, whether it had happened just now, or during the banana split, or when she finally quit, or if it had happened years ago at a point she didn't even notice.

But when he kissed her, the way he did, she knew that line would never be back again. And then she stopped thinking about any of that, because the feelings blooming inside her, and the sensations twining through her body, were just too delicious to ignore. All she knew was that, one minute, Matthias had been looking out the window and talking about Hunter, and the next, he was surrounding her.

As he kissed her, he plucked her wineglass from her hand, and she followed his mouth with hers as he bent slightly to place both their glasses on an end table beside them. Then they were both straightening again, and he was pulling her into his arms completely, opening his mouth over hers now, tasting her deeply. She felt his hands on her back, first skimming along her spine, then curling around over her nape, then tangling in her hair. Instinctively, she raised her own hands to explore him, too, touching his rough face, his hard shoulders, his silky hair, savoring the different textures and reveling in the heat, the strength, the power she encountered beneath her fingertips.

He towered over her, seeming to touch her everywhere. Every time she inhaled, she filled her lungs with the scent of him and her mouth with the taste of him. His heart thundered against her own, the rapid beating of both mixing and mingling, until she wasn't sure which was his and which was hers. Their breathing, too, grew fierce and ragged as the kiss intensified, until Kendall felt as though their breath had also joined and become one.

One hand still tangled in her hair, he moved the other to her hip, inching it slowly downward to curve over her fanny, pushing her body forward into his. Kendall responded instinctively, rubbing her pelvis against his, sinuously, seductively, loving his growl of satisfaction in response. He moved his hand higher again, bunching the fabric of her shirt in his fist and pushing upward. She felt the cool kiss of air on her heated back with every new bit of flesh he exposed. When his fingers had crept high enough for him to realize she wasn't wearing a bra, he groaned again, splaying his fingers wide over her naked skin before deepening the kiss even more.

Thinking turnabout was fair play, Kendall dipped her hand under the hem of his shirt, too, steering her fingers over the silky swell of muscle and sinew that crisscrossed his back. Then she brought her hand forward, caressing the springy hair of his chest and the taut musculature of his torso. He was hard in all the places she was soft, angled in all the places she was curved, rough in all the places she was smooth. But his skin was as hot as hers was, and his heart beat every bit as rapidly. Their differences complemented each other, but their similarities were what brought them together. They wanted each other equally. That was enough.

She felt his hand move to her waist then, squeezing between their bodies long enough to deftly flick open the fly of her jeans and tug the zipper down. Then he was at her back again, tucking his hand into the soft denim and under the fabric of her panties, curving over her bare flesh, stroking her sensitive skin again and again and again. Heat and dampness bloomed between her legs as he stroked her, then exploded when he dipped one confident finger into the delicate cleft of her behind.

"Oh," she murmured against his mouth. "Oh, Matthias…"

But he covered her mouth again before she could say more. Not that she really knew what else she wanted to say. At the moment, she only wanted to do. Do things to and with him, and have things done to her in return.

Things she had never even allowed herself to dream about, things that felt so natural, so right, now. He seemed to realize that, because he filled her mouth with his tongue, then palmed and kneaded her tender flesh, pushing her harder against his ripening erection with every stroke.

No longer content not to be able to touch him, she wedged her hand between their bodies to cup the full length of him in her palm. He murmured a satisfied sound in response and moved his hips against her hand, silently encouraging her to take her strokes farther still. Eagerly, she unfastened and opened his jeans, too, dipping her hand inside to cover him more intimately. Bare skin on bare skin, the way he was touching her. He felt so big, so powerful, so masterful in her hand, so hot, so hard, so smooth.

For long moments, they only kissed and touched each other, their pulse rates and respiration multiplying with every one that passed. When they finally started moving— slowly, deliberately, carefully—Kendall wasn't sure if it was she or Matthias who was responsible. Somehow, though, they kissed and touched and danced their way across the living room, through the door and up the stairs, until they stood in the upstairs hallway, surrounded by bedrooms. Surrounded by choices.

Only then did Matthias pull back, as if he wanted to give her time to make whatever choice she was going to make. His hesitation surprised her. Usually, he was a man who, when he wanted something, did whatever he had to do to get it. No cajoling, no seducing, no petitioning, only full-on frontal attack, damn the torpedoes or anything that got in his way. She wouldn't have been surprised if he had swept her up at the bottom of the stairs the way Rhett had Scarlett, and carried her to his room to ravish her. Especially since she'd made it clear how very much she wanted to be ravished.

Evidently, though, Matthias pursued his personal affairs with more finesse than he did his professional ones. And for some reason, realizing that just made Kendall that much more certain that allowing this next step between them, however suddenly it had come—though, somehow, it didn't feel that sudden at all—was the right thing to do.

When she said nothing to object to what he was so clearly asking her, he did take the initiative, weaving his fingers through hers and guiding her to the master bedroom. Once inside, he slipped an arm around her waist and pushed her hair aside, bending his head to place a soft, chaste kiss on her nape that, ironically, was infinitely more arousing than all the desperate hungry ones put together. He pulled her body back against his, his hard member surging against her backside, something that shot heat through her entire body. When he nuzzled the curve where her neck joined her shoulder, Kendall tilted her head to facilitate his action, then reached behind herself with both hands to thread her fingers through his hair. She purposely put herself in a vulnerable position, knowing Matthias would take advantage, which he did, covering her breasts with both hands.

As he dragged his mouth along the sensitive flesh of her neck and shoulder, he gently kneaded her breasts through the fabric of her T-shirt, bringing a sigh of pleasure from Kendall. Then he dropped his hands to the hem of the shirt and tugged it up, up, up, pulling it over her head and tossing it to the floor. Then his hands were on her bare breasts, his hot palms squeezing and stroking and caressing. As he rolled one nipple under his thumb, his other hand scooted lower, down along the bare skin of her torso, his middle finger dipping into her navel as it passed. Then Matthias pushed his hand into her panties, finding the hot damp center of her and burying his fingers in the swollen folds of flesh.

She gasped at the sensation that shot through her then, her fingers convulsing in his hair. Kneading her breast with one hand, he stroked her damp flesh with the other—long, thorough, leisurely strokes that pushed her to the brink of insanity. Her body stilled as he touched her, her breathing the only sound in the room. Little by little, he hastened his pace, moving his hand backward and forward, left to right, drawing circles and spirals until finally he touched her in that one place, with that one finger, in a way that made her shatter. Kendall was rocked by an orgasm that came out of nowhere, seizing her body and sending a crash of heat shuddering through her.

For a moment, it felt as if time had stopped, as if she would exist forever in some suspended pinnacle of emotion, her body fused to Matthias's, her heart and lungs racing alongside his. Then the moment dissolved, and so did she, and she spun around to just kiss him and kiss him and kiss him.

Somehow, they managed to undress each other without ever losing physical contact, dropping clothes left and right, leaving them where they lay. On their way to the bed, Matthias slowed long enough to light a trio of candles on the mantelpiece, something that bathed the room in the golden glow of light. They paused by the big sleigh bed, the candlelight limning everything in gold. Kendall's heart pounded faster as she took in the sight that was Matthias. Strangely, he seemed even bigger when he was naked, his broad shoulders and strong arms curved with muscle, his flat chest and torso corded with more beneath the dark hair she found so erotic.

He settled both hands on her hips as she curled her fingers over his shoulders, then sat on the edge of the bed and pulled her into his lap, facing him, her legs straddling his. Roping an arm around her waist, he kissed her again, the way he had before, hungry and urgent and deep. She moved her hand to the hard head of his shaft, palming him, then began to stroke him, leisurely, methodically, as she kissed him back. Matthias curled his hands over her fanny, matching his caresses to hers and mimicking both in the movement of his tongue inside her mouth.

He turned their bodies so that they were lying on the bed crossways, Kendall on her back and he by her side, with one heavy leg draped over both of hers and an arm thrown across her breasts. He kissed her jaw, her cheek, her temple, her forehead, then moved down to her throat, her collar-bone and her breast. There, he took his time, flattening his tongue over her nipple before drawing it into his mouth, confidently and completely. He covered her other breast with his hand, catching her nipple between the V of his index and middle fingers, squeezing gently and generating more fire inside her. Wanting more, she spread her legs and rubbed herself against his thigh, gasping at the new sensations that shot through her.

Matthias seemed to understand her needs, because after a few more dizzying flicks of his tongue against the lower curve of her breast, he moved downward again, tasting her navel this time as he passed and kissing the skin beneath. Then he was going lower still, pushing open Kendall's legs to duck his head between them, running his tongue over the warm damp folds without a single hesitation. He lapped leisurely with the flat of his tongue, then drew generous circles with the tip. Pushing his hands beneath her fanny he lifted her higher, parting her with his thumbs so that he could penetrate her with his tongue, again and again and again. Then he was penetrating her with his finger, too, deeper now, slower, more thoroughly.

Ripples of pleasure began to purl through Kendall again, starting low in her belly and echoing outward, until her body was trembling with the beginning of a second climax. Seeming to sense how close she was, Matthias moved his body again, this time kneeling before her. He parted her legs and, grasping an ankle in each hand, pulled her toward himself to bury himself inside her—deep, *deep* inside her. Hooking her legs over his shoulders, he lowered his body over hers, braced both elbows on the mattress on each side of her and thrust himself forward even deeper. Again and again, he bucked his hips against hers, going deeper with each new penetration, opening Kendall wider to receive him. She wrapped her fingers tight around his steely biceps as he thrust harder, taking him as deeply as she could, until finally, finally, they both cried out with the explosive responses that rocked them.

For one long moment, they clung to each other, his body shuddering in the last of its release, hers quaking with the remnants of her climax. Then Matthias was relaxing, falling to the bed beside Kendall, one hand draped over her waist, the other arcing over her head.

It was then that Kendall's confidence about what she had allowed to happen between them began to slip. Because she realized then that what she had thought was a crush on her boss was so much more. And although Matthias had certainly mellowed during his time at the lodge, to the point where he no longer seemed consumed by his work, he'd offered no indication that he considered anything else more important. Maybe he wasn't married to his business anymore. Maybe. But could he—would he—ever join himself to something, someone, else?

Kendall woke slowly, not sure at first where she was. The sun wasn't up yet, but there was an indistinct golden glow dancing at the foot of her bed whose origin she couldn't quite figure out, so groggy was she from sleep. She felt blissfully happy for no reason she could name and snuggled more deeply into the covers.

Why was her bed so much more comfortable than usual? she wondered blearily as she pulled the covers higher. So much warmer? So much more welcome? And why did she want nothing more than to stay here like this forever? Usually, the moment she awoke, she awoke completely, then immediately shoved back the covers and rose to face the day. She was even one of those people who immediately made the bed, so finished with it was she until nightfall came again. But today…

She sighed deeply, purring a little as she exhaled. Today, she just wanted to stay in bed until nightfall came again. Because something about the prospect of nightfall coming once more made a shudder of delight wind through her.

She was about to sigh again when her brain finally started to function—albeit none too quickly. It did get enough momentum going for her to finally realize what the light at the foot of the bed could be.

Fire. Her bedroom was on fire.

She jackknifed up to a sitting position, prepared to flee for her life, then was shocked to discover she was naked.

Why was she naked? In moving so hastily, she jostled the person next to her—why was there another person in her bed?—who, with a muffled groan, turned over and, with a muffled thump, landed on the floor. And she realized there was something very familiar about that groan…

That, finally, was when Kendall remembered. She wasn't in her bed. She wasn't in her condo. The fire in the room was the light of candles. It was perfectly safe. Perfectly lovely. Perfectly romantic. And the reason she felt so good was because—

Oh.

So *that* was why there was someone else in the bed.

She felt more than saw Matthias throw an arm up onto the mattress, but she definitely heard another soft groan as he pulled himself up off the floor. Then she heard a sound of exasperation as he crawled back into bed beside her. And then in a voice full of concern, he asked, "What's wrong?"

Oh, there were so many ways she could answer that question. Too many ways. And even so, none of them seemed quite right. Going to bed with Matthias last night had been the wrong thing to do, Kendall told herself. He was her employer again, and she was too smart to get involved with an office romance. But being in bed with Matthias this morning felt so wonderfully right. She would have been an idiot not to make love with the man last night, feeling the way she did about him.

Okay then, her feelings for him were wrong, she told herself. Falling in love with her boss? How stupid could she be? But then, only a brainless ninny would be immune to a man like him. How could she not love him?

And that was when it hit her full force. She was in love with Matthias. Probably had been for years. She just hadn't let herself admit it, because she'd been convinced he would never love her in return. And maybe he didn't love her, she thought. Just because they'd made love…more than once…with utter abandon…and not a little creativity…

Oh, God, she thought. Kendall had no idea what to think just then. So she did the only thing she could do. She lied.

"Nothing," she said, hoping Matthias didn't detect the note of alarm she heard in her voice. "Nothing's wrong. Everything's wonderful. Fabulous. Marvelous. Stupendous. Couldn't be better. In fact, everything is so perfect that I want to leave right now, before anything happens to change it. I'll see myself out. Call me when you get back to San Francisco. Goodbye."

Okay, so she lied *and* panicked. It was a perfectly justifiable response. Thankful for the darkness, she shoved the covers aside and started to rise from the bed.

Until Matthias clapped a strong hand around her wrist and pulled her back down again. Then he levered his body over hers and kissed her. Hard. Long. Deep. And then some of the tension in Kendall's body began to drain away.

Oh, all right, *all* the tension in her body drained away. In fact, by the time Matthias raised his head, she was pretty sure it was going to be hours before she moved again. Unless, you know, he kissed her like that a second time, in which case she would probably start moving *a lot.*

"Going somewhere?" he asked, his voice a velvet purr in the darkness.

Not sure she could get her tongue to work—well, not for talking, anyway—she only murmured, "Mmm-mmm."

"Good," he said. "Because we're not even close to being finished."

Oh, my, Kendall thought.

He chuckled softly. "First we have to have breakfast."

Ooooh, Kendall thought. Breakfast. Right.

"And I'm in the mood for something light, delectable and sweet."

Kendall was in the mood for something dark, delectable and spicy. They were going to need a smorgasbord for this.

No! she immediately told herself. They weren't going to have a smorgasbord. In fact, they couldn't have breakfast at all. They probably never should have had dinner last night. Or the dessert that had come after. Or the dessert after *that,* either.

She found her voice and softly said, "Matthias, we need to talk."

He cupped his hand over her breast and said, "No, we need to *not* talk."

When he started to lean down to kiss her again, she opened her hand lightly over his chest and held firm. Less softly this time, she repeated, "Matthias. We need to talk."

"Kendall—"

"Matthias."

He expelled a quiet sound of resolution, then rolled back over to his side of the bed. Enough light flickered from the candles to enable her to make out his expression. But where she might have expected him to be annoyed or unhappy, or even angry at her having halted his advance, instead, he looked kind of dejected.

Dejected, she marveled. Matthias Barton. He'd never looked dejected about anything. Because he'd never *been* dejected about anything. Then the look was gone, and she told herself she must have just imagined it.

"What do we need to talk about?" he asked. Sounding kind of dejected.

No, annoyed, she told herself. He must be feeling annoyed that instead of romping in the sheets a while longer, she wanted to do some girlie-girl thing like talk about their feelings. But she needed to know how Matthias felt. Especially since she understood how she felt herself.

Inhaling a deep breath, she said very carefully, "What exactly happened here tonight?"

He hesitated a moment before answering, as if he were trying to be careful in choosing his words, too. "Well," he began, "first we had a very enjoyable day in town, and then we came back here."

Actually, Kendall hadn't intended to go back quite that far, but he seemed to need to stall for a little more time, so she let him off the hook. Hey, it wasn't as though she knew exactly what to say, in spite of being the one who said they needed to talk.

"Then we fixed a great meal here, with a very nice cabernet—"

In which they'd probably overindulged, she couldn't help thinking.

"And then we went into the living room and looked out at the lake," he continued. "And then you kissed me—"

"No, you kissed me," she corrected him.

"And then we kissed," he went on as if she hadn't spoken, "and then we came up to the bedroom and had sex."

She was about to say something in response to that, when he continued, "Then we got hungry and went downstairs to have a snack. Only we stopped in the hallway to, um…have an appetizer."

Kendall opened her mouth to speak, but Matthias continued, "And then we had another appetizer on the landing. And then on the stairs. And then on the living room floor."

She started to talk again, but he went on. "And then we had a snack and came back upstairs and had sex in the bed again. And then we slept. And then we woke up. And now we're talking. Can we do something else now? Something *I* want to do? Like have sex?"

By the time he finished, Kendall was only half listening. Because she'd heard what she'd wanted—or, at least *needed*—to hear halfway through. "So then, it was all just sex?" she asked.

When he hesitated again, she studied his face closely, wishing the light were better. Because no matter what he said next, she wouldn't know if it was true or not unless she could look him in the eye. One thing she'd learned working closely with Matthias for five years was how to tell when he was being serious or when he was bluffing. But if she couldn't see his face…

"What do you mean *just* sex?" he asked in a voice that was void of any emotion at all, something that bothered Kendall even more than it would have bothered her had it been filled with *some*thing, even annoyance. At least then she would have known it meant something to him. "Sex isn't a *just* thing. Sex is a *spectacular* thing. And we had some pretty spectacular sex, Kendall. To reduce it to a cliché, wasn't it good for you, too?"

Oh, it had been more than good, she thought. It had been more than spectacular. Because to her, it had been special. Matthias, she feared, felt differently. And Kendall felt…

Well, she felt different, too. That was what falling in love did to a person. It made them feel different. About everything. Remembering he'd asked her a question that needed an answer, and without thinking, she told him, "It was nice."

"*Nice?*" he echoed incredulously. "Kendall, my great-aunt Viola is nice. The Beaujolais Nouveaux last year were nice. Raindrops on roses and whiskers on kittens are nice. Sex with Matthias Barton? That's not nice. That's phenomenal."

In spite of the way she was feeling inside, Kendall smiled. Then, unable to help herself, she reached over and cupped his jaw in her palm. "You were wonderful," she told him.

"Phenomenal," he corrected her.

"Phenomenal," she repeated dutifully.

He had been phenomenal, she thought. But she still didn't know if he was in love. So she turned the conversation to a topic she knew he would understand.

"Matthias," she said carefully, "have you come up with a title for the new position I'll be filling at Barton Limited?"

It wasn't as strange a question as it may have seemed. He wasn't accustomed to talking about his feelings. Although she was confident that he did indeed *have* feelings for her, she wasn't sure if they mirrored hers for him. Asking Matthias how he felt in that moment would only make him clam up. Asking him about work, on the other hand, would make him talk. After five years with him, Kendall had learned to read the subtleties of his business-speak. Matthias's reply to the question she'd just asked would tell her infinitely more than the one to "How do you feel?" would tell her.

"That's kind of a strange question to ask right now, isn't it?" he asked. "I mean, aren't you going to ask me how I feel?"

She shook her head. "I want to hear about the new position. Details this time. Not vague promises."

He expelled a soft sound of resignation, but replied, "Actually, I still haven't come up with a title."

She nodded slowly, her heart sinking a little. "Okay. Then what does the new position involve?"

He hesitated a telling moment, then said, "It's really going to challenge you. The responsibilities are awesome. There will be days when you meet yourself coming and going."

Well, that certainly sounded…vague. "Such as?" she asked.

"Well, your day will begin early," he told her. "I'll expect you at the office by seven-thirty."

"Matthias, that was what time I arrived when I worked for you before. It's not a problem." And, she couldn't help thinking a little sadly, it wasn't very awesome, either.

"Right," he said. "Of course. A typical day for you at this new job will consist of a lot of different things," he continued. "Lots of responsibilities. Awesome responsibilities."

Her heart sank more. "So you've said. You just haven't told me what the responsibilities are."

"Sure I did. They're awesome."

She expelled an impatient breath, her sadness turning to exasperation now. She was pretty sure where this was leading. Now she just wanted to get it over with. "Could you be more specific?" she asked halfheartedly.

"Well," he began in the voice he used whenever he needed to stall, "for instance, every morning, you'd be in charge of sustenance acquisition."

Any hope she might have still been harboring fled with that, and something hard and icy settled in her stomach. She eyed Matthias flatly. "Sustenance acquisition," she repeated.

"Sustenance acquisition," he told her in a more confident voice.

"In other words, getting you your coffee."

He uttered an insulted sound at that. As if he was the one who should be insulted, she thought. Right.

"No, not just getting coffee," he denied.

"Okay, a Danish, too," she conceded. "Or maybe a bagel, if you're on a health kick." He opened his mouth to object, but she cut him off with, "What other awesome responsibilities would I have?"

Not that she couldn't already guess. But she wanted to make sure before she declined the position. And then packed her bags and headed back to San Francisco. She didn't care if she had to hitchhike all the way home.

"Well, let's see," he said, feigning deep thought.

Kendall knew he was feigning it, because if he was having the thoughts she was fairly certain he was having, they weren't in any way deep. Unless they were in something for which she would have to wear waders, which, now that she thought about it, was entirely possible.

"You'd also be in charge of technology aggregation," he told her.

"You mean buying software for your laptop."

"That's way oversimplifying it," he told her.

"Right," she agreed. "Because I'd have to do all the paperwork on the warranties, too. And that sure can be awesome."

He continued gallantly, "You'd also be responsible for environmental augmentation."

"Keeping your desk tidy and well supplied," she translated.

He frowned, but added, "And client satisfaction."

"Planning cocktail parties."

"You'd be my sanitary health liaison."

"I'd make appointments for you at your barber and the gym."

"And you'd be in charge of equipment enhancement."

"Pencil sharpening," she said brightly. "Yeah, can't get enough of that."

"Kendall, it's not—"

"Yes," she said vehemently. "It is. What you're describing is exactly the job I left behind."

"All right, all right," he relented. "I want you to come back to work for me in the same capacity you were when you left. As my assistant. But I'll pay you four times what you were earning before."

"To do the same job?"

"Yes."

"Why?"

He didn't answer right away, only met her gaze levelly and studied her with a look she had no idea how to decipher. Finally, though, he told her, "Because you're the best assistant I ever had, that's why."

She closed her eyes. "I'm not an assistant, Matthias," she said. "I'm a businesswoman. That's where I want to make my mark in the world. That's what brings me satisfaction. That's what I want to be defined by." She opened her eyes again and held his gaze with hers. "I don't want to be anyone's assistant. Not even yours."

"But I can't get through the day without you, Kendall."

"Of course you can get through the—"

"No." He cut her off with even more vehemence than she'd shown herself. "I can't. You've seen me. Look, I know I'm good at what I do for a living. Hell, I'm phenomenal at that. But I can't do it by myself. If I have to be bothered with all the mundane, everyday tasks that consume so much time, I can't get anything done."

"And you think I *like* doing those things?" she asked. "You think I'm suited to that?"

"No, that's not what I meant at all."

She shook her head, not bothering to hide her exasperation now. "Face it, Matthias, you just think you're more important than me. You think you're smarter than me, and more essential than me, and more valuable than me. But here's a news flash for you. Everyone's important in some way or another. Everyone's got smarts of one kind or another. Everyone's essential in some capacity. And everyone's valuable, too." She inhaled a deep breath and finished, "I'm valuable, Matthias. For more than getting you coffee and tidying your desk and planning your parties. I can make as big a mark on the world as you have. And I will. Just watch me."

Nine

Nine

Matthias felt panic well up inside him when he realized Kendall was going to leave. Really leave this time. Not just her job, but him. And this time there would be no convincing her to come back. How could she think her job wasn't important? The work she did was crucial. And how could she think he didn't consider her valuable? She meant more to him than anything.

Anything.

And that was when it hit him. It wasn't that he needed Kendall as his assistant to keep him on track. And it wasn't that he needed her as his assistant to be successful. And it wasn't that he needed her as his assistant to make him happy. He just needed Kendall. Period. In his work, in his life, in his…

In his heart.

"Kendall, wait," he said as she pushed back the covers and scrambled out of bed.

But she ignored him, jerking the top sheet from the mattress and wrapping it around herself with an awkward sort of fury that generated a sick feeling in the pit of his stomach. After everything they'd enjoyed last night, after everything they'd discovered, she wanted to cover herself up now. She wanted to get away from him.

She wanted to leave.

"Kendall, you don't understand," he added as he rose from the bed, too. He grabbed his navy silk bathrobe from the back of the bedroom door as he followed her into the hall.

"Oh, I understand perfectly," she snapped as she went into the guest room where the bags she hadn't even unpacked still lay on the bed.

Good God, Matthias thought. She didn't even have to pack her bags. All she had to do was get dressed, and she'd be out of there. He had mere minutes before she was gone for good.

"No, you don't," he told her. "You can't understand, because I just figured it out myself."

She spun around so quickly, her hair flew over her face. Brushing it fiercely aside with one hand, her other tightened where she clutched the sheet until her knuckles were white. Her entire body quivered with her anger, he noted. Or maybe it was with something else. Maybe it was the same thing that was making his body shudder, too. The realization that he'd just found something wonderful—the most wonderful, stupendous, spectacular thing in the world—and were about to lose it, before he even had a taste.

Finally, coldly, she said, "What, Matthias? What don't I understand?"

He opened his mouth to try and explain, to try and put

into words, as eloquently as he could, all the things he needed to tell her. How much she'd come to mean to him. Not as an employee, but as a woman. How he couldn't live without her. Not because she helped him work better, but because she helped him live better. How he couldn't get through another day without her. Not because she knew how to work his BlackBerry, but because she knew how to fill all the places inside him he'd thought would be empty forever. But all he could think to tell her was—

"I love you."

She went completely still at that. But her fingers on the sheet relaxed, and her expression softened. "What?" she said, her voice a scant whisper.

"I love you," he said again.

She stiffened once more. "Don't you dare say something like that just because you're trying to—"

"I mean it, Kendall," he said. "I may be heartless when it comes to getting my way in business, but I would never put my heart on the line like this unless I was telling the truth."

He took a few experimental steps into the room, taking courage in the fact that she didn't back away from him. But neither did she reach out to him. Nor did she say a word.

"I thought I needed you to come back as my assistant, because I thought that was why you were good for me." She frowned at that, so he hurried on, "You know me, Kendall. I've always been married to my business. It never occurred to me that anything else could make me happy. I'm an idiot," he admitted. "But I'm not so stupid that I can't learn. And I finally realize, it doesn't matter what job you do, whether you program my BlackBerry or mop the floors at Barton Limited or…or come aboard as my new VP in charge of Public Relations."

She narrowed her eyes at him. "What are you talking about? You have a VP in charge of Public Relations. Mitchell Valentine."

"Yeah, well, Mitchell's wife is pregnant with twins, and he wants to be a stay-at-home dad, so he's leaving at the end of August. I was going to hire a headhunter to find someone to fill the position, but I think I already have the perfect candidate working at Barton Limited."

Her expression was cautious. "Who?"

Did she really have to ask? Well, okay, he supposed she did, since she had asked. "You," he told her. "I'd like you to come work for me as my new VP."

She said nothing in response to his offer, something he wasn't sure was good or bad. So, thinking, what the hell, he decided to go for broke. "There's just one problem," he told her.

Now her expression turned wary. "What's that?"

"Barton Limited has a policy that bars spouses from working together."

Her eyes widened at that.

"Fortunately," he added, "it's just a policy, not written in stone anywhere. Besides which, I'm the CEO, so I can do whatever the hell I want. Should, you know, two of the executives want to get…married."

It occurred to Matthias then that Kendall had never actually said she loved him, too. Not that he wasn't pretty sure she at least had *some* feelings for him. He just wasn't sure if they were as strong as his were for her.

"You really want to marry me?" she asked.

He nodded. "Yes. I do."

"You really love me?"

He nodded again. "More than anything."

This time, she nodded, too. But it was a slow nod. A thoughtful nod. The kind that indicated she was thinking, not agreeing. Finally, though, she told him, "Then I think, Matthias, before we go any further with this, we need to talk about the terms."

Good businesswoman that she was, she insisted they be dressed for their discussion. Conceding the point, Matthias decided they should also have access to coffee. So after dressing and having breakfast, he and Kendall took their coffee out to the deck, where a warm summer breeze skidded off the lake, and where the golden sun washed over them.

They took their seats on the big Adirondack love seat, settling comfortably into the patterned cushions. Matthias took solace in the fact that Kendall sat close enough to touch him, tucking her bare foot under her denim-clad leg comfortably. Her white cotton shirt was embroidered with white flowers and edged with lace, feminine enough to be unprofessional, another good sign. He, too, was barefoot, his blue jeans as worn as hers, his polo an old, lovingly faded green one that was his favorite for those few occasions when he kicked back and relaxed. They were talking terms, he thought, but for something much more important than business.

"Where would you like to start?" he asked.

She sipped her coffee and gazed out at the lake. "It occurs to me that if I agree to this merger, it's not the first time you've attempted this kind of thing. And I want to be clear that, although I'm not the first candidate for the position you've offered me, I'm your first—your only—choice."

He looked at her, confused. "I'm not sure I follow."

She sighed, then turned to face him. "Two words. Lauren Conover."

He smiled a little self-deprecatingly. "Ah. I guess that's my signal to tell you about my botched wedding attempt, isn't it?"

Kendall nodded. "I tried to be subtle, but you men just don't have the subtlety gene."

He nodded. "That explains a lot, actually. Like how my engagement happened in the first place."

He looked at Kendall, who had placed her hand on the seat cushion between them, so that her thumb touched her own thigh and her pinky touched his. Her eyes glistened in the morning light, the sun flickered in her hair, first orange then red then gold, and her cheeks had bloomed pink from the warm breeze. Her entire being seemed illuminated from within, as if it were she, not the sun, that brought warmth to the day. And to Matthias, too. Because he'd sat in the sunshine plenty of times, but never had he felt the way he did in that moment. As if everything in his life that had come before it was only preparation for this moment. As if this moment signified the beginning of something new and wonderful that would last forever.

How could he have missed Kendall's beauty all those years? he wondered. How could he have missed Kendall? How could he have not seen what should have been obvious from the first? That she was a rare, exquisite jewel amid the meaningless rubbish of his work. How could he have thought his work was the most important thing in the world, when every day she was with him was a sign of how there was so much more?

"Matthias?" she said softly.

He lifted a hand to thread his fingers through her hair, then hesitated, in case she didn't want him to. But she leaned her head forward, toward his fingers, toward him, and he closed what was left of the distance gratefully, loving the way the soft, warm tresses felt cascading over his fingertips. "Hmm?" he replied absently.

"The engagement?" she prodded gently. "You were going to tell me why it happened."

Right. He had been planning to tell her about his now-defunct engagement. Which was weird, because there was another engagement he wanted to talk about so much more. Of course, that engagement hadn't happened—yet. So maybe it would be best to divest himself completely of the old one. Then he could move ahead to the new.

"It was actually Lauren's father's idea," he began. "He and I were talking about merging our companies over dinner one night, and when the food came, the conversation turned to more personal subject matter, because it's hard to talk business when you're eating." He adopted his best professor voice as he added, importantly, "Because as everyone knows, it's an unwritten rule of business etiquette that you should never talk about important things with your mouth full. So talk about unimportant things with your mouth full instead."

Kendall chuckled at that. "Yeah, personal matters are so much less important than professional ones."

He nodded. "You learned well at my knee, grasshopper. Unfortunately, a lot of what I taught you was wrong."

She smiled at that. "As long as you understand that now."

"Oh, I understand a lot now that I was clueless about before."

She lifted her hand and cupped his cheek affectionately. A very good sign. "We can talk about that, too," she said. "In fact, I look forward to it. But first, you're talking to Conover…"

"Right. He mentioned that his daughter had just returned from Paris having canceled her wedding for the third time. Not the same wedding, mind you," he hastened to add, "but the third wedding with a third fiancé."

"Lauren Conover was engaged three times before she agreed to marry you?"

Matthias nodded. "Which was why she let her father cajole her into the whole thing. She'd gotten to the point where she didn't trust her own judgment. And Conover took advantage of that to convince her an arranged marriage would be best."

"And how did he convince you of that?" Kendall asked. "Somehow, I've never pictured you as the sort to mistrust your own judgment."

"Too true," he said. Except that, like so many other things, he'd been wrong about that, too. His judgment, at least when it came to matters of the heart, stank. Or, at least, it used to. "But Conover is a very persuasive man, and he made some excellent points about why it would be beneficial to merge our families as well as our businesses. And since I'd never planned to marry, marrying Lauren Conover made sense."

"Whoa, whoa, whoa," Kendall said. "I don't follow that logic at all."

"Of course not," he said. "You don't have the convoluted logic gene that men have."

"Ah."

"The convoluted logic goes like this," he told her, smiling. "Try to keep up. I'd never planned to marry, because I never planned to fall in love." Something else he'd been wrong about, he thought. Man. Where had he ever gotten the idea that he was savvy? "So marrying for love made no sense to me. Marrying for business, however…"

Now Kendall nodded. "Right. Got it. It's all coming clear now. Anything done for the sake of one's business makes perfect sense."

"It used to," he said. "Back before I realized what was really important. I guess I just never really thought marriage was such a big deal. And when I did think about it, it seemed like the things that screwed up a marriage always resulted from the emotional investment people made in it. I concluded that by not investing emotionally, my marriage to Lauren would be successful. As long as she and I looked at it pragmatically, everything would be fine."

"And what did Lauren think?"

"At that point, she agreed with me. Like I said, she'd been engaged three times because she thought she'd been in love, and all three times, she ended up abandoned. She hadn't wanted the arrangement to be based on love any more than I had. Until she came to her senses one day and realized how unrealistic she and I both were being about it."

"And until she met up with your brother, Luke."

Matthias waited for the stab of…something…that should have come with the comment. A stab of jealousy maybe, even if he hadn't been in love with Lauren when Luke set out to seduce her. Or a stab of anger that his brother, even though the two of them had barely been speaking at the time, would misrepresent himself as Matthias and deliberately seduce his brother's bride. Or even a stab of resentment that Luke had won some misguided competition between the two men over a woman.

But all Matthias felt was relief. Profound, unmitigated relief that Lauren, at least, had been smart enough to know they'd be making a huge mistake if they married. Then he met Kendall's gaze again, and he felt something else, too.

Something he'd never felt before, but he recognized nonetheless. Something his brother had ultimately found with Matthias's ex-fiancée, something that had made him propose to Lauren instead. Something that made Matthias realize there was a lot more to life than work.

"Love," he said aloud. "Lauren didn't just meet up with my brother, Luke. She fell in love with my brother, Luke."

Kendall said nothing in response to that, only gazed at Matthias in silence. She had to know, though, he thought. Not only had he told her, but her hands were placed right over his heart, and the way his heart was racing now, as he looked back at her, feeling what he felt, knowing what he knew, she had to feel it. She had to.

Finally, softly, she asked, "And how do you feel about that? That your brother, Luke, is going to marry a woman you once planned to marry yourself?"

"I'm happy," he told her. "Lauren's a nice woman. I'm glad she finally found someone who allows her to realize that about herself."

"And Luke?" Kendall asked. "Are you happy for him, too?"

Matthias recalled the last time he'd seen his brother, how desperate and terrified Luke had been when he thought he'd lost Lauren. Helping Luke win her back was the first time he and his brother had worked together to gain something since… He smiled. Wow. That had probably been the first time in their lives they'd ever cooperated together by themselves to achieve a common goal. That it had been to enable one brother to win the heart of the woman who'd been engaged to the other…

Well. That was actually pretty cool, now that Matthias thought about it.

Things between him and Luke were better than they'd been a few months ago, but they still weren't quite settled. Matthias wasn't sure if he and his brother could ever go back to the glory days of college, the one period in their lives when they'd been as close as, well, brothers. But he was willing to put forth the effort if Luke was. In addition to reuniting what was left of the Barton family, burying the hatchet with Luke would be a nice way to honor Hunter's memory. Hunter had been the one who reconciled the two of them at Harvard, by convincing them that brothers were supposed to be at each other's sides, not at each other's throats. Hunter had, in his way, made all of the Seven Samurai feel like brothers. Shame on all of them for not maintaining that brotherhood after his death.

And shame on Matthias and Luke in particular for allowing the gap Hunter had helped close to open again.

"I'm happy for Luke, too," Matthias said.

"Really?" Kendall asked.

He nodded. "Really. He's a good guy, even if he's acted like a lunkhead over the last several years. I guess, in a way, he had his reasons."

Of course, his reasons had been totally misguided, since he'd thought Matthias had cheated him—both years ago and as recently as a few months ago. They'd cleared the air about that two months ago, here at this very lodge. Now it was time to clear the air about everything else, too.

"Luke and Lauren both deserve to be happy," Matthias said. He smiled at Kendall. "Just like you and I deserve to be happy."

"You should call him," Kendall said.

Matthias nodded. "I will. I have a few things to talk to him about, not the least of which is to build a bridge that we should have built years ago." He met her gaze levelly now, wanting to gauge her reaction when he said the rest. "I also want to ask him about being best man at the wedding. My wedding, I mean, not his." He held his breath as he added, "Provided there's going to be a my wedding in addition to his."

She studied him in silence for a long time, her eyes never leaving his. He had no idea what she could be looking for but she must have finally found it, because she smiled. Not a big smile, but it was enough to tell Matthias that everything was going to be okay.

He hoped.

Finally, she said, "What do you mean *your* wedding? I assume there will be someone else at the altar, too, right?"

"God, I hope so," he told her. "It wouldn't be much of a wedding without her."

"It wouldn't be much of a marriage, either," she pointed out. "Since, I assume you're taking into consideration that after the wedding ends, there will be a marriage hanging around your neck."

He tilted his head to the side, feigning consideration. "Mmm, I don't know. I thought I might wear my marriage on my sleeve. Next to my heart."

Now she rolled her eyes. "No one could ever accuse you of wearing your heart on your sleeve, Matthias."

"Maybe not before," he told her. "But I do now."

She bent forward and craned her head to look first at his left arm, then at his right. "I don't see it anywhere."

Catching her under her arms, he lifted her from the love seat and into his lap, then looped both arms around her waist. Oh, yeah, he thought. Everything was going to be just fine.

"Sorry, my mistake," he said as he pulled her close. "My heart isn't *on* my arms. It's *in* them."

She smiled at that, cupping her palm softly over his cheek. "What a coincidence," she said. "My heart is surrounding me."

"So is my love," he told her.

She smiled. "I love you, too."

Very, very fine, he thought, relief—and something even more wonderful—coursing through him.

"Enough to marry me?" he asked.

"As long as it's not convenient," she replied.

He brushed his lips over hers, once, twice, three times, four, enough to get both their hearts pounding, but not enough to scramble their brains—at least not yet. Then he pressed his forehead to hers and pulled her closer still.

"I think I can safely say there will be no convenience in our marriage," he told her. "Love, honor and cherishing, but no convenience."

"Good," she said. "Because convenience just gets too messy sometimes."

He sighed. "I must be absorbing the subtlety gene through osmosis," he said, "because I'm pretty sure you just told me you won't be running Public Relations conveniently, either."

"Oh, don't you worry your handsome little head about that," she told him. "I know what I'm doing. Trust me."

He wasn't much surprised to discover that he did. He trusted Kendall implicitly. And not just with the business, either. Which meant he was so far gone on her, he was never coming back. All the more reason, he thought, to stay together forever.

"I love you, Kendall Scarborough."

"I love you, Matthias Barton."

"Then you'll marry me?"

She nodded. "As long as you promise me you'll never let anyone program your BlackBerry but me."

He chuckled and kissed her quickly on the lips. "It's a deal."

The first deal he'd ever made that would enrich his personal life instead of his professional one. A very sweet deal indeed. Starting today, Matthias Barton was no longer a man who was married to his business. Starting today, he was a man who would be marrying his love. His life. The love of his life.

Life was good, he thought as he dipped his head to Kendall's again. And from here on out, it was only going to get better.

Epilogue

"So tell me more about this picture," Kendall said.

She and Matthias stood on the stairway landing their last day at the lodge, having made their final run through the house to make sure they hadn't left anything behind. Well, other than some wonderful memories. Which, she supposed, they would actually be taking with them after all. They were dressed for the drive back to San Francisco in blue jeans and T-shirts, hers pale yellow and his navy blue, a stark contrast to the suits they'd be donning the following Monday, when they went back to work.

It would be strange, she thought, having an office on a different floor from Matthias. But at least they would still be in the same building. And the Public Relations office was only one floor down from his. They could meet for lunch regularly. And, it went without saying, play footsie under the table whenever there were meetings.

"Tell me about each of the Seven Samurai," she said now. "I know about Hunter," she added. "And obviously, I recognize you and Luke. But who are the others? Which one is Ryan?"

He looked at her askance. "How do you know Ryan's name?"

"I saw the note in the office," she confessed.

He nodded. "It was waiting for me on the desk when I arrived. Ryan obviously knew that would be the first place I went once I got settled. I tacked it up with the photographs because I figured I'd need a laugh. All that stuff about finding The One."

"You think finding 'The One' is a joke?"

He smiled down at her. "Well. I did then. She was, after all, being so uncooperative."

Kendall gaped at him. "Uncooperative? Me?"

"Hey, what else do you call a woman who leaves you high and dry when you've come to depend on her?"

"You fired me!"

"You quit!"

"But I wouldn't have left you high and dry," she told him. "If you hadn't fired me, I would have wrapped up everything I needed to before going. I tried to give you two weeks' notice, but noooooo."

"And what else do you call a woman," he continued, ignoring her, his smile growing broader, "who refuses to come back to work for you, even when you offer her her job back not once, not twice, but three times, even for quadruple her previous salary?"

"It was the job I quit," she pointed out. "Why would I come back?"

"And what would you call a woman," he went on, still

smiling, still ignoring her objections, "who makes you feel things you never thought yourself capable of feeling, who makes you think things you never thought you'd think, who makes you question everything you thought you knew about yourself, everything you thought was universally true."

She brushed her lips lightly over his. "You guys were in college when you made those universal truths," she reminded him. "You didn't know jack about women then."

"We don't know jack about women now," he told her with a laugh.

She shook her head. "You know enough. Because you know how to make us happy. Now, then," she added, pointing to the photo again. "Tell me who all these guys are."

He sighed, but this time when he looked at the picture, the sadness she'd seen in him before was gone, replaced by an unmistakable wistfulness that was captured in his voice. "This is Ryan," he said, pointing to the young man on the far right. "He was here last month and met a woman named Kelly Hartley, who I understand decorated the place."

"She's good," Kendall said.

"Ryan seems to think so, too. They're engaged."

Kendall grinned at that.

"This guy—" he went on to the next young man in the group "—is Nathan Barrister. He was the first one to stay here at the lodge. Then he stayed longer out of the lodge, because he ended up marrying the mayor of Hunter's Landing."

"That was fast," Kendall said.

"Nathan's always been the kind of guy to know what he wants, and he does whatever he has to to get it. Her," he quickly corrected himself. "You know what I mean."

"Boy, do I," she said with a laugh.

"And this," Matthias continued, smiling at the comment and moving to the guy next to Nathan, "is Devlin Campbell. He was always the dutiful one. Still is, evidently. He just got married to a woman who's having his baby. Not that he married her out of duty," he hastened to add. "When Ryan called this place a 'love shack' it was for good reason. Dev met Nicole because she was working in a casino near here."

"Hmm," Kendall mused, "and didn't Luke meet Lauren because she came to the lodge looking for you?"

Matthias nodded. "He did indeed."

"So then this *is* a love shack."

"Only in the literal sense," he said.

"So who's this last guy?" Kendall asked.

"That's Jack Howington. Excuse me. I mean Jack Howington the third. Gotta get those three *I*s in there. He was Special Forces after college, but these days, he owns a consulting firm where he takes what he learned in the service and helps people keep their businesses safe in dangerous parts of the world. Interesting guy."

"Sounds like it."

"He'll be staying here after I leave."

Kendall studied the man in the picture carefully. He was, like the rest of them, very handsome. But where the others all seemed to be generous with their smiles, Jack's was a bit more reserved. Maybe mysterious, she decided. Hard to tell.

"I wonder what his experiences in the love shack will be," she said.

Matthias shook his head. "I don't know. But that reminds me. I need to leave him a note, too."

He turned and made his way up to the office loft, Kendall following in his wake. He withdrew a pad of paper from the desk drawer and plucked a pen from a container full of them, then folded himself into the chair. He tapped his mouth lightly with the pen as he thought about what to write, then smiled. Kendall moved to stand behind him, watching him as he wrote, his strong hand moving slowly, as if he were giving great thought to what he was writing. As he moved down the page, she read what he'd written so far.

Jack—

When I read Ryan's note that called this place a "love shack," my first thought was, "What a load of B.S." But now I think he may be on to something. He was also right about how wrong we were when we compiled our universal truths about women. Remember those? Yeah? Well, now you can forget 'em. We had no idea.

Kendall smiled at that, then continued to read.

As for me, here's what I learned during my month at the lodge: The most important work you'll ever do has nothing to do with the job. And it's work you can't do by yourself. But when you find a partner you can trust, and the two of you do that work together, it pays better than any career you could imagine. And perks? You have no idea…

    Have a good month, pal.

She noticed that he hesitated before signing it, then finally dashed off, "Matt."

"Matt," she said aloud. "When I first saw that on the note Ryan wrote to you, I couldn't imagine anyone calling you that. But now I think it kind of fits."

"No one but family and close friends has ever called me that," he told her. Then, after another small hesitation, he added, "But if you'd like…"

She didn't have to hesitate at all. "I do like," she told him. "Matt."

She pushed herself up on tiptoe to kiss him, then, as one, they turned to make their way down the stairs. The car was packed, the lodge was empty. They'd left the key on the kitchen table, as the caretaker had asked them to. Kendall told herself not to feel too sad as they closed the front door behind them and checked to make sure it was locked. She would be coming back in a couple of months to see the place again. To meet Matthias's—no, Matt's—friends. To see fulfilled the dream the Seven Samurai had made in college. She was a part of that dream now, she realized as they made their way down the steps. Part of Matt's dream. Part of his life, just as he was part of hers.

No, not part of it, she realized. And not two lives. They were one now. In work. In life. In love.

And that, she thought, was exactly where they needed to be.

* * * * *

IN BED WITH
THE DEVIL

BY
SUSAN MALLERY

Susan Mallery is the *New York Times* bestselling author of over one hundred romances and she has yet to run out of ideas! Always reader favorites, her books have appeared on the *USA Today* bestseller list and, of course, the *New York Times* list. She recently took home the prestigious National Reader's Choice Award. As her degree in Accounting wasn't very helpful in the writing department, Susan earned a Masters in Writing Popular Fiction.

Susan makes her home in the Pacific Northwest where, rumor has it, all that rain helps with creativity. Susan is married to a fabulous hero-like husband and has a six-pound toy poodle…who is possibly the cutest dog on the planet.

Visit her website at www.SusanMallery.com

To the fabulously talented authors in this series. Thank you so much for inviting me along for the ride. It was wonderful fun and I would do it again in a heartbeat!

One

Eleven years ago…

Meredith Palmer spent the afternoon of her seventeenth birthday curled up on her narrow bed, sobbing uncontrollably. Everything about her life was a disaster. It was never going to be better—and what if she was one of the unlucky people who peaked in her teenage years? What if this was the *best* it was going to be?

Seriously, she should just throw herself out her dorm room window and be done with it. Of course, she was only on the fourth floor, so she was not going to actually kill herself. The most likely event was maiming.

She sat up and wiped her face. "Given the distance to the ground and the speed at impact," she murmured to herself, then sniffed. "Depending on my position…" She reached for a piece of paper. "If I fell feet first— unlikely, but it could happen—then the majority of the stress would be on my…"

She started doing the calculations. Bone density versus a hard concrete landing or a softer grass landing. Assuming a coefficient of—

Meri threw down the pencil and paper and collapsed back on her bed. "I'm a total freak. I'll never be anything but a freak. I should be planning my *death,* not doing math. No wonder I don't have any friends."

The sobs returned. She cried and cried, knowing that there was no cure for her freakishness. That she was destined to be one of those scary solitary people.

"I'll have to get cats," she cried. "I'm allergic to cats."

The door to her room opened. She kept her face firmly in her pillow.

"Go away."

"I don't think so."

That voice. She knew that voice. The owner was the star of every romantic and semisexual fantasy she'd ever had. Tall, with dark hair and eyes the color of the midnight sky—assuming one was away from the city, where the ambient light emitted enough of a—

Meri groaned. "Someone just kill me now."

"No one's going to kill you," Jack said as he sat next to her on her bed and put a strong, large hand on her back. "Come on, kid. It's your birthday. What's the problem?"

How much time did he have? She could make him a list. Given an extra forty-five seconds, she could index it, translate it into a couple of languages, then turn it into computer code.

"I hate my life. It's horrible. I'm a freak. Worse, I'm a fat, ugly freak and I'll always be this way."

She heard Jack draw in a breath.

There were a lot of reasons she was totally in love with him. Sure, he was incredibly good-looking, but that almost didn't matter. The best part of Jack was he took time with her. He talked to her as if she was a real person. Next to Hunter, her brother, she loved Jack more than anyone.

"You're not a freak," he said, his voice low.

She noticed he didn't say she wasn't fat. There was no getting around the extra forty pounds on her five-foot-two-inch, small-boned frame. Unfortunately he also didn't tell her she wasn't ugly. Jack was kind, but he wasn't a liar.

Between her braces and her nose—which rivaled the size of Io, one of Jupiter's moons—and her blotchy complexion, she had a permanent offer from the circus to sign on up for the sideshow.

"I'm not normal," she said, still speaking into her pillow because crying made her puffy and she didn't need for Jack to see her looking even *more* hideous. "I was planning my death and instead I got caught up in math equations. Normal people don't do that."

"You're right, Meri. You're not normal. You're way better than that. You're a genius. The rest of us are idiots."

He wasn't an idiot. He was perfect.

"I've been in college since I was twelve," she mumbled. "That's five years. If I was really smart, I'd be done now."

"You're getting a Ph.D., not to mention your, what, third masters?"

"Something like that." Unable to be in the same room with him and not look at him, she flipped onto her back.

God, he was so amazing, she thought as her chest tightened and her stomach turned over a couple of times. Technically the organ in question couldn't turn over. What she felt was just—

She covered her face with her hands. "I have to find a way to turn off my brain."

"Why? So you can be like the rest of us?"

She dropped her hands to her side. "Yes. I want to be a regular girl."

"Sorry. You're stuck being special."

She loved him so much it hurt. She wanted him to think she was more than his best friend's kid sister. She wanted him to see her as a woman.

Right, and while she was having a fantasy moment…

maybe he could see her as a beautiful woman he ached for. As if!

"I don't have any friends," she said as she did her best to ignore the need to tell him she would love him forever. "I'm too young, especially in the Ph.D. program. They all think I'm some upstart kid. They're waiting for me to crash and burn."

"Which isn't going to happen."

"I know, but between my academic isolation and my lack of a female role model since the death of my mother, the odds of my maturing to a normal functioning member of society grow more slim each day. Like I said—I'm a freak." Tears rolled down her temples to get lost in her hair. "I'll never have a boyfriend."

"Give it a couple of years."

"It's not going to happen. And even if some guy does take pity on me and ask me out, he'll have to be drunk or stoned or something to want to kiss me, let alone have sex with me. I'm going to d-die a virgin."

The sobs began again.

Jack pulled her into a sitting position and wrapped his arms around her. "Hell of a birthday," he said.

"Tell me about it."

She snuggled close, liking how strong and muscular he felt. He smelled good, too. If only he were desperately in love with her, the moment would be perfect.

But that was not meant to be. Instead of declaring undying devotion and ripping off both their clothes or even kissing her, he shifted back so they weren't even touching.

"Meri, you're in a tough place right now. You don't fit in here and you sure don't fit in with kids your own age."

She wanted to protest she was almost his age—there were only four years between them—and she fit with him just fine. But Jack was the kind of guy who had dozens of women lining up to be with him. Pretty, skinny girls she really, really hated.

"But you're going to get through this and then life is going to be a whole lot better."

"I don't think so. Freakishness doesn't just go away."

He reached out and touched her cheek. "I have high hopes for you."

"What if you're wrong? What if I do die a virgin?"

He chuckled. "You won't. I promise."

"Cheap talk."

"It's what I'm good at."

He leaned toward her, and before she knew what he was going to do, he kissed her. On the mouth!

She barely registered the soft, warm pressure of his lips on hers and then the kiss was over.

"No!" She spoke without thinking and grabbed the front of his sweatshirt. "Jack, no. Please. I want you to be my first time."

She'd never seen a man move so fast. One second he was on her bed, the next he was standing by the door to her dorm room.

Shame and humiliation swept through her. She would have given a hundred IQ points to call those words back. Heat burned her cheeks until she knew she would be marked by the embarrassment forever.

She'd never meant him to know. He'd probably guessed she had a massive crush on him, but she'd never wanted him to be sure.

"Jack, I…"

He shook his head. "Meri, I'm sorry. You're…you're Hunter's little sister. I could never… I don't see you like that."

Of course not. Why would he want a beast when there were so many beauties throwing themselves at him?

"I understand. Everything. Just go."

He started to leave, then turned back. "I want us to be friends. You're my friend, Meri." And with those horrifying words, he left.

Meri sat on the edge of her bed and wondered when she would stop hurting so much. When would she fit in?

When would she stop loving Jack? When would she be able to walk in a room and not wish for the floor to open up and swallow her whole?

Automatically she reached under her bed and pulled out the plastic storage container filled with her snacks. After grabbing a frosted cupcake, she unwrapped it.

This was it—she'd officially hit bottom. Nothing would ever be worse than this exact moment. It was like dark matter in the universe. The absolute absence of anything. It was the death of hope.

She took a bite of the cupcake. Shame made her chew fast and swallow. When the sugar and fat hit her system, she wouldn't hurt so bad. She wouldn't feel so lonely or totally rejected by Jack Howington III. Damn him.

Why couldn't he love her back? She was a good person. But she wasn't busty and blond and tiny, like the girls he dated and slept with.

"I have a brain," she murmured. "That scares guys."

She said the words bravely, but she knew it was more than her incredible IQ that chased off boys. It was how she looked. How she'd allowed food to be everything, especially after her mom died four years ago. It was turning down her father's badly worded offer to take her to a plastic surgeon to talk about her nose. She screamed that if he really loved her, he would never, ever talk about it again, when in truth she was scared. Scared of changing and scared of being the same.

She stood and stared at the closed dorm room door. "I hate you, Jack," she said as tears slipped down her cheeks. "I hate you and I'll make you suffer. I'm going to grow up and be so beautiful you have to sleep with me. Then I'm going to walk away and break your heart. Just watch me."

Present day

Jack Howington III had driven two days straight to get to Lake Tahoe. He could have flown his jet, then picked up a rental car for the month he was going to be forced to stay at Hunter's house, but he'd needed the downtime to clear his head.

His assistant had been frantic, unable to reach him in the more rural parts of the country, but he'd enjoyed the silence. There hadn't been enough silence in his life for a long, long time. Even when he was alone, there were still the damn ghosts to contend with.

He drove down a long driveway toward a barely visible log house. The place stood surrounded by trees with a view of the lake behind. There were windows and stone steps, along with a heavy double wood door.

Jack parked, then climbed out of his Mercedes. Hunter's house had been built just recently, nearly ten years after the death of his friend, but Jack had a feeling that Hunter had left detailed instructions on what it should look like. The place reminded him of Hunter, which was both good and bad.

It was just a month, he told himself as he walked around to the trunk and grabbed his suitcase and computer bag. If he stayed in here for a month, per the terms of Hunter's will, the house would be converted to a place for cancer patients and survivors to come for free. Twenty million would be given to the town or charity or something like that. Jack hadn't paid attention to the details. All he knew was that Hunter had asked him for one last favor. Jack had failed his friend enough times to know that this time he had to follow through.

He took a single step toward the house, then stopped as the front door opened. The lawyer's letter had promised quiet, an office he could work in and a housekeeper to take care of day-to-day necessities.

Easy duty, Jack had thought at the time. Now, as a petite, pretty woman stepped onto the porch, he wasn't so sure.

Next to Hunter, who was long dead, she was about the last person he wanted to see.

"Hello, Jack," she said.

"Meredith."

Her blue eyes widened in surprise. "You recognize me?"

"Sure. Why not?"

She drew in a breath. "It's been a long time. We've both changed."

"I'd know you anywhere."

Which wasn't exactly the truth. He'd kept tabs on Meri over the years. It was the least he could do after he'd promised Hunter he would look after his sister. Jack hadn't been able to deal with her in person, but distance made things safer. Easier. The regular reports from his staff meant he wasn't the least bit surprised by her appearance. Although she looked more…feminine than usual. He'd known she'd been working in California on a temporary assignment with JPL—Jet Propulsion Laboratory, but not the details. He hadn't known she was *here.*

She muttered something under her breath, then said, "Good to know."

Her eyes were still as blue as he remembered. The same color as Hunter's eyes. The same shape. Other than that and an easy laugh, the siblings had had little in common.

He hadn't seen her in years. Not since Hunter's funeral. And before that—

He pushed the memory of her heartfelt declaration and his piss-poor handling of it out of his mind. Let's just say they'd both traveled a lot of years and miles, he told himself.

She'd grown up, he thought as she walked down the stairs and stood in front of him. The baby fat was gone. She looked like what she was—a beautiful, sexy woman who was confident of her place in the world.

Under other circumstances, he could have appreciated the changes, but not with her. Not with the promises he'd made.

"Obviously you received the letter from the lawyer or you wouldn't be here," she said. "You're required to stay for a month. At the end of that time, there will be a brief but meaningful ceremony deeding the house to the town, handing over the keys and the money. You and the other Samurai are free to mingle and catch up, then you're free to go." She glanced at the single suitcase and computer bag. "You travel light."

"Makes it easier to move around."

"But it doesn't give you many choices for that unexpected costume party."

"Is there going to be one?"

"Not that I know of."

"Then I'm good."

She tilted her head slightly, a gesture he remembered. Funny how he could still see the girl in the woman. He'd always liked the girl. He didn't plan to get to know the woman.

He looked her over, then frowned. Was it just him or were her shorts way too short? Not that he didn't appreciate the display of leg, but this was Meredith—Hunter's baby sister. And should her shirt really be that...revealing?

"I'm staying here, too."

Her voice was low and sexy, and had she been anyone else, he would have welcomed the distraction.

"Why?" he asked bluntly.

"I'm the housekeeper. The one you were promised. I'm here to make your life...easier."

There was almost a challenge in the statement. "I don't need a housekeeper."

"You're not being given a choice. I come with the property."

"That's ridiculous," he said flatly. He happened to know she worked for a D.C. think tank and was currently on loan to JPL and some private company, helping them develop a better solid rocket fuel.

"Such language," she scolded gently, then smiled. "It's what Hunter wanted. We're both here because of him."

He frowned. He didn't buy her story. Why would Hunter want his sister at the house for a month? But then, he'd asked all his friends to spend time here, so it was possible. Besides, it wasn't as if Meri would *want* to be in the same house as him. Not after what had happened on her seventeenth birthday.

He'd hurt her. He hadn't meant to, but he had, and after the fact he'd been unable to figure out a way to make things better. Then Hunter had died and everything had changed.

Or maybe he was making too big a deal out of all this. Maybe Meri didn't give a damn about what had happened…or not happened…between them.

"Let's go inside," she said and led the way.

They walked into a large entryway with a staircase and a stone floor. The place was welcoming and masculine. It might not be the house he would have built, but it wasn't going to drive him crazy with lots of frills and smelly bowls of dried flowers.

"You'll get your exercise climbing the stairs. Your room is on the next floor."

He glanced around. "You're down here?"

She smiled. "No, Jack. I'm on the second floor, next to the master. We're only a wall apart."

Meri deliberately widened her eyes and leaned toward him as she spoke. She wanted the invitation to be clear. After what Jack had put her through eleven years ago, he deserved to squirm.

She started down the hall before he had a chance to respond. "There's an office loft area," she continued. "You can use that. It's set up with Internet access, a fax. I'll be in the dining room. I like to spread out when I work. I tend to get really…involved."

She emphasized the last word, then had to consciously keep herself from laughing. Okay, this was way more fun than she'd thought it would be. She should have punished Jack a long time ago.

She made sure she swayed her hips as she climbed and bent forward slightly so he would be sure to notice her very short shorts. She'd worn them deliberately, along with the halter top that left very little to the imagination. It had taken her nearly two days to come up with the perfect outfit, but it had been worth the time.

The shorts clung to her and were cut high enough to show the bottom of her butt. Tacky but effective. Her sandals had a spiked heel that was practically a weapon, but they made her legs look long—a serious trick for someone as short as her.

The halter was so low-cut that she'd had to hold it in place with double-sided tape. She had fresh highlights, sultry makeup and long, dangling earrings that almost touched her nearly bare shoulders.

If the guys back at her science lab could see her now, they would probably implode from shock. Around them she only wore tailored suits and lab jackets. But for the next month she was dressing as a sex kitten and she planned to enjoy every minute of it.

She deliberately sped up at the end of the hall, then stopped suddenly. Jack ran into her. He reached out to steady himself or maybe her. She'd planned that he would, so she turned and held in a grin as the palm of his hand landed exactly on her left breast.

He stiffened and pulled back so fast he almost fell. Meri tried to decide if she minded seeing him in a crumpled heap on the polished hardwood floor.

"Sorry," he muttered.

"Jack," she purred. "Are you coming on to me? I have to say, that's not very subtle. I would have expected better."

"I'm not coming on to you."

"Really?" She put her hands on her hips as she faced him. "Why not? Aren't I your type?"

He frowned. "What the hell is this all about?"

"So many things. I'm not sure where to start."

"Try at the beginning. It usually works for me."

The beginning? Where was that? At conception, where some quirk of the Palmer gene pool had decided to produce a child with an exceptional IQ? Or later, when Meri had first realized she was never going to fit in anywhere? Or perhaps that long-ago-but-never-forgotten-afternoon when the man she loved had so cruelly rejected her?

"We're spending the month together," she told him. "I thought we could have more fun if we played. I know you like to play, Jack."

He swore under his breath. "This isn't like you, Meri."

"How can you be sure? It's been a long time. I've grown up." She turned slowly. "Don't you like the changes?"

"You look great. You know that. So what's the point?"

The point was she wanted him desperate. She wanted him panting, begging, pleading. Then she would give in and walk away. It was her plan—it had always been her plan.

"I'm not going to sleep with you," he said flatly. "You're Hunter's sister. I gave him my word I'd look after you. That means taking care of you, not sleeping with you."

She'd meant to keep her temper. Honestly she'd even written it on her to-do list. But it was simply impossible.

"Take care of me? Is that what you call disappearing two seconds after Hunter's funeral? All of you left—all of his friends. I expected it of them but not of you. Hunter told me you would always be there for me no matter what. But you weren't. You were gone. I was seventeen, Jack. My father was a basket case, I was a total social outcast with no friends and you disappeared. Because that was easier than facing your responsibility."

He put down his luggage. "Is that why you're here? To tell me off?"

He had no idea, she thought, still furious and wishing she could breathe fire and burn him into a little stick figure, like in the cartoons.

"That's only part of the fun."

"Would it help if I said I was sorry?"

"No, it wouldn't." Nothing would change the fact that he'd abandoned her, just like everyone else she'd ever loved.

"Meri, I know we have some history. But if we're stuck here for a month, we need to find a way to get along."

"Be friends, you mean?" she said, remembering how he'd said he would always be her friend, right after rejecting her.

"If you'd like."

She took a deep breath, then released it. "No, Jack. We'll never be friends. We'll be lovers and nothing else."

Two

The next morning Meri woke up feeling much better about everything. After leaving out food for Jack, she'd escaped to her room, where she'd had a bath and a good cry. Some of her tears had been about her brother, but a lot of them had been for herself. For the geek she'd been and the losses she'd suffered.

After Hunter had died, their father had totally lost it. He'd been less than useless to her. Within a year he'd started dating nineteen-year-olds, and in the nine years since, his girlfriends had stayed depressingly young.

She'd been on her own and she'd survived. Wasn't that what mattered? That she'd managed to get the help she'd needed to move forward and thrive?

She turned on her clock's radio and rocked her hips to the disco music that blasted into the room. She was sorry she'd missed the disco years—the music had such a driving beat. Of course, she was a total spaz on the dance floor, but what she lacked in style and grace she made up for in enthusiasm.

After brushing out her hair, she braided it, then dressed in a sports bra, tank top and another pair of skimpy shorts. Ankle socks and athletic shoes completed her outfit.

Humming "We Are Family" under her breath, she left her room and prepared to implement the next part of her plan for revenge.

Jack was in the kitchen. She walked up to him and smiled.

"Morning," she said, reaching past him for the pot of coffee. She made sure she leaned against him rather than going around. "How did you sleep?"

His dark eyes flickered slightly, but his expression never changed. "Fine."

"Good. Me, too."

She poured the coffee, then took a sip, looking at him over the mug.

"So," she said. "A whole month. That's a long time. Whatever will we do with it?"

"Not what you have planned."

She allowed herself a slight smile. "I remember you saying that before. Did you always repeat yourself? I remember you being a whole lot more articulate. Of course, I was younger then, and one looks at one's elders with the idealism of youth."

He nearly choked on his coffee. "Elders?"

"Time has been passing, Jack. You're, what, nearly forty?"

"I'm thirty-two and you know it."

"Oh, right. Thirty-two. Time has been a challenge for you, hasn't it?"

She enjoyed baiting him too much, she thought, knowing she was being totally evil and unable to help herself. The truth was, Jack looked amazing. Fit, sexy—a man in his prime. The good news was that sleeping with him wouldn't be a hardship.

"You gave up on seducing me?" he asked.

"Not at all. But this is fun, too."

"I'm not sleeping with you."

She glanced around the kitchen, then looked back at him. "I'm sorry, did you say something? I wasn't listening."

"You're a pain in the ass."

"But it's a darned nice ass, isn't it?" She turned to show him, patted the curve, then faced front again. "Okay, go get changed. I'll take you to the nearest gym. You can get a thirty-day membership. Then we'll work out together."

"There's no equipment here?"

She smiled. "I guess Hunter didn't think of everything after all. It's a good thing I'm around."

He stared at her. "You think you're in charge?"

"Uh-huh."

He put down his mug, then moved close and stared into her eyes. "Be careful, Meri. You're playing a game you don't know how to win. I'm out of your league and we both know it."

A challenge? Was he crazy? She always won and she would this time. Although there was something about the way he looked at her that made her shiver. Something that told her he was not a man to be toyed with.

But he *was* just a man, she reminded herself. The sooner she got him into bed, the quicker she could get on with her life.

Jack followed Meri into the large gym overlooking the lake. The facility was light and clean, with only a few people working out. Probably because it was midday, he thought as he took in the new equipment and mentally planned his workout.

Back in Dallas, he worked out in his private gym, built to his specifications. But this would do for now.

"So we can circuit-train together," she said brightly, standing close and gazing up at him with a teasing smile. "I'm great at spotting."

She was trying to push his buttons. He was determined not to react, regardless of what she said or did. Meri was playing a game that could be dangerous to her. He might not have taken care of her the way he should have, but he *had* looked out for her. That wasn't going to stop just because she was determined to prove a point.

"Want to warm up with some cardio first?" she asked. "We can race. I'll even give you a head start."

"I'm not going to need it," he told her as he headed over to the treadmills, not bothering to see if she followed.

"That's what you think."

She stepped onto the machine next to his and set it for a brisk warm-up pace. He did the same, not bothering to look at her speed.

"You didn't used to exercise," he said conversationally a few minutes later as he broke into a jog.

Meri punched a few buttons on her treadmill and matched his speed. "I know. I was much more into food than anything else. Not surprising—food was my only friend."

"We were friends," he said before he could stop himself. He'd liked Meri—she was Hunter's little sister. She'd been like family to him.

"Food was the only friend I could depend on," she said as she cranked up her treadmill again. She was breathing a little harder but barely breaking a sweat. "It didn't disappear when I needed it most."

No point in defending himself. She was right—he'd taken off right after Hunter's funeral. He'd been too devastated by loss and guilt to stick around. A few months later he'd realized he needed to make sure Meri was all right. So he'd hired a P.I. to check in on her every few months. The quarterly reports had given him the basics about her life but nothing specific. Later, when he'd started his own company, he'd gotten his people to keep tabs on her and he'd learned a lot more about her. He'd learned that she'd grown up into a hell of a woman. Obviously she hadn't needed him around, taking care of things.

"The downside of food as a friend," she continued, "is that there's an ugly side effect. Still, I couldn't seem to stop eating. Then one day I made some new friends and I stopped needing the food so much." She grinned. "Okay, friends and some serious therapy."

"You were in therapy?" The reports hadn't mentioned that.

"For a couple of years. I worked through my issues. I'm too smart and weird to ever be completely normal, but these days I know how to pass."

"You're not weird," he said, knowing better than to challenge her brain. Meri had always been on the high side of brilliant.

"A lot you know," she said. "But I like who I am now. I accept the good points and the bad."

There were plenty of good points, he thought, doing his best not to look at her trim body. She had plenty of curves, all in the right places.

They continued to jog next to each other. After another five minutes, Meri increased the speed again and went into a full-out run. Jack's competitive side kicked in. He increased not only the speed but the incline.

"You think you're so tough," she muttered, her breath coming fast and hard now.

"You'll never win this battle," he told her. "I have long legs and more muscle mass."

"That just means more weight to haul around."

She ran a couple more minutes, then hit the stop button and straddled the tread. After wiping her face and gulping water, she went back onto the treadmill but at a much slower pace. He ran a few more minutes—because he could—then started his cooldown.

"You're in shape," he told her as they walked over to the weight room.

"I know." She smiled. "I'm a wild woman with the free weights. This is where you really get to show off, what with having more upper-body strength. But pound for pound, I'm actually lifting nearly as much as you. Want me to make a graph?"

He grinned. "No, thanks. I can see your excuses without visual aids."

"Reality is never an excuse," she told him as she collected several weights, then walked over to a bench. She wiped her hands on the towel she'd brought.

"I can't be too sweaty," she said. "If my hands are slick, it gets dangerous. About a year ago, I nearly dropped a weight on my face. Not a good thing."

"You should be more careful," he said.

"You think? I paid a lot of money for my new nose. You never said anything. Do you like it?"

He'd known about the surgery. She'd had it when she was twenty. He supposed the smaller nose made her a little prettier, but it wasn't that big a change.

"It's fine," he said.

She laughed. "Be careful. You'll turn my head with all that praise. My nose was huge and now it's just regular."

"You worry too much about being like everybody else. Average is not a goal."

She looked at him. "I haven't had enough coffee for you to be philosophizing. Besides, you don't know anything about normal. You were born rich and you're still rich."

"You're no different."

"True, but we're not talking about me. As a guy, you have different standards to live up or down to. If you have money, then you can be a total loser and you'll still get the girl. But for me it was different. Hence the surgeries."

"You had more than one?" he asked, frowning slightly. He knew only about her nose.

She sat up and leaned toward him. "Breasts," she said in a mock whisper. "I had breast implants."

His gaze involuntarily dropped to her chest. Then he jerked his head to the right and focused on the weight bench next to him.

"Why?" he asked, determined not to think about her body and especially not her breasts, which were suddenly more interesting than he wanted them to be.

"After I lost weight, I discovered I had the chest of a twelve-year-old-boy. I was totally flat. It was depressing. So I got implants. I went for a jumbo B—which seemed about right for my newly skinny self."

She stood and turned sideways in front of the mirror. "I don't know. Sometimes I think I should have just gone for it and ordered the centerfold breasts. What do you think?"

He told himself not to look, but it was like trying to hold back the tide. Against his will, his head turned and his gaze settled on her chest. Meri raised her tank top to show off her sports bra.

"Are they okay, Jack?"

A guy walking by did a double take. "They're great, honey."

She dropped her shirt and smiled. "Thanks."

Jack glanced at the guy and instantly wanted to kill him. It would be fast and relatively painless for the bastard. A quick twist of the neck and he would fall lifeless to the ground.

Meri dropped her shirt. "I love being a girl."

"You're still playing me. I'm going to ignore you."

"I'm not sure you can," she teased. "But you can try. Let's change the subject. We can talk about you. Men love to talk about themselves."

He grabbed a couple of weights and sat on a bench. "Or we could focus on our workout."

"I don't think so." She lay on her back and did chest presses. "What have you been up to for the last ten years? I know you went into the military."

"Army," he said between reps.

"I heard it was Special Forces."

"That, too."

"I also heard you left and started your own company dealing with corporations that want to expand into the dangerous parts of the world."

Apparently he wasn't the only one who had done some research.

"It's impressive," she said. "You've grown that company into quite the business."

"I'm doing okay." Five hundred million in billing in the past year. His accountants kept begging him to go public. They told him he could make a fortune. But he already had more than he needed, and going public meant giving up control.

"Are you married?" she asked.

He looked over at her. She'd shifted positions and was now doing bicep curls. Her honey-tanned skin was slick with sweat, her face flushed, her expression intense. She was totally focused on what she was doing.

Would she be like that in bed? Giving a hundred percent, really going for it?

The thought came from nowhere and he quickly pushed it away. Meri could never be more than Hunter's baby sister. She could dance around naked and beg him to take her—they were never going there.

"Jack? You gonna answer the question?"

Which was? Oh, yeah. "No, I'm not married."

"You're not gay, are you? Hunter always wondered."

He ignored her and the question. If he didn't react, she would get tired of her game and move on to something else.

She sighed. "Okay, that was funny only to me. So there's no wife, but is there someone significant?"

"No."

"Ever been anyone?"

"There have been plenty."

She looked at him. "You know what I mean. A relationship where you're exchanging more than bodily fluids. Have you ever been in love?"

"No," he said flatly. Women tried to get close and he didn't let them.

"Me, either," she said with a sigh. "Which is deeply tragic. I want to be in love. I've been close. I thought I was in love, but now I'm not so sure. I have trust and commitment issues. It's from losing my mom when I was young and then losing Hunter. Isn't it interesting that knowing what the problem is doesn't mean I can fix it?"

He didn't know what to say to that. In his world, people didn't talk about their feelings.

"You lost a brother when you were young," she said. "That had to have affected you."

No way he was thinking about that. He stood. "I'm done. I'm going to take a shower."

She rose and moved close. "Want to take one together?"

He had an instant image of her naked, water pouring over her body. How would she feel? His fingers curled slightly, as if imagining cupping her breasts.

Damn her, he thought. She wasn't going to win. It was time to stop playing nice.

He moved forward, crowding her. She stepped back until she bumped into a weight bench, then she dropped into a sitting position. He crouched in front of her.

"You do not want to play this game with me," he told her in a low voice. "I'm not one of your brainy book guys. I have seen things you can't begin to imagine, I have survived situations you couldn't begin to invent. You may be smart, but this isn't about your brain. You can play me all you want, but eventually there will be consequences. Are you prepared for that, little girl?"

"I'm not a little girl."

He reached behind her and wrapped his hand around her ponytail, pulling just hard enough to force her head back. Then he put his free hand on her throat and stroked the underside of her jaw.

Her eyes widened. He sensed her fighting fear and something else. Something sexual.

He knew because he felt it, too. A pulsing heat that arced between them. Need swirled and grew until he wanted to do a whole lot more than teach her a lesson.

Then she smiled. "I'm getting to you, aren't I?"

He released her. "In your dreams."

* * *

Back at the house, Meri went up to her room to change clothes. She didn't offer to help Jack with his. After their close encounter at the gym, she needed a little time to regroup.

There had been a moment when Jack had touched her that had if not changed everything then certainly captured her attention. A moment when she'd been aware of him as being a powerful man and maybe the slightest bit dangerous.

"I'm not impressed," she told herself as she brushed out her hair, then slipped into a skimpy sundress that left her arms bare. "I'm tough, too." Sort of.

Jack was right. He'd been through things she couldn't begin to imagine. While they'd both changed in the past eleven years, she wondered who had changed more on the inside. Was the man anything like the boy she'd both loved and hated?

Before she could decide, she heard the rumble of a truck engine. A quick glance at her watch told her the delivery was right on time.

"It's here! It's here!" she yelled as she ran out of her room and raced down the stairs. "Jack, you have to come see. It's just totally cool."

She burst out of the house and danced over to the truck. "Were you careful? You were careful, right? It's very expensive and delicate and I can't wait until you set it up. You're going to calibrate it, right? You know how? You've been trained?"

The guy with the clipboard looked at her, then shook his head. "You're a scientist, aren't you?"

"Yes. How'd you know?"

"No one else gets that excited about a telescope." He pointed back at the compact car parked behind the truck. "He calibrates it. I just deliver."

Jack walked outside and joined her. "A telescope?"

"I know—it's too exciting for words. It was very expensive, but the best ones are. You won't believe what we'll be able to see. And it's so clear. How long until sunset?"

She looked at the sky. It would be too long but worth the wait.

"You bought a telescope for the house?" he asked.

"Uh-huh."

"We already have one."

She wrinkled her nose. "It's a toy. This is an instrument."

"But you're only here for a month."

Less if her plan went well. "I know, but I want to see the stars. Everything is better when there are stars to look at."

"You're leaving it in place, aren't you?"

"For the families," she said, watching anxiously as the ramp was lowered on the truck. "I'll write up some instructions, although it's computer-guided. They won't have to do anything but type in what they want to see, then stand back and watch the show. Not that we'll be using the program. I can find whatever you want to see."

"I have no doubt."

She glanced at him. "What?"

"Nothing. Just you."

Which meant what? Not that Jack would tell her if she asked.

"Hunter would have loved this," she said absently, knowing her brother would have made fun of her, then spent the whole night looking at the sky.

Thinking about her brother was both wonderful and filled with pain. While she appreciated all the memories she had, she still had a hole in her heart from his passing.

"I think about him every day," she told Jack. "I think about him and wish he were here. Do you think about him much?"

Jack's expression closed and he turned away. "No. I don't think about him at all."

She knew he couldn't be telling the truth. He and Hunter had been close for a long time. They'd been like brothers. Jack couldn't have forgotten that.

Her instinct to be compassionate battled with her annoyance. Temper won.

"Most people improve with age," she said. "Too bad you didn't. You not only break your word but you're a liar, as well."

Three

Jack spent a couple of hours in the loft office, working. He called his assistant back in Dallas.

"They're building more roads in Afghanistan," Bobbi Sue told him. "They're looking at maybe an eighteen-month contract, but we all know those things take longer. And Sister Helena called. They want to take in another convoy of medical supplies."

His business provided protection in dangerous parts of the world. His teams allowed building crews to get their jobs done and get out. The work was dangerous, often a logistical nightmare and extremely expensive. His corporate clients paid well for what they got.

The corporate profits were channeled into funding protection for those providing relief efforts in places often forgotten. He'd grown up in the shadow of the

Howington Foundation, a philanthropic trust that helped the poor. Jack hated having a number after his name and had vowed he would make his own way.

He had. He'd grown his company from nothing, but he couldn't seem to escape that damn sense of duty. The one that told him he needed to use his profits for something other than a flashy lifestyle.

His critics said he could afford to be generous—he had a trust fund worth nearly a billion dollars. What they didn't know is he never touched it. Another vow he'd made to himself. He'd grown up with something to prove. The question was whether or not he would have achieved enough to let that need go.

"Get Ron on the contract," Jack told his assistant. "The usual clauses. Tell Sister Helena to e-mail the best dates for the convoy and we'll get as close to them as possible."

"She's going to want to leave before you're back from your vacation in Tahoe."

"I'm not on vacation."

"Hmm, a month in a fancy house with nothing to do with your time? Sounds like a vacation to me."

"I'm working."

"Talk, talk, talk."

Bobbi Sue had attitude, which he put up with because she was the best at her job. She was also old enough to be his mother, a fact she mentioned on a regular basis, especially when she hounded him on the topic of settling down.

"Someone else will have to take Sister Helena's team in," he said. "See if Wade's available." Wade was one of his best guys.

"Will do. Anything else?"

"Not from my end."

"You know, I looked up Hunter's Landing on the Internet, and the place you're staying isn't that far from the casinos."

"I'm aware of that."

"So you should go. Gamble, talk to some people. You spend too much time alone."

He thought about Meri, sleeping in the room next to his. "Not anymore."

"Does that mean you're seeing someone?"

"No."

"You need to get married."

"You need to get off me."

Bobbi Sue sighed. "All right, but just in the short term."

Jack hung up. He glanced at his computer, but for once he didn't want to work. He paced the length of the spacious bedroom, ignoring the fireplace, the view and the television. Then he went downstairs to confront the woman who seemed determined to think the worst of him.

Not that he cared what she thought. But this wasn't about her—it was about Hunter.

He found Meri in the kitchen, sitting on the counter, eating ice cream out of a pint-size container.

"Lunch?" he asked as he entered the room.

"Sort of. Not exactly high in nutrition, but I'm more interested in sugar and fat right now."

He stared at her miniature spoon. "That's an interesting size."

She waved the tiny utensil. "It's my ice-cream-eating spoon. I try to avoid using food as an emotional crutch, but sometimes ice cream is the only solution. I use this spoon because it takes longer to eat and I have a better chance of getting disgusted with myself and stopping before finishing the pint. A trick for keeping off the weight. I have a thousand of them."

"This situation required ice cream?"

She licked the spoon. He did his best to ignore the flick of her tongue and the sigh that followed, along with the rush of unwelcome heat in his body.

"You pissed me off," she told him.

Translation: he'd hurt her. Hunter was her brother. She wouldn't want to think his friends had forgotten him.

He leaned against the counter as he considered what to do. His natural inclination was to walk away. Her feelings didn't matter to him. At least they shouldn't. But this was Meri, and he was supposed to be looking out for her. Which meant not making a bad situation worse.

Maybe a small concession was in order. "I don't want to think about Hunter," he admitted. "I've trained myself not to. But he's there. All the time."

She eyed him. "Why should I believe you?"

"I don't care if you do."

She surprised him by smiling. "Okay. I like that answer. If you'd tried to convince me, I would have known you were just placating me. But your stick-up-the-butt attitude is honest."

"Excuse me?"

"You're excused."

He frowned. Had she always been this irritating?

"You getting much work done?" she asked as she checked her watch. "I'm not. There's so much going on right now and I really need to focus. But it's tough. Being here, seducing you—it's a full time job."

He folded his arms over his chest. "You need to let that go."

"The seduction part? I don't think so. I'm making progress. You're going on the defensive. What happened in the gym was definitely about taking charge. So that means I'm getting to you." She held out the ice cream container. "Want some, big guy?"

She was mocking him. She was irreverent and fearless and determined. All good qualities, but not in this situation. She was right. He wanted to get control. And he could think of only one way to do that.

He moved close and took the ice cream from her. After setting it and the spoon on the counter, he cupped her face and kissed her.

He took rather than asked. He claimed her with his lips, branding her skin with his own. He leaned in, crowding her, showing her that she hadn't thought her plan through.

She stiffened slightly and gasped in surprise. He took advantage of the moment and plunged his tongue into her mouth.

She was cool from the ice cream, cool with a hint of fire. She tasted of chocolate and something that had to be her own erotic essence. He ignored the softness of her skin, the sensual feel of her mouth and the heat that poured through him.

She pulled back slightly and gazed into his eyes. "Is that the best you can do?" she asked before she put her arms around his neck and drew him in.

She kissed him back with a need that surprised him. She opened for him and then met his tongue with darting licks of her own.

She'd parted her legs, so he slipped between her thighs. Although she was much shorter, with her sitting on the counter, he found himself nestled against her crotch.

Blood pumped, making him hard. Desire consumed him. Desire for a woman he couldn't have. Dammit all to hell.

Then he reminded himself that his reaction was to an attractive woman. It wasn't specific. It wasn't about Meri. As his assistant enjoyed pointing out, he'd been solitary for a long time. Even brief sexual encounters no longer intrigued him. He'd been lost in a world of work and nothing else.

He had needs. That was all this was—a scratch for an itch.

He pulled back. "Interesting."

She raised her eyebrows. "It was a whole lot more than interesting and you know it."

"If it's important for you to believe that, go ahead."

"I don't mind that you're not making this easy," she told him. "The victory will be all the sweeter." She picked up her ice cream and put the cover back. "I'm done."

"Sugar and fat needs met?"

"I no longer need the comfort. My bad mood is gone."

So like a woman, he thought as he leaned against the counter. "Because I kissed you?"

She smiled and jumped to the floor, then walked to the freezer. "Because you liked it."

He wasn't going to argue the point.

She closed the freezer door with her hip, then looked at him. "Tell me about the women in your life."

"Not much to tell."

"It's tough, isn't it?" She leaned against the counter opposite his. For once, her eyes weren't bright with humor or challenge. "Being who we are and trying to get involved. The money thing, I mean."

Because they both came from money. Because they'd been raised with the idea that they had to be careful, to make sure they didn't fall for someone who was in it for the wrong reasons.

Without wanting to, Jack remembered sitting in on a painful conversation between Hunter and Meredith. He'd tried to escape more than once, but his friend had wanted him to stick around to make sure Meri really listened.

"Guys are going to know who you are," Hunter had told her. "You have to be smart and not just think with your heart."

Meri had been sixteen. She'd writhed in her seat as Hunter had talked, then she'd stood and glared at him. "Who is going to want me for anything else?" she demanded. "I'm not pretty. I'll never be pretty. I'm nothing more than a giant brain with braces and a big nose. I'm going to have to buy all my boyfriends."

Hunter had looked at Jack with an expression that begged for help, but Jack hadn't known what to say either. They were too young to be guiding Meri through life—what experiences did they have to pass on? Doing twins from the law school hardly counted.

"I have it easier than you do," he said, forcing himself back to the present, not wanting to think about how he'd failed both Hunter and Meri. "The women I go out with don't know who I am."

"Interesting point. I don't talk about my family, but word gets out. I've actually reached the point in my life where I have to have men investigated before I start dating them. It's not fun."

"You're doing the right thing." Not that she was the only one checking out her dates. He ran a check on all of them, too. For casual dates, he only bothered with a preliminary investigation, but if it looked like things were getting serious, he asked for a more involved report.

She glanced at her watch again.

"You have an appointment?" he asked.

She grinned. "I have a surprise."

"Another one?"

"Oh, yeah. So there's no little woman waiting in the wings?"

"I told you—I'm not the little-woman type."

"Of course. You're the kind of man who enjoys a challenge. Which is what I am."

Okay, so kissing her hadn't gotten her to back off. He needed another direction. He refused to spend the next three and a half weeks dodging Meri. All he needed was a plan. He'd never been defeated before and he wasn't about to be defeated now.

"But I want something different from the men in my life," she continued. "Maybe my tastes have matured, but I'm looking for someone smart and funny—but normal-smart. Not brainy. I could never marry another genius. We'd have a mutant child, for sure."

He chuckled. "Your own version of genetic engineering?"

"Sort of. I made a list of characteristics that are important to me. I used to have a whole program I wrote one weekend, but that seemed so calculated. A list is more ordinary."

"Not if you wrote it in binary code."

She rolled her eyes. "Oh, please. I'd never do that. C++ maybe."

He was going to guess C++ was another computer language, but he could be wrong.

"Not that I needed a computer program to know Andrew is a great guy."

Jack stared at her. "Andrew?"

"The man I've been dating for a while now. He checked out great, and things are getting serious."

Jack didn't remember hearing about any guy named Andrew. Not that he got personally involved unless things were heating up—which, apparently, they were. Why hadn't he been told?

"How serious?" he asked as he heard the sound of a truck heading toward the house.

"I'm probably going to marry him," Meri said, then ran out of the kitchen. "You hear that? They're here!"

Marry him?

Before he could react to that, he found himself following her to the foyer and beyond that to the front of the house. A shuttle van pulled to a stop in front of the porch, and the door eased open.

"Who's here?" he asked, but Meri wasn't listening. She bounced from foot to foot, then threw herself into the arms of the first person off the shuttle. He was short, skinny and wearing glasses thick enough to be portholes. Nothing about him was the least bit threatening, and Jack immediately wanted to kill him.

"You made it," Meri said, hugging the guy again. "I've missed you so much."

The guy disentangled himself. "It's been a week, Meri. You need to get out more."

She laughed, then turned to the next person and greeted him with exactly the same enthusiasm. Okay. So nerd guy wasn't Andrew. Good to know.

Meri welcomed all eight visitors with exactly the same amount of enthusiasm, then she turned to Jack.

"Everybody, this is Jack. Jack, this is my team."

"Team for what?" he asked.

She grinned. "Would you believe me if I said polo?"

Judging from their pale skin and slightly peering gazes, he was going to guess none of them had ever seen a horse outside of the movies or television.

"No."

"I didn't think so. This is my solid-rocket-fuel team. We're working on ways to make it less toxic and more efficient. There's a technical explanation, but I don't want to watch your eyes glaze over."

"I appreciate that. What are they doing here?"

"Don't freak. They're not all staying in the house. Only Colin and Betina. The rest are staying at nearby hotels."

Jack didn't like the idea of anyone else hanging around. He needed to concentrate on work. Of course, if Meri were distracted by her friends, she wouldn't be such a problem for him.

"Why are they here?" he asked.

"So we can work, I can't leave the mountain, so they agreed to a field trip." She leaned toward him and lowered her voice. "I know you're going to find it difficult to believe, but this is a really fun group."

Most of her colleagues were squinting in the sun and looking uncomfortable. "I can only imagine."

She walked over to the oldest woman in the group—a slightly overweight, stylishly dressed blonde—linked arms with her and led her forward.

"Jack, this is my friend Betina. Technically she's a liaison—she stands between the team and the real world, taking care of all the details the scientifically gifted seem to be so bad with. In reality, she's my best friend and the reason I'm just so darned normal."

He eyed the other woman and wondered how many of Meri's secrets she knew.

"Nice to meet you," he said as he shook hands with Betina.

Betina smiled. "I'm enjoying meeting you, as well," she said. "Finally."

Finally?

Meri grinned. "Did I tell you or what?"

Tell her what? But before Jack could ask, the group went into the house. He was left standing on the porch, wondering when the hell his life had gotten so out of his control.

Meri sat cross-legged in the center of the bed while her friend unpacked. "He's gorgeous. Admit it—you saw it."

Betina smiled. "Jack is very nice-looking, if you

enjoy the tall, dark and powerful type. He wasn't happy about us arriving."

"I know. I didn't tell him you were coming. It was fabulous. I wish you'd seen the look on his face when I explained why you were here. Of course, it was right after I told him I might marry Andrew, so there it was a double-thrill moment for me."

Betina unpacked her cosmetics and carried them into the attached bathroom. "You know you're not marrying Andrew. You're baiting Jack."

"It's fun and I need a hobby." Meri flopped back on the bed. "Why shouldn't I bait him? He deserves it. He was mean to me."

"He was in college. At that age, men are not known for their emotional sensitivity. Actually, they're not known for it at any age. But the point is, you bared your heart and soul and he reacted badly. I agree some punishment is in order, but you're taking it all too far. This is a mistake, Meri."

Meri loved Betina like a sister…sometimes like a mom. There were only twelve years between them chronologically, but in life experiences they were light-years apart.

Betina had been the project manager's assistant at the think tank that had first hired Meri. The second week Meri had been there, Betina had walked into her lab.

"Do you have anything close to a sense of humor?" the other woman had asked. "I don't mind that you're brilliant, but a sense of humor is required for any kind of a relationship."

Meri hadn't known what to say. She'd been eighteen

and terrified of living on her own in a strange city. Money wasn't an issue—the think tank had hired her for more than she'd ever thought she would earn and she had a family trust fund. But she'd spent that last third of her life in college. What did she know about furnishing an apartment, buying a car, paying bills?

"I don't know if I would qualify as funny," Meri had said honestly. "Does sarcasm count?"

Betina had smiled. "Oh, honey, sarcasm is the best."

At that moment their friendship had been born.

Betina had been turning thirty and on her own for over a decade. She'd shown Meri how to live on her own and had insisted she buy a condo in a good part of D.C.

She'd taken care of Meri after both her surgeries, offered fashion advice, love life advice and had hooked her up with a trainer who had pummeled her into shape.

"Why is getting revenge a mistake?" Meri asked as her friend finished unpacking. "He's earned it."

"Because you're not thinking this through. You're going to get into trouble and I don't want that to happen. Your relationship with Jack isn't what you think."

Meri frowned. "What do you mean? I totally understand my feelings about Jack. I had a huge crush on him, he hurt me and, because of that, I've been unable to move on. If I sleep with him, I'll instantly figure out that he's not special at all. He's just some guy and I'll be healed. The benefit is I get to leave him wanting more."

Betina sat next to her and fluffed her short hair. "I hate travel. I always get puffy." Then she drew in a breath. "You didn't have a crush on Jack. You were in love with him then and you're still in love with him.

You're emotionally connected to him, even if you refuse to admit it. Sleeping with him is only going to confuse the matter. The problem with your plan is that, odds are, the person left wanting more could easily be you."

Meri sat up and took Betina's hands. "I love and admire you, but you are desperately wrong."

"I hope so, for your sake."

But her friend sounded worried as she spoke. Meri appreciated the show of support. They were never going to agree on this topic. Better to move on.

She released Betina's hands and grinned. "So Colin is right next door. Whatever will the two of you get up to late at night?"

Betina flushed. "Lower your voice," she whispered. "He'll hear you."

"Oh, please. He wouldn't hear a nuclear explosion if he was focused on something else, and when I walked by his room, he was already booting his laptop. We're safe. Don't you love how I got the two of you into the house while everyone else is far, far away?"

"I guess," Betina said with uncharacteristic indecision. "I know something has to happen soon or I'll be forced to back the car over him. He's such a sweetie. And you know I really like him, but I don't think I'm his type."

Meri groaned. "He doesn't have a type. He's a nerd. Do you think he dates much?"

"He should. He's adorable and smart and funny."

Her friend had it bad, Meri thought happily. And she was pretty sure that Colin found Betina equally intriguing. Usually Betina simply took what she wanted in the man department. But something about Colin made her nervous.

"He's afraid of being rejected," Meri told her. "Something I can relate to."

"I wouldn't reject him," Betina said. "But it will never work. We're on a project together. I'm too old for him and I'm too fat."

"You're six years older, which is nothing, and you're not fat. You're totally curvy and lush. Guys go for that."

They always had. Meri had spent the last decade marveling at the number of men her friend met, dated, slept with and dumped.

"Not Colin. He barely speaks to me."

"Which is interesting," Meri said. "He talks to everyone else."

It was true. Colin was tongue-tied around Betina. Meri thought it was charming.

At first, when her friend had confessed her interest in Colin, Meri had been protective of her coworker. Colin might enjoy the ride that was Betina, but once dumped, he would be heartbroken. Then Betina had admitted her feelings went a whole lot deeper. The L word had been whispered.

After getting over the idea of her friend being in love with anyone, Meri had agreed to help. So far, she'd been unable to think of a way to bring the couple together. Hunter's lodge had offered the perfect opportunity.

"You have time," Meri pointed out. "Jack and I never come down here, so you have the whole floor to yourselves. You can talk to each other in a casual setting. No pressure. It will be great."

Betina smiled. "Hey, it's *my* job to be the positive, self-actualized one."

"I know. I love being the emotionally mature friend. It doesn't happen often."

"It happens more and more."

Meri leaned in and hugged her friend. "You're the best."

"So are you."

Jack looked up as he heard footsteps on the stairs. Seconds later, Meri appeared in his loft office.

She'd changed into a tight skirt and cropped top, curled her hair and put on makeup. Always pretty, she'd upped the stakes to come-get-me sexy.

A quick bit of research on the Internet had told him that the guy she'd mentioned wasn't one of her scientists. Instead he worked for a D.C. lobbyist and was safely several thousand miles away. Not that Jack cared one way or the other. The only issue for him was researching the man more thoroughly. If things were getting serious, it was his job to make sure Meri wasn't being taken.

His low-grade anger was something he would deal with later. He didn't know why he minded the thought of her marrying some guy, but he did.

"We're going to dinner," she announced when she stopped in front of his desk. "You might not believe this, but we're actually a pretty fun group. You're welcome to join us."

"Thanks, but no."

"Want me to bring back something? The fridge is still fully stocked, but I could stop for chicken wings."

"I'm good."

She turned to leave. He stopped her with, "You should have mentioned you were engaged."

She turned back to him. "Why? You claim you're not sleeping with me. What would an engagement matter one way or another?"

"It makes a difference. I wouldn't have kissed you."

"Ah. Then I'm glad you didn't know." Her blue eyes brightened with amusement. "Does the fact that I belong to someone else make me more tempting? The allure of the forbidden?"

He had to consciously keep from smiling. She'd always been overly dramatic.

"No," he told her. "Sorry."

"You're not sorry. And, for what it's worth, the engagement isn't official. I wouldn't be trying to sleep with you if I'd said yes."

A cool rush of relief swept through him. "You said no?"

"I didn't say anything. Andrew hasn't actually proposed. I found a ring." She shifted on her high heels. "I didn't know what to think. I'd never thought about getting married. I realized we had unfinished business, so here I am. Seducing you."

He ignored that. "You're sleeping with him." The point was obvious, so he didn't make it a question.

She leaned forward and sighed. "It bothers you, doesn't it? Thinking about me in bed with another man. Writhing, panting, being taken." She straightened and fanned herself. "Wow, it's really warm here at the top of the house."

He didn't react, at least not on the outside. But her words had done what she'd wanted them to do. He reacted on the inside, with heat building in his groin.

She got to him. He would give her points for that. But she wouldn't win.

"So no on dinner?" she asked.

"I have work."

"Okay. Want a goodbye kiss before I go?"

He hated that he did. He wanted to feel her mouth on his, her body leaning in close. He wanted skin on skin, touching her until he made her cry out with a passion she couldn't control. "No, thanks," he said coolly.

She eyed him for a second, then grinned. "We both know that's not true, don't we, Jack?"

And then she was gone.

Four

Meri arrived home from dinner with her team feeling just full enough, with a slight buzz. They'd taken the shuttle van into town, and that had meant no one had to be a designated driver. Wine had flowed freely. Well, as freely as it could given no one drank more than a glass, preferring the thrill of intellectual discussion to the mental blurriness of too much alcohol.

But just this once Meri had passed up the wine and gone with a margarita. That was fine, but she'd ordered a second one and was absolutely feeling it as she climbed the stairs to her bedroom.

As she reached the landing, she saw two doors and was reminded that it was also the same floor with Jack's bedroom.

What an interesting fact, she thought as she paused

and stared at the firmly closed door. He was in there. By himself, she would guess. So what exactly was he getting up to?

She was pretty confident he was stretched out on the bed, watching TV or reading. But this was her buzz, and she could imagine him waiting for her in the massive tub in front of the fireplace if she wanted to. Because in her fantasy, he wanted her with a desperation that took his breath away. In her fantasy, he was deeply sorry for hurting her and he'd spent the past eleven years barely surviving because his love for her had been so great it had immobilized him.

"Okay, that last one is total crap," she whispered to herself. "But the other two have possibilities."

She walked to his door, knocked once, then let herself in before he could tell her to go away.

A quick glance around the room told her that he wasn't about to fulfill her bathtub fantasy. Probably for the best. She was really feeling the margarita, and drowning was a distinct possibility.

Instead of being naked and in water, Jack sat in a corner chair, his feet up on the leather ottoman, reading. At least he'd been reading until she'd walked in. Now he set the book on his lap and looked at her expectantly.

She swayed as she moved toward the bed and sank down on the edge. She pushed off her sandals and smiled at him.

"Dinner was great. You should have come."

"I'll survive the deep loss."

She smiled. "You're so funny. Sometimes I forget you're funny. I think it's because you're so intense and macho. Dangerous. You were always dangerous. Before, it was just about who you were as a person, but now you have access to all kinds of weapons. Doubly dangerous."

His gaze narrowed slightly. "You're drunk."

She waved her left hand back and forth. "*Drunk* is such a strong term. Tipsy. Buzzed. Seriously buzzed. I had a second margarita. Always a mistake. I don't drink much, so I never build up any tolerance. And I'm small, so there's not much in the way of body mass. I could figure out the formula if you want. How many ounces of alcohol per pound of human body."

"An intriguing offer, but no."

She smiled. "It's the math, huh. You're scared of the math. Most people are. I don't know why. Math is constant, you know. It's built on principles, and once you learn them, they don't change. It's not like literature. That's open to interpretation and there's all that writing. But math is clean. You're right or you're not. I like being right."

"It's your competitive streak," he said.

She swayed slightly on the bed. "You think I'm competitive?"

"It's in your blood."

"I guess. I like to be right about stuff. I get focused. I can be a real pain." She grinned. "Doesn't that make me even cuter? How can you stand it?"

"I'm using every ounce of willpower not to attack you this very moment."

"You're so lying, but it's sweet. Thank you."

She stared at him. If eyes were the windows to the

soul, then Jack's innermost place was a dark and protected place.

Secrets, she thought. They all had secrets. What were his?

Not that he would tell her. He kept that sort of thing to himself. But if he ever did decide to trust someone, it would be forever, she thought idly. Or maybe that was another of her fantasies.

"You need to help me with Betina and Colin," she told him. "We're going to get them together."

One dark eyebrow rose. "I don't think so."

"Oh, come on. Don't be such a guy. This could be fun. Just think of it—we could be part of a great love match."

"Colin and Betina?" He sounded doubtful.

"Sure. Betina has a serious thing for Colin. I was skeptical at first because Betina changes her men with the rhythm of the tide. A long-term relationship for her is a week. But that's because she's afraid to really care about someone. She had a bad early marriage years ago. Anyway, she's liked Colin for a long time, and that liking has grown into something more. Something significant."

She paused, waiting for him to grasp the importance of the information. Obviously he missed it, because he said, "I'm not getting involved."

"You have to. It's not like you're doing anything else with your time."

"We're going to ignore my work and the effort I put into avoiding you?"

"Oh, yeah. There's hard duty. A beautiful single woman desperately wants you in her bed. Poor Jack. Your life is pain."

She could think of a thousand ways he could have reacted, but she never expected him to smile.

"You think of yourself as beautiful?" he asked quietly, sounding almost pleased.

Meri shifted on the bed. "It was a figure of speech."

"The last time we talked about your appearance, you said you were a freak."

She didn't want to think about that, but if he insisted… "The last time we talked about my appearance, you emotionally slapped me, trampled my heart and left me for dead."

His smile faded. "I'm sorry. I should have handled that differently."

"But you didn't. I wasn't asking for sex right that moment." She didn't want to be talking about this. It was too humiliating. "My point is, Betina is crazy about Colin and I'm pretty sure he likes her. Which is where you come in. I want you to find out for sure."

"What? No."

"Why not? You're a guy, he's a guy. You can ask him if he likes Betina."

"Should I pass you a note in homeroom?"

"I don't care how I get the information, I just need confirmation."

"You're not getting it from me."

She remembered his being stubborn but never this bad. "Have I mentioned you're annoying? Because you are."

"I live to serve."

"If only that were true. Look, they're both great people. They deserve to be happy. I'm just giving them a little push."

"Did you need a push with Andrew?"

She sighed. "I wondered when you'd bring him up."

"You're nearly engaged. Why wouldn't I be curious?"

She tried to figure out what he was thinking from his tone of voice, but as usual, Jack gave nothing away. It was one of his more annoying characteristics.

"We met at a charity auction," she said. "There was a pet fashion show to start things off. Somehow I got tangled up in the leashes and nearly fell. Andrew rescued me. It was very romantic."

"I can only imagine."

She ignored any hint of sarcasm in his voice. Maybe knowing there was another man in her life would make him a little less arrogant.

"He was funny and charming and I liked him right away. We have so much in common. What movies we like, where we go on vacation. It's been really fun."

It *had* been fun, she thought, remembering all the good times with Andrew. But she'd been on this coast for nearly six months. They'd had a chance to get together only a few times, although they talked regularly. Their relationship seemed to be on hold and she obviously didn't mind. Something she was going to have to think about.

"Is he a genius, too?" Jack asked.

"No, he's delightfully normal. Smart but not too smart. I like that in a guy."

"What do you know about him? Did you check him out?"

"Of course. He's just a regular guy. Not in it for money." Her good mood faded. "Is that your point? That no one could possibly want me if it wasn't for the money?"

"Not at all. I just want you to be happy."

"I am happy. Blissfully so. Andrew's the one. We'll be engaged as soon as I get back to D.C." Which wasn't actually true but it sounded good.

"Congratulations."

Jack had ruined everything, she thought bitterly as she stood. Her buzz, her great evening.

"Just because you don't believe in letting yourself care about people doesn't mean the feelings aren't real," she told him. "Some of us want to connect."

"I hope you do. I hope this is everything you want."

"Why don't I believe you? What aren't you saying?"

"That if Andrew was so important to you, you wouldn't stay away from him for six months."

She walked to the door. "Who says I have?"

With that, she walked out and closed the door behind her.

It was only a few steps to her room, and she was grateful for the solitary quiet when she entered. After flicking on a few lights, she crossed to the window and stared out at the night sky.

It was a perfect night for viewing the stars, but she wasn't in the mood. Not even on her brand-new telescope. She hurt too much and it was hard to say why.

Maybe because Jack was right. If Andrew was that important to her, she wouldn't stay away from him for six months. But she had, and it had been relatively easy. Too easy. If she were really in love with him, wouldn't she be desperate to be with him?

Finding the engagement ring had shocked her. She hadn't known what to think about his proposing. She'd been happy, but a part of her had known that it was time to put off the inevitable. That closure with Jack was required.

She'd known about Hunter's friends coming to stay at the house. She'd taken the consulting job in California, hired on as the caretaker of the house and had waited to confront the man who was holding her back. Once she got her revenge on Jack, she would be fine.

"That's what's wrong," she whispered to herself. "I'm still waiting to punish him. Once Jack is reduced to dust, I'll be able to give my whole heart to Andrew. It's just going to be another week or so. Then I'll be happy."

Jack spent a restless night. He told himself it was because he'd had coffee too late in the day, but part of the problem was Meri's words. Her claim that he didn't connect.

Late the next morning, he saved the files on his computer and opened the top desk drawer in his temporary office. There was an envelope inside, along with a letter.

The letter had been waiting for him the first day he'd arrived. He'd recognized the distinctive handwriting and had known it was from Matt. The battered appliances in the kitchen had been another clue. His friend might be able to program a computer to do heart surgery, but Matt couldn't do something simple like work an electric can opener.

For some reason, Jack had avoided the letter. Now he opened the envelope and pulled out the single sheet of paper.

Jack—

When I read Ryan's note that called this place a "love shack," my first thought was, what a load of BS. But now I think he may have been onto something. He was also right about how wrong we were when we compiled our universal truths about women. Remember those? Yeah? Well, now you can forget 'em. We had no idea.

As for me, here's what I learned during my month at the cabin: the most important work you'll ever do has nothing to do with the job. And it's work you can't do by yourself. But when you find a partner you can trust and the two of you do that work together, it pays better than any career you could imagine. And the perks? You have no idea….

Have a good month, pal.

Matt.

Jack read the letter again. He'd figured out a long time ago that he didn't know squat about women. Not that it mattered, as he never got involved. As for Matt and his other friends, sometimes he allowed himself to miss them. To wonder what it would have been like if Hunter hadn't died. Because Hunter was the one who had held them all together. Without him, they'd gone their separate ways. There were times when he—

He stood and shook his head. Okay, he needed more coffee or something, because there was no way he was spending the rest of the morning in his head.

He went downstairs and poured himself coffee. He could hear Meri and her team talking in the dining room.

"String theory is ruining theoretical physics," one of the guys said. "Everything has to be defined and explained, which is wasting a lot of time. Sure there's a why and a how, but if there's no practical application, then why bother?"

"Because you can't know the practical application until you understand the theory."

"It's not a theory. It's equations. Compare string theory to something else. Something like—"

They kept on talking, but even thought Jack knew they were probably speaking English, he had no idea what they were saying. He knew string theory had nothing to do with strings and maybe something to do with the universe. The word *vibrating* was attached to the idea in his head, but whether that meant string theory was about vibrations in the universe or just so above him that it made his teeth hurt, he wasn't sure.

"All very interesting," Meri said loudly over the argument. "But it has little to do with the project at hand. Get back to work. All of you."

There was a little grumbling, but the discussion shifted back to something that sounded a lot like solid rocket fuel. Not that Jack could be sure.

After grabbing his mug, he stepped out onto the deck. Hunter would be proud of Meri. She'd turned into a hell of a woman.

He pulled out his cell phone and hit redial. Bobbi Sue answered on the first ring. "You've got to stop calling me," she told him by way of greeting. "I swear, you're starting to get on my nerves. We're all capable here. We can do the job. You're just bored, and let me tell you, I don't like being punished for your mood swings."

He ignored her. "I want you to check out someone Meri's seeing. Andrew Layman. His address is on file. I want to know everything about him. Apparently it's gotten serious, and I want to make sure Meri isn't getting involved with a guy after her money."

"I swear, Jack, you have got to stop spying on this girl. If you're so interested, date her yourself. Otherwise get out of her life."

"I can't. She's a wealthy heiress. That makes her a target. Besides, I gave my word."

"I wish you were here so you could see how unimpressed I am by you giving your word. This just isn't healthy." Bobbi Sue sighed. "I'll do it, but only because it's my job and, for the most part, I respect you."

He grinned, knowing Meri would adore his secretary. "Your praise is all that matters."

"As if I'd believe that. This'll take a couple of days."

"I'm not going anywhere."

"I hear that. You need to get out. Find a woman. I mean it, Jack. Either get involved with Meri or leave the poor girl alone. You have no right to do this."

"I have every right." Meri might not know it, but she needed him. Someone had to keep her safe.

He hung up and returned to the kitchen for more coffee. Meri entered from the dining room.

"Hi. How's your day going?" she asked as she pushed past him and walked into the pantry. "Have you seen the box of pencils I put in here? Colin insists on fresh pencils when he works. Betina thinks it's charming, but I have to tell you, his little quirks are a pain in the butt. There was a whole new box. I swear."

He heard her rummaging around, then she gasped. He stepped to the pantry door and saw her crouched by the bottom shelf.

"What?" he demanded. "Did you hit your head?"

"No," she whispered and slowly straightened. She held a box in her hand, but it wasn't pencils. Instead it was a shoe box covered with childish stickers of unicorns and stars and rainbows.

"This is mine," she breathed. "I haven't seen it in years. I'd forgotten about it. How did it get here?"

As he didn't know what "it" was, he only shrugged.

Meri looked up at him, her eyes filled with tears. "It's pictures of Hunter and my mom and all of us."

She set the box on the counter and opened the top. There were old Polaroid photos of a very young Hunter standing in front of some church. Probably in Europe. He looked about fourteen or fifteen. He had his arm around a much younger Meredith.

"God, I miss him," Meri whispered. "He was my family."

Betina walked into the kitchen. "It's pencils, Meri. You're supposed to be the smart one. Are you telling me you can't find a—" Betina stopped. "What happened?" She turned on Jack. "What the hell did you do to her?"

"Nothing," Meri said before he could defend himself. "It's not him. Look."

Betina moved close and took the photo. "That's you. Is that Hunter?"

"Uh-huh. I think we're in France." She pulled out more pictures. "I can't believe it. Look at how fat I am. Did anyone stop to say, 'Gee, honey, you should eat less'?"

"Food is love," Betina told her and fanned out the pictures on the counter. "You're adorable and Hunter is quite the hunk."

Several more members of Meri's team wandered into the kitchen. Soon they, too, were looking over pictures and talking about Hunter as if they'd known him.

Jack hung back. As much as he wanted to see his friend, he didn't want to open old wounds. For a second he wondered if Meri would need comforting, then he looked at all the people around her. She didn't need him at all. Which was for the best. He didn't want to get involved.

Meri paid the driver, then carried the bag of Chinese food into the house. "Dinner," she yelled in the general direction of the stairs, not sure if Jack would come down or not. She was gratified to see him walk into the kitchen a couple of minutes later.

"Why aren't you out with the nerd brigade?" he asked as she pulled a couple of plates out of the cupboard.

"Nerd brigade?" She smiled. "They'd like that. It sounds very military. They're all going to a club in Lake Tahoe and I'm not in the mood. Plus, I knew you were lonely, so I stayed home to keep you company."

"I'm not lonely."

He sounded annoyed as he spoke, which made her want to giggle. Jack was really easy to rile. It was that stick up his butt—if he would just let it go, he could be a regular person. Of course, his macho I'm-in-charge attitude was part of his appeal.

"Can you reach those?" she asked, pointing to the tall glasses some idiot had put on the top shelf. She could never have left them there.

While he got them for her, she carried the plates and food over to the table in the kitchen, then went to the refrigerator for a couple of beers.

When they were seated across from each other, she said, "So are we invading you too badly?"

"Do you care if you are?"

She considered the question and went with the honest answer. "Not really, but it seemed polite to ask."

"Good to know. I'm getting work done."

"Your company specializes in protecting corporations in scary parts of the world, right?"

He nodded.

"An interesting choice," she said. "But then, you have all that Special Forces training."

Again with the look.

She passed him the kung pao chicken. "I know a few things," she said.

"Yes, that's what my company does. When I left the Army, I wanted to start my own firm. Being a consultant didn't give me enough control. Someone has to rebuild roads in places like Iraq, and our job is to keep those people safe."

"Sounds dangerous."

"We know what we're doing."

"Weren't you supposed to be a lawyer?" she asked.

"I joined the Army after Hunter died."

An interesting way to cope with grief, she thought. But then, maybe the point had been to be so busy he could just forget.

"What do your parents have to say about all this?"

"They're still hoping I'll take over the Howington Foundation."

"Will you?" she asked.

"Probably not. I'm not the foundation type."

She wasn't either, but so far it wasn't an option. Her father seemed content to spend his money on the very young women in his life. Hunter's foundation ran smoothly. She had her trust fund, which she never touched, and a nice salary that covered all of her needs. If Hunter were still alive…

"You have to deal with your grief sometime," she said.

"About the foundation? I'm over it."

"No. Hunter."

Jack's mouth twisted. "I've dealt. Thanks for asking."

"I don't think so. There's a whole lot there under the surface." He'd let down his best friend. That had to bug him. Jack had let her down, too, but for once she wasn't mad at him. Maybe because she'd had a good cry after looking at all the pictures she'd found and felt emotionally cleansed.

She looked at him. "On my bad days I tell myself you're a selfish bastard who played us all. On my good days I tell myself you wanted to stay but couldn't handle what you were going through. Which is it?"

"Both."

* * *

Meri waited until nearly midnight, then climbed the stairs to Jack's office, prepared to let herself out onto the balcony and enjoy the beauty of the heavens. She didn't expect to find him on his laptop.

"You're not supposed to be here," she grumbled as he glanced up. "It's late. You need your rest."

"I see you've changed your seduction techniques. These are interesting. Less effective, in case you were wondering."

"I'm not here to seduce you. I have more important things to do with my time."

He glanced out the French doors toward the sky. "I see. And I would get in the way?"

"You're going to ask a lot of irritating questions. You won't be able to help it. I'll try to be patient, but I'll snap and then you'll get your feelings hurt. I'm just not in the mood to deal with your emotional outbursts."

Instead she wanted to stare at the sky and let the vast beauty heal her soul. Okay, yes, getting Jack into bed was her ultimate goal, but there was a time and place for work and this wasn't it.

"I suspect my feelings will survive just fine," he said.

"No way. You'll go all girlie on me."

She shouldn't have said it. She knew that. She hadn't actually meant to challenge him—she was simply impatient to get out into the night and use the telescope.

He stood without speaking and moved around the desk until he was standing in front of her. Looming, actually. She had to tilt her head all the way back to see into his eyes.

"You think I'm girlie?" he asked in a low, slightly dangerous voice. A voice thick with power. A voice that made her realize he was a whole lot bigger than her and that there were a couple of floors between her and help.

"Not at all," she said quickly. "I didn't mean to say it. The words just slipped out. Bad me. You should probably stalk out and teach me what for by leaving me alone."

Instead he tucked a strand of hair behind her ear. "Do you play all the men in your life?"

She swallowed. "Pretty much."

"Does it work?"

"Mostly."

"Not this time."

He cupped her cheek with his hand, bent down and kissed her.

She'd sensed he was going to and should have had time to brace herself. It was just a kiss, right? No big deal. They'd kissed before, and while she'd liked it, she'd managed to keep perfect control...sort of.

But not this time. The second his mouth touched hers, she started dissolving from the inside out. Technically that couldn't be true, but it *felt* true. Heat poured through her, making her want to move closer. Again something that didn't make sense. The closer she got to Jack, the more their shared body temperature would rise. Wait—it wouldn't rise exactly, it would...

He moved his mouth against hers. This wasn't the angry, something-to-prove kiss he'd given her at the gym. That had been easy to deal with. This kiss was different. It offered instead of taking. He applied just enough pressure to make her want to lean in and do a little demanding of her own.

Without meaning to, she reached up and rested her hands on his shoulders. He pulled her close until they were touching all over. Shoulder to knee, man to woman. He was hard and unyielding, a combination she found wildly erotic.

One of his hands slipped through her hair, tangling in the waves. The other moved up and down her back. Slowly, so slowly. Not touching anything significant, but still…touching.

He continued to brush his mouth against hers, keeping the kiss chaste yet arousing her until she wanted to grab him, shake him and tell him to get on with it already.

When he licked her bottom lip, she nearly groaned in relief. Fortunately she managed to hold in the sound. She even waited a nanosecond before parting for him. She didn't want to seem *too* eager. But then his tongue was touching hers, and staying cool was the last thing on her mind. Not when her blood rushed through her body at Mach 1 and every interesting female part of her began to tingle and ache and move toward begging to be touched.

He kissed her deeply, exploring, teasing, circling. She met him stroke for stroke, wanting to arouse him as much as he aroused her. Not to prove a point, for once, but because a kiss this good should be shared. Because it felt right.

She breathed in the scent of his body. She wished she were physically capable of crawling inside of him so she could know what he was feeling at that exact moment.

Instead she tilted her head and continued to kiss him as if this had been her plan all along.

She felt the hardness of his arousal pressing into her midsection. He wanted her. There was physical proof.

It should have been a moment of rejoicing. She should have pulled away and crowed about her victory. She was more than halfway there. But while she did pull back, she didn't say a word. Instead she stared into his dark eyes, at the fire there, the fire that matched the one raging inside her.

Then she did the only thing that couldn't possibly make sense. She turned and ran.

Five

If there wasn't twenty million for charity on the line, not to mention the house itself, Jack would have been on the road back to Texas the next morning. But he was stuck for the month. All the other guys had survived their time at Hunter's Landing, so he would, too. But he would bet a lot of money that their weeks had been a whole lot less hellish than his.

He didn't want to think about his most recent kiss with Meri, but he couldn't seem to think about anything else. It had been different. He'd felt the power of his need for her all the way down to his bones. He'd ached for her in a way that was more than unsettling.

Trouble. Meri was nothing but trouble. She'd been a whole lot easier to handle when she'd been a teenager.

He walked into the kitchen, intent on coffee, only to

find one of her team members pouring a cup. Jack frowned slightly, trying to put a name with the face.

"Morning," the guy said and held out the pot for Jack.

"Morning…Colin," he added, remembering the smaller man from his arrival.

"Right." Colin pushed up his glasses and smiled. "Great house."

"I agree."

"It belongs to your friend, right? Meri's brother? The one who died."

Casual, easy words. *The one who died.* They cut through him like a razor and left wounds only he could see. "Yes. Hunter had this house built."

"Meri said this house was being turned over to the town or something. That it's going to be a place where sick people can recover and regroup. That's cool."

It was pure Hunter. Wanting to make a difference even after he was gone.

"How's the work coming?" Jack asked, not wanting to talk about his friend anymore. "Making progress?"

"Not yet. Theoretically there is a way to increase thrust within the confines of a safe formulation, but the nature of our planet seems to be that going faster and longer always means creating something toxic. Meri is determined to change that. When we consider the finite nature of our resources and the vastness of space, there are going to have to be some spectacular breakthroughs before we'll ever have a chance to explore our solar system, let alone the galaxy."

Colin took a quick gulp of his coffee. "The truth is, the next few generations are going to be like the early

Vikings. Going off on the rocket equivalent of rafts into a great unknown. If you consider their total lack of technology, the analogy is even more interesting. Because we consider ourselves cutting-edge, but compare what we have now to the first Russian launches. It's like they used paper clips and rubber bands to hold the whole thing together. But if they hadn't launched first, would Kennedy have pushed space flight? If you knew the number of modern innovations that came out of the space program…" He trailed off and looked slightly confused. "What were we talking about?"

"How your work was going."

"Oh, yeah. Sorry. I get carried away." Colin shifted slightly. "I like your car."

"Thanks." The sleek sports car wasn't practical, but it was fun to drive.

"Get good mileage with that?"

Jack grinned. "No."

"I didn't think so. I'd like a car like that."

"So buy one," Jack told him. Someone with Colin's brain had to make enough money.

"I'd like to, but it's not a good idea. I'm not a great driver." Colin shrugged. "I get easily distracted. You know, I'll be going along just fine and then I think about something with work and—zap—I'm just not paying attention. I've had a couple of accidents. I drive a Volvo. It's safer for me and the rest of the world."

"Okay, then." A sports car was not a good idea. At least Colin understood his limitations.

"Meri said you own a company that works in dangerous parts of the world," Colin said. "Interesting work?"

"More of a logistical challenge. People need to be able to work in dangerous parts of the world. My teams make sure they stay safe."

"Sounds exciting."

"It's an easy way to get dead. You have to know what you're doing."

Colin nodded slowly. He was blond and pale, with light blue eyes and a slightly unfocused expression. "Military background?" he asked.

"Special Forces."

Colin sighed. "I wanted to go to West Point. At least when I was a kid. But I was already in college by the time I was thirteen. Besides, I don't think I would have survived the physical training."

Jack had spent his six years of service staying out of any kind of officer training. "It's all a matter of discipline."

Colin smiled. "Maybe for you. For some of us there's an issue of natural ability. Or lack thereof. Meri talks about you a lot. I decided she had to be making it up, but she wasn't. You really are dynamic and powerful. Probably good with women."

Colin seemed to shrink as he spoke. Jack wasn't sure how to respond to his comments. What most interested him was the fact that Meri talked about him. Unfortunately that was the one question he couldn't ask.

"You have a thing for Meri?"

"What?" Colin's eyes widened. He pushed up his glasses again. "No. She's great, don't get me wrong, but we're just friends. She's not anyone I would…you know…be attracted to."

Jack's first instinct was to grab the little weasel by

the throat and ask him what the hell he thought was wrong with Meri. Then he got a grip and told himself to back off.

His second instinct was to walk away, because he didn't do personal conversations. But then he remembered Meri's insistence that they help Colin and Betina get together.

He refused to play matchmaker, but maybe a couple of questions couldn't hurt.

"You're a lucky guy," he said. "Surrounded by beautiful women."

Colin blinked. "Betina's beautiful."

"Yes, she is. Meri mentioned she wasn't one of the scientists?"

"Oh, no. She coordinates the project. She's just a normal person. She keeps us on track with our time and our budget. She takes care of things." His voice had a dreamy quality. "She always smells good. It's not always the same scent. Some of it is perfume, but there's an intriguing quality to her skin…."

"Sounds like someone worth getting to know."

"She is," Colin said, then paused. "What do you mean?"

"Is she seeing anyone?"

"What? I don't think so. But Betina has a lot of men. Practically a different man every week. She's always fun. I don't think the two of you would get along at all."

Jack held in a grin. "You're probably right. Have you two ever…?"

"Oh." Colin took a step back. "No. We've never dated or anything."

"Not your type either?"

"Uh, no. Probably not." But Colin sounded more resigned than anything else. As if he'd given up hope on the one thing he wanted.

Jack heard the shuttle van arriving and excused himself. He took the stairs up to his office, but as he passed the landing for the bedrooms, he paused. Meri liked to just pop into his room without warning. Maybe it was time to play the same game with her. Last night's kiss had obviously rattled her. He should press his advantage.

He crossed to her room and opened the door without knocking. Meri stood beside her bed.

The drapes were open and sunlight streamed into the room, illuminating every inch of her. Her hair fell in a wavy mass down her back. Her skin gleamed as if it had been dusted with starlight. She wore nothing but a tiny pair of bikini panties.

He stared at her nearly naked body, taking in the dip of her waist, the narrow rib cage and her perfect breasts. She held a bra in each hand, as if she'd been trying to decide which one to wear.

At last he raised his gaze to her face. She looked confused and apprehensive. There was none of her usual sass or spark.

Wanting slammed into him, nearly knocking him over with its intensity. On the heels of that came guilt. He'd promised Hunter he would keep Meredith safe from predators. Men exactly like himself.

"I'm sorry," he said and backed out of the room.

Meri dressed quickly, then stood in the center of her room, not sure what to do. Last night's kiss had been upsetting enough. She'd reacted to it with a passion that had stunned her. She'd wanted him, and nothing in her revenge plan was supposed to be about wanting.

She'd tried to convince herself that her reaction had been perfectly natural. Jack was a good-looking guy she liked a lot. She used to have a crush on him. It had been illogical to assume she could seduce him and not get aroused herself. End of story.

But she hadn't been able to totally believe herself. Now, having seen the need in his eyes, she knew the wanting wasn't all one-sided.

She left her room and went upstairs to his office. Sure enough, Jack was at his computer, staring at the screen as if it were the only thing that mattered.

"We have to talk," she said.

"No, we don't."

"I'm not leaving. You want me. I saw it in your eyes."

"I walked in on a beautiful naked woman. It was a biological reaction to a visual stimulus. Nothing more. I would have wanted anyone who fit the description."

She considered his words. Was he telling the truth? Was that all it was? Biology at work?

"I don't think so," she said. "It was more specific than that. You don't want any woman. You want me."

He finally looked up from the computer. "I've never understood why anyone would bang their head against a wall to make the pain go away, but I do now."

She smiled. "It's just part of my charm. Come on, Jack. You want me. Why can't you admit it?"

He sucked in a breath. She held hers, waiting for the words that would make her want to party like it was 1999.

"I talked to Colin about Betina," he said instead.

She sank into the chair opposite his desk. All thoughts of wanting and sex disappeared as she leaned forward eagerly. "Really? What did he say?"

"Nothing specific. You're right—he has a thing for her, but he thinks he's totally out of her league."

She groaned. "Of course he does."

"Why?" Jack asked. "He's got a lot going for him. He's smart and he has a good job. He seems nice. He should be like catnip."

"It's not that simple. Colin is like me—book-smart, world-stupid. Betina is one of those funny, social people who makes life a party wherever she goes. Colin bonds with the potted plant in the room. Trust me, I've been there."

"You were never that bad."

"I was worse. I had a wild crush on a guy I could never have. Then he broke my heart."

Jack looked out the window, then back at her. "I've apologized for that. I can't take it back."

"I know, but I like punishing you for it over and over again. The point is, being that smart isn't easy. I always knew I didn't fit in, and Colin feels the same way. We're bright enough to see the problem, but we can't seem to fix it."

"You're saying Colin can't take the steps to tell Betina he's interested?"

"He won't see himself as capable."

"Then maybe they shouldn't be together."

"I don't accept that," Meri told him. "Colin is a sweetie. And Betina is my best friend. I owe her everything. I want her to be happy. I'm going to make this happen."

"You shouldn't get involved."

"Too late. Thanks for your help."

"I didn't help."

She smiled. "You so did. When we go to their wedding, you can tell everyone how you had a hand in getting them together."

He groaned. "Or you could just shoot me now."

"Where's the fun in that?"

Six

"I have happy news," Meri told Betina that afternoon when they'd finished working for the day.

Betina glanced out the kitchen window to where the rest of the team had walked down to the water. "You're giving up your ridiculous quest to sleep with Jack?"

"Never that," Meri told her. "I'm actually getting closer by the day. He's weak with desire. I'm sure you've noticed him limping."

"You're a nut."

"Maybe, but I'm a nut with fabulous news about Colin. He likes you."

Betina had traveled the world, dated a European prince and had a very wealthy sheik invite her into his harem. She had a tattoo, knew how to do henna and had explained the intricacies of sex to Meri in such detail that her first time had been a breeze. But she'd never once, in all the years Meri had known her, blushed.

Betina ducked her head. "I don't think so."

"He does. He talked to Jack about you. He thinks you're great. He's just lacking in confidence. But you have enough confidence for two people, so you're a perfect match."

Betina raised her head. "You dragged Jack into this?"

"I didn't drag him. He wanted to help. Sort of. That's so not the point. Isn't this fabulous? Aren't you happy?"

Betina didn't look the least bit thrilled. Her friend walked over to the kitchen table and sat down. "I'm not sure I want things to change."

Meri sank down across from her. "What? Are you crazy? We're talking about Colin."

"Exactly. He's really special. Right now he's my friend and I can depend on him to always be my friend. If I change that relationship, there's no going back."

"Is that a bad thing?"

"I don't know and neither do you. Meri, there are consequences for everything we do. What if Colin and I don't hit it off? What if he's not who I think he is? Then I'll lose the friendship and have nothing."

Meri didn't understand. "I thought you were in love with him."

"I am. That's what makes this so hard. I'd rather just be his friend than not have him in my life at all."

"But you could be more. You could have it all. I don't understand. You've always been a risk taker."

"Not when something important is on the line. There I'm nothing but a coward."

This was news, Meri thought, confused by her friend. "I don't get it. You're in love with him. There's a very good chance that he's in love with you. And yet you're not going to do anything about it? You'd rather have a skinny piece of pie than the whole thing?"

"It's better than no pie."

"But if you don't try, you'll always wonder. You'll have regrets—and, believe me—those are the worst."

"How would you know?"

Meri smiled sadly. "I grew up the queen of regrets. There were so many things I wanted to do when I was growing up. But I was always afraid. I didn't fit in and I wasn't willing to risk being rejected. So I never tried. I was miserable in college, so sure no one would ever want to be my friend. Looking back, I can see a few times when people approached me. But I blew them off. It was easier to be right than to risk. But it was a high price. Like you said, there are always consequences."

"What are the consequences of sleeping with Jack?" Betina asked.

"So now we're talking about me?"

"I have more confidence in the subject."

Meri considered the question. "I finally get to move on with my life. He was my first crush and then he hurt me. I've grown up and matured, but I've never been able to let him totally go. He's always lurking in the back of my mind. If I can get over him, I can move on. He's the reason I've never been able to fall in love."

"I thought you were in love with Andrew."

Was she? Meri didn't know what real, adult love felt like. She enjoyed Andrew's company. She liked being with him. Six months ago she would have said yes, she was pretty sure she was almost in love with him. Today she was less sure.

"I haven't missed him enough," she said softly. "I've seen him only a couple of times in the past six months. Shouldn't I be destroyed without him?"

"Nothing about you is normal. Andrew seems like a good guy. You'll hook up again when you go back to D.C. You can figure out your feelings then. Assuming you're not in love with Jack."

What? "No way. I don't love him. I want to hurt him. I want to make him crawl and beg and then I want to walk away."

"That's sure the story," Betina said calmly. "The one you've been telling yourself for years. But is it the truth?" She shrugged. "I have my doubts. I think you've never gotten over Jack. I don't think any of this is about revenge. You can't accept you still love him so this is the story you tell yourself. But be careful. You're not into casual relationships. What happens if you sleep with him and then can't walk away? You want him to break your heart twice?"

In love with Jack? "Never. He can't hurt me. I won't let him. He's little more than a symbol of the issues in my childhood. Once I prove I've outgrown him, I can let my past go."

"An excellent theory. You'll have to tell me how that works out for you."

Meri hated her friend's doubts. Betina was her oracle, the keeper of social and romantic knowledge. They'd never disagreed on anything significant before.

"I have to do this," Meri said. "I've waited too long to walk away now. I have to go for it. You should, too. Tonight."

Betina laughed. "You're a brave woman. Braver than me."

"That's not true."

"It is when it comes to matters of the heart. You're willing to risk it all to get what you want, and I'm not."

Jack walked into his room that night weary from too many hours at the computer. He pulled the hem of his shirt out of his jeans and started unbuttoning it, only to stop when he heard something in the bathroom.

He turned and saw the door was closed but light shone from underneath. What the hell?

But as quickly as the question formed, it was answered. There was only one person who would be hanging out in his bathroom. Meri.

He hesitated as he tried to figure out the best way to handle the situation. With his luck, she was probably naked. Maybe in the tub. Waiting for him. She'd been doing her best to seduce him, and he hated to admit that she'd done a damn fine job. He was primed and ready. It wouldn't take much to push him over the edge.

The question was, did he want to fall?

He owed Hunter his loyalty. He'd given his word and he hadn't done much of a job of seeing it through. All his friend had asked was for him to protect his sister. Instead Jack had cut and run. Sure, he'd kept tabs on Meri from a distance, but that was taking the easy way out.

Which meant now was the time to make good on his

promise. He would walk into the bathroom, tell Meredith to get the hell out of there, explain nothing was ever going to happen between them and grit his teeth for the rest of the time he was stuck up here in the lodge.

A least it was a plan.

He sucked in a breath and walked into the bathroom.

It was as he'd expected. Candles glowing, rose petals scattered, the fire flickering and a very naked Meri in the tub.

She'd piled her hair on top of her head, exposing the sexy line of her neck. Bubbles in the bath floated across the water, giving him a quick view of her nakedness before moving to cover the scene. Her perfect breasts floated, a siren's lure calling to him.

He was hard in a heartbeat. Hard and ready to take her every way he knew how.

It wasn't her pale skin or the music playing in the background that got to him. It wasn't the way she'd set the scene or the fact that he knew she wasn't just willing, she was determined. He could have resisted all of that, even her slightly pouting lips.

What he couldn't resist was the book she was reading. She'd set out to seduce him and had gotten so caught up in a textbook on nuclear fission that she hadn't even heard him walk into the bathroom. That was the very heart of Meri. A walking, breathing genius brain trapped in the body of a centerfold. Who else could possibly appreciate the magic that was her?

Meri sighed as she turned the page. Why did Jerry have to go out of his way to make a perfectly mesmerizing topic boring? She'd been a little nervous when he'd asked her to read his latest textbook, and now that she was into it, she realized she'd been wary for a reason. Nuclear fission was one of the great discoveries of the twentieth century. Shouldn't that be celebrated? Shouldn't it at least be interesting? But noooo. Jerry wrote down to his audience and had taken what was—

The book was ripped from her hands. Meri blinked in surprise to find Jack standing beside the tub. Tub? She was in a tub? When had that happened?

She blinked again and her memory returned. Right. She'd planned on seducing him tonight. She glanced around and saw the candles and rose petals. At least she'd done a nice job.

"Hi," she said as she smiled up at Jack. "Surprise."

"You sure are that."

She braced herself for him to yell at her or stalk off or explain for the four hundredth time why this was never going to work. She didn't expect him to pull her to her feet, drag her out of the bath and haul her against him.

She was stunned. In a good way. She liked how he stared into her eyes as if she were prime rib and he were a starving man. She liked how his hands moved up and down her back, then slipped lower, to her butt.

She was totally naked. A fact he seemed to appreciate.

"But I'm all wet," she whispered.

"I hope that's true," he said before he bent his head and kissed her.

His mouth was firm and sure, claiming her with a kiss that demanded a response. She tilted her head and parted for him, wanting to get the party started with some soul-stirring kisses.

He didn't disappoint. He moved into her mouth, brushing her tongue with his, moving leisurely, as if arousing her was the only thing on his mind. Heat poured through her.

Not that she was cold. Not with the fire to her back and Jack pressing against her front.

As he kissed her over and over again, he moved his hands over her body. He touched her shoulders, her back, her hips, tracing her skin, igniting nerve endings everywhere he went.

She raised her hands to his shoulders, then slid her fingers through his hair. She touched his cheeks, feeling the stubble there, before exploring his chest.

He was strong and masculine. When he cupped her rear, she arched against him and felt the hard thickness of his erection. A thrill of anticipation shot through her. She shivered.

He pulled back a little. "Cold?"

"No."

He stared into her eyes. She stared back, wondering what he was thinking. He'd been resisting her best efforts for a while now. Did he regret giving in? Not that she was going to ask. There were some things it was best not to know.

He didn't act like a man with regrets. He bent down, but instead of kissing her lips, he pressed his mouth to her neck and nibbled his way to her collarbone.

His hands rested lightly on her waist. As he teased her neck, licked her earlobe, then gently bit down, he moved his hands up her rib cage, toward her breasts.

Before her surgery she'd been warned that she might

lose some of the sensitivity in her breasts, but she'd been one of the lucky ones. She could feel everything—every touch, every kiss, every whisper of breath. She tensed in anticipation of how Jack would make her tingle.

When he reached her curves, he cupped them gently. He explored her skin, then swept his thumbs across her nipples. Her insides tightened.

He kissed his way down to her breasts and drew her left nipple into his mouth. She leaned her head back as he circled her, then sucked and licked. Ribbons of need wove through her body, settling in her rapidly swelling center. The dull ache of arousal grew.

He turned his attentions to her other nipple, teasing and kissing until her breathing came in pants and her legs began to tremble.

Even as he continued to tease her breasts, he slipped one hand lower and lower, down her belly, toward the promised land. She parted her legs and braced herself for the impact his touch would have on her. Only he didn't touch her *there*. Instead he stroked her thighs and played with her curls. He ran his fingers along the outside but never dipped in.

She shifted impatiently, wondering if shaking him would get the message across. There! He needed to touch her *there*.

But he ignored that place where she was wet and swollen and desperately ready. He squeezed her bottom, he circled her belly button, he touched everywhere else.

Just when she was about to issue a complaint in writing, he pulled back a little, bent down and gathered her in his arms. Before she could catch her breath, he'd carried her into the bedroom and placed her on the bed. Then he was kneeling between her legs, his fingers parting her as he gave her an intimate, six-second-to-climax openmouthed kiss.

The combination of tongue and lips and breath made her moan in delight. He licked her with the leisurely confidence of a man who knows what to do and likes doing it. She gave herself over to the steady stroking and the easy exploration.

Tension invaded her. Each clench of her muscles pushed her higher and closer. One summer while she was still in college, she'd played with the idea of becoming a doctor, so she'd read several medical textbooks. She knew the biological steps leading to an orgasm—the arousal, how the blood made the area feel hot, the mechanism involved in swelling, the response of the sympathetic nervous system.

But none of those words could begin to describe what it felt like to have Jack suck on the most nerve-filled place in her body. How there seemed to be a direct connection between that engorged spot between her legs and the rest of her. How each flick of his tongue made her stomach clench and her heels dig into the bed.

She felt herself getting closer and closer. He moved patiently, slowly, drawing out the experience. Taking her to the edge, then pulling back just enough to keep her from coming.

Again and again she caught sight of her release, only to have it move out of reach.

Then, without warning, he went faster. The quick

flicks of his tongue caught her off guard. She had no time to prepare, no way to brace herself for the sudden explosion of pleasure that tore her apart.

Wave after wave of release swept through her. She pressed down, wanting to keep the feelings going. He gentled his touch but didn't pull away. Not until she experienced the last shudder and was able to finally draw in a breath.

She opened her eyes and found him looking at her. Under any other circumstance, his smug grin would have annoyed her, but considering what he'd just done, she decided he'd earned it.

She grabbed him by his shirt front and urged him to slide up next to her. When he would have spoken, she touched his mouth with her fingers, telling him to be quiet. While she loved a good relationship conversation as much as the next woman, this was a time for silence.

When he was on his back, she unbuttoned his shirt, then kissed her way down his chest to his belly. He was warm and he tasted sexy and faintly sweet. She nipped at his side, which made him both laugh and groan, then she went to work on his jeans.

He was so hard she had trouble with the zipper but finally managed to get it unfastened. He helped her push down his jeans and briefs.

She knelt between his legs, taking in the beauty that was his aroused naked body. His erection called to her. She reached out and touched him, then stroked his length. He put his hand on top of hers.

"I don't have any protection," he said.

She smiled. "Come on, Jack. It's me. When have I not prepared for every contingency?"

She leaned forward and opened his nightstand, then pulled out the condoms she'd put there before she'd started her bath.

Seconds later, the condom in place, she eased herself onto him.

He was big and thick and he filled her, stretching her inside in the most delicious way possible. She braced herself on her hands and knees, settling in for the ride.

His dark gaze met hers. "You really think I'm going to let you be on top?" he asked.

"Uh-huh."

He reached for her breasts. "You're right."

She laughed, then rocked back and forth, easing herself onto him, then off. At the same time, he cupped her breasts, teasing her nipples and providing a heck of a distraction.

She forced herself to concentrate on that place where they joined, but it got more and more difficult as her body got lost in the pleasure. With each stroke, she drove herself closer to another orgasm.

She felt him tense beneath her. She rode him faster, taking them higher and harder, pushing toward their mutual goal.

He abandoned her breasts and grabbed her hips, holding her tightly enough to control the pace. It was just slow enough to make her whimper.

So close, she thought as she concentrated on the feel of him pushing inside of her again and again. So…

And then she was coming. Her release rushed

through her, urging her on. Faster and faster until she felt him hold her still as he shuddered beneath her.

On and on their bodies joined, until they were both still.

Jack rolled her onto her side and withdrew. They stared at each other in the soft light of the room. He touched her face.

"I wasn't going to let you do that," he murmured.

"I know. You mad?"

"Not at you."

At himself? Because he'd betrayed his promise to Hunter? Meri started to tell him it didn't matter when it suddenly occurred to her that maybe it did. To him, at least. That maybe he regretted letting his friend down and that this had been the last promise he'd been able to keep.

Only he hadn't.

"Jack…" she began.

He shook his head. "Don't go there. Wherever you're going, don't."

She opened her mouth, then closed it. She didn't want to apologize. Not exactly. But she felt as if she should say something.

"I should go," she murmured

"You don't have to."

She stared into his dark eyes and knew she wanted to stay. Even if it was just one night, she wanted to spend the time with him.

"I went to a psychic once," she told him. "She told me that one day I would be in bed with the devil. I always knew she meant you. It's not your fault you gave in. It was destiny."

He smiled faintly. "You believe in psychics?"

"I believe in a lot of things. I'm very interesting."

"Yes, you are."

She sighed and snuggled close. "Are we going to make love again tonight?"

"Yes."

"You can be on top this time if you want."

He chuckled. "You're not in charge."

"Of course I am. I'm also totally irresistible. Right now you're wondering how you resisted me for so long."

"It's like you can read my mind."

She closed her eyes and breathed in the scent of him. Everything about this moment felt right, she thought. As if this was what she'd been waiting for. As if—

Wait a minute. She wasn't supposed to *like* having sex with Jack. She was supposed to be getting her revenge and moving on. They weren't supposed to connect.

They weren't, she told herself. She was just emotionally gooey from the afterglow. It was a biological response. Her body's attempt to bond with a man who was genetically desirable. Come morning, she would be totally over him and this and be ready to walk away. Her plan would go on as scheduled and she would be free to move forward with her life.

"I'm healed," Meri told Betina the next morning as she poured milk over her cereal. "Seriously, if I had a limp, it would be gone."

Betina looked her over. "Based on the smirk and the glow, I'm going to guess you and Jack did the wild thing last night."

Meri sighed with contentment. "We did. It was fabulous. Better than I imagined, which is hard to believe. I feel like a new woman. A new woman with really, really clear skin!"

Betina laughed. "Okay. Good for you."

"Any progress with Colin?"

"No. I watched a movie and he spent the evening on his computer. Then we went to bed separately."

Meri felt her fabulous mood fade a little. "That sucks. You need to talk to him."

"I'm not taking advice from you."

"Why not? My plan is working perfectly. Jack has had me and now he wants more. But he's not going to get any more. I'm walking away."

"Really?"

"Absolutely."

"And you don't feel a thing?"

"I'm a little sore," Meri said with a grin.

Betina slowly shook her head. "Okay. Then I was wrong. I guess you don't have any feelings for him. If you're not thinking about being with him again or wanting to hang out with him, then you are healed. Yay you."

Her friend poured coffee and walked out of the kitchen. Meri stared after her.

She didn't have feelings for Jack. Okay, sure, he was a friend and, as such, she would always have a soft spot for him. She was also willing to admit that not sleeping with him again might be difficult, but only because it had been so darned good. Not because she felt any kind of emotional connection.

But as she thought the words, she felt a little *ping* in her heart. One that warned her something might not be right.

"I don't care about him," she told herself. "I don't."

Which was a good thing, because falling for him would totally ruin her attempts at revenge.

She finished her cereal, rinsed the bowl and put it in the dishwasher. Then she walked into the dining room.

Someone rang the bell at the front door. She frowned. It was too early for the rest of the team, not to mention a delivery. So who on earth…?

She walked to the front of the house and opened the door. Her mind went blank as she stared at the man standing there. The man who swept her into his arms and kissed her.

"Hey, babe," he said.

She swallowed. "Andrew. This is a surprise."

Seven

When Jack finished getting dressed after his shower, he debated going downstairs for coffee or heading up to the loft to check in with his office.

Coffee won, mostly because he hadn't gotten much sleep the previous night. Sharing a bed with Meri had been anything but restful.

He walked out of his bedroom, then paused at the landing to look at the picture he'd mostly avoided since arriving at the house. It showed him and his friends during college. When everything had been easy and they'd called themselves the Seven Samurai.

Hunter laughed into the camera, because he'd always enjoyed whatever he was doing. Luke and Matt—twins who couldn't be more different—held Ryan in a headlock, while he and Devlin poured beer over the group. He knew that just outside the view of the camera sat a teenage girl on a blanket, her head buried in a book. Because Meri had never quite fit in.

Hunter had worried about her, especially after he'd found out he was dying. That's when he'd asked Jack to take care of her.

"Hell of a job," Jack muttered to himself as he turned away from the picture. Sure, Meri was all grown up now, a woman who made her own choices. That was her excuse for what had happened the previous night. What was his?

He'd wanted her. Who wouldn't? She was smart and funny and pretty as hell. She challenged him the way no one else dared. She was sexy and irreverent and so filled with life and ideas. Hunter would have been proud of her. Then he would have turned on Jack like a rabid dog and beaten the crap out of him. Or at least he would have tried. Knowing it was all his fault, Jack knew he just might have let him.

So now what? Meri had claimed she wanted to seduce him, which she probably thought she had. Did they just move on now? Pretend it hadn't happened? Because it shouldn't have, no matter how good it had been. If he could turn back time…

Jack shook his head. No point in lying to himself. If he could turn back time, he would do it all over again. Which made him a pretty big bastard and a sorry sort of friend.

He glanced back at the photo. Now what?

He heard footsteps on the stairs. But instead of a petite blonde with an attitude, he saw Betina climbing toward him.

"Morning," he said.

She reached the landing and looked at him. There was something in her eyes—something that warned him she was not happy about certain events.

"What?" he asked.

"That would be my question to you." She drew in a breath. "Look, it's not my business—"

Great. She was going to get protective. "You're right. It's *not* your business."

She glared at him. "Meredith is my friend. I care about her. I don't want her to get hurt."

"What makes you think that's going to happen?"

"It's in your nature. You're the kind of man who is used to getting what he wants and walking away."

True enough, he thought, not sure what that had to do with anything. "Meri's not in this for the long term," he said.

"That's what she keeps telling me, but I'm not so sure. I think she's in a position where she could get her heart broken."

"Not by me."

Betina rolled her eyes. "Are all men stupid about women or is it just the ones in this house?"

"You expect me to answer that?"

"No. I expect you to respect someone you're supposed to care about. You've known Meri a long time. She's not like the rest of us. She didn't grow up with a chance at being normal. She managed to fit in all on her own."

"I heard you had a part in making that happen."

Betina shrugged. "I gave her direction. She did the

work. But she's not as tough as she thinks. What she had planned for you was crazy—and I told her that, but she wouldn't listen."

"Typical."

"I know. My point is I don't want anything bad to happen to her. If you hurt her, I'll hunt you down like the dog you are and make you pay."

He gave her a half smile. "Going to hire someone to beat me up?"

"No, Jack. I'm going to tell you exactly how much she's suffering. I'm going to point out that you were her brother's best friend and that he asked only one thing of you and you couldn't seem to do it. Not then and not now. I'm going to be the voice in your head—the ugly one that never lets you rest."

He met her steady gaze with one of his own. "You're good."

"I care about her. She's part of my family. She deserves someone who loves her. Are you that guy?"

He didn't have to think about that. "No." He'd never loved anyone. He refused to care. It cost too much.

"Then leave her alone. Give her a chance with someone else."

"Someone like Andrew?" Jack had a bad feeling about him. He would get his report soon enough and then figure out what to do.

"Funny you should mention him," Betina said, looking amused. "I guess you don't know."

"Know what?"

"He's here."

* * *

Meri pulled back, stood in front of the open door and wondered if she looked as guilty as she felt. While she and Andrew had agreed that they were on a relationship hiatus, saying the words and having him show up less than four hours after she and Jack had made love for the third time of the night was a little disconcerting.

"You're here," she said, feeling stupid and awkward and really, really guilty.

"I missed you." He smiled that easy Andrew smile—the one that had first drawn her to him. The one that told the world he was pleasant, charming and curious about everything. "Did you miss me?"

She'd spent five months working on her plan to seduce Jack Howington III and nearly a week putting that plan into action. In her free time she'd been consulting for two different defense contractors and working on her solid-rocket-fuel project. Who had time to miss anyone?

"Of course," she said, resisting the urge to fold her arms over her chest and shuffle her feet.

"Good." He stepped into the house and put his arm around her. "So this is where you've been hanging out."

"I've actually been down in Los Angeles a lot. Remember? The consulting."

"I know. Is your team here?"

"They'll arrive in an hour or so."

"How fortunate." He pulled her close again. "So we have time to get reacquainted."

Ick and double ick. She couldn't get "reacquainted" with Andrew right after having seduced Jack. It was wrong on many, many levels.

She stepped away and looked at him. Andrew was tall like Jack but not as muscular or lean. His brown hair was longer, his blue eyes lighter. Jack was a sexy version of the devil come to life. He played every hand close and gave nothing away. Andrew was open and friendly. He assumed the world liked him—and most of the time it did.

Which didn't matter, she told herself. There was no need for comparisons. She had a relationship with Andrew and she had nothing with Jack. They'd been friends once, she'd proved her point and now she was moving on. She should be happy Andrew was here. He was part of the moving-on bit, wasn't he?

Andrew's blue eyes clouded. "What's wrong, Meredith? Aren't you happy to see me? It's been weeks since we met at The Symposium in Chicago. I've missed you. You said you wanted time for us both to be sure about our feelings. I'm still sure. Are you?"

Life was all about timing, Meredith thought happily as Colin walked into the room, saw Andrew and grimaced.

"Oh. You're here," he grumbled. Colin had never been a fan.

It wasn't anyone's fault, Meri told herself. Andrew was inherently athletic and Colin…wasn't. She wasn't either, but she tried and she always forced her team to attempt something new a couple of times a year. She ignored the complaints and reminded them it was good for them.

"Colin!" Andrew said cheerfully, ignoring the other man's obvious irritation at his presence. "Haven't seen you in a long time. How's it hanging?"

Colin looked Andrew over with the same enthusiasm one would use when seeing a cockroach in one's salad. "It's hanging just fine."

Colin poured his coffee and left.

"I think he's starting to like me," Andrew said in a mock whisper. "We're really communicating."

Despite everything, Meri laughed. "You're an optimist."

"Hey, you like Colin and I like you. Therefore I must like Colin. Isn't that some kind of math logic? You should appreciate that."

She should, and she mostly did. She appreciated that Andrew was never tense or intense. She enjoyed his humor, his spontaneity and how he seemed to live a charmed life. According to every women's-magazine survey she'd ever taken, Andrew was perfect for her.

So how had she been able to be apart from him for six months only seeing him for a few days at a time and not really mind?

Before she could figure out the answer, she heard more footsteps on the stairs. She turned, expecting to see Betina, who would be a great distraction. Instead Jack walked into the kitchen.

The room got so quiet Meri could actually hear her heart pumping blood through her body. She felt herself flush as she tried to figure out what on earth she was supposed to say.

Andrew stepped forward, held out his hand and smiled. "Andrew Layman. I'm Meredith's boyfriend."

Jack looked him over. "Jack Howington the third. Friend of the family."

Meri stared in surprise. Jack had used his full name, including the number. Why? He never did that.

The two men shook hands. When they separated, it seemed that they were both crowding her a little.

"So you know Meredith's dad?" Andrew asked. "You mentioned you were a friend of the family, but she hasn't mentioned you before."

"I knew her brother. Meri and I were friends in college. We go way back."

"Interesting. You never came to D.C.," Andrew said easily. "I know all of Meredith's friends there."

"Sounds like you keep a close watch on her."

"I care about her."

"Apparently not enough that you mind a six-month absence," Jack told him. "You haven't met all of Meri's friends here."

"I already know them."

"You don't know me."

"You're the past."

Jack's gaze was steady. "Not as much as you might think. Meri and I have a history together."

Meri rolled her eyes. It was as though they were a couple of dogs and she were the favorite tree they both wanted to pee on. While she was sure Jack was more than capable of winning the contest, she was surprised he would bother to play. She also hadn't expected Andrew to get drawn in. Since when had he become competitive?

"There's a little too much testosterone in here for me," she said as she stepped back. "You two boys have fun."

* * *

Meri made her way to Betina's room and found her friend typing on her laptop.

"Girl emergency," Meri said as she closed the bedroom door and sat on the edge of the bed. "How could he be here?"

"Andrew?"

Meri nodded. "I had no idea. We've been staying in touch via e-mail and we've talked a little on the phone, but there was no warning. He just showed up. How could he do that?"

"He got on a plane and flew here. It's romantic. Does it feel romantic to you?"

"I don't know," Meri admitted, still unclear how she felt. "It's been weeks and weeks. I thought he was going to propose and I thought maybe I would say yes. Shouldn't I be excited that he's here? Shouldn't I be dancing in the streets?"

"We don't have much in the way of streets, but maybe if you danced in the driveway, it would be enough."

Meri started to laugh, then sucked in a breath as she suddenly fought tears. "I'm so confused."

"You slept with Jack. That was bound to change things."

"It was supposed to make them more clear. I was supposed to be healed."

"Maybe the problem is you were never broken."

Meri nodded slowly. Maybe that *was* the problem. She'd always thought there was something wrong with her and that it could be traced back to Jack's painful rejection. But what if that had just been a normal part of growing up and, because of her freakishness, she hadn't been able to see it? What if she'd made it too big a deal?

"You don't think I needed closure with Jack?" Meri asked. "You don't think getting revenge on him will move me to a higher plane?"

Betina sighed. "I don't think anything negative like revenge is ever healthy. You've felt emotionally stalled and unable to commit. Was that about what Jack did or was it simply that you needed more time to integrate who you were with who you wanted to be? Being book-smart doesn't help you grow up any faster or better. Sometimes it just gets in the way."

"I figured that out a while ago," Meri grumbled. "You'd think I could deal with it by now." She drew in a deep breath. "I was so *sure* that revenge was the right way to go. I knew that if I could just make him want me, then walk away, I'd be happy forever."

"Maybe that's still true."

Meri wasn't sure. "Like you said—it's not healthy to be so negative."

"But it is done," Betina reminded her. "Deal with what you have now. Closure. So on to Andrew—if that's where you want to go."

An interesting idea. The only problem was Meri wasn't sure what she thought about anything anymore.

"I need to clear my head. I'm going to run. Could you get the group started without me?"

Betina grinned. "I love it when you leave me in charge."

Later that morning, Jack went looking for Meri. She wasn't in the dining room with her team, although

Betina had told him she was in the house somewhere. He checked out his bathroom, but no beautiful, naked women waited for him. Damn. There were days a guy couldn't cut a break. Then he saw something move on the balcony and stepped out to find her sitting on a chair, staring out at the view.

She looked up as he joined her. "I was going to use the telescope, but it's kind of hard to see the stars with all the sunshine getting in the way."

He glanced at the bright blue sky. "I can see where that's a problem."

"I thought about spying on our neighbors—you know, catch someone sunbathing nude. But I just can't seem to get into it."

Her big eyes were dark and troubled. The corner of her mouth drooped. She looked sad and uncomfortable, which was so far from her normal bouncy self that he found himself saying, "You want to talk about it?"

She shrugged. "I'm confused. And before you ask why, I'm not going to tell you."

"Makes it hard to help if I don't know what's wrong."

"Maybe you're the problem."

"Am I?"

She sighed. "Not really. A little, but it's mostly me."

He took the chair next to hers and stared out at the lake. It was huge, stretching for miles. "Did you know Lake Tahoe is nearly a mile deep?"

The droopy corner turned up. "Someone's been reading the chamber of commerce brochure."

"I got bored."

She looked at him. "Why aren't you married?"

The question made him shrug. "No one's ever asked."

"Oh, right. Because you're so eager to say yes?"

"Probably not. I'm not the marrying kind."

Now she smiled for real. "Sure you are. You're rich and single. What was it Jane Austen said? Something about any single man of good fortune must be in search of a wife? That's you. Don't you want to get married?"

"I never much thought about it. My work keeps me busy."

"Meaning, if you have too much time to think, you take on another job."

How had she figured that out? "Sometimes."

He liked to stay busy, involved with his business. He had some guys he hung out with occasionally. That was enough.

"No one gets close?" she asked.

"No."

"Because of Hunter?"

He stretched out his legs in front of him. "Just because we slept together doesn't mean I'm going to tell you everything I'm thinking."

"Okay. Is it because of Hunter?"

He glanced at her. "You're annoying."

"So I've been told. Do I need to ask again?"

"I should hire you to do interrogations. And, yes, some of it is because of Hunter."

"People die, Jack."

"I know. I lost my brother when he was still a kid. It changed everything."

He hadn't meant to say that, to tell her the truth. But now that he had, he found he didn't mind her knowing.

"It was like with Hunter," he said quietly. "He got sick and then he died. We'd been close and it hurt like hell that he was gone."

The difference was he hadn't kept his brother from going to the doctor. When Hunter had first noticed the dark spot on his shoulder, Jack had teased him about being a wimp for wanting to get it checked out. So Hunter had waited. What would have happened if the melanoma had been caught before it had spread?

"You didn't kill Hunter," Meri told him. "It's not your fault."

Jack stood. "I'm done here."

She moved fast and blocked the door. She was small enough that he could have easily pushed past her, but for some reason he didn't.

"You didn't kill him," she repeated. "I know that's what you think. I know you feel guilty. So what's the deal? Are you lost in the past? Are you afraid to fall for someone because you don't want to lose another person you love? Or do you think you're cursed or something?"

Both, he thought. And so much more. He wasn't allowed to love or care. It was the price he had to pay for what he'd done. Or, rather, what he hadn't done.

"I'm not having this conversation with you," he said.

"Wanna bet?"

She probably thought she looked tough, but she was small and girlie and he could take her in half a second. Or a nanosecond, to talk like her.

"Get out of my way," he growled.

She raised her chin. "Make me."

She was like a kitten spitting at a wolf. Entertaining and with no idea of the danger she was in.

"You don't scare me," he told her.

"Right back at you." Then she smiled. "But you probably want to kiss me now, huh?"

She was impossible. And, damn her, he *did* want to kiss her. He wanted to do a lot of things to her, some of which, if they stayed out here on the balcony, would violate the town's decency code.

So instead of acting, he went for the distraction. "Andrew seems nice."

"Oh, please. You hate him."

"Hate would require me thinking about him. I don't."

"So macho. What was up with the I-know-Meribetter game?"

"I have no idea what you're talking about," he said, even though he did. Establishing dominance early on was the best way to win.

"And they say women are complicated," she murmured.

Eight

Meri came downstairs and found Andrew waiting for her in the living room and her team hard at work in the dining room. The choice should be simple. Work or the man who had traveled so far to see her.

She debated, then ducked into the kitchen, found the phone book in the pantry and made a couple of quick calls.

"We're taking the afternoon off," she announced as she walked in on her team.

"Oh, good," Andrew said, coming up behind her and putting his hand on her shoulder. "Alone at last."

"Not exactly," she said with a grin. "Everyone, the shuttle will be here shortly to take you back to your hotel. I want you to put on bathing suits and beach clothes. Plenty of sunscreen."

Donny grimaced. "You're going to make us be out-doors again, aren't you?"

"Uh-huh."

There was a collection of grumbles, but everyone knew better than to argue.

"At least we'll get it over with," someone said. "Then we can work."

"You're taking them to the lake?" Andrew asked when the team had left. "Are you sure about this?"

"They can swim," she told him. "They might not be great at it, but they can. It's not healthy for us to sit in this room day after day. Being outside clears the mind. Physical activity is good for them."

He pulled her close. "You're good for me. Haven't you missed me, Meredith?"

"Yes, but maybe not as much as I should have," she told him honestly.

His blue gaze never wavered. "So I left you alone for too long. I knew I shouldn't have listened to you when you said you wanted to take a break."

"I had some things I had to do." Things she wasn't comfortable thinking about with an actual boyfriend in the wings.

She braced herself for his temper or at least a serious hissy fit. Instead he touched her cheek. "I guess I'm going to have to win you back."

Words that should have melted her heart—emotion-ally if not physically. Because the temperature required to melt a body part would cook it first, and that was gross, even for her twisted mind. So what was wrong with her? Why wasn't Andrew getting to her?

A question that seriously needed an answer.

* * *

An hour later they were down at the edge of the lake. Meri counted heads to make sure no one had ducked out of what she had planned and was surprised to see Jack had joined them.

"Colin told me I wouldn't want to miss it," he said when she approached.

"He's right." She had a little trouble speaking, which was weird but possibly explained by how great Jack looked in swim trunks and a T-shirt. He was tanned—mostly all over, she remembered from the previous night.

Bad memory, she told herself. Don't think about making love with Jack. Think about Andrew and how sweet he is. Although sweet Andrew had chosen not to show up for her afternoon of fun on the lake.

"So what are we doing?" Betina asked. She wore shorts and a bikini top.

Meri was momentarily distracted by amazing curves a couple of hours of surgery hadn't begun to give her. And Betina's assets were all natural.

"Um, that." Meri pointed out to the water, where four guys rode toward them on Jet Skis.

"Nerds on water," Colin muttered. "What were you thinking?"

"That you'll have fun."

"I'll get a sunburn."

Jack moved close. "I like it," he said. "Will they give them lessons?"

"Yes. And make them wear life jackets. It will be fun."

He raised his eyebrows. "Do you always bully them into some physical activity?"

"Pretty much. I'm not athletically gifted either, but I try. We can't spend out whole lives inside. It makes us pasty. This is better."

"Last year she made us ski," Colin said absently as he eyed the Jet Ski. "Norman broke his leg."

"It's true," Betina said. "To this day, the man walks with a limp."

Meri put her hands on her hips. "But he had fun. He still talks about that day, okay? We're doing this. Don't argue with me."

Jack liked the way she stood up to everyone and how they reluctantly agreed. Meri was an unlikely leader, but she was in charge.

"So where's Allen?" he asked.

"Andrew," she corrected. "He doesn't like group sports."

"Not a team player?"

"He plays tennis."

"I see."

She glared at him. "What does that mean?"

He held up both hands. "Nothing. I'm sure he has a great backhand."

"He belongs to a country club. He nearly went pro."

"Afraid of messing up his hair?"

She sniffed. "No. He wanted to do something else with his life."

"Oh. He couldn't make the tour."

"He came really close."

"I'm sure that brings him comfort."

"Look," she said, poking her finger at his chest. "We can't all be physically perfect."

He liked baiting her and allowed himself a slight smile. "You think I'm perfect."

"You're annoying. And you're not all that."

"Yes, I am."

She turned her back on him. He liked getting to her almost as much as he didn't like Andrew. Jack was still waiting on Bobbi Sue's report on the man. His gut told him it wasn't going to be good news. Would Meri listen when he told her the truth?

He refused to consider that Andrew might be an okay guy.

The instructors rode their Jet Skis to the shore. "We're looking for Meri," the tallest, tannest and blondest one said.

"I'm here." She waved. "This is my team. They're really smart but not superathletic. Sort of like me."

She grinned and the guy smiled back. He looked her up and down, then whipped off his sunglasses and moved toward her.

Jack stepped between them. He put his hand on the other guy's shoulder. "Not so fast."

Surfer dude nodded and took a step back. "Sorry, man."

"It's fine."

Meri raised her eyebrows. "You're protecting me from a guy on a Jet Ski. It's almost romantic."

"I was impressed," Betina said. "He could have carried you off to the other side of the lake. We might never have seen you again."

He eyed them both, not sure of their point.

"You overreacted," Betina said in a loud whisper. "She could have handled him herself."

"Just doing my job."

"Sure you were," Betina told him with a wink. "You're not subtle. I'll give you that."

"Didn't know I was supposed to be."

Meri sighed. "While this is lovely, let's get on with the activity. You'll take people out with you and make sure they know what they're doing before setting them loose with the moving equivalent of a power tool, right?"

"Sure thing," surfer dude said.

Jack grabbed Meri by the hand and led her over to one of the Jet Skis. "You can go with me."

"Are you being all macho and take-charge? It's unexpected—but fun."

Now she was baiting him. Which was fair, he thought as he put on a life jacket, pushed the Jet Ski back into the lake, then straddled it. If she had been anyone else, he would have thought they were a good team. But he wasn't interested in being on a team, nor was he interested in Meri. Not that way.

She stepped into the lake and shrieked. "It's cold."

"Snow runoff and a mile deep. What did you expect?"

"Eighty degrees. I'll freeze."

He gunned the Jet Ski. "You'll be fine. Hop on."

She slid behind him, put her feet on the running board and wrapped her arms around his waist.

When she was settled, he twisted the accelerator and they took off across the water.

They bounced through the wake of a boat, then settled onto smoother water. Meri leaned against him, her thighs nestling him. The image of her naked, hungry and ready filled his mind. For once, he didn't push it away. He let it stay there, arousing him, making him want to pull into shallow waters and make the fantasy real.

He didn't. Instead he headed back to the beach, where her friends were being shown the right way to board a Jet Ski.

There was also a new addition to the group. A dinghy had been pulled up on the beach, and Andrew stood slightly to the side, staring at Meri.

"How about something with a little more power?" he said, pointing to the twenty-five-foot boat anchored offshore.

She climbed off the Jet Ski and pulled off her life jacket.

"I need to stay here," she told him. "This was my idea."

Andrew glanced around. "The nerd brigade will be fine." He grabbed her hand. "Come on. It'll be fun."

Jack wanted to step between them the way he had with surfer dude. But this was different. This was the guy Meri thought she wanted to marry. And until he, Jack, had proof that Andrew was only in it for her money, he couldn't do a damn thing to stop her.

"Go ahead," he told her, consciously unclenching his jaw. "I'll take care of them."

"We don't need taking care of," Colin protested, then shrugged. "Okay. Maybe we do."

Meri looked at Jack. "Are you sure?"

"Go. We'll be fine."

She nodded slowly, helped Andrew push the dinghy back into the water, then climbed on board. Andrew started the engine and then they were gone.

Colin stared after them. "I hate it when he takes her away. It's never the same without her."

Jack hated that he wanted to agree.

Meri scraped the dishes into the garbage disposal, then stacked them on the counter by the sink. She was pleasantly full from the Mexican food they'd brought in for dinner and just slightly buzzed from the margarita. Hmm, her team had had liquor twice in a week. If she wasn't careful, they were going to get wild on her.

She smiled at the idea, then caught her breath as someone came up behind her and wrapped his arms around her waist. Her first thought was that it was Jack, who'd mostly ignored her all afternoon. But then she inhaled the scent and felt the pressure of the body behind her and knew it wasn't.

"Andrew," she said as she sidestepped his embrace. "Come to help me with the dishes?"

"No. You don't need to do that. Let someone else clean up."

"I don't mind. I was gone all afternoon."

"You say that like it's a bad thing. Didn't you have fun with me?"

"Sure."

They'd taken the boat to the middle of the lake, dropped anchor and enjoyed a light lunch in the sun, then stretched out for some sunbathing. What was there not to like?

She would ignore the fact that she'd kept watching the shore to see what was going on there. To make sure her friends were all right, she reminded herself. She hadn't been looking to see if Jack stuck around. Even though he had.

"Too bad about the cabin onboard," Andrew said.

"Uh-huh."

It had been small and cramped, and when Andrew had tried to take her down below, she'd nearly thrown up. The combination of confined spaces, movement on water and her tummy wasn't a happy one.

"Let's go have more fun," he said, reaching for her hand. "Back at my hotel."

She sidestepped him. "I need to stay here."

"Why?"

"I was gone all afternoon."

"They survived. Meredith, you're not their cruise director."

"I know, but I'm responsible for them."

"Why? They're adults."

True, but they were her team. "Look, I want to stay here."

He stared into her eyes. "How am I going to win you back if you refuse to be alone with me?"

An interesting point. Did she want to be won back?

Of course she did, she told herself. This was Andrew, the man she'd thought she might marry. She'd slept with Jack; she was over him and ready to move on with her life. She could emotionally engage now. Why not with Andrew?

"I have a great suite," he told her. "With a view. If you don't want to go back to my room, we could go to a casino and go gambling. You know how you like to play blackjack."

It was true. She didn't actually count cards, but she had a great memory and there were usually only a half dozen or so decks in play at any one time. How hard could it be to keep track of three hundred and twelve cards?

Jack walked into the kitchen. He smiled pleasantly at Andrew. "You're still here?"

Andrew stepped close to her. "Trying to get rid of me?"

"I'll let Meri do that herself." He turned to her. "We're about to play Truth or Dare. I know it's your favorite. Want to join us?"

"We're going to state line to the casinos," Andrew said.

Meri glanced between the two men. They were both great in their own ways. Different but great.

"I'm tired," she told Andrew. "I'd really like to stay in tonight."

His expression tightened. "I'm not interested in hanging out here. I'll go to the casino without you."

She touched his arm. "You don't have to do that. You could stay."

He glanced toward the dining room, where she could hear Colin arguing theoretical equations.

"No, thanks," Andrew told her. He started for the door.

She turned to Jack. "This is all your fault."

"What did I do?"

She huffed out a breath, then hurried after Andrew.

"Don't be like this," she told him on the front porch.

"Like what? Interested in spending time with you alone? I haven't seen you in weeks. The last time we talked on the phone, you said everything was fine. But now I find out it isn't. Were we taking a break, Meredith, or were you trying to break up with me? If that's what you want, just say so."

She opened her mouth, then closed it. Andrew was perfect for her in so many ways. He was exactly the man she was looking for. Added to that was the fact that she'd had him investigated and there was nothing in his past to indicate he gave a damn about her inheritance. Men like that were hard to find.

Six months ago she'd been almost sure. So what was different now?

Stupid question, she thought. Jack was different. Being with Jack was supposed to make things more clear, and it hadn't.

"I'm not trying to break up with you," she told him. "I'm glad you're here. I just need some time to get used to us being a couple."

"Hard to do when we're apart."

"So stay."

"Come back to my hotel with me, Meredith."

"I can't."

"You won't."

She wouldn't. He was right.

"Andrew…"

He walked to his car. "I'll be back, Meredith. I think you're worth fighting for. The question you need to answer is, do you want me to keep trying?"

She watched him drive away. The front door opened and Betina stepped out next to her.

"Man trouble?" her friend asked.

"When does my romantic life flow smoothly?"

"Practically never. You're always interesting, I'll grant you that. So what has his panties in a snit?"

Meri looked at her. "You never liked him. Why is that?"

"I don't mind him. I think he's too impressed with himself. But he's good to you and he passed your rigorous inspection, so that's all I need to know."

"But you don't like him."

"Do I have to?" Betina asked.

Meri shrugged. "Do you like Jack?"

"Are you doing a comparison?"

"No. I'm just curious."

Betina considered the question. "Yes, I like Jack."

"Me, too." Meri held up her hand. "Don't you dare start in on me that you knew I would fall for him, blah, blah, blah. I haven't fallen for him. It's just different now."

"What are you going to do about it?"

"Nothing. Jack and I are friends. The bigger question is, what do I want from Andrew?"

"How are you going to figure that out?"

"I haven't got a clue."

She followed Betina back inside, where everyone sat around on the oversize sofas. Two bowls filled with pieces of paper stood in the middle of the coffee table. They would be the "truth" and "dare" parts of the game.

Meri had learned not to mess with dare with this group. Not when they wanted things like mathematical proof that the universe existed. Answering personal, probably embarrassing questions was a whole lot easier.

As Jack was new to the game, they let him go first.

He pulled out a question and read it aloud. "Have you ever gone to a convention in any kind of costume?"

He frowned and turned to her. "This is as wild as you guys get?"

She laughed. "It's not a big deal for you, but—trust me—there are people in this room with guilty *Star Trek* secrets."

Jack put down the paper. "No."

Colin groaned. "You weren't supposed to get that question."

"Which means there's another one in the bowl about doing it with twins," Meri told him with a grin.

She reached into the bowl and pulled out a paper. "Have you ever been stood up?"

The room seemed to tilt slightly. She remembered being eighteen, wearing her prettiest dress, although a size eighteen on her small frame was anything but elegant. She'd had her hair done, actually put on makeup and gone to the restaurant to meet a guy from her physics lab. She'd waited for two hours and he'd never shown up.

The next day he'd acted as if nothing had happened. She'd never had the courage to ask if he'd forgotten or done it on purpose or for sport.

Jack leaned over and grabbed the paper from her. "She's not answering the question. This is a stupid game."

"I don't mind," she told him.

"I do. I'll tell them about the twins."

All the guys leaned forward. "For real?" Robert asked. "Twins?"

She shook her head. "Jack, it's okay."

"It's not. What happened is private."

What happened? How could he know she'd been stood up? He'd been gone for months. Actually, the nondate had gotten her to think about changing. She'd joined a gym the next day.

She started to tell him that, then found she couldn't speak. Her throat was all closed, as if she had a cold…or was going to cry. What was wrong with her?

"Excuse me," she said and ducked out of the room. She hurried into the kitchen to get a glass of water.

It was stress, she told herself. There was too much going on.

She heard footsteps and turned to find Colin entering the room.

"You okay?" he asked. "I'm sorry about the question. It wasn't for you. I was hoping Betina would get it."

Something inside Meri snapped. "I've had it with you," she said. "Look, you're a grown single man interested in a woman who obviously thinks you're hot. For heaven's sake, do something about it."

He opened his mouth, then closed it. "I can't."

"Then you don't deserve her."

Nine

Meri needed coffee more than she needed air. It had been another long night but not for any fun reasons. She'd tossed and turned, not sure what to do with her life—something she hadn't wrestled with in years.

She was supposed to have things together by now. She was supposed to know her heart as well as she knew her head. Or did being so damned smart mean she was destined to be stupid in other ways?

The coffee had barely begun to pour through the filter when someone rang the doorbell. She hadn't seen anyone else up yet so she walked to the front door and opened it.

Andrew stood on the porch. He held a single red rose in one hand and a stuffed bright-green monkey in the other.

"It's possible I behaved badly yesterday," he said

with a shrug. "More than possible. I want things to work between us."

She didn't know what to say. While she was relieved to not be fighting, she wasn't exactly in the mood to throw herself into his arms. Which meant that there was a whole lot more for them to deal with.

"Andrew, this is really confusing for me," she said. "You're right. We were apart too long. Things have changed."

"Is there someone else?"

"No," she said without thinking, then had to wonder if that was true.

Not Jack, she told herself. Okay, yes, they'd gotten intimate, but just the one time and nothing since. He was her past. The problem was Andrew might not be her future.

He handed her the monkey. "I brought you this. I thought it would make you smile."

She took the ridiculous stuffed toy. "He's adorable. What about the rose?"

"That's for me. I plan to wear it in my teeth."

He bit down on the stem, which made her laugh. Andrew always made her laugh. Wasn't that a good thing? Shouldn't she want to be with him?

"You want some coffee?" she asked. "I have a pot going."

"Sure." He took a step inside, then grimaced as his cell phone rang. "Sorry. I'm dealing with some stuff at work. Give me ten minutes?"

She nodded and stepped inside. Still carrying the monkey, she returned to the kitchen. Only this time she wasn't alone. Colin stood pouring coffee. He wore jeans, an unbuttoned shirt and nothing else. But it wasn't his unusual outfit that got her attention. Instead there was something about the way he stood. Something in the tilt of his head or the set of his shoulders.

"Colin?"

He turned and smiled at her. "Morning."

A single word but in a voice she'd never heard from him. It was low and confident. He was a man at peace with himself and the universe.

She felt her mouth drop open. "You had sex with Betina."

Colin didn't even blush. "It wasn't sex, Meri. It was making love. And, yes, we did. She's amazing. She's the woman I've been waiting for all my life."

With that, he collected two cups of coffee and carried them back to his room.

Meri laughed out loud. She set the monkey on the counter, then turned to find someone to share the good news with.

But she was alone in the kitchen, so she ran upstairs, taking them two at a time, then burst into Jack's office. He was on the phone but hung up when he saw her.

"You look happy," he said. "So it's not bad news."

"I know. It's fabulous. I saw Colin. He's someone completely different. He and Betina slept together and I think they're seriously in love. Isn't that fabulous? Are you jazzed?"

One corner of Jack's mouth turned up. "Good for Colin. I didn't think he had it in him."

"Oh, there was a tiger lurking behind those silly plaid shirts. And we're a part of it. We got them together."

Jack held up his hands in the shape of a T. "There's no 'we' in all this. They got themselves together."

"Don't be silly. We pushed. And I mean *we*. You were a part of it. You acted like a matchmaker. I'm so proud."

He groaned. "Leave me out of it."

She crossed to the window, then turned back to face him. "This is great. They may get married. We can go hang out at the wedding and take all the credit."

"I don't think so."

She wrinkled her nose. "You're not getting in the spirit of this. It's happy news."

She spun in a circle, holding her arms out and tilting back her head. Soon the room was turning and turning. She lost her balance and started to fall. Which should have worried her, except Jack was there to catch her.

She collapsed against him, then smiled up into his face. He had the most amazing eyes, she thought absently, then she dropped her gaze to his mouth. That part of him wasn't so bad either.

"You need to slow down," he told her.

"No way. Light speed isn't fast enough."

"You'll get hurt."

What were they talking about? She found she didn't know and she sort of didn't care. Not as long as he held her.

"Jack," she breathed.

He released her and stepped back. "Meri, this isn't a good idea."

Then it hit her. She'd run to Jack instead of Andrew.

That couldn't be good. Had Betina been right all along? Had there been more on the line that getting revenge or closure or any of the other reasons she'd given herself for wanting to sleep with Jack? Dear God, what had she done?

"I have to go," she whispered and hurried out of the room. She ran all the way to her bedroom, then closed the door behind her and leaned against it. Where did she go from here?

Jack poured coffee. As he raised his mug, Colin walked into the kitchen.

Meri was right—there was something different about the guy. An air of confidence. He wasn't just a nerd anymore.

The love of a good woman, Jack thought humorously. Apparently the old saying about it being able to transform a man was true. Lucky for him, he'd escaped.

"How's it going?" Colin asked.

"Good. With you?"

"Great."

"No one seems to be talking trash in the dining room today," Jack said.

"Meri gave us the day off."

Probably to ensure that Betina and Colin spent more time together. It was just like her.

"Andrew was here before," Colin said.

"What happened?"

"Something with his office. He had to leave."

"You sound relieved."

Colin shrugged. "He's not my favorite."

"Mine either."

They were an interesting group, these scientists, Jack thought. Brilliant and humble, funny, determined and willing to make fools of themselves on Jet Skis. They looked out for Meri. Hunter would have liked them a lot.

"What?" Colin asked. "You have a strange look on your face."

"I was thinking about Meri's brother. He would have liked you. All of you."

"Meri talks about him. He sounds like a great guy."

"He was. A group of us became friends in college. We called ourselves the Seven Samurai. It was dumb but meaningful to us. Hunter was the connection we all had with each other. He brought us together. Held us together."

Then he'd died and they'd drifted apart.

Jack thought about his friends—something he didn't usually allow himself to do—and wondered how they'd enjoyed their months in Hunter's house. Had their worlds been flipped around and changed or had the weeks passed quietly?

"It's good to have friends like that," Colin said. "Meri's a lot like him. She draws people together. Gets them involved. She handpicked the team for this project. They let her do that because she's so brilliant."

Jack nodded. Meri's brain was never in question. "She's more outgoing than she used to be."

"She's grown up. It's hard for us, the freaks." Colin grinned. "That's what she calls us and herself. We all had to deal with not fitting in and stuff. Meri wants us to put that aside and deal with life as it is. Look forward. That sort of thing."

There was affection in his voice, but not the romantic

kind, so Jack didn't have to kill him. He realized that the reports might have told him the specifics but they hadn't allowed him to get to know the woman she'd become.

"I was thinking about your business," Colin said. "There's some new military software that could help with your security issues."

"Military software? Is it classified?"

Colin grinned. "Sure, but I know the guy who wrote it. There's a couple of beta versions floating around. I might be able to get you a copy to test out—you know, as a service to your government."

"Lucky me." Jack eyed the other man. "You're a lot more dangerous than you look."

Colin grinned. "I know.

"Left foot green," Betina called.

Meri looked down at the Twister sheet on the floor and groaned. "I'm not built to bend that way."

"The very reason I don't try to play the game. But so not the point."

"You're basically mean," Meri muttered. "I don't know why I didn't see that before. Sorry, Robert. I'm going to have to slide under you."

Robert arched his back as best he could. "Good luck with that. You do realize you're in danger of hyperextending your shoulder."

Colin looked up from his awkward position. "I'm not sure she would hyperextend it. Technically speaking—"

"Stop!" Meri yelled. "I don't want any technical talk right now. Let's pretend to be normal."

Colin and Robert both frowned at her. "Why?"

She started laughing, which made bending and stretching impossible. But she still tried, because the big green dot was just out of—

She wobbled, leaned, then collapsed, bringing everyone down with her. She landed on Robert, and Colin sank down on top of her.

"I'm not sure I approve of this," Betina said from the sidelines. "Colin, do we need to talk about fidelity?"

"Not really." He grunted as he rolled off Meri, then scrambled to his feet. "Unless you want to spank me."

Meri gagged. "I so did not want to know that about you two."

"I'm surprised," Robert said from his place on the floor. "Usually men who enjoy domination have powerful positions in their work life. It's an attempt to obtain balance and let someone else take responsibility."

Meri looked at him. "Is there anything you don't know?"

"How to get the girl. Any girl."

"We'll talk later," Meri said, offering her hand and helping him to his feet. "I'm on a roll. Are you interested in anyone in particular?"

Before he could answer, Jack walked into the room. There was something about his expression that warned Meri he didn't have good news.

"What's wrong?" she asked. "Is someone hurt?"

"No, but we need to talk."

He took her arm and led her into the kitchen. She didn't like anything about this.

After folding her arms over her chest she said, "So talk."

His dark eyes were unreadable. "Andrew isn't who you think."

She'd thought maybe her father had been in an accident or had a heart attack. But Andrew?

"Not who I think? You mean like secretly a woman?"

"I'm serious, Meri. I have some information on him. His background. He's not the man he's pretending to be. He's in it for the money."

A thousand different thoughts flashed through her brain. At any other time she would have paused to marvel at the exquisite structure of the human mind—of how it could hold so many contradictory ideas at any single moment. But right now all she cared about was being strong enough to punch Jack in the stomach.

"What the hell are you going on about?" she asked, her voice low and cold. "Why would you know anything about Andrew?"

"I had him investigated."

Anger burned hot and bright. "You have no right to get involved in my personal life. Who do you think you are?"

"I know you're upset—"

"Upset? You have no idea. Dammit, Jack, this is wrong on so many levels." She glanced toward the door to the living room and lowered her voice. "Just because we slept together doesn't mean you get to tell me what to do. You gave up that right the day you walked out on me after Hunter died. You were supposed to be there for me and you weren't. So I don't care what you think about anything."

She started to walk away. He grabbed her arm and held her in place.

"You have to listen to me," he said.

"No, I don't. Not that it matters, but I already had Andrew investigated. Thoroughly. He's clean. He comes from a comfortable background. He doesn't have my trust fund, but he's not hurting for money. He's a good man."

"He's married."

Her entire body went cold. She knew intellectually that her core temperature was what it had been five seconds ago, but the sensation of being on the verge of turning to ice was incredibly real.

"You're wrong," she breathed. "My investigator—"

"Did exactly what I did the first time I learned about Andrew. A basic investigation. That's usually good enough. But when you said you were thinking of marrying this guy, I had my people dig deeper. It was eight years ago. They hooked up and conned an old man out of about two million dollars. Three years ago, they took another heiress for the same amount. I'm guessing you were their next target."

She couldn't deal with the news about Andrew, so she turned on Jack. "You dug into his background? What gives you the right?"

"Someone has to look out for you. Your father is useless. With Hunter gone, there was only me." His gaze was steady. "I couldn't do what Hunter asked—I couldn't stay in your life. I was too destroyed by what had happened. Still, I had a responsibility to look out for you. So I did. From a distance."

"You spied on me?"

"Call it what you want. I made sure you didn't get into trouble."

He'd paid people to watch her? To poke into her private life? But he'd never cared enough to get involved himself?

"Bastard," she breathed and raised her hand to slap him.

He grabbed her by the wrist and held her still. "It was for your own good."

"That's a load of crap. You were trying to assuage your guilt by doing the least you could. You weren't a good friend to my brother and you sure as hell weren't a friend to me. You don't get to do this, Jack. You aren't running my life. I'll marry Andrew if I want and you can't stop me."

"Bigamy is illegal in all fifty states."

Andrew—married? She couldn't believe it. He might not be the handsome prince she'd first imagined, but married?

"He's not playing me," she insisted even as she wondered if he was.

"How do you know? At least look at the report. Then make your own decision."

There was nothing to look at, she thought sadly as she pulled her hand free of his grip. Nothing to consider. She wasn't in love with Andrew. She'd been fighting that truth since he'd shown up here. Their time apart had demonstrated that big-time. She hadn't missed him.

Had she ever been in love with him? Did it matter? If he was married and playing her, then he was nothing but a weasel.

"Your gender sucks," she muttered.

"I agree."

"You most of all. I will never forgive you for spying on me. For spending the last eleven years hiding in the shadows."

"I cared about what happened to you."

"Is that what you call it? I would say you were nothing more than a coward trying to quiet a ghost. But I know my brother. I know Hunter would never stop haunting you. He expected more, Jack. And so did I."

Ten

Meri lay on her bed facedown, fighting tears. Betina sat next to her, lightly rubbing her back.

"I can't believe it," Meri said into her pillow. "I can't believe he did that."

Betina patted her shoulder. "*I* can't believe I have to ask, but who are we talking about? Andrew or Jack?"

"Both of them," Meri muttered, then rolled onto her back and wiped away her tears. "That's my current life. I have two men betraying me."

She could say the words, but she didn't believe them. She couldn't believe any of this. How had everything gone so wrong?

Betina sighed. "I'm shocked by what Jack found out about Andrew. Do you believe him?"

Meri nodded. "He wouldn't lie about that. He said

Andrew and his wife had a whole scam going. I'm not sure what his plan was with me. He couldn't have married me, and I wouldn't have given him money for anything."

Although, now that she thought about it, he had mentioned a few investment opportunities right before she'd left.

Her stomach hurt from all the emotional churning.

"I thought about marrying him," she admitted. "When I found the ring, I knew he was going to propose and I thought about saying yes."

"You didn't."

"He didn't ask. I don't know what would have happened. Maybe he was planning to propose, then tell me I had to pay off his wife so he could get a divorce." She shuddered. "It's awful. I slept with him. I slept with a married man. I would never do that."

"You didn't know. He tricked you. You're the innocent party in all this."

Meri didn't feel very innocent. She felt dirty and gross and confused.

"I liked him," she said. "I don't know if I ever really loved Andrew, but I liked him. Shouldn't I have known? Shouldn't I have sensed something wasn't right?"

Betina shook her head. "Why? He set out to deceive you. You're a decent person who accepts people for who and what they are. You did a regular background check on him and it came back clean."

"I'm never using that investigation agency again," Meri said. "I wonder if Andrew found out the name of the guy and bought him off."

"Very possibly."

"I hate Andrew."

"No, you don't."

Meri wiped away more tears. "I don't. I can't care enough about him to hate him. I feel disgusted and I'm sick that I let myself get played. That's what hurts about him. That he used me and I was too stupid to recognize what was going on. I hate being stupid."

"No one is smart all the time. Meri, it's awful. It sucks big-time. But here's the thing—you escaped Andrew relatively unscathed. Nothing bad happened. The only thing hurt is your pride, and not even very much at that."

Meri knew her friend was right. Still, memories of all the time she spent with Andrew flashed through her head.

"I introduced him to my friends. You guys never liked him. I should have paid attention to that."

"We have amazing insight. What can I say?"

Meri started to laugh, but the sound turned into a sob. She rolled onto her side.

"Jack was spying on me. He watched me from a distance. He never cared enough to even take me to lunch, damn him. How could he do that? It's gross and creepy."

It was more than that. It was painful to think that Jack would keep his word to Hunter enough to pay others to keep tabs on her but that he didn't care enough to do it himself.

"He was wrong to act like that," Betina said soothingly.

Meri raised his head. "You're going to defend him, aren't you? You're going to say he did the best he could with what he had. You're going to say he was hurting, too, that he blamed himself for Hunter's death. He does, you know. Blame himself. Hunter had melanoma. He saw this weird black thing on his shoulder and wanted to go to the doctor. Jack teased him about being a girl and worrying about nothing."

"That can't be easy to live with."

Meri sniffed. "Statistically, getting the diagnosis a few weeks earlier wouldn't have made any difference in the end. Hunter was going to die. Not that Jack would care about that. He would still blame himself, because that's who he is."

"I don't have to defend him," Betina told her. "You're doing it for me."

"I'm not. He's a low-life who cared only about himself. I was totally alone. My mother was dead, my father is possibly the most emotionally useless man on the planet. I was seventeen. I had no one. No friends, no family to speak of. I was alone in the world and he abandoned me."

"He should have stayed," Betina said. "He should have stayed and taken care of you. I wonder why he didn't."

"Guilt," Meri said with a sigh. "Guilt about Hunter and maybe guilt about me. About how he handled things." Betina knew all about Meri's pathetic attempt to seduce Jack years ago and how badly he'd reacted.

"He was twenty-one and nowhere near grown-up enough to be responsible for a seventeen-year-old with a crush on him. So he left and I had to deal on my own."

"You did a hell of a job," her friend told her. "Hunter would be proud."

Meri considered that. "He wouldn't like my plan to get revenge on Jack."

"Brothers rarely enjoy thinking about their sisters having sex with anyone."

That made Meri almost smile. "You don't approve of it either."

"I don't approve one way or the other. I'm worried about you. I think you wanted to sleep with Jack for a lot of reasons, and none of them have anything to do with punishing him."

"You think I'm still in love with him."

"It would explain a lot."

Meri rolled onto her back and stared up at the ceiling. In love with Jack. Was it possible? The way her personal life was going, it made sense. He'd spent the last ten years doing the least he could justify when it came to her, and she might have spent the same amount of time desperate to give her heart to him.

Jack was staring at his computer screen when Colin walked into his office.

"What's up?" he asked.

"You hurt Meri," Colin said. "That's not right. You can't be so insensitive that you wouldn't know how much the information about Andrew would bother her. Not to mention the fact that someone she respected and thought of as a friend had been spying on her."

"You're not telling me anything I don't already know," Jack told him.

Colin moved closer to the desk. "That's not good enough."

Was Colin trying to intimidate him? Jack didn't think it was possible, but Colin was a changed man since his night with Betina.

"She had to learn the truth about Andrew. She said

things were getting serious. Andrew could have taken her for a lot of money."

"It's not about the money," Colin told him. "It's about trust and caring and being there for someone. She expected more of you, and you let her down."

Small words. Unimportant words, yet they made their point, Jack thought grimly.

"I was trying to protect her," he said, knowing it wasn't enough of an answer.

"There were a lot of different ways to do that. Did you have to pick one that hurt?"

"How the hell was I supposed to tell her the truth about Andrew without hurting her?"

"I'm not talking about Andrew."

Jack nodded slowly. "You're right. I should have thought through telling her that I'd been keeping an eye on her. I did it for her own good."

"No one believes that. You did what was easy, and that's not allowed. You can't go around hurting people like that. It's wrong. Meri matters to me, and I'm going to protect her—even from you."

Jack stood. He was a good half head taller than Colin and about thirty pounds of muscle heavier. He wanted to tell himself that Colin's threats were pitiful. The man couldn't hurt him if he were armed and Jack was unconscious. But he was oddly touched by Colin's bravery in the face of certain defeat. The man took care of the people who mattered, no matter what it might cost him personally.

"It wasn't my intention to hurt Meri," Jack said slowly. "But I'm going to have to do it again."

Colin narrowed his gaze. "What do you mean?"

"I'm going to make Andrew go away."

Colin nodded slowly. "I'd like to be there when that happens."

Andrew's hotel room overlooked the lake. All the right trappings were there—the computer, the lobbying magazines. He looked the part and he played it well. He'd fooled a lot of people.

"This is a surprise," Andrew said as he held open the door, a tacit invitation to Jack and Colin. "To what do I owe this honor?"

"I'm here to run you out of town," Jack said, his voice calm and pleasant. "Colin's going to watch."

Nothing about Andrew's expression changed. "I have no idea what you're talking about."

"Sure you do. I don't know how you passed the preliminary background check. Maybe you're that good at covering your tracks. You might have paid off Meri's investigator, although you couldn't have paid off mine. So I'll give you credit for creating a good front."

Andrew sat on the sofa across from the small fireplace. He waved at the two chairs opposite.

"I'll stand," Jack said.

"Me, too," Colin told him.

"As you prefer," Andrew said. "I have to tell you, this is all fascinating. So what do you think you've found out about me?"

"That you're married. That you and your wife con people for money. You know Meri is worth nearly a billion dollars. She must have been a hell of a prize for the two of you."

Andrew's expression never changed. "I have no idea what you're talking about. I've never been married."

"I have copies of the certificate in the car. Do I have to send Colin to get it? I also have the police statements from the people you two duped. Lucky for you, you didn't break any actual laws. It's not a crime to be stupid."

"You have me confused with someone else," Andrew said calmly. "I care about Meredith. We've been dating for a long time. The relationship is serious. As for your ridiculous claims, ask her yourself. I've never once talked to her about money."

"It was all just a matter of time until you did. Or it would have been."

Andrew was a pro—Jack would give him credit for that. But he was still a rat rooting in garbage.

"It's all just your word against mine," Andrew said. "I'm assuming you told Meredith all this?"

Jack nodded.

"She won't believe you."

"You sound confident," Jack said. "Funny she hasn't phoned you."

"She will."

Would she? Was she mad enough at Jack to want to get back with Andrew? How far would she take things?

He didn't have an answer, so he did the only thing he could think of to protect her.

"How much?" he asked. "Give me a number."

Andrew smiled. "You want to pay me off."

"If that's what it takes. How much?"

The other man hesitated, and in that moment Jack knew he'd been right. If Andrew had been who he claimed, he would have refused any payment.

"Ten million," Andrew said. "Ten million and I'll sign anything you want."

"Five million and you'll still sign."

Andrew smiled. "Done."

Twenty minutes later Jack and Colin were back in Jack's car.

"You paid him off," Colin said. "I thought you'd just beat the crap out of him and be done with it."

"That would have been my preference. But he's good at what he does. He could have gone back to Meri and convinced her I was the jerk in all this. This way, she'll never want him back. He can't ever hurt her."

He had a copy of the check he'd written to Andrew, along with a signed letter saying Andrew was freely taking the money in exchange for never seeing Meri again. Just to be safe, Jack had insisted on a thumbprint under the signature.

"So it's done," Colin said. "She's safe."

"It's not done," Jack told him. "Now I have to tell her what happened."

The house was quiet when they returned. Colin disappeared downstairs, probably to fill Betina in on what had happened. The nerd brigade hadn't shown up for work, which had probably been previously arranged to give Meri some time alone. Better for him, he thought.

He walked up the stairs to the bedroom level and

walked to her closed door. After knocking, he pushed
it open.

She'd pulled a chair over to the window. She sat
curled up in the chair, staring out at the lake.

"Go away," she said without looking at him.

"How do you know I'm not Betina or Colin?"

"I recognized your footsteps."

"Not my 'foul stench?'"

She turned to look at him. Her face was pale, her eyes
red and swollen. "Don't you dare quote *Star Wars* to me,
Jack. You haven't the right."

She was hurt. He could see it, but worse, he could feel
it. Her pain was a tangible creature in the room. It didn't
attack him. Instead it lived and breathed, reminding him
that he'd let her down...again.

"We have to talk," he told her.

"No, thanks. I have nothing to say to you."

"That's okay. I'll do the talking. You just listen."

She shrugged, then turned her head back so she was
facing the window. He didn't know if she was looking
out or not. He had a feeling she was crying, which made
him feel like crap.

"Andrew's gone," he said.

"Let me guess. You bought him off."

"I didn't trust him to leave any other way."

"And you didn't trust me to be able to resist him?
Do you think he's that charming or that I'm that
weak?"

"You're pissed at me. I didn't know how far you'd
go to punish me."

She drew her knees to her chest. "I wouldn't give myself to a man who lied to me or tried to play me. You're not worth that."

"I wasn't sure."

"How much?"

He could have lied. He could have said there wasn't money involved. But he wanted to be honest with her.

"Five million."

She didn't react. "I'll have my accountant send you a check."

"You don't need to pay me back. I wanted to keep you safe. That's what I've always wanted."

"Because of your promise to Hunter?"

"Yes."

"But not because of me."

He didn't know what she was asking so he couldn't respond. She looked at him again.

"How many others have you paid off?" she asked. "How many other times have you gotten involved in my life?"

"Twice before."

She sucked in a breath. "The ones who just disappeared? Who broke up with me for no reason?"

"I guess. I wasn't involved in the details."

She stood and faced him. "Of course not. Why would you bother when you have a staff? It must have been desperately uncomfortable to be so close now. Distance makes things tidy. You don't have to deal with emotion."

She put both her hands flat on his chest and shoved him hard. He didn't move.

"Damn you," she cried. "I hate this. Do you know how

much I hate this? I wasn't even a person to you. I was a project. You couldn't be bothered to get involved yourself."

"It wasn't like that. I wanted you to be safe. I didn't want you with the wrong guy."

"And you know who that is?"

"Yes."

She dropped her arms to her sides, then stared up at him with tears in her eyes. "So who's the right guy? Or does he exist?"

"I don't know."

"It's not you."

She wasn't asking a question, but he answered it anyway. "No. I'm not him."

"Just the devil?"

"I'm not that bad."

"You are to me," she said and turned away. "You shouldn't have done it, Jack. It's a zero-sum game. All or nothing. You can't hide in the middle. Hunter would be disappointed, and so am I. It would have been better to just disappear. At least that would have been honest. I could have respected that."

"I don't need your respect," he said, then realized that maybe he did. For some reason, Meri's opinion mattered. As did Hunter's.

He started to leave, then paused at the door. "I didn't know how to be there for you, Meri. I didn't know how to look at you from across Hunter's grave and tell you I was sorry. I didn't know how to be what you needed. So, yeah, I left. But you were never alone. I was always looking out for you."

"That wasn't much consolation when I sat by myself

in a dorm room on Christmas Eve, with nowhere else to go," she said. "And it was more than feeling guilty about Hunter's death. You hated that I had a crush on you."

He thought about that afternoon when she'd turned seventeen and had cried her heart out.

"I didn't know how to help. I couldn't be the guy you wanted me to be."

Her mouth twisted. "Tell the truth, Jack. You couldn't stand me because I was fat and ugly."

Her pain had grown until it threatened to suck all the air out of the room. He felt it and ached for her. He'd always had a rule of never letting anyone get close. Never letting anyone see the truth about him—not the emptiness of his heart or the darkness of his soul.

He walked over and grabbed her arms, forcing her to face him. "Did it occur to you that I liked you a lot? That I saw the woman you would become and knew that I would never measure up? Did you ever once think that by letting Hunter down I knew I'd lost both of you forever?"

Tears filled her eyes. "Don't be cruel. Don't pretend I mattered."

"You did matter. We were friends. Could there have been more as you'd gotten older? I always thought so. Until it was impossible because of what I'd done. I let him down. I let you down. I knew it and I couldn't face either of you."

He turned away and walked to the door. "I lied to you before. About Hunter. I think about him every damn day."

He reached for the door handle but instead felt something warm. Somehow Meri had gotten in front of him. She touched his face, his shoulders, his chest.

"Jack, you have to let it go. You didn't do anything wrong. Hunter would never want you to suffer like this."

"I don't know how else to make it right," he admitted.

"So you're going to punish yourself forever?"

He nodded slowly.

"You're right," she whispered. "I am the bright one in this relationship." Then she leaned in and kissed him.

He told himself to resist. That being with her was the last thing he had the right to do. But her mouth was soft and insistent, and her hands urged him forward. She was beautiful and caring and sexy and smart. How was he supposed to resist her?

She touched her tongue to his bottom lip, then nipped at his flesh. Fire shot through him. Fire and need and the knowledge that for a few minutes he could forget the past and live only in the present.

"You're a hard man to convince," she murmured as she grabbed his hand and placed it on her breast.

He caressed the curve. "But at least I'm hard."

Eleven

Meri laughed softly as Jack swept her into his arms, then carried her to the bed. He set her down, bent over her and kissed her with a hot need that made her want to forget everything but the moment, the man and how he made her feel.

His mouth was firm, his tongue insistent. He touched her everywhere, his hands tugging at clothing, pulling it off until she was naked. He stroked her body, caressing her bare skin, arousing her with a quick touch of her breast, fingers teasing the curve of her hip, dipping between her legs, then moving away.

It was like being attacked by a sensual, marauding beast who took what he wanted in sneak attacks. A tickle at the back of her thighs, a quick lick on her nipple, a puff of hot breath against her neck. Over and over he touched her, then moved on before she could get lost in the moment.

She writhed beneath him for several minutes, alternately laughing, then moaning. She finally drew him to a stop by wrapping her legs around his hips and holding him in place on top of her.

He braced himself above her, his dark eyes bright with passion, his mouth tempting.

"You're playing with me," she murmured.

One corner of his mouth turned up. "Tell me you don't like it."

"I can't."

"Meredith."

He breathed her name like a prayer. The sound caught her off guard, seeping inside of her, making her strain toward him. But for what? Sexual release? Or something far more dangerous?

Before she could decide, he bent down and kissed her. She parted for him, welcoming the stroke of his tongue and the arousal his touch brought. She reached between them and tugged at his shirt. She unfastened the buttons and he shrugged it off.

His jeans went next, and his briefs. He'd walked in barefoot. When he was as naked as she, he leaned toward her nightstand and opened the drawer. The condoms she'd bought were under the book she'd been reading.

But instead of putting one on, he dropped the protection on the corner of the nightstand, then shifted onto his side. He bent down and took her right breast in his mouth, at the same time reaching between her thighs to tease the most sensitive part of her.

She parted her legs and tried to catch her breath as he explored her swollen center, then dipped inside. He mimicked the act of love with his fingers before easing up to that one important spot and circling it.

He rubbed her gently, then harder and faster. He moved so he was kissing her mouth, even as he continued to touch her there. Around and around, taking her higher with each stroke, keeping ahead of her somehow, so she was the one chasing him. Chasing the sensations that made her body tense and promised a release that would shatter her world.

She tried to catch her breath, but there was a tightness in her chest that made it hard to breathe. The closer she got, the more her heart seemed to squeeze until, as she reached the point of no return, the pain gave way.

She shattered, both inside and out. Her orgasm claimed her in a rush that erased every thought in her head but one: she loved Jack.

Through the waves of pleasure, that single truth grew until she wondered how she'd ever convinced herself otherwise. Of course she loved him. She'd loved him from the first moment she'd met him and for all the eleven years they'd been apart. She'd never loved anyone else.

Her body slowed and relaxed, but not her mind. Not even when he put on the condom, then eased between her legs and filled her until she knew she was going to come again.

He made love to her with a steady rhythm designed to spin her into madness, and she went willingly, wanting to get lost in the sensation.

But the feel of his body on hers wasn't enough to clear her mind. Nor were the waves of release, the heat, the sound of his gasps for air or the pounding of *his* heart.

Meri clung to him for as long as he would let her, holding him close, wanting time to stand still. If only she could believe that was possible. But it wasn't. She knew enough about the universe to know all things were in motion—at their most basic level. That nothing was static.

Which meant, in time, with luck, her pain would fade. Because the other thing she knew down to the cellular level was that Jack would never love her back.

Jack breathed in the scent of Meri's body as he stroked her face. She was so beautiful. She'd always been beautiful.

He slid off her so he wouldn't snap a rib, then propped his head up on his hand and wondered what the hell he was supposed to say. What happened now?

She sat up and reached for her clothes.

"Where are you going?" he asked. "An appointment?"

He smiled as he spoke, but when she looked at him, his smile faded. There was something wrong—he could see it in her blue eyes.

"What?" he asked.

"I have to go."

"Where?"

"Away. We both know this is not what you want or need. You've never been the guy to settle down. I don't know if you can't or you won't. Some of it is your guilt over Hunter and some of it is...honestly I don't have a clue what it is."

She blinked several times, then swallowed. "I can't stay with you, Jack."

He hadn't thought about her leaving until she said she had to, and now he didn't want her to go.

She scrambled out of the bed and pulled on her clothes. "This is crazy. All of it. I don't know what I was thinking. I had this great plan. Betina warned me, but did I listen? And I'm supposed to be the smart one."

"What are you talking about?"

She slid on her T-shirt, then looked at him. "You have to stop it, Jack. You're not allowed to spy on me anymore. I know you'd call it looking after me. Whatever it is, you have to stop. I'm a grown woman and I can take care of myself. If there are mistakes to be made, then I'll make them. Stop protecting me."

"I don't want to."

"This isn't about you."

He didn't understand. They'd just made love. It had been great. So why was she leaving? And when the hell had it gotten so cold in this room?

"Just like that?" he asked, getting angry because it was easy and something he could understand.

She slipped her feet into her sandals. "Just like that. Goodbye, Jack."

Then she was gone.

He stared at the door. What was going on? What had just happened? She couldn't leave. Not like this.

He swore, then scooped up his clothes and put them on. He had no idea what she wanted that she hadn't gotten. Was she still pissed about Andrew? About the fact that he, Jack, had watched out for her?

She should be grateful, he told himself as he stalked up the stairs to his office. He'd taken care of her. He'd kept her safe. That had to be worth something. She was just too stubborn to admit it.

Still angry, he opened his computer and did his damnedest to get lost in work. It was the only safe place he could think to go.

Meri burst into Betina's room without knocking. It was only after she heard scrambling that she realized she might have interrupted something.

"I'm sorry," she said, turning away. She hadn't seen anything—the tears had blinded her.

"Wait," Betina said. "You don't have to go."

"I'm in the way."

"You're not."

Her friend grabbed her and pulled her close. Meri went willingly, needing the support. She had a vague impression of her friend in a robe and a guy hovering in the background, then the tears began again.

"What happened?" Betina asked as she stroked Meri's hair. "What did Jack say?"

"Nothing. He didn't have to. I get it. I've been so stupid. You were right about everything. I didn't want revenge or closure. I'm in love with him. I have been for years. He's the reason I can't seem to commit to anyone else. I love him. I was afraid to admit that, so I came here with my crazy idea of showing him. I think I secretly thought he'd take one look at the new and improved me and be struck by lightning or something."

Meri sank onto the floor and let the tears flow. She

hurt so much. It felt as if someone had cracked open her chest and ripped out her heart.

"How can I be so smart and so stupid at the same time?" she asked.

"Because you're human and no one is smart when it comes to matters of the heart."

Made sense, she thought, wishing it were a year from now and the pain had lessened. Not that she expected it ever to go away. She had a bad feeling she would love Jack forever.

"He doesn't want me," she whispered. "He never did. I thought it was about the age difference or how I looked, but now I'm not so sure. I think maybe it was just me."

Which made it hurt. She couldn't change who she was any more than she already had. He didn't want the very essence of her being. What else was left?

"He's an idiot," Betina murmured.

"No. He's just a man who can't pretend to be in love with me." Meri sucked in a breath. "I have to go. I can't stay here. We'll need to regroup somewhere else. Maybe down south. Pasadena or something."

"Don't worry about it. Do you want me to go with you?"

Meri managed a smile as she looked at her friend. "No. I want you to stay with Colin and be in love for the both of us."

Jack worked until dark. When he finally realized he couldn't see anything other than his computer screen anymore, he stood and stretched. It was only then he noticed the silence of the house.

Uneasiness slipped through him as he went downstairs and pushed open the door to Meri's room.

The furniture was exactly as he remembered—with the exception of the bed. Someone had stripped off the sheets and left the blankets neatly folded. The closet was empty, as were the drawers. She was gone.

He raced down to the main floor, where he found Betina packing up the notes from the dining room.

"What are you doing?" he demanded.

"Leaving." She didn't bother to look at him.

"All of you?"

She nodded. "We'll finish the work elsewhere."

Work? He didn't care about the work. He cared about Meri. "Where is she? She can't leave. She has to stay the month."

He'd known that from the beginning. That she was stuck here, too. Just like him. They couldn't escape each other. Hadn't that been the point?

Betina looked at him. "She doesn't have to stay here. That was just something she told you. Hunter's donation has nothing to do with her. It was always about his friends."

She'd lied about having to stay? Why? So he wouldn't force her to leave? To make him think he had time?

"Where is she?" he asked again.

"I'm not going to tell you. If she wants you to know, she'll get in touch with you herself."

He didn't understand any of this. Why had Meri been here in the first place? What had she wanted? Why leave now?

"Is it Andrew?" he asked. "Is she upset because I told her what he was?"

Betina's expression was almost pitying. "It's a guy thing, right? This failure to comprehend the most basic of human emotions? It has to be. I can't believe you're honestly that stupid." She smiled, then shook her head. "It always comes down to smart and stupid. How strange."

"What are you talking about?"

"Nothing," she told him. "Meri came here because she thought she wanted closure. She got it, in a way. She's been in love with you all these years. But the man wasn't really you. He was someone better. The person she thought you would be. Meri embraces life. She loves and is loved. She cares about people. She thought you were all those things, too. But she was wrong. And now she's gone."

Meri loved him? She couldn't. Not after what he'd done. Not after he'd let her down time after time.

"She can't," he whispered.

"That's what I keep telling her, but does she listen?" Betina closed the box. "I'm done here. Colin and I will be gone within the hour. Then you can have the house to yourself. You've got a few weeks left, right? I hope you enjoy your time here."

She started to leave. He grabbed her arm. "You can't leave it like that. There has to be more."

"Why? You don't want there to be more. It's not like you really care about her. She's just Hunter's little sister, right? An annoying responsibility. Your problem is you didn't know what you had until you lost it, and now she's gone forever. Goodbye, Jack."

He released her and let her go because there was nothing left to say.

Fine. He could be fine his last few weeks here. It was just three weeks, and then he'd go back to Texas and bury himself in his work. He would stay busy and he would forget. He was good at forgetting.

Three days later, Jack knew he was damn close to slipping into madness. The house was empty. Too empty. The silence mocked him. Worse, he found himself missing Meri's nerd friends. He missed the arguments about string theory and the scraps of paper with equations that had dotted every surface. He missed walking into a room and not understanding a word of what was being said despite the fact that everyone was speaking English.

He missed the closeness, the way Meri bullied everyone to get outside, to live life. He missed her insisting on a better telescope because the stars were so beautiful. He missed the sound of her voice, her laughter, the way her body moved. He missed her quirky sense of humor, her brilliance and how her smile could light up a room. He missed *her.*

She wasn't the teenager he'd known all those years ago. The young woman who had intrigued him and at the same time scared the hell out of him. Not just because she was Hunter's sister but because there was a quality about her that warned him she would expect only the best of herself and those in her world.

For a while he'd thought maybe he could live up to those expectations, but then Hunter had gotten sick and he'd known he would only hold her back.

He'd let her go for a thousand reasons that made

sense at the time. She didn't need him. She had to grow up on her own. She was better off without him. He was afraid. They'd both been so young and his feelings for Meri had been confused. So he'd walked away and stayed away. He'd kept tabs on her from a distance. He'd taken the coward's way out.

He hadn't expected to ever see her again. Then she'd been here and he'd been thrown. She'd wanted to seduce him and he knew he couldn't let that happen. Because of what he owed both her and Hunter.

He walked into the empty living room and stared at the perfectly arranged furniture. It was all so comfortable. He wanted to throw things, break things, mess it all up. Because life wasn't tidy or comfortable. It was a pain in the ass.

He turned to leave, then spotted a DVD case on the floor, by the sofa. Someone had dropped it. Or left it on purpose. Meri? Betina? Hunter?

He picked it up and stared at the plain black cover. Someone had stuck on a piece of paper covered with a single word.

Hunter.

Against his better judgment, Jack walked to the DVD player and put in the disk. Then he turned on the television and braced himself for the pain.

Someone had taken the time to transfer Hunter's home movies, he thought as he watched snippets of the first confusing days at Harvard. There were shots of Hunter's friends. All of them. And Meri. She was always hanging on the fringes.

She'd been the one to show them around, list the

best places to get pizza at three in the morning. She'd been there since she was a kid.

There were shots of snowball fights and a late-night party by a bonfire.

He leaned back against the sofa and lost himself in the images. A vacation here, a camping trip there. Seven guys who had become friends. No. Brothers. Brothers he hadn't seen or talked to in years.

The scene shifted to a yacht vacation they'd all taken one spring break. The camera panned to show the guys stretched out in the sun after a very late night. Meri walked on deck and paused, looking awkward and unhappy. She turned her gaze to him. He had his eyes closed and didn't see the look on her face. The one that clearly showed she loved him.

He felt it then, the cold slice of pain that was almost familiar. It took him a second to place it and then he remembered the knife attack in a Central American jungle. At first there had been nothing—just a breath of expectation, followed by the warm sensation of liquid as his blood flowed out. Then there had been the sharp sting that had quickly grown into agony.

It was the same today. As if razors had sliced his heart and his soul, as he realized he'd lost something precious. Something he could never replace.

He picked up his cell phone and pressed the buttons that connected him to his office.

"I don't have anything," Bobbi Sue snapped by way of greeting. "If you'd stop calling me, I might get a chance to find her."

"She has to be somewhere."

"You think I don't know that? She turned in the rental car at the airport in Los Angeles, but she didn't get on a plane. If she's in a hotel somewhere, she's using cash and a false name. I'm checking all her friends to see if they've used their names to register her. It's taking time."

He didn't have time. He had to find her *now*. He'd spent every minute of the past three days thinking he had to go after her himself, but leaving meant blowing the donation, and Meri would hate him for that.

"Keep looking," he said and hung up. To give his assistant the time she needed.

Jack stood and paced the length of the living room. He wanted to be doing the search himself, but he was trapped in this damn house. Trapped with memories and ghosts and a burning need he'd acknowledged three days too late.

He loved her. He had for a long time. In college, he'd assumed she would grow up and they'd get together. The plan had existed in the back of his mind, as if he'd known they were meant for each other. Then Hunter had died and everything had changed.

His cell rang. He reached for it.

"You found her?"

"I'm not looking for her."

The voice was familiar. "Colin?"

"Uh-huh. So you're looking for Meri?"

"I have my entire staff on it."

"You won't figure it out. Besides, what does it matter?"

"It matters more than anything."

"I *want* to believe you."

Because Colin had information. Why wouldn't he?

Meri would tell Betina where she was going and Betina would tell Colin.

"I have to find her," Jack said hoarsely. "I love her."

"What if that's too little too late?"

"I'll convince her."

There was an excruciating minute of silence.

"I kind of believe you," Colin said. "Okay. When your month is up there, I'll tell you where she is."

"What?" Jack roared. "You'll tell me now."

"Sorry. No. You have to stay. It's a lot of money on the line."

"I'll pay them the difference myself."

"Okay, yeah. You're probably good for it. But leaving now violates the spirit of what Hunter was trying to do. You really think Meri will be happy about that?"

"You think she's happy thinking I don't care about her?"

"Good point, but I'm not going to tell you. Not until the time is up."

The call ended. Jack picked up the coffee table and threw it through the sliding glass door. The glass shattered with a satisfyingly destructive sound.

"Dammit all to hell," he yelled into the subsequent silence.

And no one answered.

Twelve

Meri was thinking maybe she should get a dog. One of those small ones she could travel with. From her corner room at the Ritz-Carlton in Pasadena she could see down into a beautiful grassy area, with plants and paths where people walked their small dogs several times a day. At least then there would be something else alive in the room with her.

She glanced at her watch, then sighed. Her team wouldn't arrive for another half hour, which meant time to kill. Maybe it was just her, but the days had gotten much longer in the past few weeks. The things she loved no longer made her as happy as they once had. She found it more difficult to laugh and sleep and be really excited about Colin and Betina's announcement that they were getting married.

Not that she wasn't thrilled for her friends. There was nothing she wanted more than their happiness. It was just…

She missed Jack. Yes, that was crazy and made her an idiot, but there it was. She missed him—his voice, his touch, his laugh. The way he took charge and wasn't the least bit intimidated by her. She'd loved him most of her life. How was she supposed to stop loving him?

"Therapy," she murmured as she continued to stare out the window. It had helped her before—to figure out what normal was. Maybe talking with a paid professional could help her get over Jack. Maybe she could find a really cute male therapist and do a little emotional transference, because getting over anyone else had to be so much easier than getting over Jack.

She closed her eyes against the pain. He would be gone by now. His month at Hunter's house had ended at midnight. Had he already started back to Texas or was he just getting on the road? What was he thinking of her? Would she ever be the one who got away or was that just wishful thinking on her part? She knew he would come back for the reunion, but for now, he was gone.

There was a knock at the door. Housekeeping, she thought. Okay. That was fine. They could clean while she walked the grounds and made friends with the little dogs. Maybe an owner or two could give her some advice on which kind to get.

Jack would be a big-dog kind of guy, she thought absently. Of course, if she had his feelings to consider, she wouldn't need a dog in the first place. She would have a husband and a family, although a dog would be nice, too. Maybe one of—

She opened the door and stood staring. "You're not housekeeping."

Jack pushed past her into the room and shrugged. "I can go get you more towels if you need them."

"I don't need towels."

She stared at him, unable to believe he was here. He looked good—tired and maybe thinner but still powerful and sexy and the man of her dreams.

"You're supposed to be heading home," she said. "Your four weeks are up."

He looked at her. "Is that what you think? That I'd put in my time, then walk away?"

"Sure."

"Because it's what I've always done. Put in my time, kept my distance, not gotten involved."

Her stomach flipped over a couple of times. Okay, physically it couldn't turn, but the churning caused by anxiety did a really great imitation.

She wanted to throw herself into his arms. She wanted him to hold her and tell her it was going to be all right. Only he wouldn't, because nothing in her life had ever been that easy. She had no idea why he was here. Maybe to offer her some advice or something. She would smile politely, listen, push him out the door, then have a private breakdown. She was getting good at those.

"How did you find me?" she asked.

"Colin told me."

"What? He didn't."

"Oh, yeah. But he did it in a way you can totally

respect. He tortured me first. He called right after you left and said he knew where you were but he wasn't going to tell me until my month was up. Something about a donation and that damn house."

Colin had called Jack? She wasn't sure if she should be happy or planning to return the engagement present she'd already bought.

"You were looking for me?" she asked cautiously.

Jack touched her face. "What do you think?"

"I don't know."

"You must have had an idea. You went to a lot of trouble to stay hidden."

"I don't want your pity," she admitted. "I don't want you watching over me anymore. I don't want to be a project or Hunter's little sister."

His eyes were dark and unreadable. Something flashed through them.

"Would you settle for being the woman I love?"

She heard the words. The vibration of sound worked its way through her ears and was transmitted through her brain via—

"What?" she asked, suddenly not caring about the hows and whys of her body. "What?"

"I love you, Meri. I have for a long time. I always thought…" He shrugged. "I thought there was something between us back then. But you were young and I was young and then Hunter got sick. I couldn't deal, so I ran. You know all this. I ran, but I couldn't let go. I took the coward's way out. I spied on you. You were right to call it that. I kept track from a distance, where it was safe. Where I was safe."

She had to sit down. Her legs felt weak and the room was spinning. Instead she reached for him, and he caught her and held her as if he might never let go.

"I missed you," he murmured, speaking into her hair. "I missed you so much. Not just the past three weeks, although they were hell, but for the past eleven years. I'm sorry I didn't know before. I love you, Meri. I want to be with you. I want to make this right."

He grabbed her by her upper arms and held her in front of him. "Can you forgive me? Can you tell me what to do to make it right? Can you ever care about me?"

She began to laugh and cry and went back into his arms, where he held her so tight she couldn't breathe.

It felt good. It felt right.

"Of course I love you," she said, her voice shaking. "What did you think all this was about?"

"You're a complicated woman. I had no idea. You left. That confused me."

"I wanted to leave before you could dump me. I couldn't have my heart broken again."

"I'll never leave you," he promised. "I love you. I want to be with you always. Marry me?"

It was as if someone had injected fizz into her blood. She felt light and bubbly and more happy than she'd ever been.

"What kind of dogs do you like?" she asked.

"Whichever ones makes you happy."

She smiled. "Good answer."

The first time Hunter Palmer had gone into the light, he hadn't known what to expect. Until he'd been diagnosed and told he had weeks to live, he'd never thought about having a soul or what it meant to die. Now, ten years later, he had all the answers. But there were still questions. Questions only his friends could answer.

He moved through the reception celebrating the dedication of Hunter's House, unseen, unfelt but very much there—for his friends. Once they had been the Seven Samurai—men who had vowed friendship forever. After he'd died, they'd gotten lost. Now they'd found their way back.

Hunter moved close to Nathan Barrister.

Six months ago Nathan had never heard of Hunter's Landing. Now he was married to Keira, the mayor of Hunter's Landing, and dividing his time between a house in Knightsbridge, London, and Keira's house here in the mountains.

His life was rich and full and more than he could have ever imagined. And he owed it all to Hunter. All of them did. Nathan closed his eyes and whispered his thanks to the friend who had somehow made all of this possible. And somehow he was sure Hunter heard him.

"What're you smiling about?" Keira asked, leaning into his shoulder, tipping her face up to his.

"You," he said, wrapping his arm around her and holding on tightly. "I'm smiling because of you."

"Ooh, that's what I like to hear." She turned to look at the remaining Samurai and the women who had saved them—loved them. "It's a wonderful day. I think your friend Hunter would have approved."

"Are you kidding? He would have loved this. All of us together again. Whole again." With Keira in his arms,

Nathan looked out at his friends and the women who had become the heart of the Samurai. They weren't the same, any of them. Somehow, through the magic of this place, they'd all become *more*. Smiling down at his wife, Nathan said, "I just don't think it's possible to be any happier than I am at this moment."

"Wanna bet? I have a surprise for you," she said, wrapping her arms around his middle and staring up into his eyes. "And I think today is the perfect day for this announcement."

"Yeah?" He looked at her and thought about the coming night, when he could hold her close in their bed, lose himself in the wonder of loving and being loved. "I love a good surprise."

"We're going to have a baby."

"We're what?"

"You're going to be a daddy."

"When?" His heart jolted, then kicked into a gallop. "How? What?"

"Surprise!"

She looked so happy. So beautiful. And she'd given him everything.

"I love you," he said, cupping her face between his palms. "Thanks for loving me back."

"My pleasure. Believe me."

He did. He believed her. Just as he believed that his life, his world, was only going to get better and better. Holding on to his wife, he tipped his head back, looked to heaven and said again, "Thanks, Hunter. I really owe you for this."

Hunter touched his friend's shoulder and moved on…to Luke.

It was just the kind of event Hunter would have enjoyed, Luke thought. Plenty of cold beer, good food and beautiful girls.

Make that beautiful *women*. Their time in the house had brought each of the remaining Samurai a lover with whom the men intended to spend the rest of their lives. Hunter couldn't have known that would happen...or could he?

Luke grinned at his fanciful thought, then caught Lauren's eye. "Hey, do you think we'll have time later for a round or two at the Game Palace?"

"Pool during the reunion?" She twisted one of her blond curls around her finger.

"Why not? We'll invite Matt and Kendall along and we can kick their butts. How much do you want to bet she's never played?"

Lauren frowned. "I thought you were giving up your competitive ways."

Luke snagged her in one arm and drew her close. "You know that won't happen. I've just learned to temper them with a little perspective. And with a lotta love from you, honey."

"And from Matt."

Luke gazed over the top of her head at his twin brother, who looked equally relaxed and equally loved by his Kendall. He and Matt had spent a lot of their lives as each other's enemies, but their time at Hunter's House had resolved their conflicts and returned them to a brotherhood that Luke appreciated more each day.

From across the room Matt looked up as if he'd heard

Luke's thoughts. Like many twins, they could communicate without a sound. His brother lifted his sweating beer in a little toast, and Luke returned it. Then he directed another toast heavenward.

Thank you, Hunter. I vow to live a better, fuller life.

Then he looked back down at the woman who owned his heart. "Speaking of vows…"

She tilted her head. "What?"

"A little birdie told me that a couple in this room is planning on sneaking off to Reno on Sunday to tie the knot."

"Really?"

He nodded, then captured her left hand so he could rub his thumb over the engagement ring he'd placed there. Yes, he was living a better, fuller life, but oh, how he still enjoyed winning. "Now, if we make a quick dash tonight, my sweet, sweet Lauren, we could just beat them to the altar…."

Hunter laughed quietly as he moved away. Luke would never change. Of course, Lauren didn't want him to, which was why they were so happy together.

He looked around the room and saw Devlin Campbell looking uncharacteristically worried.

As happy as Devlin was to see his old friends, he was more anxious to get home. Nicole's obstetrician had forbidden her to travel by plane with the baby so close to being born, and he missed her.

Ryan wandered over, Devlin's best man and the same guy who had declared he was swearing off women for the month he was to be at the lodge. But the Love Shack had weaved its magic on Ryan as it had the rest of them. He'd found true love, too.

"What's right with this picture?" Devlin asked Ryan as they glanced around the room.

Ryan smiled. "Yeah. Amazing. And you're missing Nicole, I'll bet."

"As much as I've liked getting together with all the Samurai, I want to be home."

"Think we'll do this again sometime? A gathering of the clan?"

"We should. Maybe a golf weekend somewhere once a year."

"It would take some doing, coordinating our schedules."

"One thing I've learned, Ryan—you have to make time for what's important. My wife, the Samurai. You're important."

"Let's go propose the idea while the wives are around to hear. They'll force the issue. Women like that kind of bonding stuff."

As if on cue, Devlin's cell phone rang. Panic struck him full force when he saw it was Nicole. Had she gone into labor without him?

"You okay?" he asked.

"I love you. I miss you. That's all."

He relaxed. She loved him and missed him. *That's all.* Such an elemental part of his life now. His beautiful wife, her love and devotion. But *that's all?*

On second thought, maybe it *was* that simple. Maybe that was the secret of life. The best things weren't complicated.

Hunter nodded. He touched Devlin's arm to ease his worry. Nicole would be fine. Then he followed Ryan across the room.

His arm draped around Kelly's shoulders, Ryan looked around at the Seven Samurai who'd finally gathered together again. He said *seven* because he knew Hunter was here in spirit. In fact, Hunter had brought about this reunion, thanks to his will.

Hunter had always been the glue that had bound them together, and now they were his legacy.

Ryan looked down at Kelly. They'd been married just weeks, but they'd been the best damn weeks he'd had in a long time. Since before his mother and Hunter had died, in fact. He felt alive again.

They'd gotten married in an intimate ceremony in California's Napa Valley. Erica and Greg had served as the matron of honor and best man. Because it was summer break, he'd been able to fly them in, along with their kids, for a family vacation. He grinned thinking about how thrilled Kelly's friends had been to get away to a romantic place, even if it was with the kids in tow.

He and Kelly would be in the same situation in a few years, especially if they kept having the same steamy nights they'd been having the past few weeks.

Kelly glanced up at him. "Why are you grinning?"

He bent and murmured something sinful in her ear.

She went still, looked embarrassed, then swatted him playfully. "Behave."

He laughed as he straightened because she'd given him exactly the reaction he would have predicted.

"Impossible with you, Venus," he responded irrepressibly.

Hunter chuckled, patted his friend on the back, then walked toward Luke's twin.

It was strange, Matthias thought, seeing all six of them together again after so many years. Even stranger that they were here without Hunter. Though, in a way, maybe Hunter *was* here with them. Maybe he'd been with them all along. And it was fitting that Hunter had been the one to bring them all together again, since he'd been the one who'd united them in college. They were still the Seven Samurai, Matthias supposed, but now one was missing. And somehow the Six Samurai just didn't seem right.

Then he realized they weren't six anymore. They were twelve. And they weren't Samurai anymore, either. Samurai were warriors, always prepared for death. Matthias, Luke, Ryan, Jack, Nathan and Devlin were family men now, focused on their lives ahead with the women who had made them complete.

That was what Kendall had done for him, anyway. Completed him. Filled in all the empty places that he hadn't wanted to admit were empty.

As if she'd sensed something, Kendall looked up at him, narrowing her gaze thoughtfully. "What are you thinking about?" she asked. "You look…happy."

"That's what I'm thinking about."

"Not the Perkins contract?"

"Nope."

"Not the Endicott merger?"

"No."

"Not the Sacramento conference?"

He tightened his fingers around hers. "I'm thinking about our life together. And I'm thinking about how we need to get right to work on that."

"You're the boss."

He shook his head. "No. We're a newly announced partnership. One that's going to take the world by storm."

She pushed herself up on tiptoe and brushed her lips over his. "I'll prepare the memo at once."

"We'd better make it a PowerPoint demonstration," he told her. "This is going to be big."

Hunter nodded with pleasure. Everything had turned out the way he'd hoped. The possibilities had been there, of course, but his friends had been the ones to take the right steps.

Last he turned to Meri, his sister. He'd missed her, but he was proud of the woman she'd become. It had taken her and Jack far too long to find each other, but at last they had.

He eased close, wishing he could hug her and tell her how much he loved them both.

"There's something about the house," Meri told Jack. "All these people falling in love. It's almost scary."

"You scared to be in love with me?"

She smiled. "Never. I'm used to it. I've loved you a lot longer than you've loved me."

"Have not."

"Have to."

Jack grinned. "Are all our fights going to be this mature?"

"I hope so." She leaned close to him. "I love you,

Jack. I think Hunter would be very happy to know we're together."

Jack nodded. "I agree. I know it's strange, but there's a part of me that thinks he wanted this all along."

If Hunter had eyes to roll, he would have done it. Then he cuffed his friend on the shoulder. What else would he have been talking about when he'd made Jack promise to take care of his sister?

It had all worked out in the end. For each of his friends. When he'd known he was dying, he'd vowed to find some way to make sure they stayed together—brothers. He'd been afraid that guilt and time and distance would pull them apart. On a sleepless night weeks before his death, the idea of the house had been born.

Now, ten years later, he was content. His sister was finally where she belonged and his brothers had become the men he knew they could be. He would tell them everything…eventually.

He smiled at them. His work here was done. He would wait for them on the other side, in a better place than they could begin to imagine. Hunter turned then, moving into the light…this time to stay.

* * * * *

Read on for a sneak preview of Carol Marinelli's
PUTTING ALICE BACK TOGETHER!

Hugh hired bikes!

You know that saying: 'It's like riding a bike, you never forget'?

I'd never learnt in the first place.

I never got past training wheels.

'You've got limited upper-body strength?' He stopped and looked at me.

I had been explaining to him as I wobbled along and tried to stay up that I really had no centre of balance. I mean *really* had no centre of balance. And when we decided, fairly quickly, that a bike ride along the Yarra perhaps, after all, wasn't the best activity (he'd kept insisting I'd be fine once I was on, that you never forget), I threw in too my other disability. I told him about my limited upper-body strength, just in case he took me to an indoor rock-climbing centre next. I'd honestly forgotten he was a doctor, and he seemed worried, like I'd had a mini-stroke in the past or had mild cerebral palsy or something.

'God, Alice, I'm sorry—you should have said. What happened?'

And then I had had to tell him that it was a self-diagnosis. 'Well, I could never get up the ropes at the gym at school.' We were pushing our bikes back. 'I can't blow-dry the back of my hair…' He started laughing.

Not like Lisa who was laughing at me—he was just laughing and so was I. We got a full refund because we'd only been on our bikes ten minutes, but I hadn't failed. If anything, we were getting on better.

And better.

We went to St Kilda to the lovely bitty shops and I found these miniature Russian dolls. They were tiny, made of tin or something, the biggest no bigger than my thumbnail. Every time we opened them, there was another tiny one, and then another, all reds and yellows and greens.

They were divine.

We were facing each other, looking down at the palm of my hand, and our heads touched.

If I put my hand up now, I can feel where our heads touched.

I remember that moment.

I remember it a lot.

Our heads connected for a second and it was alchemic; it was as if our minds kissed hello.

I just have to touch my head, just there at the very spot and I can, whenever I want to, relive that moment.

So many times I do.

'Get them.' Hugh said, and I would have, except that little bit of tin cost more than a hundred dollars and, though that usually wouldn't have stopped me, I wasn't about to have my card declined in front of him.

I put them back.

'Nope.' I gave him a smile. 'Gotta stop the impulse

spending.'

We had lunch.

Out on the pavement and I can't remember what we ate, I just remember being happy. Actually, I can remember: I had Caesar salad because it was the lowest carb thing I could find. We drank water and I *do* remember not giving it a thought.

I was just thirsty.

And happy.

He went to the loo and I chatted to a girl at the next table, just chatted away. Hugh was gone for ages and I was glad I hadn't demanded Dan from the universe, because I would have been worried about how long he was taking.

Do I go on about the universe too much? I don't know, but what I do know is that something *was* looking out for me, helping me to be my best, not to **** this up as I usually do. You see, we walked on the beach, we went for another coffee and by that time it was evening and we went home and he gave me a present.

Those Russian dolls.

I held them in my palm, and it was the nicest thing he could have done for me.

They are absolutely my favourite thing and I've just stopped to look at them now. I've just stopped to take them apart and then put them all back together again and I can still feel the wonder I felt on that day.

He was the only man who had bought something for me, I mean something truly special. Something beautiful, something thoughtful, something just for me.

© Carol Marinelli 2012
Available at millsandboon.co.uk

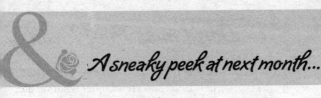

A sneaky peek at next month...

By Request

RELIVE THE ROMANCE WITH THE BEST OF THE BEST

My wish list for next month's titles...

In stores from 17th February 2012:

❏ His Suitable Bride – Cathy Williams,
Abby Green & Kate Walker

❏ Monte Carlo Affairs

– Emilie Rose

3 stories in each book - only £5.99!

In stores from 2nd March 2012:

❏ Capturing the Crown – Marie Ferrarella.
Karen Whiddon & Linda Winstead Jones

Available at WHSmith, Tesco, Asda, Eason, Amazon and Apple

Just can't wait?

Don't miss Pink Tuesday
One day. 10 hours. 10 deals.

PINK TUESDAY
IS COMING!

10 hours...10 unmissable deals!

This Valentine's Day we will be bringing
you fantastic offers across a range of
our titles—each hour, on the hour!

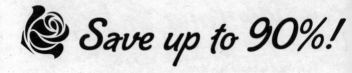

Save up to 90%!

Pink Tuesday starts
9am Tuesday 14th February

Find out how to grab a Pink Tuesday deal—
register online at **www.millsandboon.co.uk**

*Visit us
Online*

0212/PM/MB362

 *Have Your Say*

*You've just finished your book.
So what did you think?*

We'd love to hear your thoughts on our
'Have your say' online panel
www.millsandboon.co.uk/haveyoursay

- 🌹 Easy to use
- 🌹 Short questionnaire
- 🌹 Chance to win Mills & Boon® goodies

 Visit us Online Tell us what you thought of this book now at
www.millsandboon.co.uk/haveyoursay

Special Offers

Every month we put together collections and longer reads written by your favourite authors.

Here are some of next month's highlights— and don't miss our fabulous discount online!

On sale 17th February

On sale 17th February

On sale 17th February

On sale 2nd March